image comics presents

CHEW

created by John Layman & Rob Guillory

Flambé

written & lettered by
John Layman
drawn & coloured by
Rob Guillory

Color Assists by Steven Struble & Taylor Wells

IMAGE COMICS, INC.

Robert Kirkman - chief operating officer
Erik Larsen - chief financial officer
Todd McFarlane - president
Marc Silvestri - chief executive officer
Jim Valentino - vice-president

Eric Stephenson - publisher
Todd Martinez - sales & licensing coordinator
Sarah deLaine - pr & marketing coordinator
Branwyn Bigglestone - accounts manager
Emily Miller - administrative assistant
Jamie Parreno - marketing assistant
Kevin Yuen - digital rights coordinator
Tyler Shainline - production manager
Drew Gill - art director
Jonathan Chan - senior production artist
Monica Garcia - production artist
Vincent Kukua - production artist
Jana Cook - production artist

www.imagecomics.com

CHEW, VOL. 4: FLAMBÉ. First printing. September 2011. Published by Image Comics, Inc. Office of publication: 2134 Allston Way, 2nd Floor, Berkeley, CA 94704. Copyright © 2011 John Layman. Originally published in single magazine form as CHEW #16-20 by Image Comics. All rights reserved. CHEW™, its logos, and all character likenesses herein are trademarks of John Layman, unless expressly indicated. Image Comics® and its logos are registered trademarks and copyright of Image Comics, Inc. All rights reserved. No part of this publication may be reproduced or transmitted, in any form or by any means (except for short excerpts for review purposes) without the express written permission of John Layman or Image Comics, Inc. All names, characters, events, and locales in this publication, except for satirical purposes, are entirely fictional, and any resemblance to actual persons (living or dead) or entities or events or places is coincidental or for satirical purposes. Printed in the U.S.A. For information regarding the CPSIA on this printed material call: 203-595-3636 and provide reference # EAST – 396011

International Rights Representative: Christine Meyer (christine@gfloystudio.com)   ISBN: 978-1-60706-398-8

Dedications:

JOHN: To John Nee, Scott Dunbier and Jim Lee, the unholy trinity who brought me down this dark path.

ROB: For Thomas. Thanks for everything. See ya later.

Thanks:

Taylor Wells and Steven Struble, for the color assists
Tom B. Long, for the logo.
Comicbookfonts.com, for the fonts

And More Thanks:

Drew, Tyler, Branwyn, Sarah, eric and the Image Gang, as always, and Valerie Artigas, Roman Stepanov, Joshua Williamson, Anthony Bozzi, Lance Curran, April Hanks and Kim Peterson. And Aiden Guillory, for making Rob smile.

threadless®

Olive Chu's wardrobe provided by Threadless.com
Designs by Travis Pitts Marcelo Jimenez and Glenn Jones.

Chapter 1

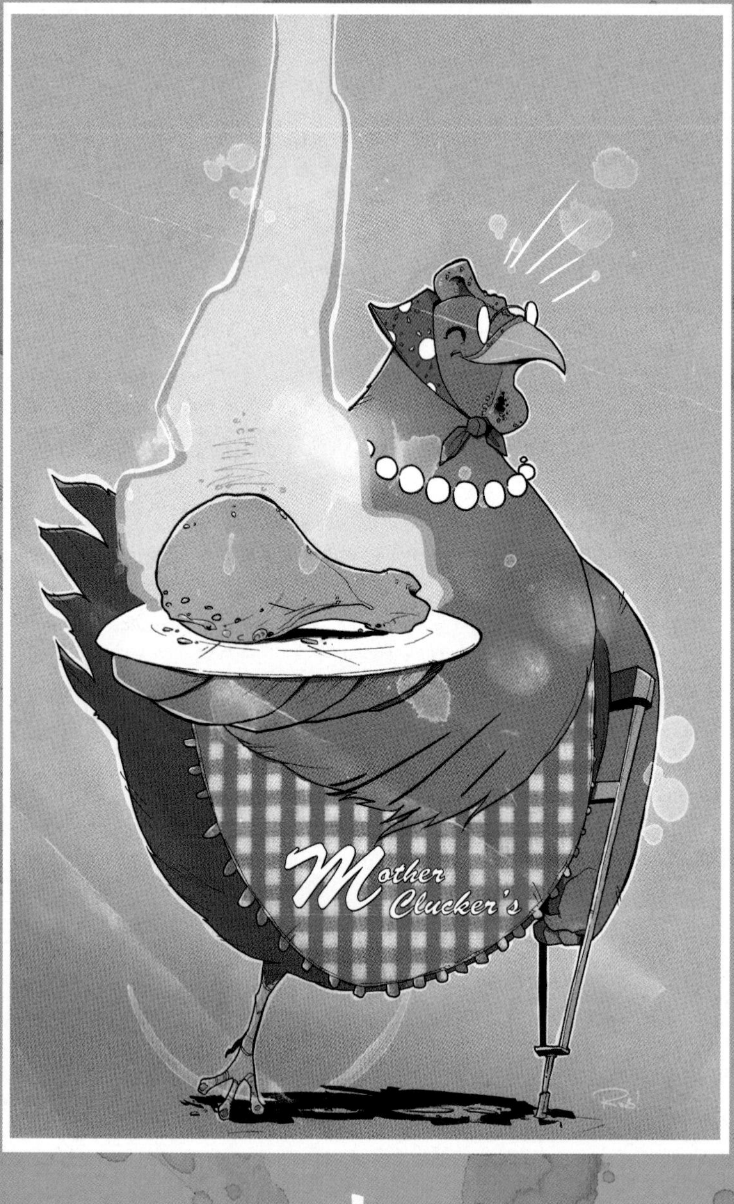
Mother Clucker's

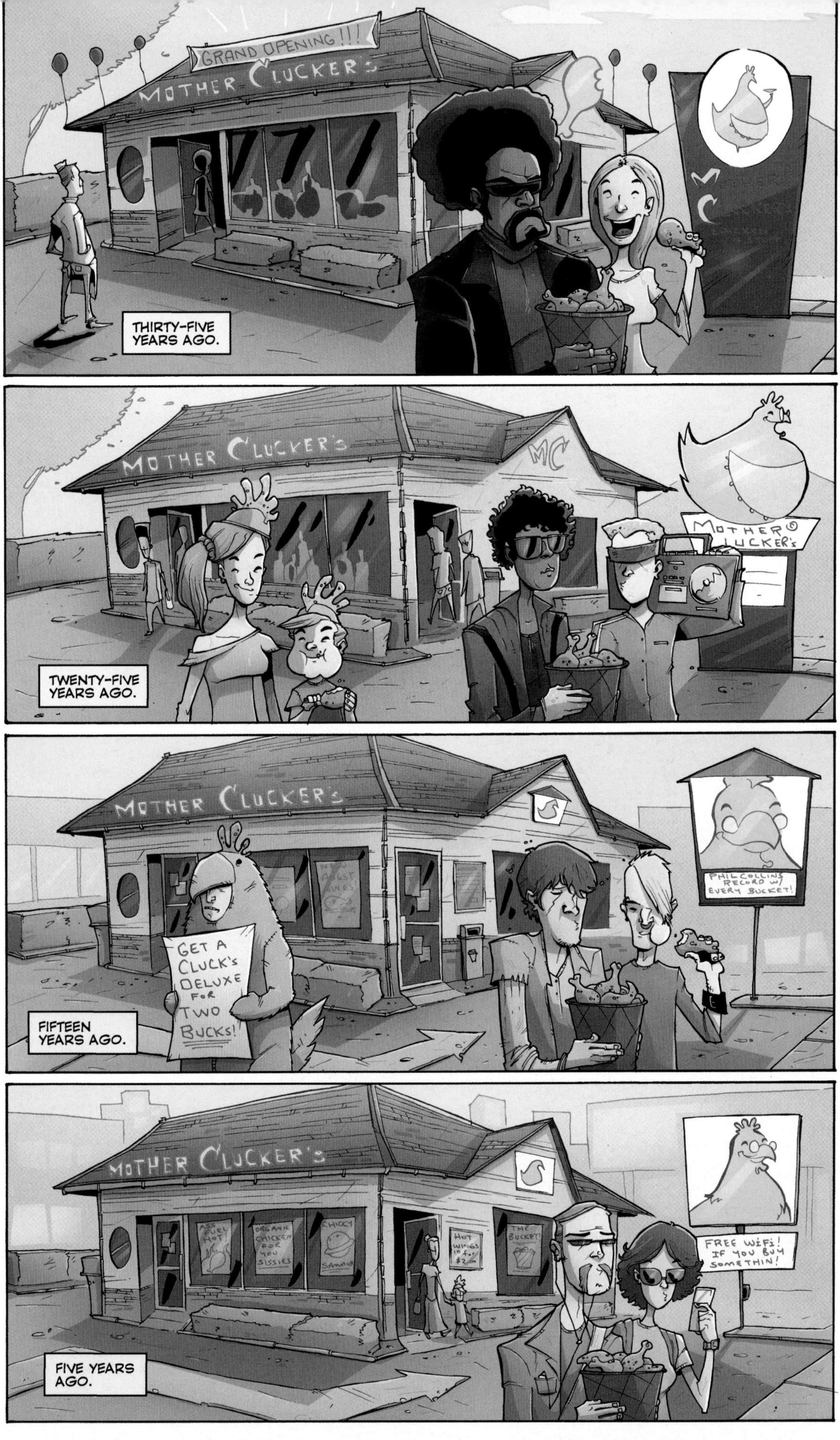
GRAND OPENING!!!
MOTHER CLUCKER'S
THIRTY-FIVE YEARS AGO.
MOTHER CLUCKER'S
MC
MOTHER® CLUCKER'S
TWENTY-FIVE YEARS AGO.
MOTHER CLUCKER'S
PHIL COLLINS RECORD w/ EVERY BUCKET!
GET A CLUCK'S DELUXE FOR TWO BUCKS!
FIFTEEN YEARS AGO.
MOTHER CLUCKER'S
ASS FUEL HOT!
ORGANIC CHICKEN FOR YOU SISSIES
CHICKY SAMMICH
HOT WINGS 10 for $2.00
THE BUCKET!
FREE WiFi! IF YOU BUY SOMETHIN'!
FIVE YEARS AGO.

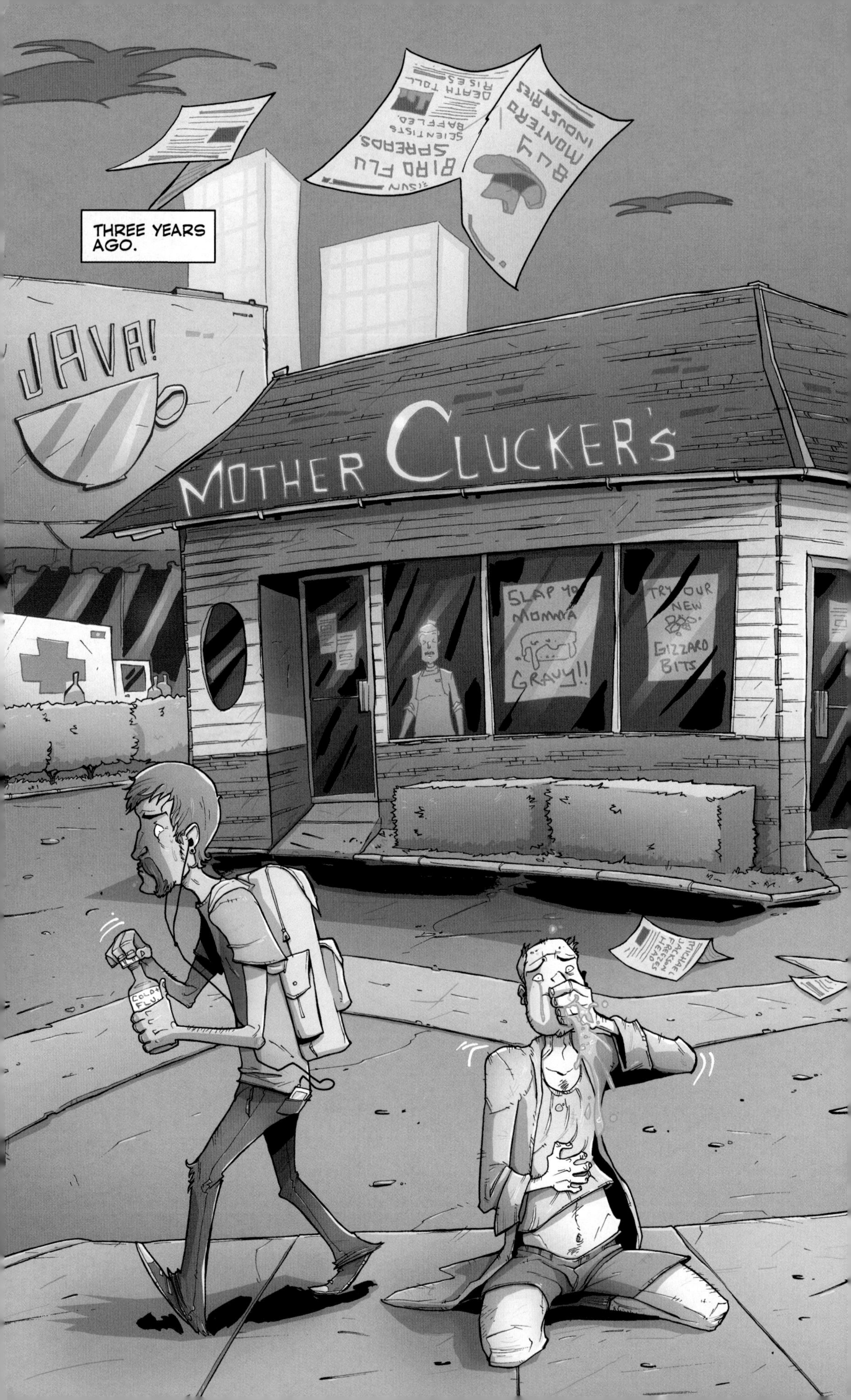
THREE YEARS AGO.
BIRD FLU SPREADS
SCIENTISTS BAFFLED.
DEATH TOLL RISES
BUY MONTERO INDUSTRIES
JAVA!
MOTHER CLUCKER'S
SLAP YO MOMMA GRAVY!!
TRY OUR NEW GIZZARD BITS
COLD + FLU
MICHAEL JACKSON FREEZES HEAD

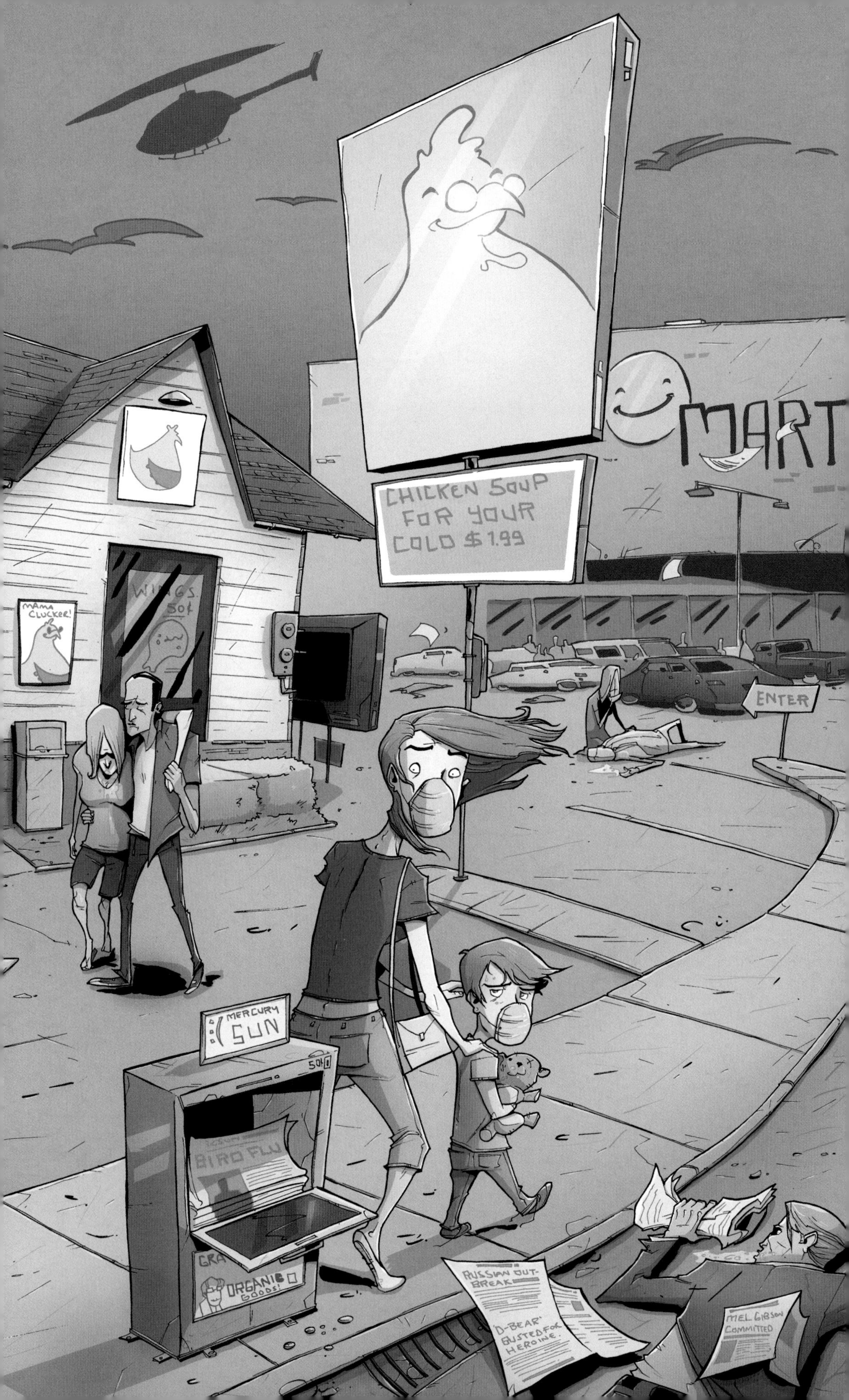
CHICKEN SOUP
FOR YOUR
COLD $1.99
MART
MAMA CLUCKER!
WINGS.
50¢
ENTER
MERCURY
SUN
50¢
BIRD FLU
ORGANIC
GOODS!
RUSSIAN OUT-BREAK
'D-BEAR' BUSTED FOR HEROINE
MEL GIBSON COMMITTED

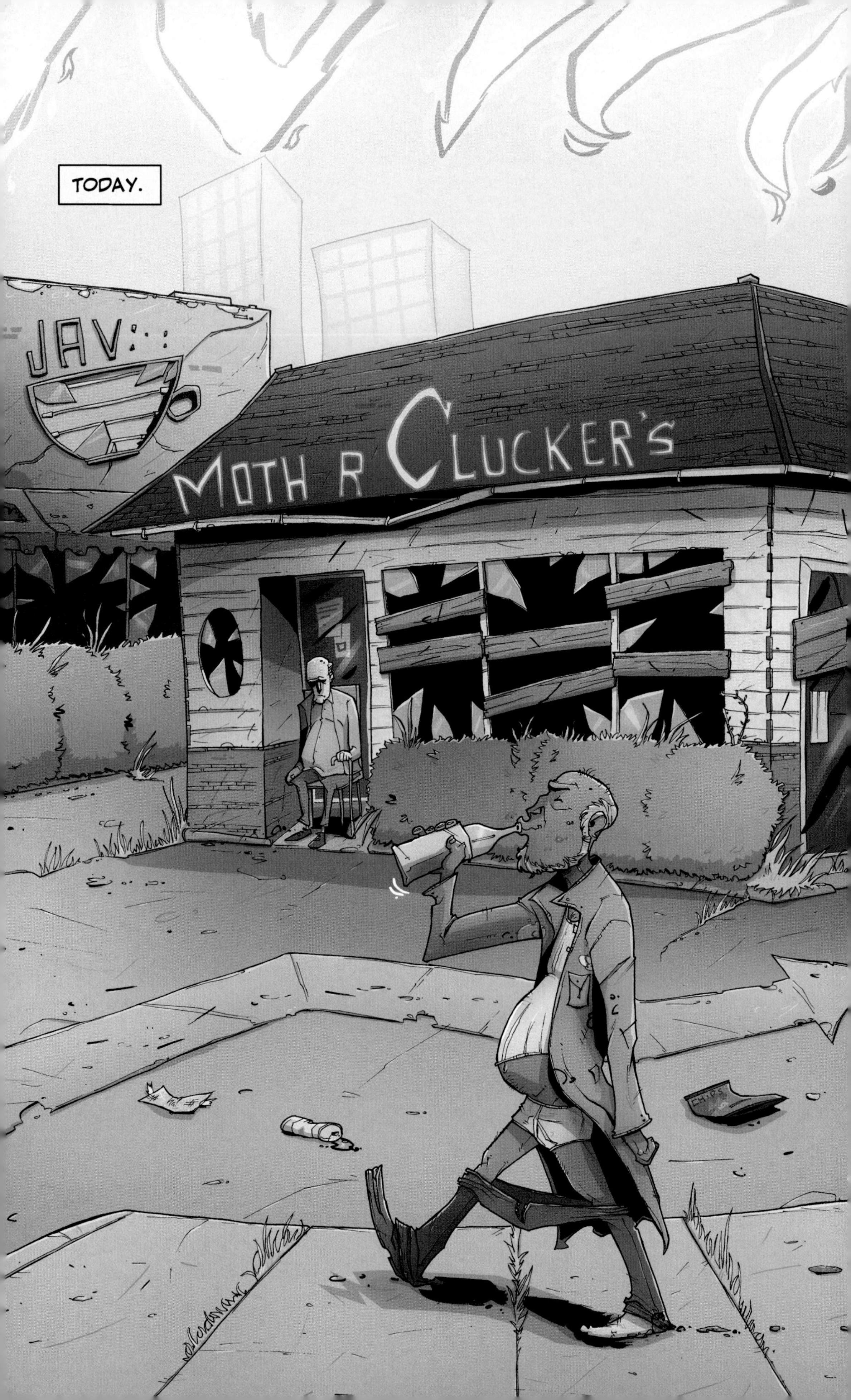
TODAY.
JAV
MOTH R CLUCKER'S

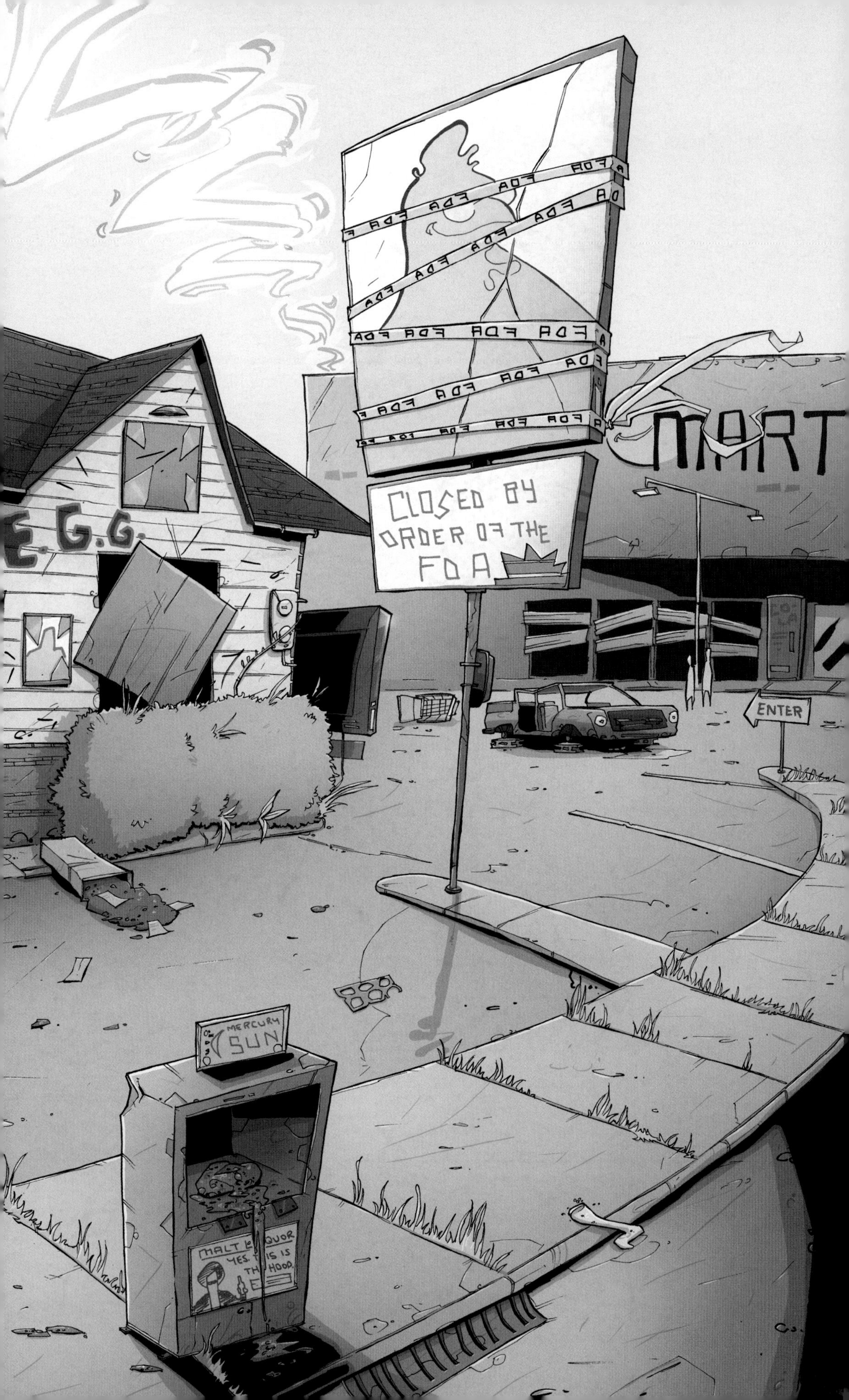
FDA
CLOSED BY ORDER OF THE FDA
E.G.G.
MART
ENTER
MERCURY SUN

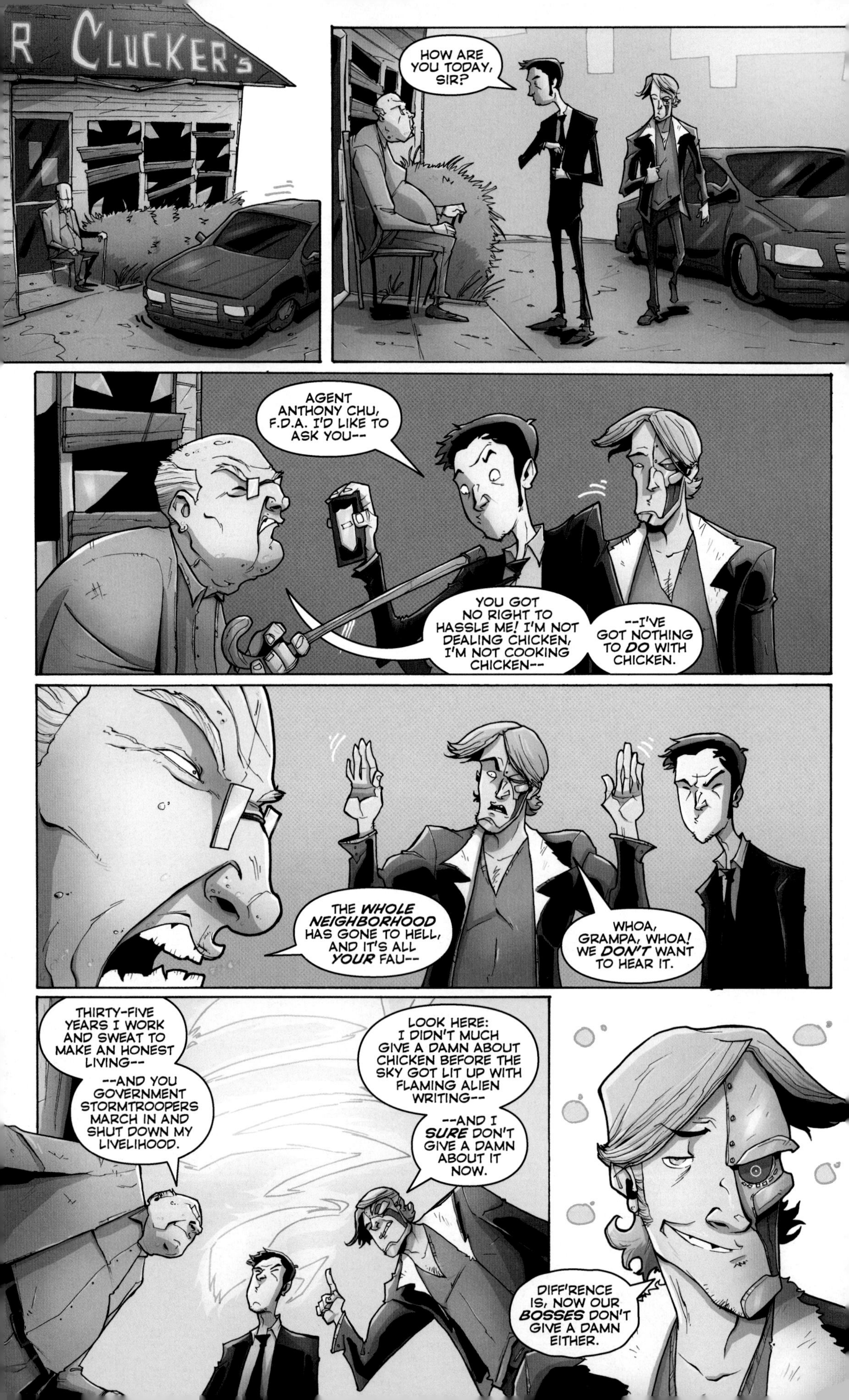
R CLUCKER'S
HOW ARE YOU TODAY, SIR?
AGENT ANTHONY CHU, F.D.A. I'D LIKE TO ASK YOU--
YOU GOT NO RIGHT TO HASSLE ME! I'M NOT DEALING CHICKEN, I'M NOT COOKING CHICKEN--
--I'VE GOT NOTHING TO *DO* WITH CHICKEN.
THE ***WHOLE NEIGHBORHOOD*** HAS GONE TO HELL, AND IT'S ALL ***YOUR*** FAU--
WHOA, GRAMPA, WHOA! WE ***DON'T*** WANT TO HEAR IT.
THIRTY-FIVE YEARS I WORK AND SWEAT TO MAKE AN HONEST LIVING--
--AND YOU GOVERNMENT STORMTROOPERS MARCH IN AND SHUT DOWN MY LIVELIHOOD.
LOOK HERE: I DIDN'T MUCH GIVE A DAMN ABOUT CHICKEN BEFORE THE SKY GOT LIT UP WITH FLAMING ALIEN WRITING--
--AND I ***SURE*** DON'T GIVE A DAMN ABOUT IT NOW.
DIFF'RENCE IS, NOW OUR ***BOSSES*** DON'T GIVE A DAMN EITHER.

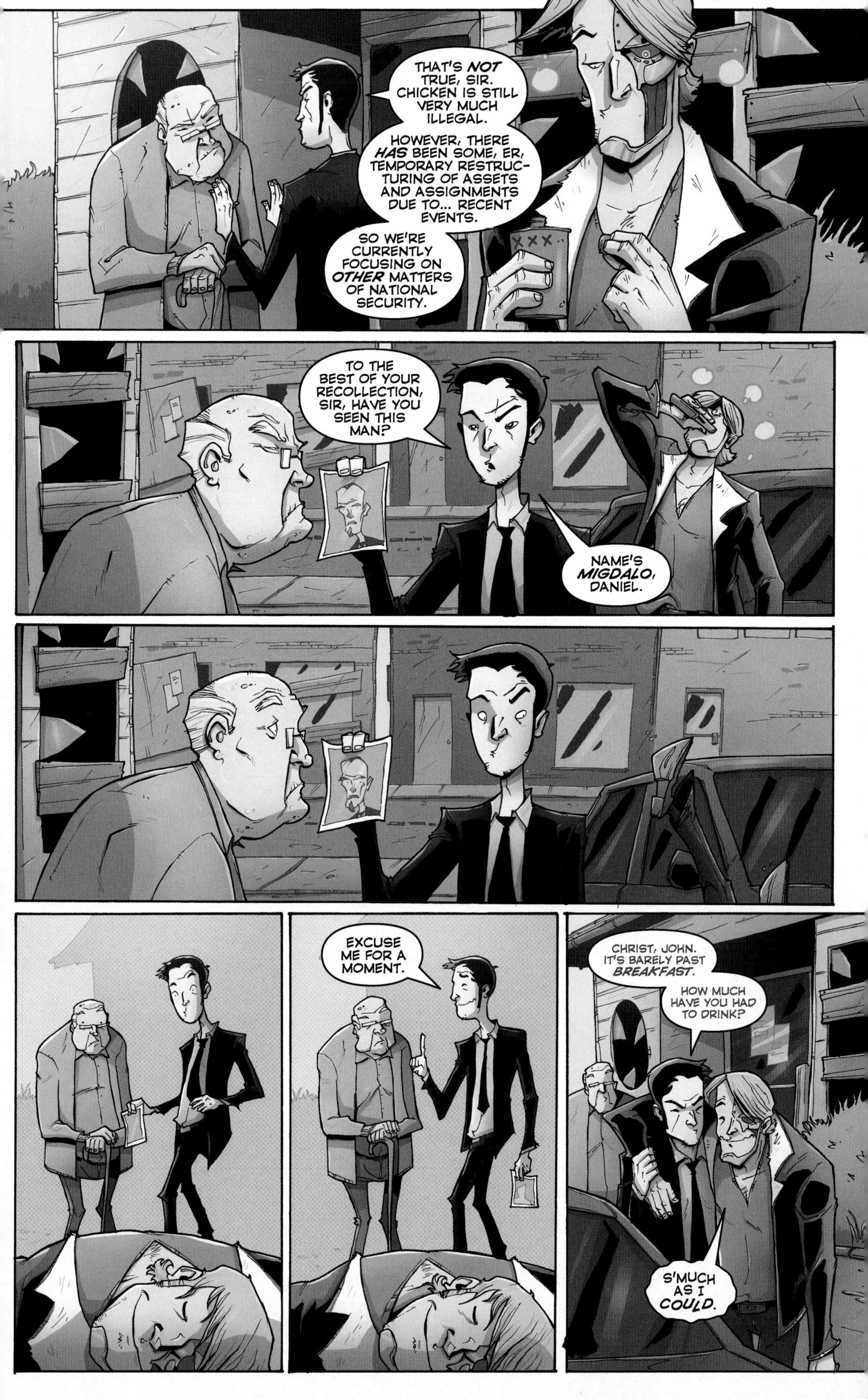
THAT'S NOT TRUE, SIR. CHICKEN IS STILL VERY MUCH ILLEGAL.
HOWEVER, THERE HAS BEEN SOME, ER, TEMPORARY RESTRUCTURING OF ASSETS AND ASSIGNMENTS DUE TO... RECENT EVENTS.
SO WE'RE CURRENTLY FOCUSING ON OTHER MATTERS OF NATIONAL SECURITY.
TO THE BEST OF YOUR RECOLLECTION, SIR, HAVE YOU SEEN THIS MAN?
NAME'S MIGDALO, DANIEL.
EXCUSE ME FOR A MOMENT.
CHRIST, JOHN. IT'S BARELY PAST BREAKFAST.
HOW MUCH HAVE YOU HAD TO DRINK?
S'MUCH AS I COULD.

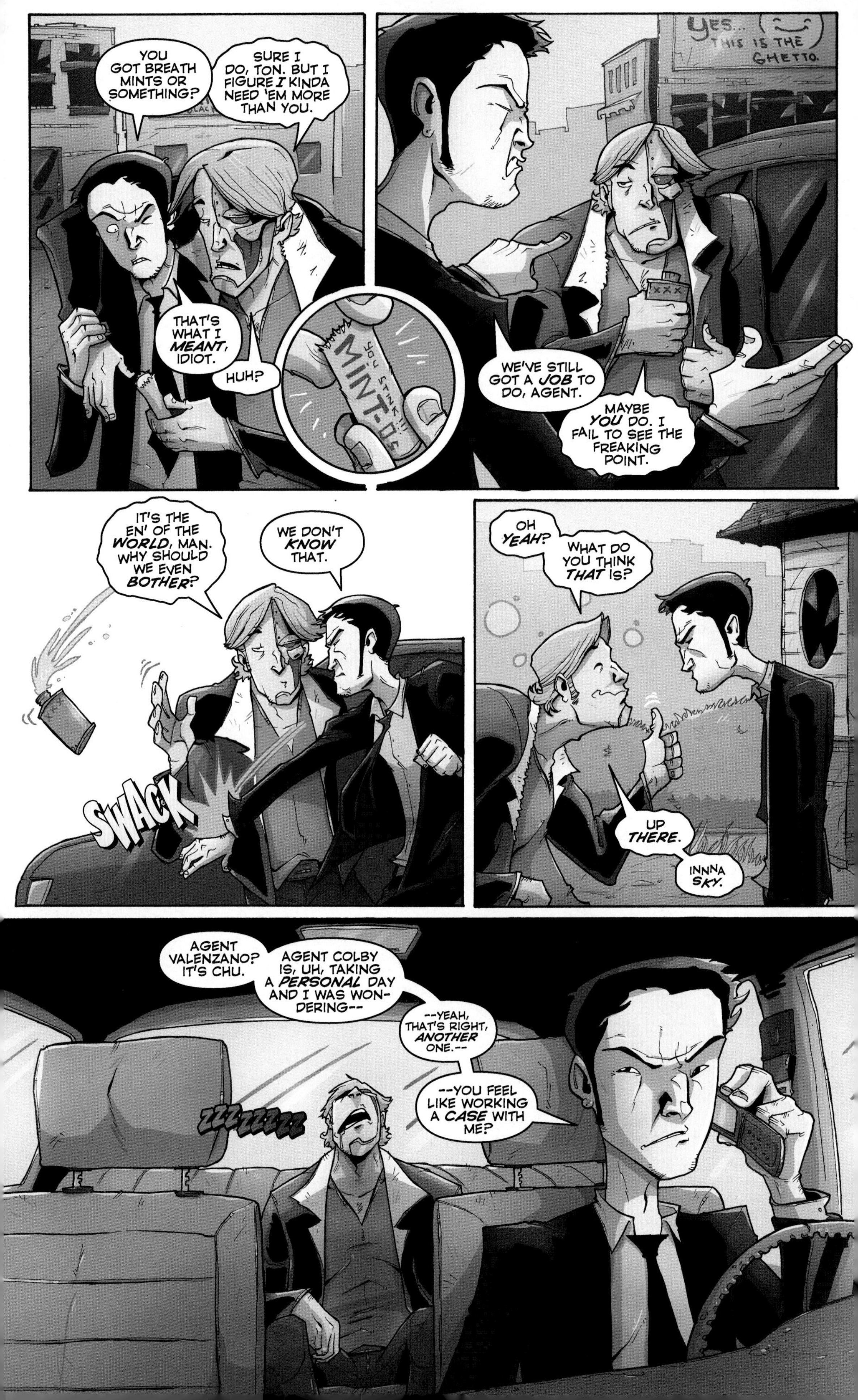
YOU GOT BREATH MINTS OR SOMETHING?
SURE I DO, TON. BUT I FIGURE *I* KINDA NEED 'EM MORE THAN YOU.
THAT'S WHAT I *MEANT*, IDIOT.
HUH?
YOU STINK! MINT-OS
YES... THIS IS THE GHETTO.
WE'VE STILL GOT A *JOB* TO DO, AGENT.
MAYBE *YOU* DO. I FAIL TO SEE THE FREAKING POINT.
IT'S THE EN' OF THE *WORLD*, MAN. WHY SHOULD WE EVEN *BOTHER*?
WE DON'T *KNOW* THAT.
SWACK
OH *YEAH*?
WHAT DO YOU THINK *THAT* IS?
UP *THERE*.
INNNA *SKY*.
AGENT VALENZANO? IT'S CHU.
AGENT COLBY IS, UH, TAKING A *PERSONAL* DAY AND I WAS WONDERING--
--YEAH, THAT'S RIGHT, *ANOTHER* ONE.--
--YOU FEEL LIKE WORKING A *CASE* WITH ME?
ZZZZZZZZ

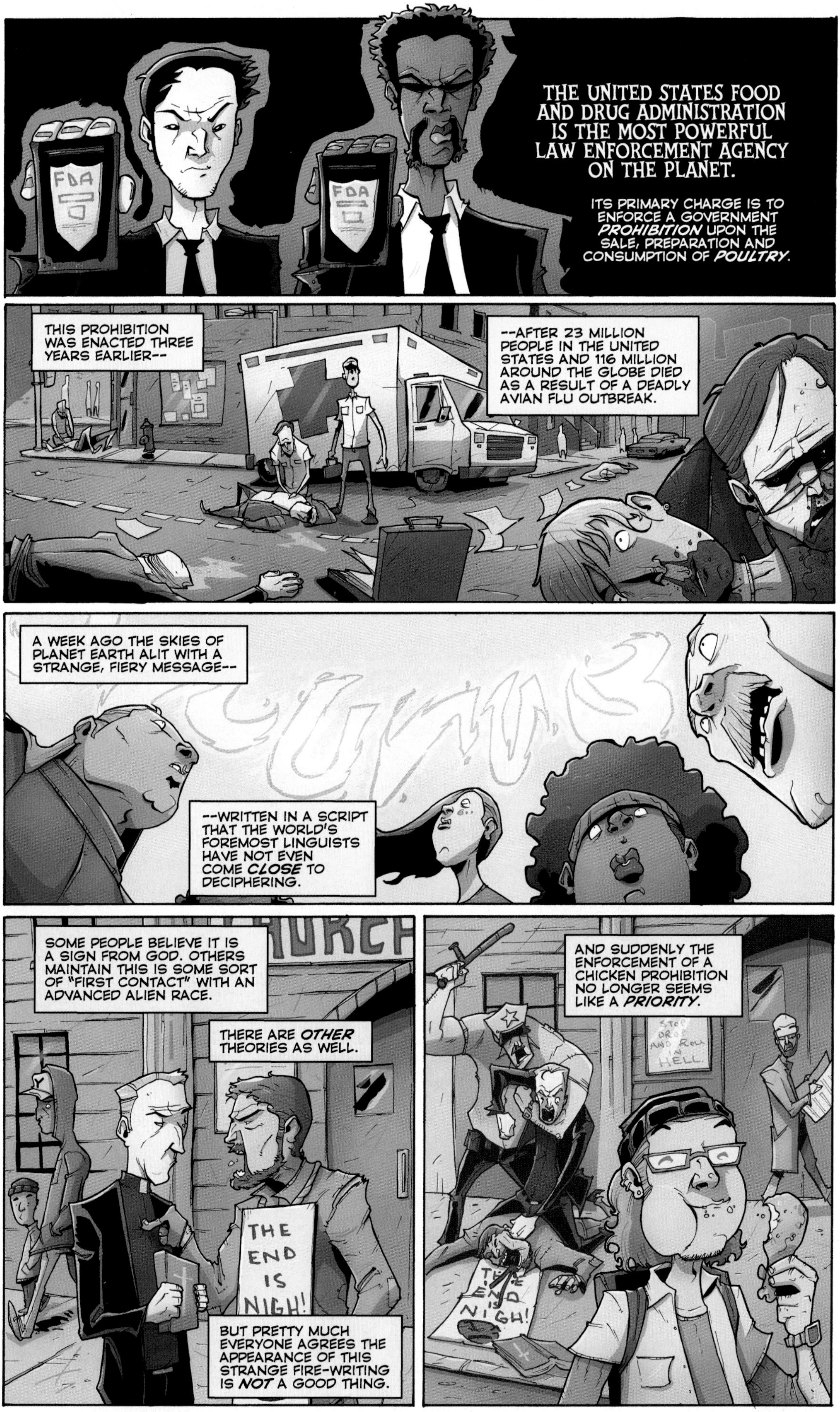

FDA
FDA
THE UNITED STATES FOOD AND DRUG ADMINISTRATION IS THE MOST POWERFUL LAW ENFORCEMENT AGENCY ON THE PLANET.
ITS PRIMARY CHARGE IS TO ENFORCE A GOVERNMENT PROHIBITION UPON THE SALE, PREPARATION AND CONSUMPTION OF POULTRY.
THIS PROHIBITION WAS ENACTED THREE YEARS EARLIER--
--AFTER 23 MILLION PEOPLE IN THE UNITED STATES AND 116 MILLION AROUND THE GLOBE DIED AS A RESULT OF A DEADLY AVIAN FLU OUTBREAK.
A WEEK AGO THE SKIES OF PLANET EARTH ALIT WITH A STRANGE, FIERY MESSAGE--
--WRITTEN IN A SCRIPT THAT THE WORLD'S FOREMOST LINGUISTS HAVE NOT EVEN COME CLOSE TO DECIPHERING.
SOME PEOPLE BELIEVE IT IS A SIGN FROM GOD. OTHERS MAINTAIN THIS IS SOME SORT OF "FIRST CONTACT" WITH AN ADVANCED ALIEN RACE.
THERE ARE OTHER THEORIES AS WELL.
THE END IS NIGH!
BUT PRETTY MUCH EVERYONE AGREES THE APPEARANCE OF THIS STRANGE FIRE-WRITING IS NOT A GOOD THING.
AND SUDDENLY THE ENFORCEMENT OF A CHICKEN PROHIBITION NO LONGER SEEMS LIKE A PRIORITY.
STOP DROP AND ROLL IN HELL.
THE END IS NIGH!

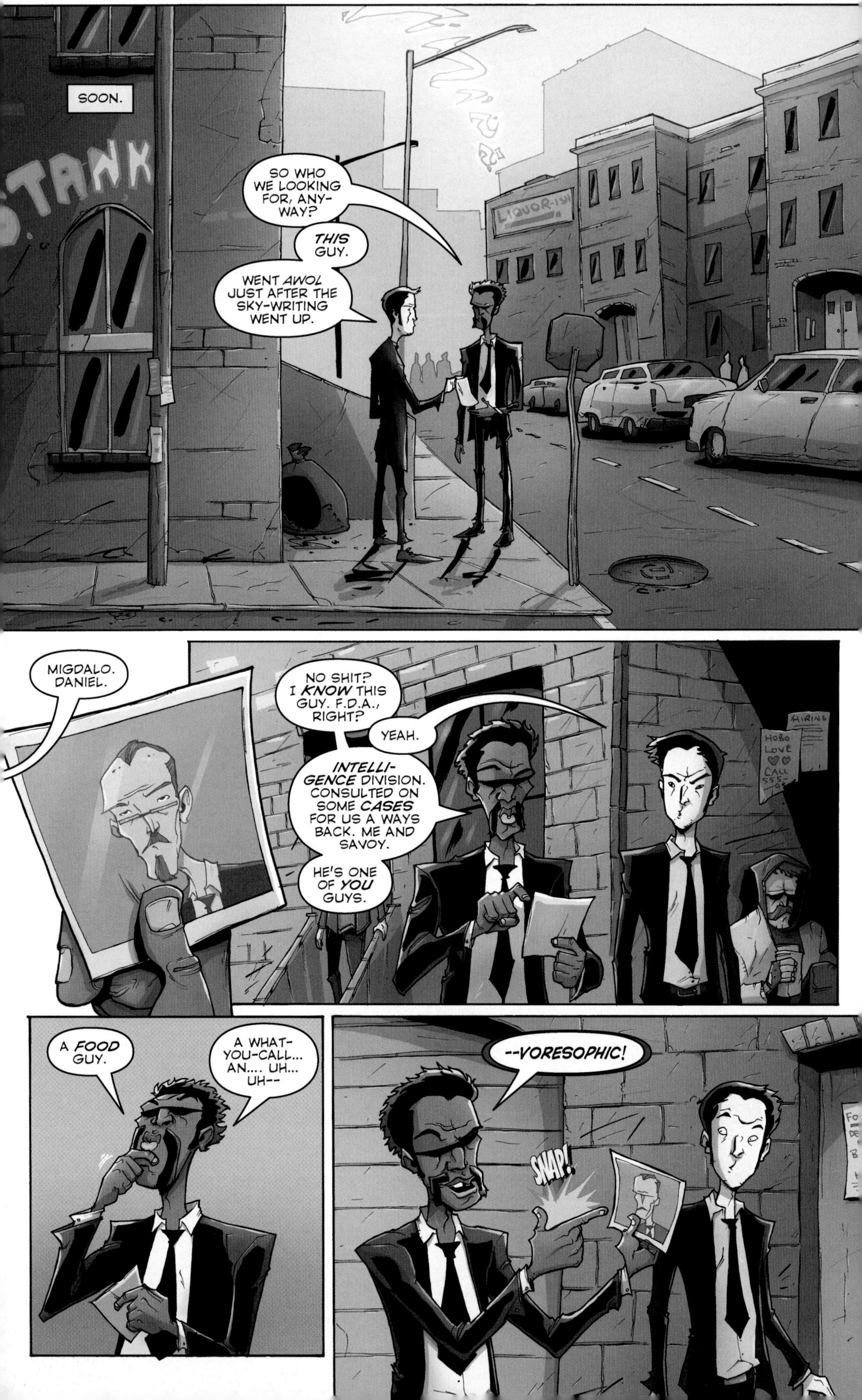
SOON.
SO WHO WE LOOKING FOR, ANYWAY?
THIS GUY.
WENT AWOL JUST AFTER THE SKY-WRITING WENT UP.
LIQUOR-ISH
MIGDALO. DANIEL.
NO SHIT? I KNOW THIS GUY. F.D.A., RIGHT?
YEAH.
INTELLIGENCE DIVISION. CONSULTED ON SOME CASES FOR US A WAYS BACK. ME AND SAVOY.
HE'S ONE OF YOU GUYS.
HIRING
HOBO LOVE
A FOOD GUY.
A WHAT-YOU-CALL... AN.... UH... UH--
--VORESOPHIC!
SNAP!

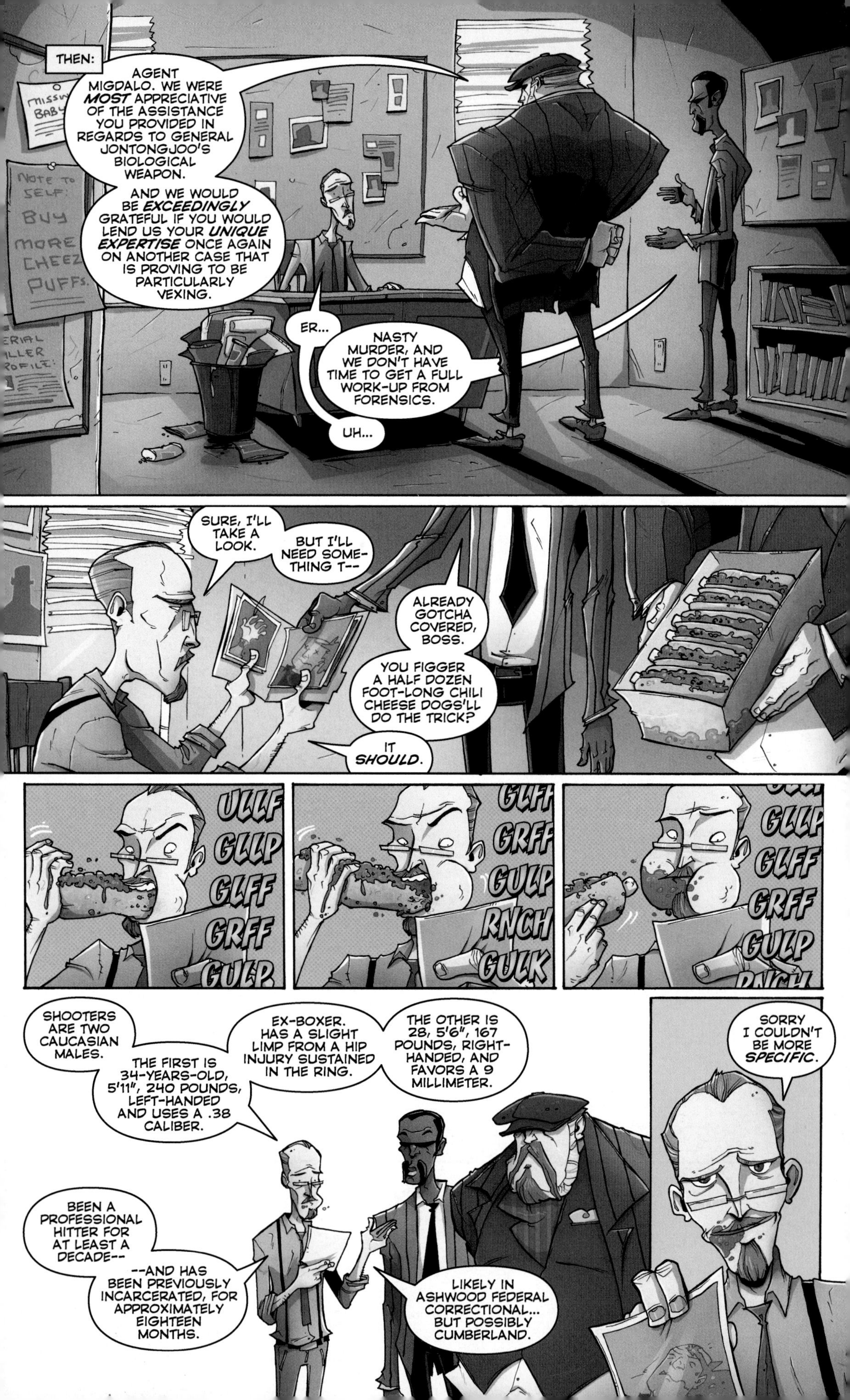
THEN:
AGENT MIGDALO. WE WERE *MOST* APPRECIATIVE OF THE ASSISTANCE YOU PROVIDED IN REGARDS TO GENERAL JONTONGJOO'S BIOLOGICAL WEAPON.
AND WE WOULD BE *EXCEEDINGLY* GRATEFUL IF YOU WOULD LEND US YOUR *UNIQUE EXPERTISE* ONCE AGAIN ON ANOTHER CASE THAT IS PROVING TO BE PARTICULARLY VEXING.
NOTE TO SELF: BUY MORE CHEEZ PUFFS.
ER...
NASTY MURDER, AND WE DON'T HAVE TIME TO GET A FULL WORK-UP FROM FORENSICS.
UH...
SURE, I'LL TAKE A LOOK.
BUT I'LL NEED SOME-THING T--
ALREADY GOTCHA COVERED, BOSS.
YOU FIGGER A HALF DOZEN FOOT-LONG CHILI CHEESE DOGS'LL DO THE TRICK?
IT *SHOULD*.
ULLF GLLP GLFF GRFF GULP
GRFF GULP RNCH GULK
GLLP GLFF GRFF GULP
SHOOTERS ARE TWO CAUCASIAN MALES.
THE FIRST IS 34-YEARS-OLD, 5'11", 240 POUNDS, LEFT-HANDED AND USES A .38 CALIBER.
EX-BOXER. HAS A SLIGHT LIMP FROM A HIP INJURY SUSTAINED IN THE RING.
THE OTHER IS 28, 5'6", 167 POUNDS, RIGHT-HANDED, AND FAVORS A 9 MILLIMETER.
BEEN A PROFESSIONAL HITTER FOR AT LEAST A DECADE--
--AND HAS BEEN PREVIOUSLY INCARCERATED, FOR APPROXIMATELY EIGHTEEN MONTHS.
LIKELY IN ASHWOOD FEDERAL CORRECTIONAL... BUT POSSIBLY CUMBERLAND.
SORRY I COULDN'T BE MORE *SPECIFIC*.

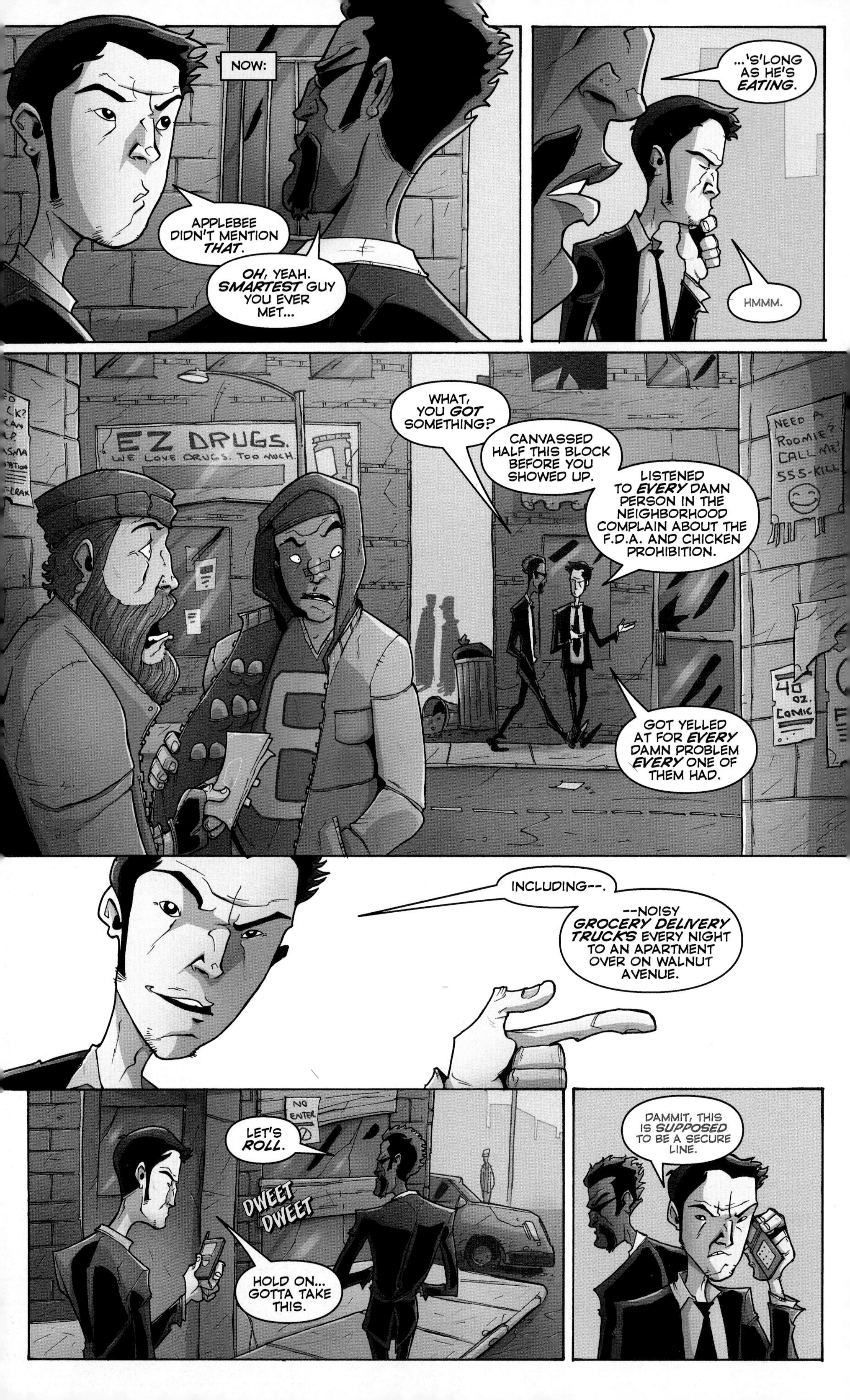
NOW:
APPLEBEE DIDN'T MENTION *THAT*.
OH, YEAH. *SMARTEST* GUY YOU EVER MET...
...'S'LONG AS HE'S *EATING*.
HMMM.
EZ DRUGS.
WE LOVE DRUGS. TOO MUCH.
NEED A ROOMIE? CALL ME! 555-KILL
40 OZ. COMIC
WHAT, YOU *GOT* SOMETHING?
CANVASSED HALF THIS BLOCK BEFORE YOU SHOWED UP.
LISTENED TO *EVERY* DAMN PERSON IN THE NEIGHBORHOOD COMPLAIN ABOUT THE F.D.A. AND CHICKEN PROHIBITION.
GOT YELLED AT FOR *EVERY* DAMN PROBLEM *EVERY* ONE OF THEM HAD.
INCLUDING--.
--NOISY *GROCERY DELIVERY TRUCKS* EVERY NIGHT TO AN APARTMENT OVER ON WALNUT AVENUE.
NO ENTER
LET'S *ROLL*.
DWEET DWEET
HOLD ON... GOTTA TAKE THIS.
DAMMIT, THIS IS *SUPPOSED* TO BE A SECURE LINE.

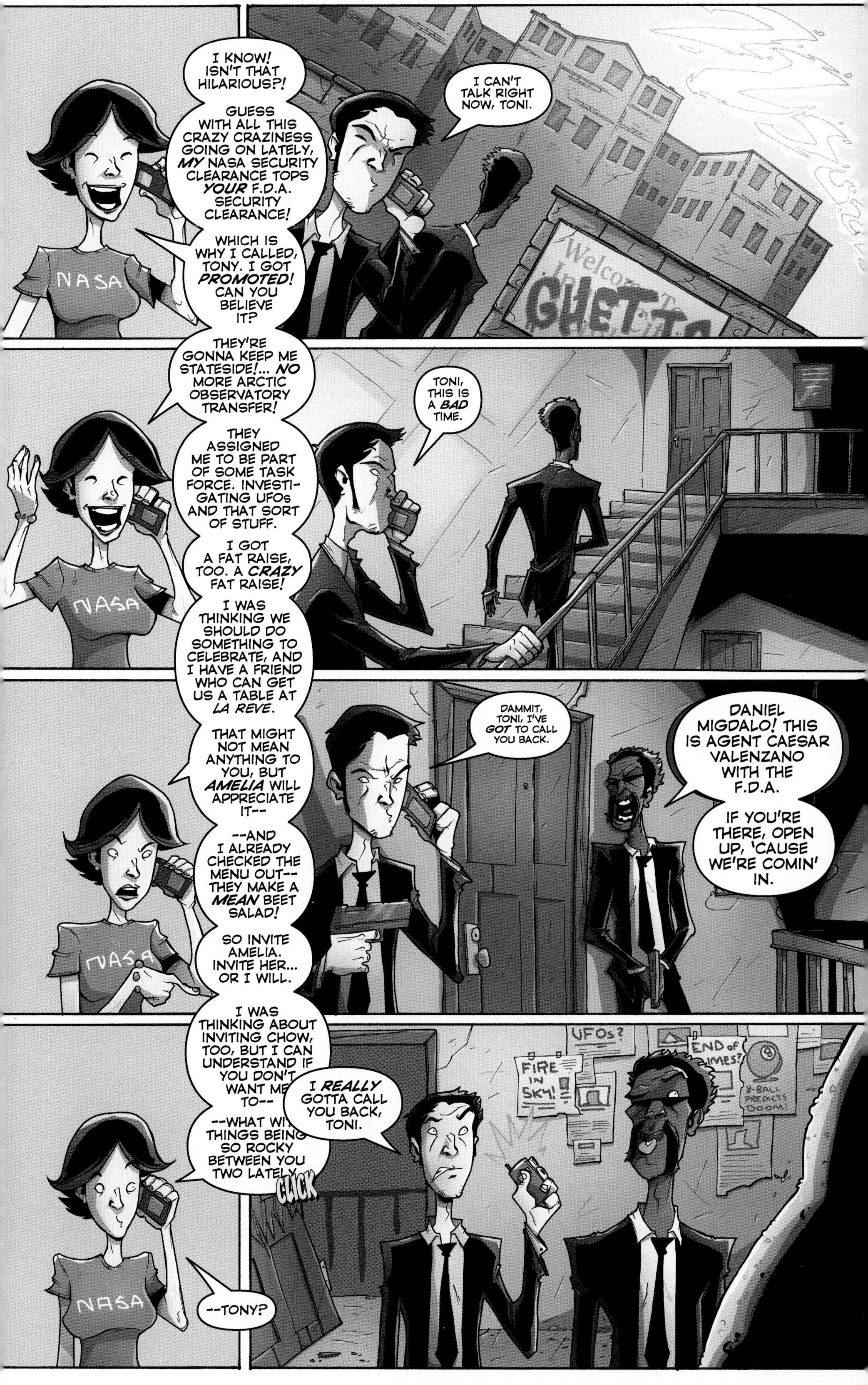

I KNOW! ISN'T THAT HILARIOUS?!
GUESS WITH ALL THIS CRAZY CRAZINESS GOING ON LATELY, *MY* NASA SECURITY CLEARANCE TOPS *YOUR* F.D.A. SECURITY CLEARANCE!
WHICH IS WHY I CALLED, TONY. I GOT *PROMOTED!* CAN YOU BELIEVE IT?
I CAN'T TALK RIGHT NOW, TONI.
NASA
Welcome To
GHETTO
THEY'RE GONNA KEEP ME STATESIDE!... *NO* MORE ARCTIC OBSERVATORY TRANSFER!
THEY ASSIGNED ME TO BE PART OF SOME TASK FORCE. INVESTI-GATING UFOs AND THAT SORT OF STUFF.
I GOT A FAT RAISE, TOO. A *CRAZY* FAT RAISE!
I WAS THINKING WE SHOULD DO SOMETHING TO CELEBRATE, AND I HAVE A FRIEND WHO CAN GET US A TABLE AT *LA REVE*.
TONI, THIS IS A *BAD* TIME.
NASA
THAT MIGHT NOT MEAN ANYTHING TO YOU, BUT *AMELIA* WILL APPRECIATE IT--
--AND I ALREADY CHECKED THE MENU OUT-- THEY MAKE A *MEAN* BEET SALAD!
SO INVITE AMELIA. INVITE HER... OR I WILL.
DAMMIT, TONI, I'VE *GOT* TO CALL YOU BACK.
DANIEL MIGDALO! THIS IS AGENT CAESAR VALENZANO WITH THE F.D.A.
IF YOU'RE THERE, OPEN UP, 'CAUSE WE'RE COMIN' IN.
NASA
I WAS THINKING ABOUT INVITING CHOW, TOO, BUT I CAN UNDERSTAND IF YOU DON'T WANT ME TO--
--WHAT WITH THINGS BEING SO ROCKY BETWEEN YOU TWO LATELY
I *REALLY* GOTTA CALL YOU BACK, TONI.
CLICK
UFOs?
END of TIMES?
FIRE IN SKY!
8-BALL PREDICTS DOOM!
NASA
--TONY?

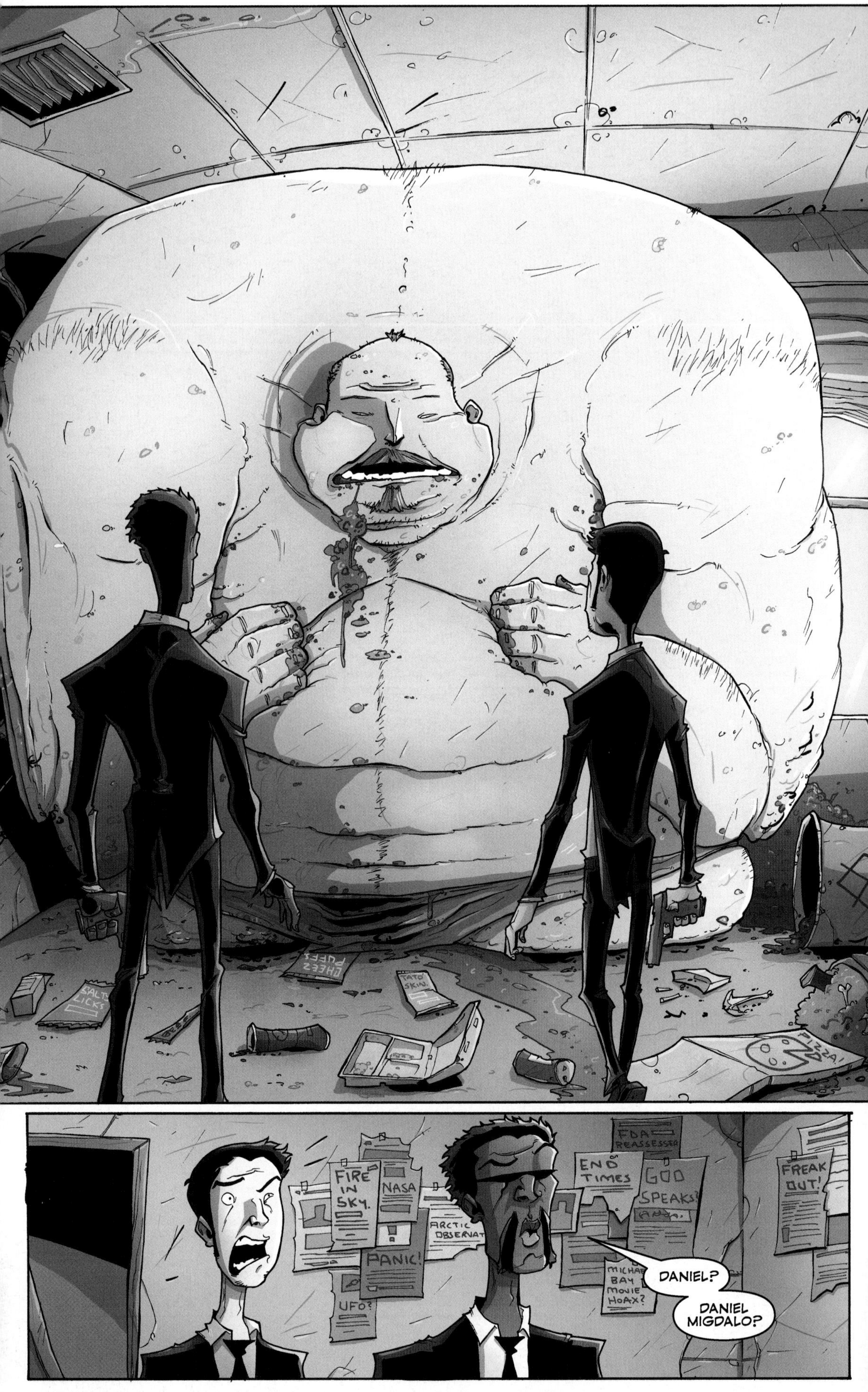
CHEEZ PUFFS
SALTY LICKS
TATO SKIN.
PIZZA!
FDA REASSESSES
FIRE IN SKY.
NASA
ARCTIC OBSERVAT
PANIC!
UFO?
END TIMES
GOD SPEAKS!
MICHAEL BAY MOVIE HOAX?
FREAK OUT!
DANIEL?
DANIEL MIGDALO?

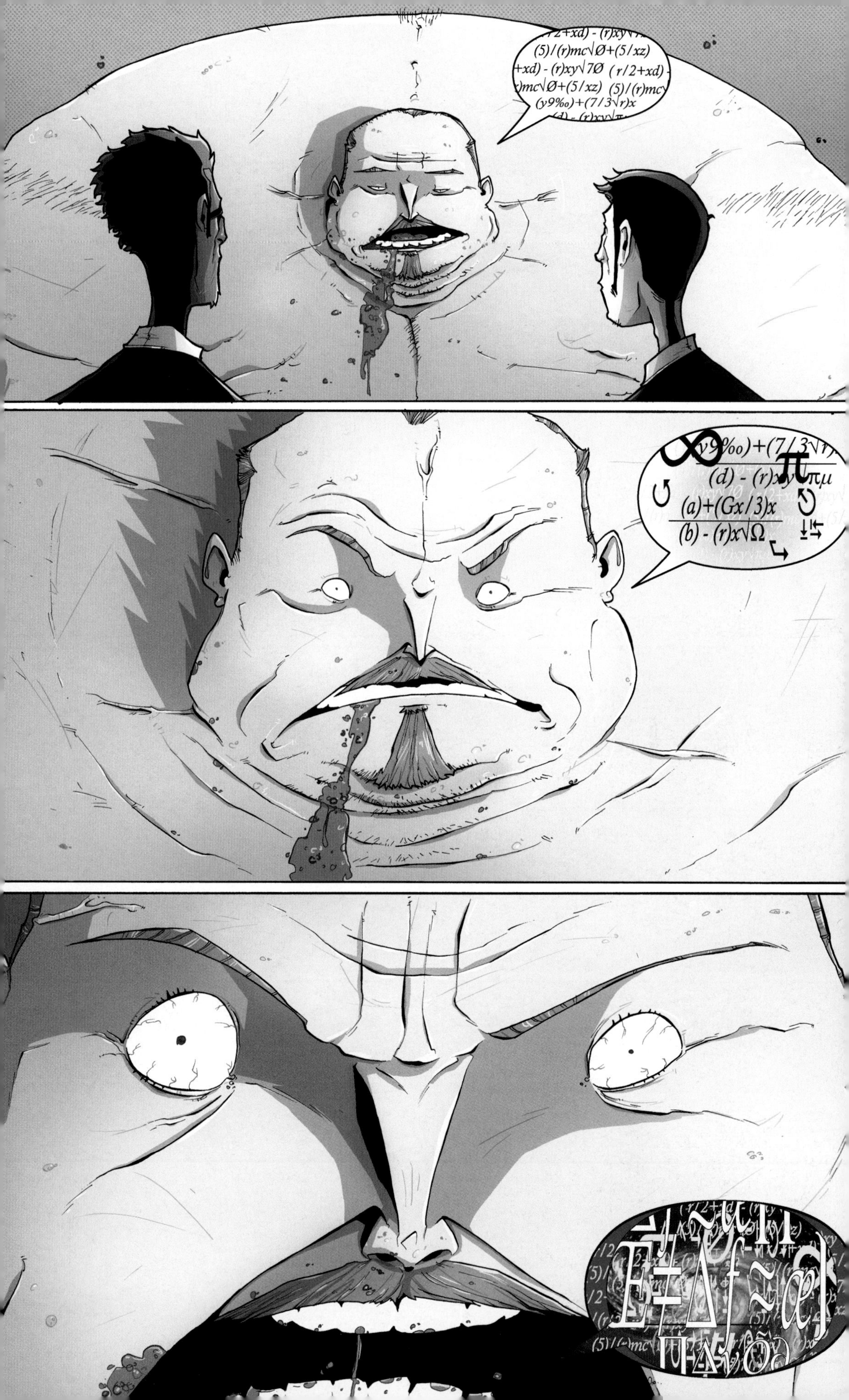
(5)/(r)mc√Ø+(5/xz)
+xd) - (r)xy√7Ø (r/2+xd) -
)mc√Ø+(5/xz) (5)/(r)mcy
(y9‰)+(7/3√r)x
(a)+(Gx/3)x
(b) - (r)x√Ω

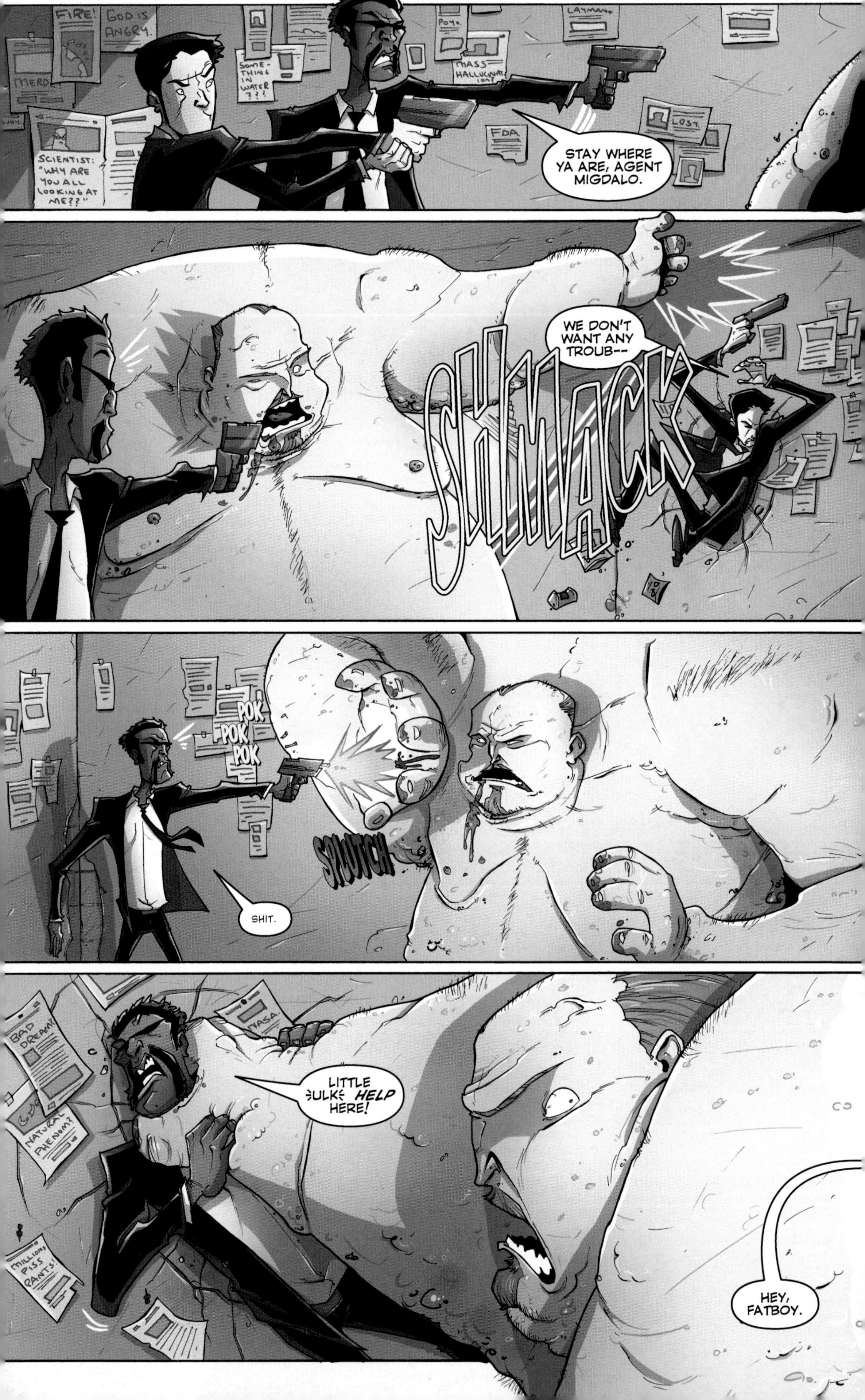
FIRE!
GOD IS ANGRY.
SOME-THING IN WATER???
MASS HALLUCINATION?
FDA
LOST.
SCIENTIST: "WHY ARE YOU ALL LOOKING AT ME??"
STAY WHERE YA ARE, AGENT MIGDALO.
WE DON'T WANT ANY TROUB--
SHMACK
POK
POK
POK
SPLUTCH
SHIT.
BAD DREAMS?
NASA.
NATURAL PHENOM?
MILLIONS PISS PANTS!
LITTLE ULK *HELP* HERE!
HEY, FATBOY.

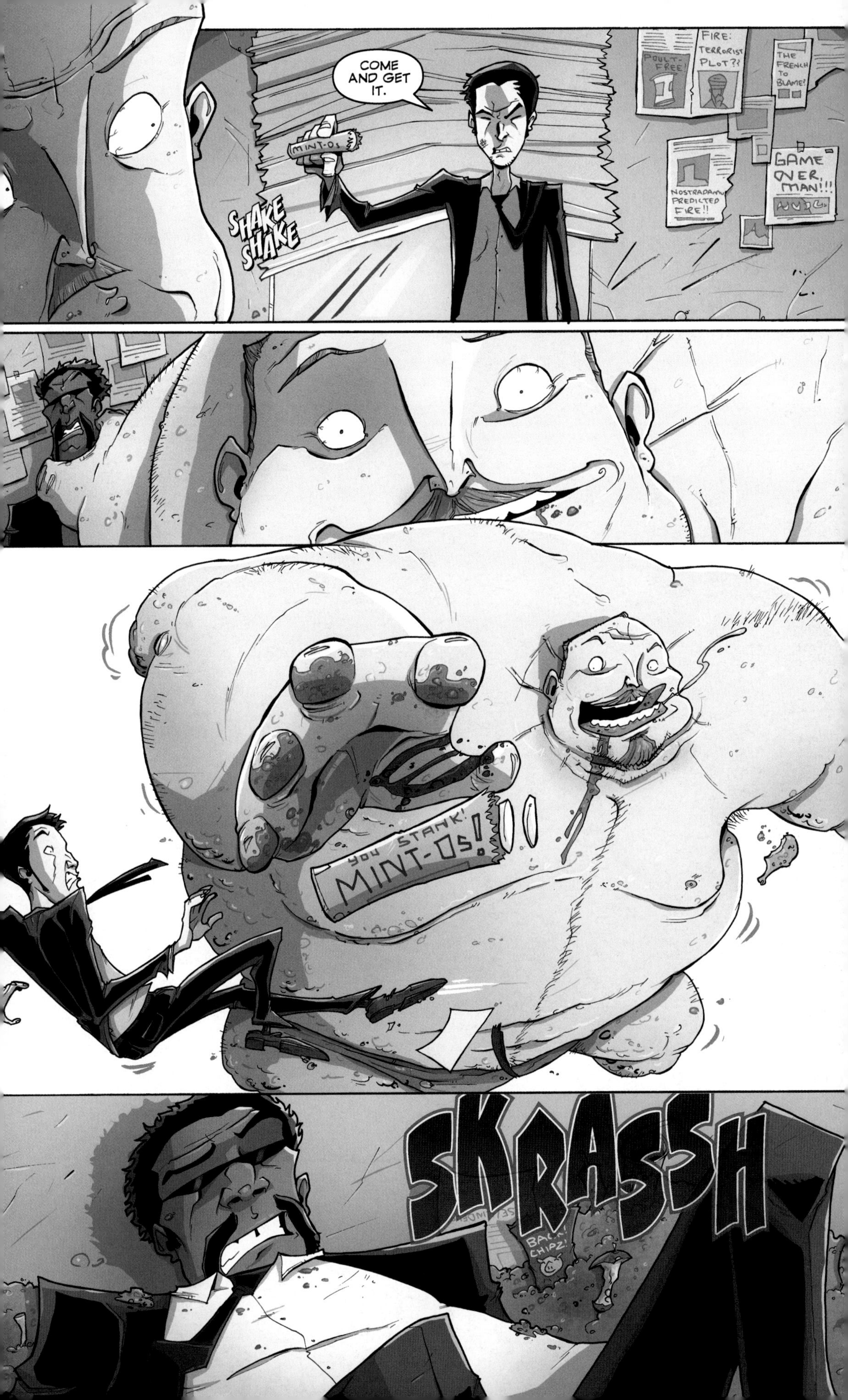
COME AND GET IT.
MINT-OS
SHAKE SHAKE
POULT-FREE!
FIRE: TERRORIST PLOT??
THE FRENCH TO BLAME!
NOSTRADAMU PREDICTED FIRE!!
GAME OVER, MAN!!!
YOU STANK! MINT-OS!
SKRASSH

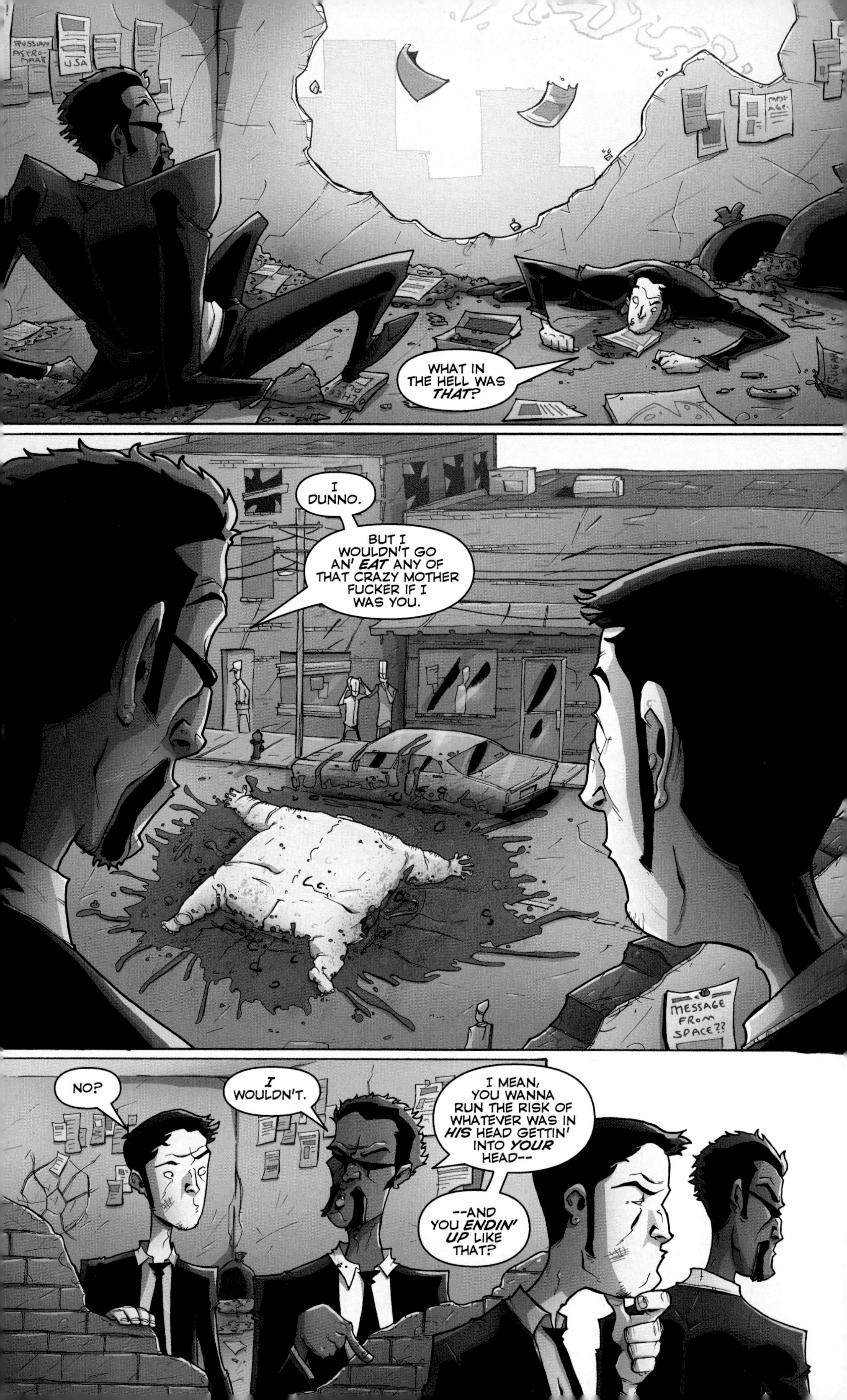
WHAT IN THE HELL WAS *THAT*?
I DUNNO.
BUT I WOULDN'T GO AN' *EAT* ANY OF THAT CRAZY MOTHER FUCKER IF I WAS YOU.
MESSAGE FROM SPACE??
NO?
I WOULDN'T.
I MEAN, YOU WANNA RUN THE RISK OF WHATEVER WAS IN *HIS* HEAD GETTIN' INTO *YOUR* HEAD--
--AND YOU *ENDIN' UP* LIKE THAT?

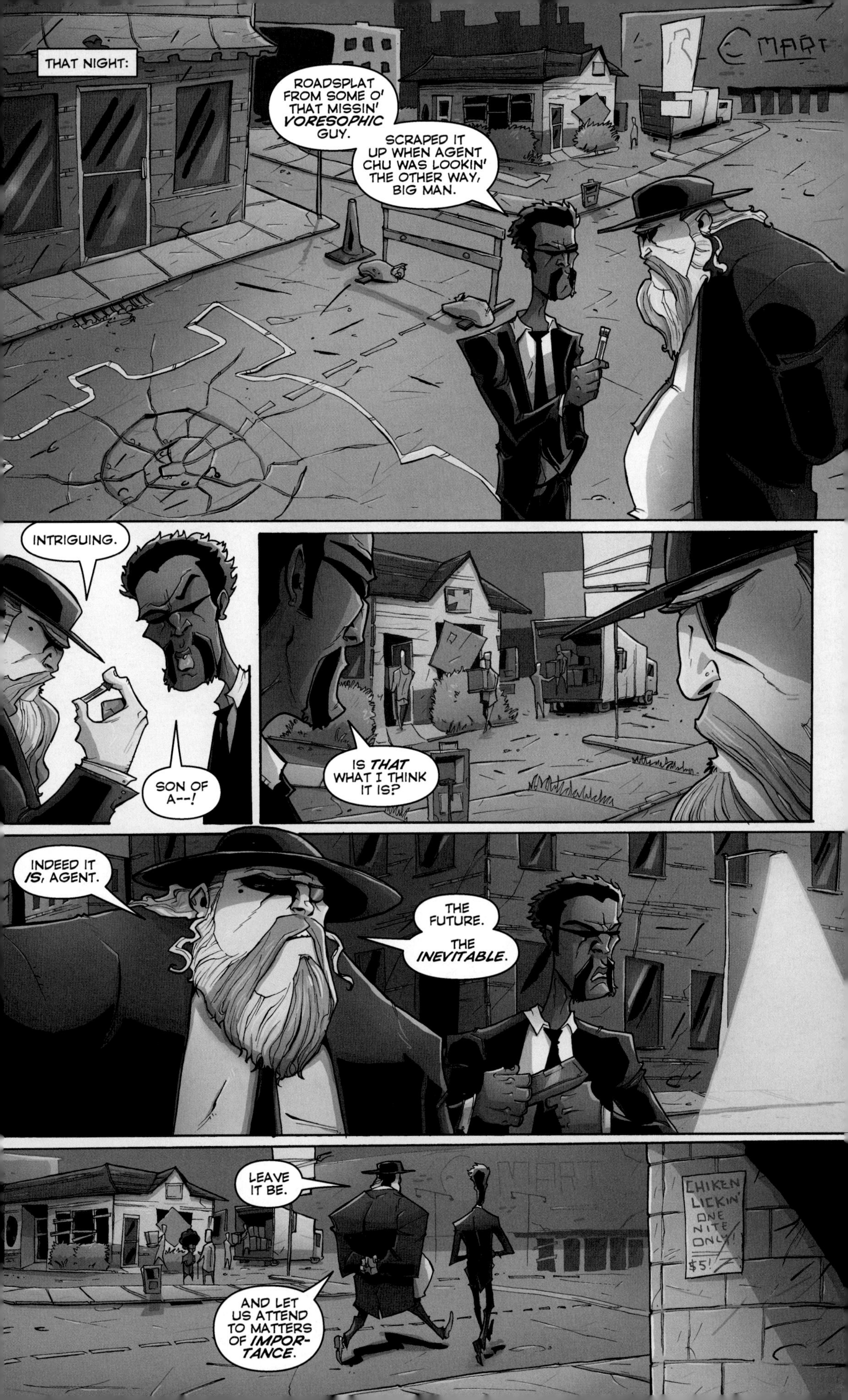
THAT NIGHT:
ROADSPLAT FROM SOME O' THAT MISSIN' *VORESOPHIC* GUY.
SCRAPED IT UP WHEN AGENT CHU WAS LOOKIN' THE OTHER WAY, BIG MAN.
C MART
INTRIGUING.
SON OF A--!
IS *THAT* WHAT I THINK IT IS?
INDEED IT *IS*, AGENT.
THE FUTURE.
THE *INEVITABLE*.
LEAVE IT BE.
AND LET US ATTEND TO MATTERS OF *IMPORTANCE*.
CHIKEN LICKIN' ONE NITE ONLY! $5!

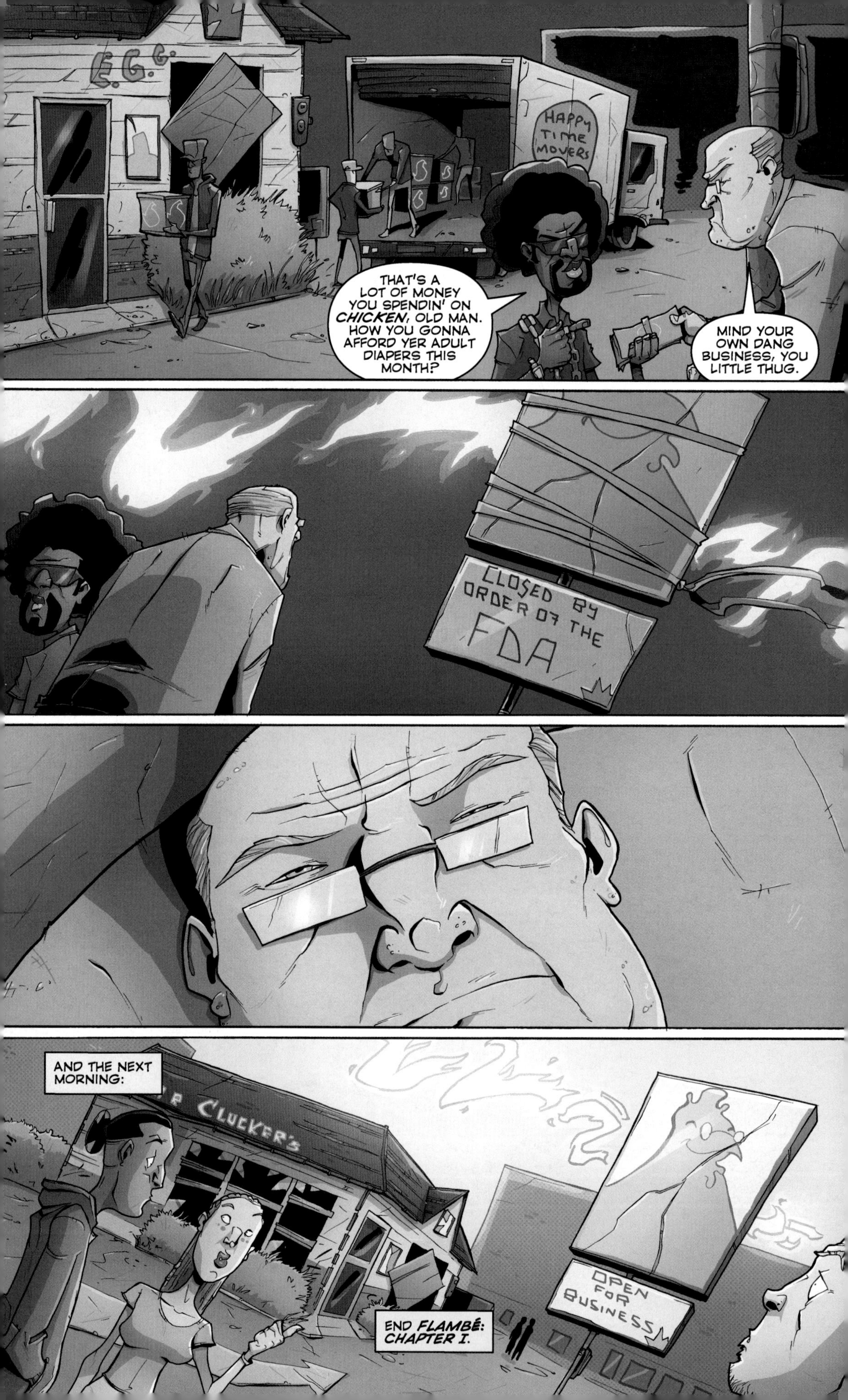
E.G.
HAPPY TIME MOVERS
THAT'S A LOT OF MONEY YOU SPENDIN' ON ***CHICKEN***, OLD MAN. HOW YOU GONNA AFFORD YER ADULT DIAPERS THIS MONTH?
MIND YOUR OWN DANG BUSINESS, YOU LITTLE THUG.
CLOSED BY ORDER OF THE FDA
AND THE NEXT MORNING:
CLUCKER'S
OPEN FOR BUSINESS
END ***FLAMBÉ: CHAPTER I.***

Chapter 2

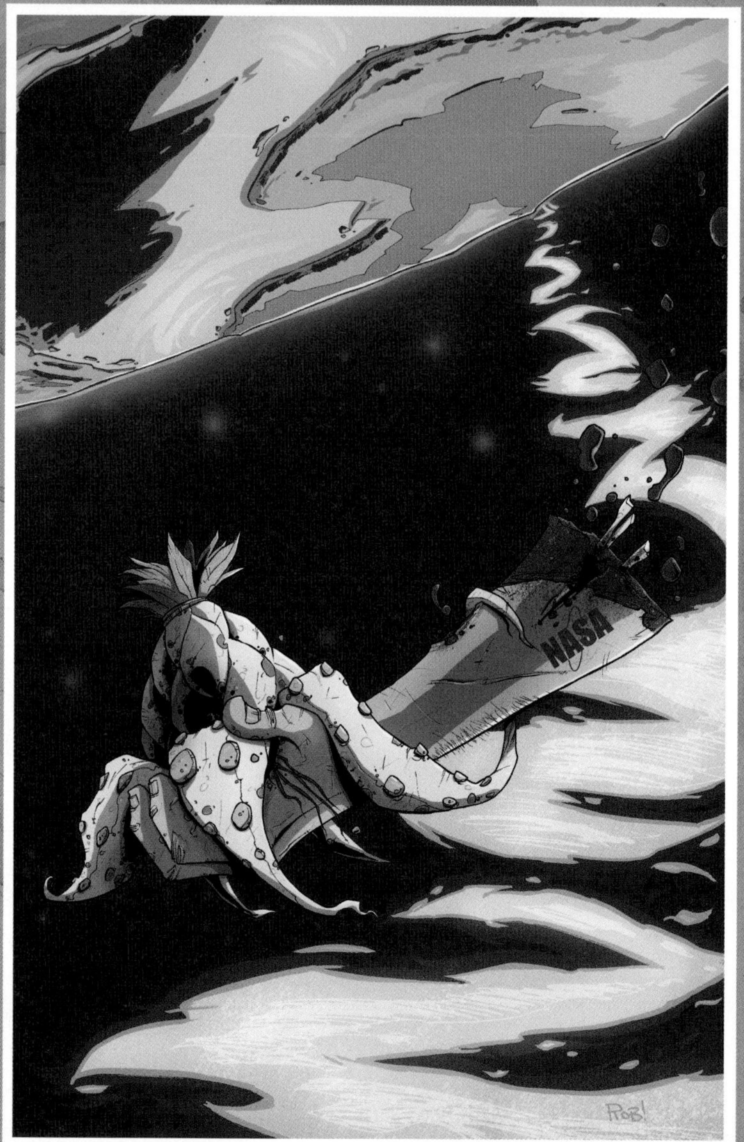
NASA

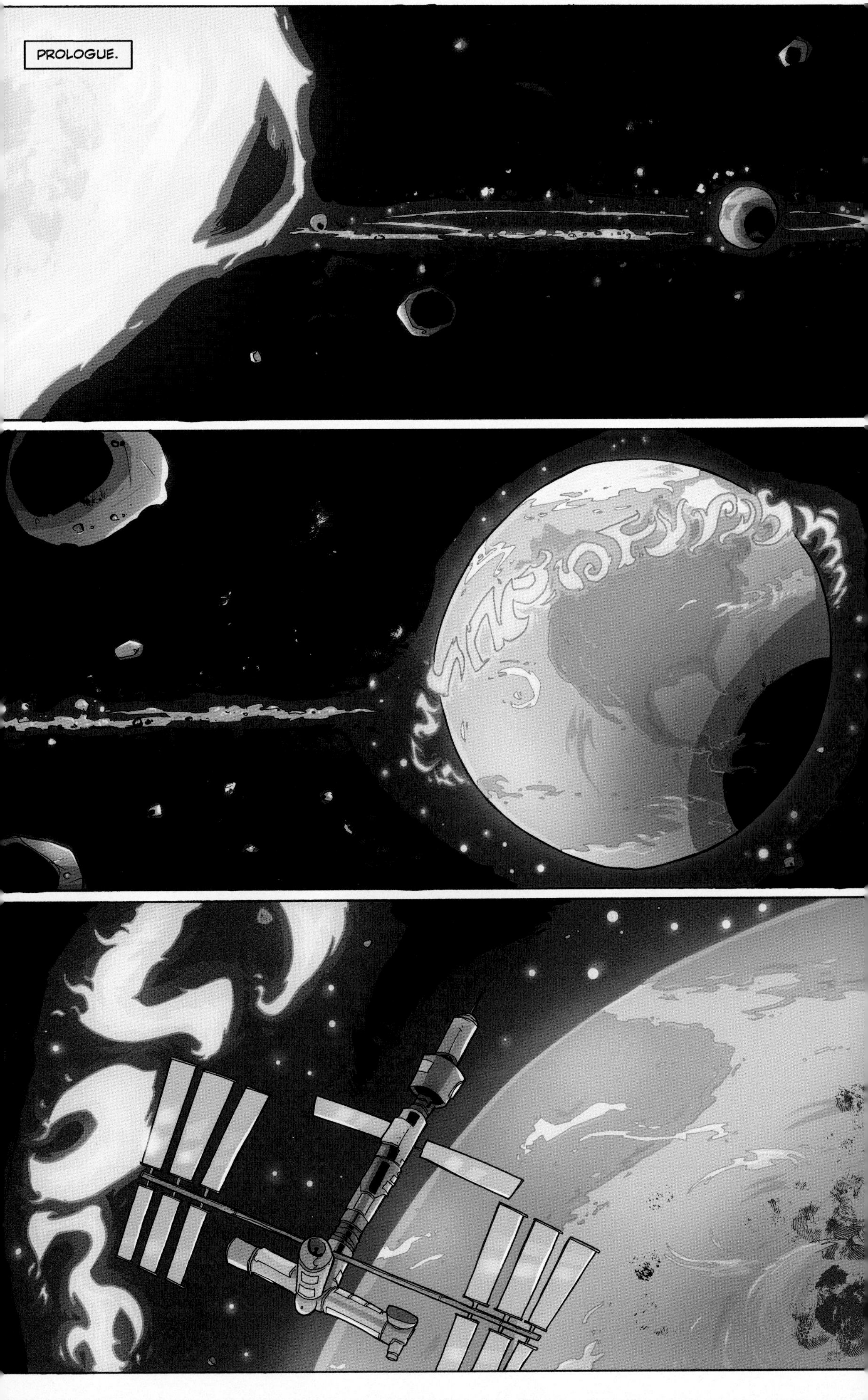
PROLOGUE.

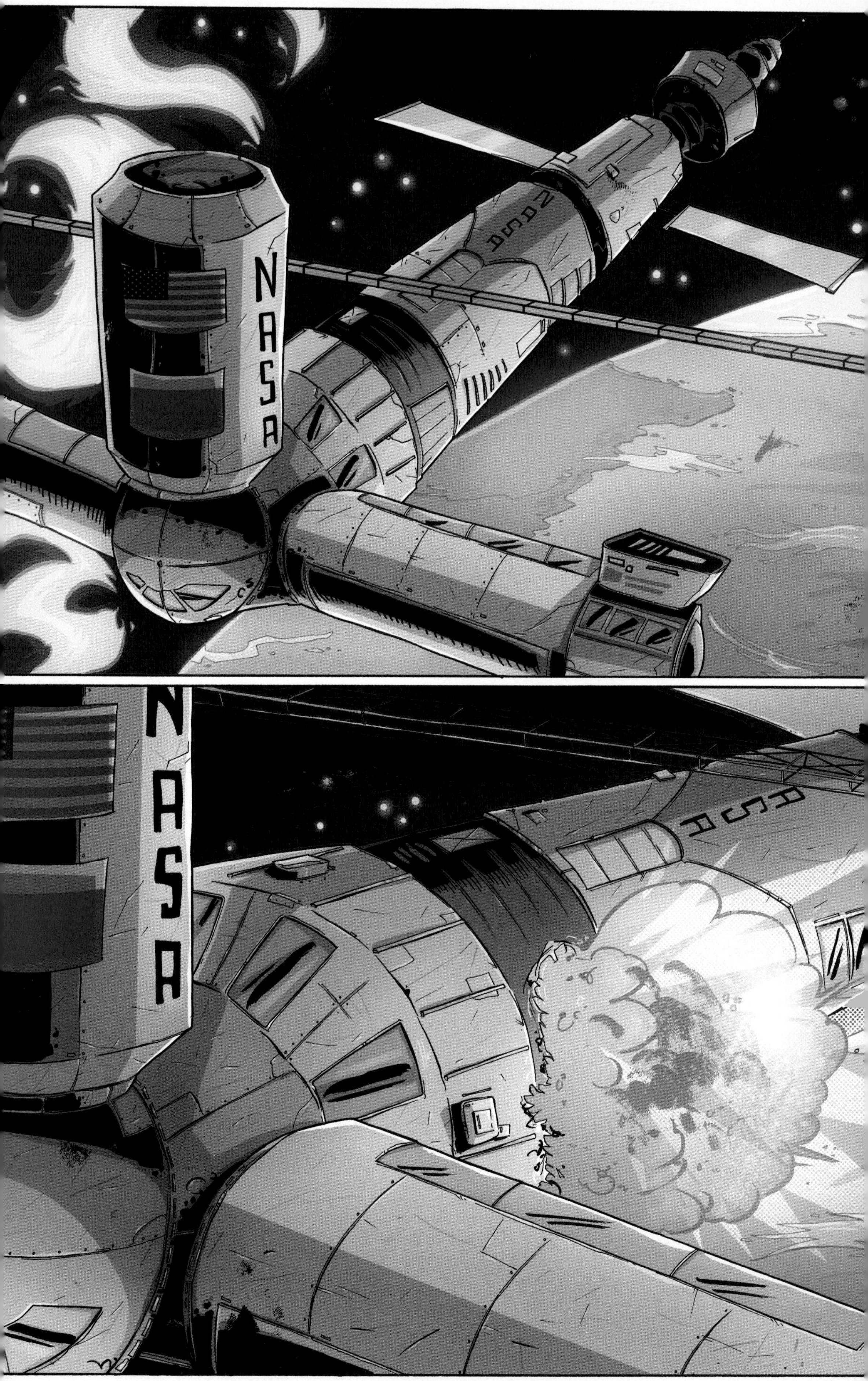
NASA

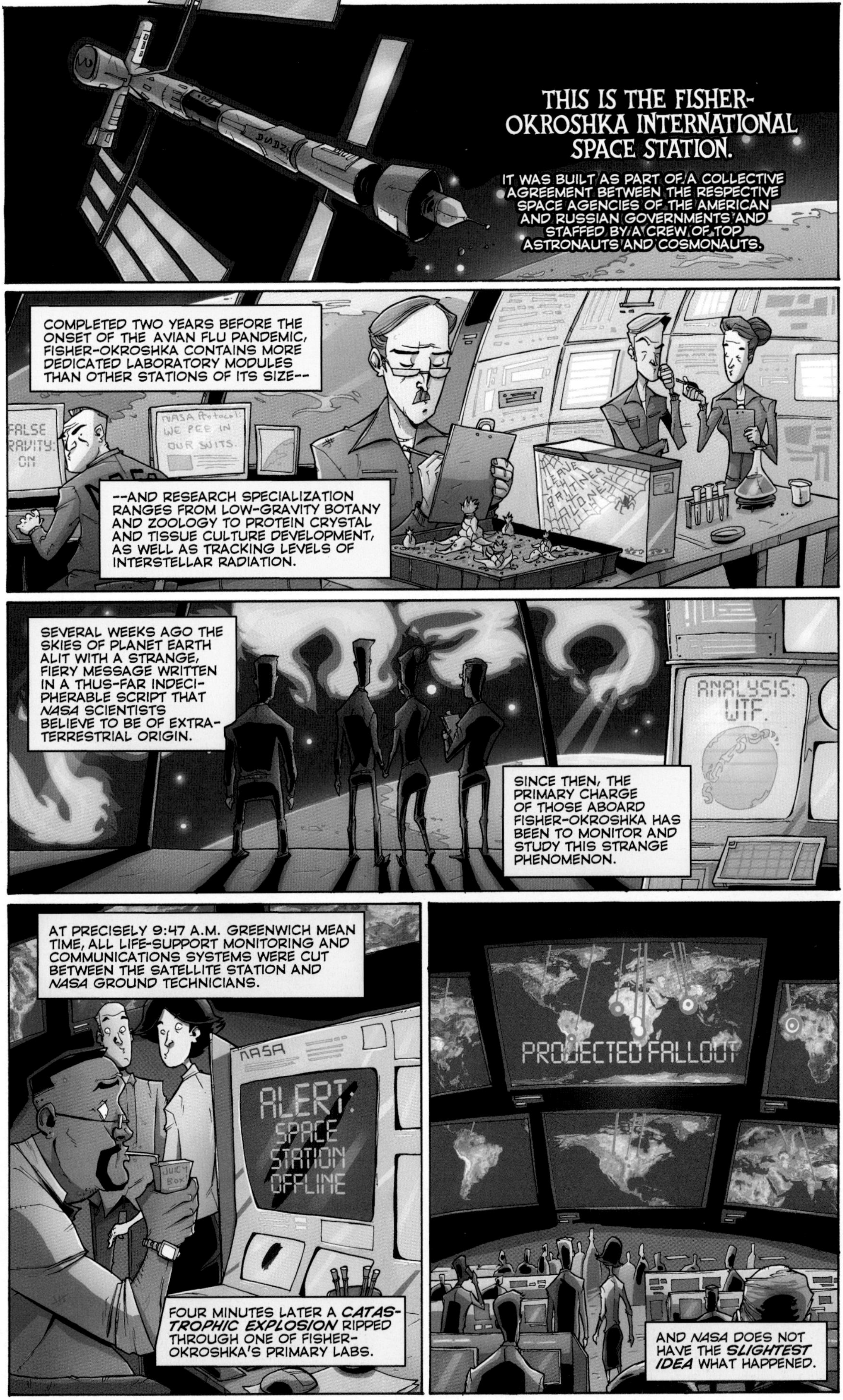
THIS IS THE FISHER-OKROSHKA INTERNATIONAL SPACE STATION.
IT WAS BUILT AS PART OF A COLLECTIVE AGREEMENT BETWEEN THE RESPECTIVE SPACE AGENCIES OF THE AMERICAN AND RUSSIAN GOVERNMENTS AND STAFFED BY A CREW OF TOP ASTRONAUTS AND COSMONAUTS.
COMPLETED TWO YEARS BEFORE THE ONSET OF THE AVIAN FLU PANDEMIC, FISHER-OKROSHKA CONTAINS MORE DEDICATED LABORATORY MODULES THAN OTHER STATIONS OF ITS SIZE--
FALSE RAVITY: ON
NASA Protocol: WE PEE IN OUR SUITS.
LEAVE BRITNEY ALONE
--AND RESEARCH SPECIALIZATION RANGES FROM LOW-GRAVITY BOTANY AND ZOOLOGY TO PROTEIN CRYSTAL AND TISSUE CULTURE DEVELOPMENT, AS WELL AS TRACKING LEVELS OF INTERSTELLAR RADIATION.
SEVERAL WEEKS AGO THE SKIES OF PLANET EARTH ALIT WITH A STRANGE, FIERY MESSAGE WRITTEN IN A THUS-FAR INDECIPHERABLE SCRIPT THAT NASA SCIENTISTS BELIEVE TO BE OF EXTRATERRESTRIAL ORIGIN.
ANALYSIS: WTF.
SINCE THEN, THE PRIMARY CHARGE OF THOSE ABOARD FISHER-OKROSHKA HAS BEEN TO MONITOR AND STUDY THIS STRANGE PHENOMENON.
AT PRECISELY 9:47 A.M. GREENWICH MEAN TIME, ALL LIFE-SUPPORT MONITORING AND COMMUNICATIONS SYSTEMS WERE CUT BETWEEN THE SATELLITE STATION AND NASA GROUND TECHNICIANS.
NASA
ALERT: SPACE STATION OFFLINE
JUICY BOX!
FOUR MINUTES LATER A CATASTROPHIC EXPLOSION RIPPED THROUGH ONE OF FISHER-OKROSHKA'S PRIMARY LABS.
PROJECTED FALLOUT
AND NASA DOES NOT HAVE THE SLIGHTEST IDEA WHAT HAPPENED.

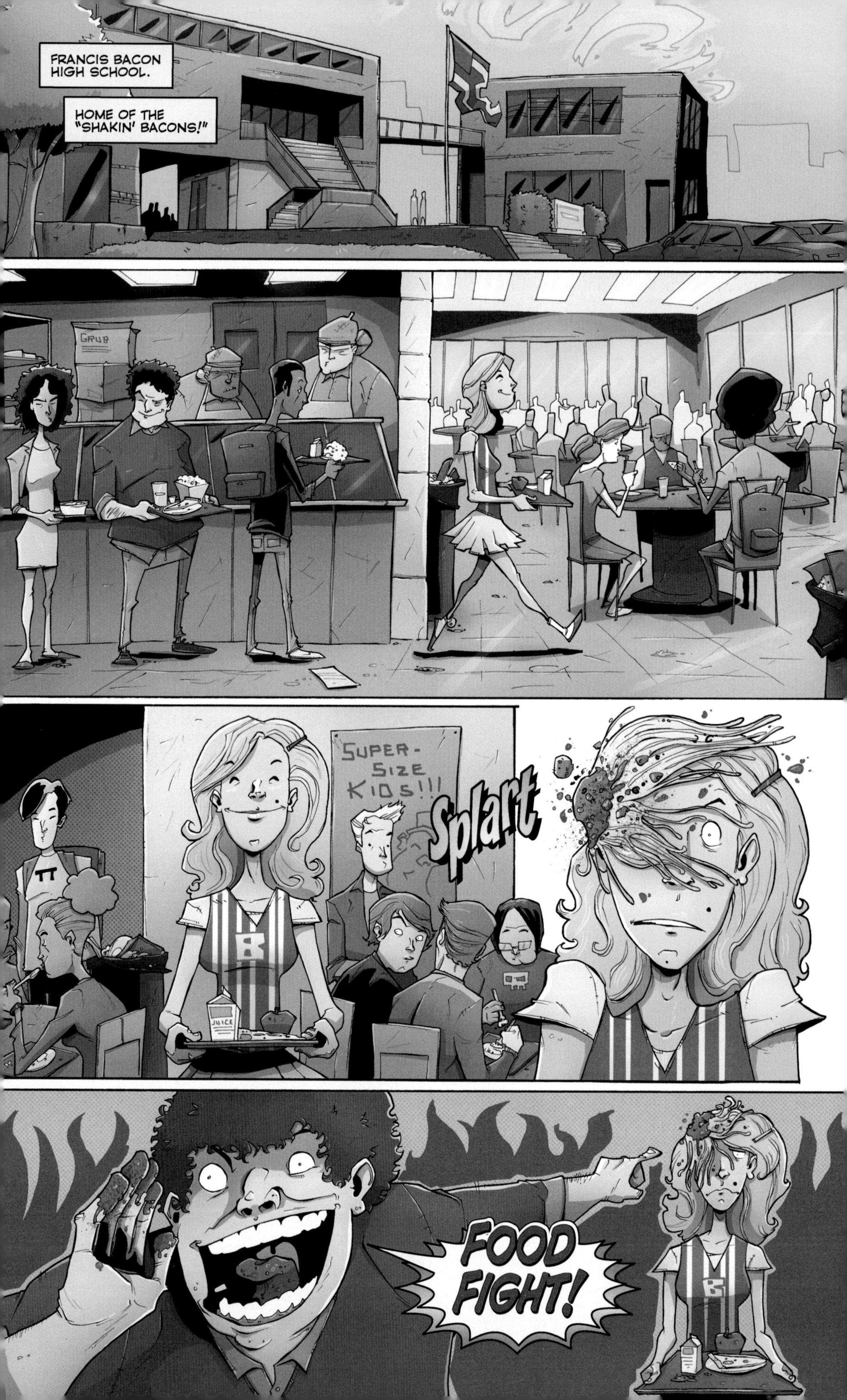
FRANCIS BACON HIGH SCHOOL.
HOME OF THE "SHAKIN' BACONS!"
GRUB
SUPER-SIZE KIDS!!!
JUICE
Splart
FOOD FIGHT!

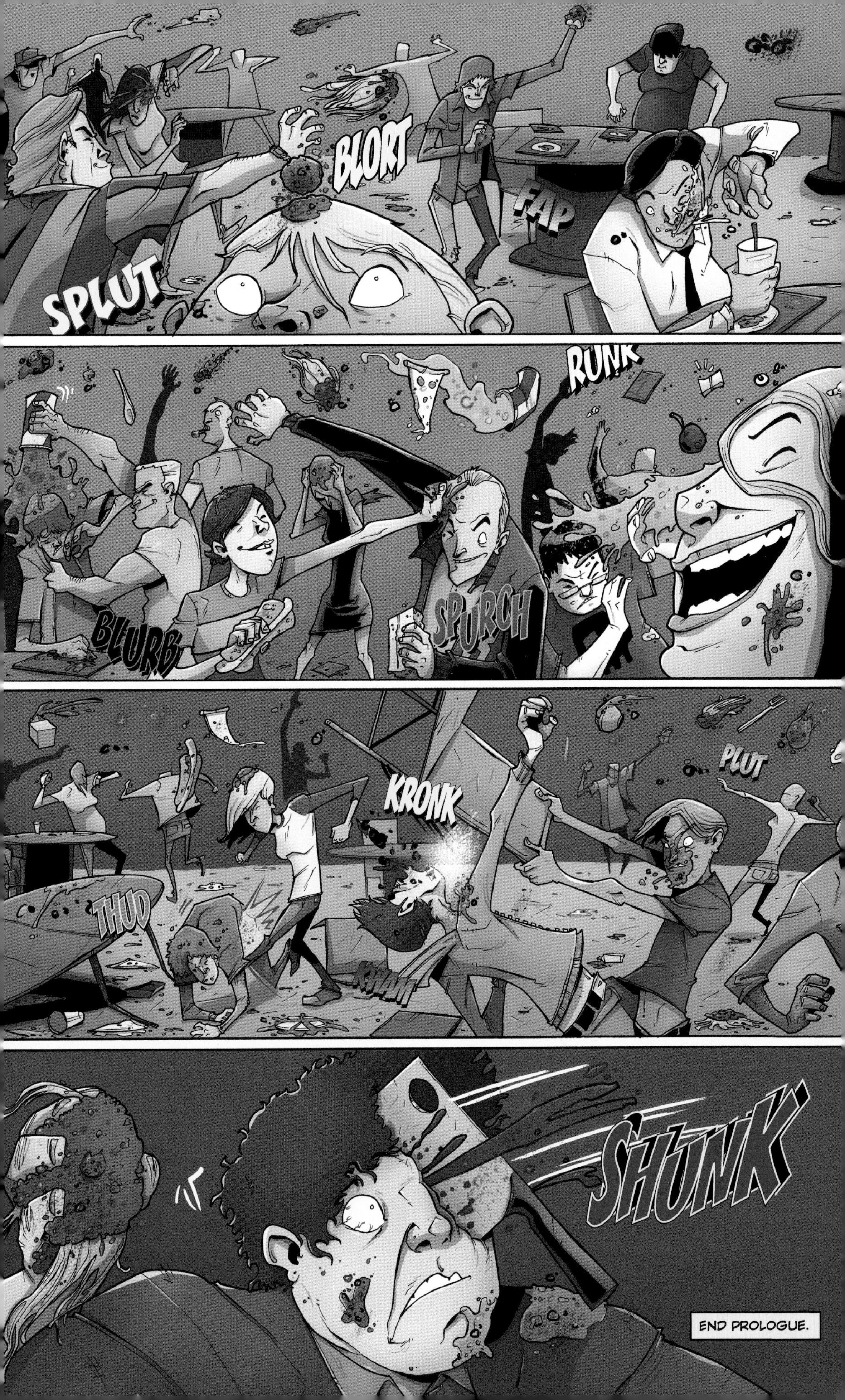

SPLUT
BLORT
FAP
RUNK
BLURB
SPURCH
KRONK
PLUT
THUD
KWAM
SHUNK
END PROLOGUE.

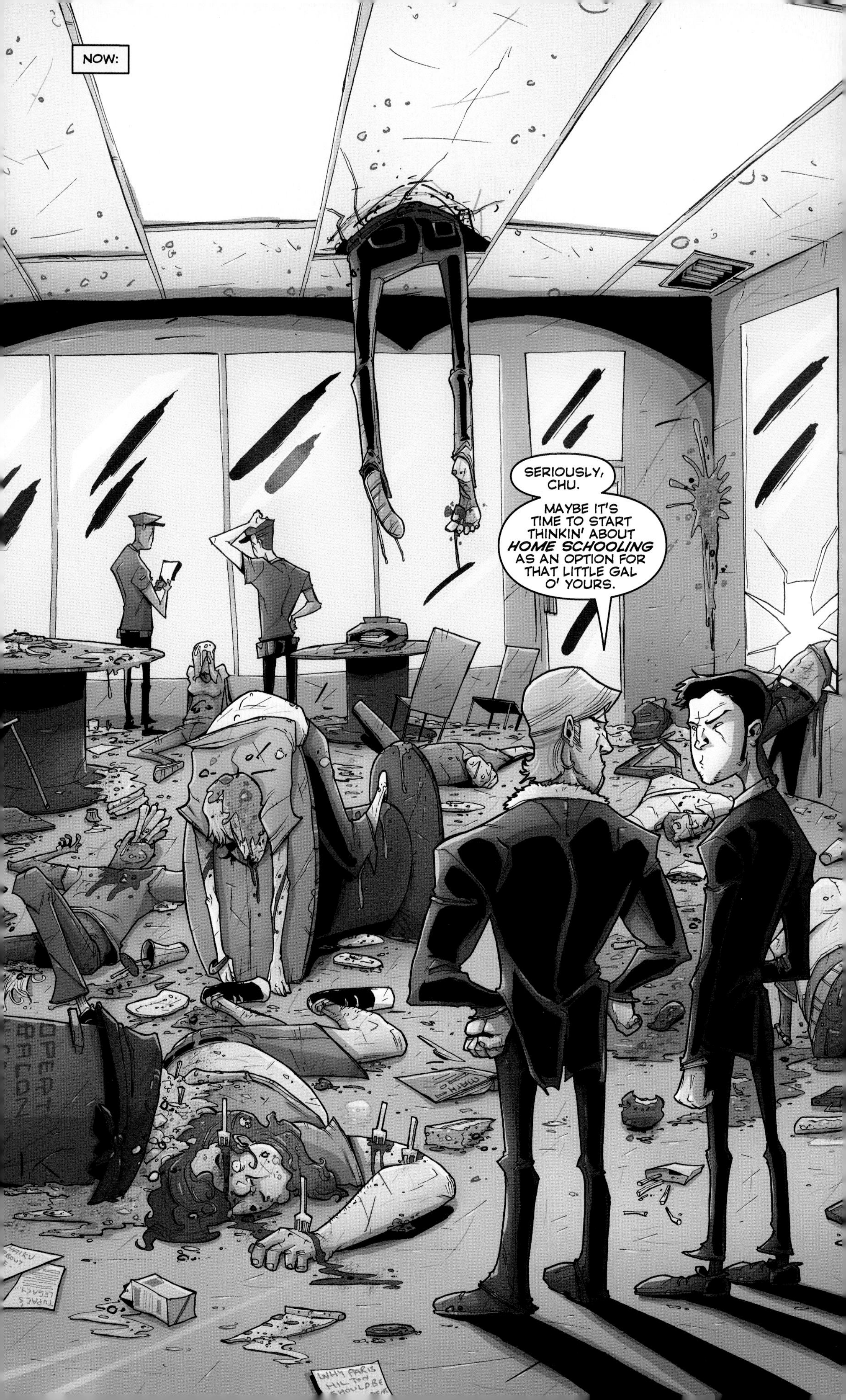
NOW:
SERIOUSLY, CHU. MAYBE IT'S TIME TO START THINKIN' ABOUT *HOME SCHOOLING* AS AN OPTION FOR THAT LITTLE GAL O' YOURS.

WE GOT A *MOTIVE* HERE?

WEDGIE!

Scrippp

SPAFLURSH

SWIRLIE!

LOCKERBOX!

LUNCH MONEY LARCENY!

Clang ta-Klang

SPLORSH

PROM PRANK PIG'S BLOOD!

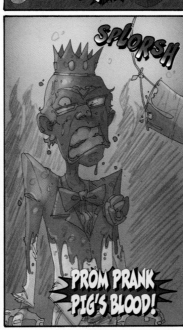

<snicker>

<guffaw>

PHOTOSHOP SLANDER!

ABOUT WHAT YOU'D *EXPECT.*

HOW ABOUT A *NAME?*

PETER. PETER *PILAF.*

POOR BASTARD. NAME LIKE THAT, EVEN *I* WANNA BEAT HIM UP AND STUFF 'IM IN A TRASH CAN.

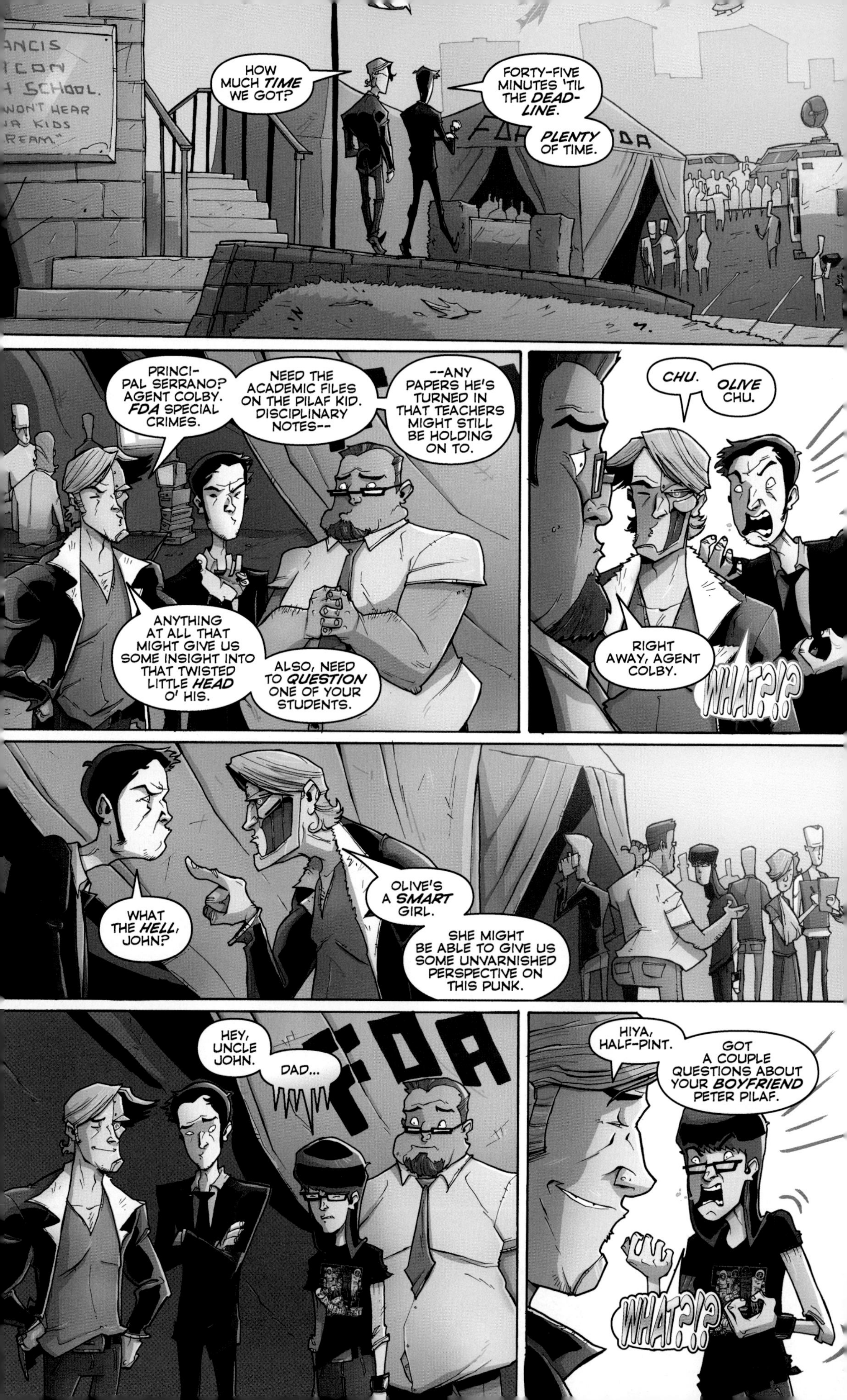

"FRANCIS ... ICON ... SCHOOL. ... WON'T HEAR ... KIDS ... REAM."
HOW MUCH *TIME* WE GOT?
FORTY-FIVE MINUTES 'TIL THE *DEAD-LINE*.
PLENTY OF TIME.
PRINCI-PAL SERRANO? AGENT COLBY. *FDA* SPECIAL CRIMES.
NEED THE ACADEMIC FILES ON THE PILAF KID. DISCIPLINARY NOTES--
--ANY PAPERS HE'S TURNED IN THAT TEACHERS MIGHT STILL BE HOLDING ON TO.
ANYTHING AT ALL THAT MIGHT GIVE US SOME INSIGHT INTO THAT TWISTED LITTLE *HEAD* O' HIS.
ALSO, NEED TO *QUESTION* ONE OF YOUR STUDENTS.
CHU.
OLIVE CHU.
RIGHT AWAY, AGENT COLBY.
WHAT?!?
WHAT THE *HELL*, JOHN?
OLIVE'S A *SMART* GIRL.
SHE MIGHT BE ABLE TO GIVE US SOME UNVARNISHED PERSPECTIVE ON THIS PUNK.
HEY, UNCLE JOHN.
DAD...
FDA
HIYA, HALF-PINT.
GOT A COUPLE QUESTIONS ABOUT YOUR *BOYFRIEND* PETER PILAF.
WHAT?!?

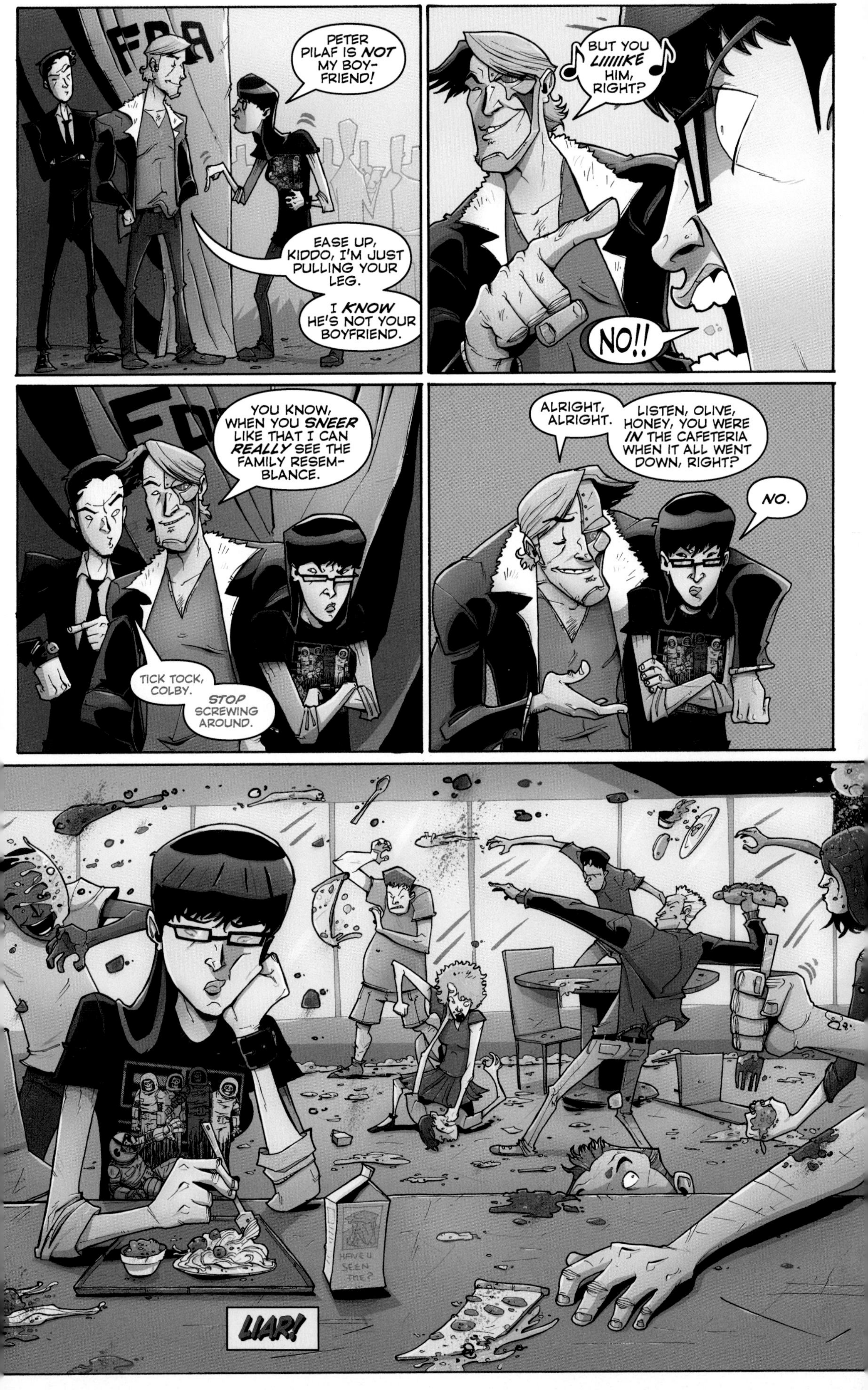
PETER PILAF IS NOT MY BOY-FRIEND!
EASE UP, KIDDO, I'M JUST PULLING YOUR LEG.
I KNOW HE'S NOT YOUR BOYFRIEND.
BUT YOU LIIIIIKE HIM, RIGHT?
NO!!
YOU KNOW, WHEN YOU SNEER LIKE THAT I CAN REALLY SEE THE FAMILY RESEM-BLANCE.
TICK TOCK, COLBY.
STOP SCREWING AROUND.
ALRIGHT, ALRIGHT.
LISTEN, OLIVE, HONEY, YOU WERE IN THE CAFETERIA WHEN IT ALL WENT DOWN, RIGHT?
NO.
HAVE U SEEN ME?
LIAR!

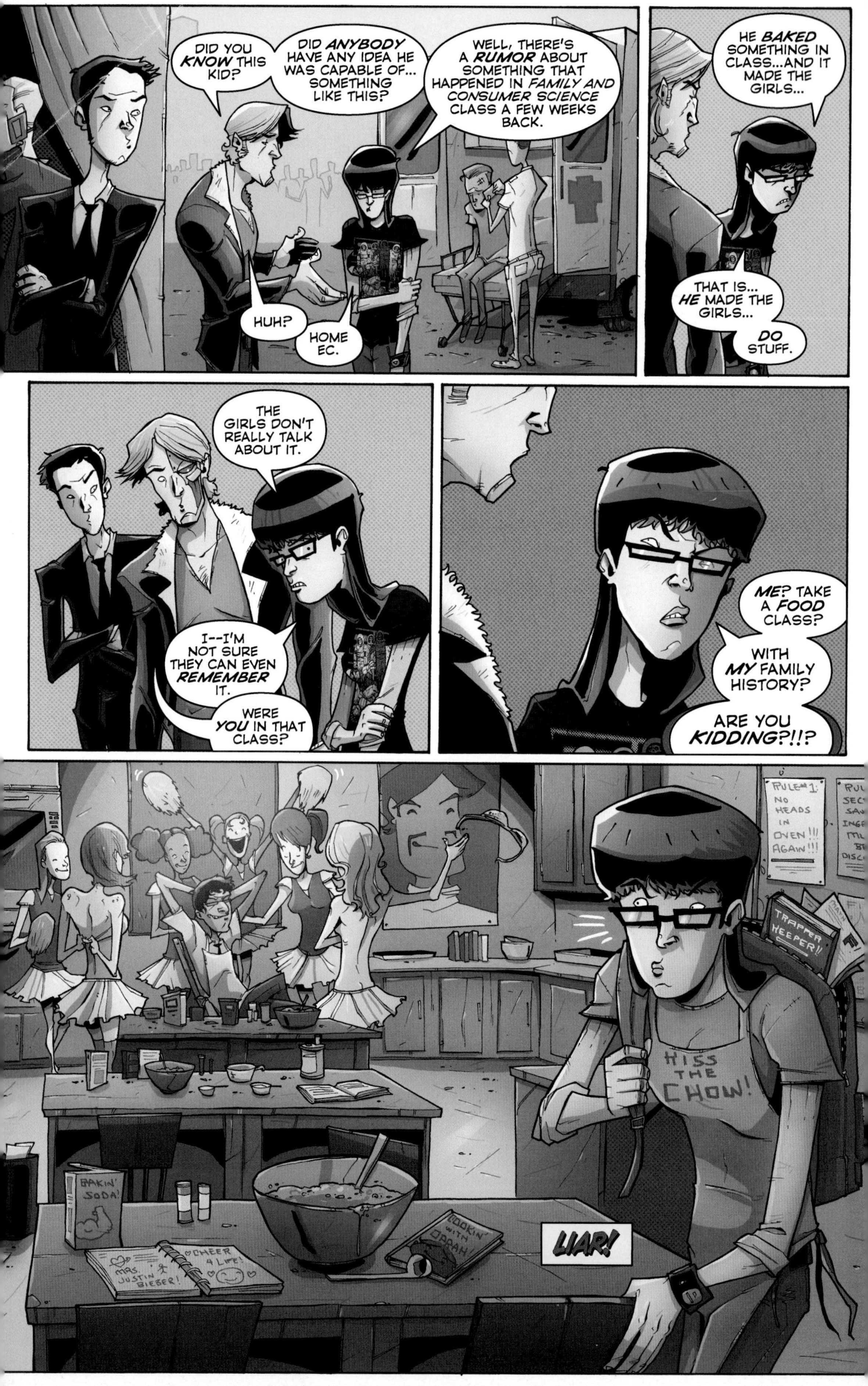
DID YOU KNOW THIS KID?
DID ANYBODY HAVE ANY IDEA HE WAS CAPABLE OF... SOMETHING LIKE THIS?
WELL, THERE'S A RUMOR ABOUT SOMETHING THAT HAPPENED IN FAMILY AND CONSUMER SCIENCE CLASS A FEW WEEKS BACK.
HUH?
HOME EC.
HE BAKED SOMETHING IN CLASS...AND IT MADE THE GIRLS...
THAT IS... HE MADE THE GIRLS...
DO STUFF.
THE GIRLS DON'T REALLY TALK ABOUT IT.
I--I'M NOT SURE THEY CAN EVEN REMEMBER IT.
WERE YOU IN THAT CLASS?
ME? TAKE A FOOD CLASS?
WITH MY FAMILY HISTORY?
ARE YOU KIDDING?!!?
RULE#1: NO HEADS IN OVEN!!! AGAIN!!!
TRAPPER KEEPER!!
KISS THE CHOW!
BAKIN' SODA!
MRS. JUSTIN BIEBER!
CHEER 4 LIFE!
COOKIN' WITH OPRAH!
LIAR!

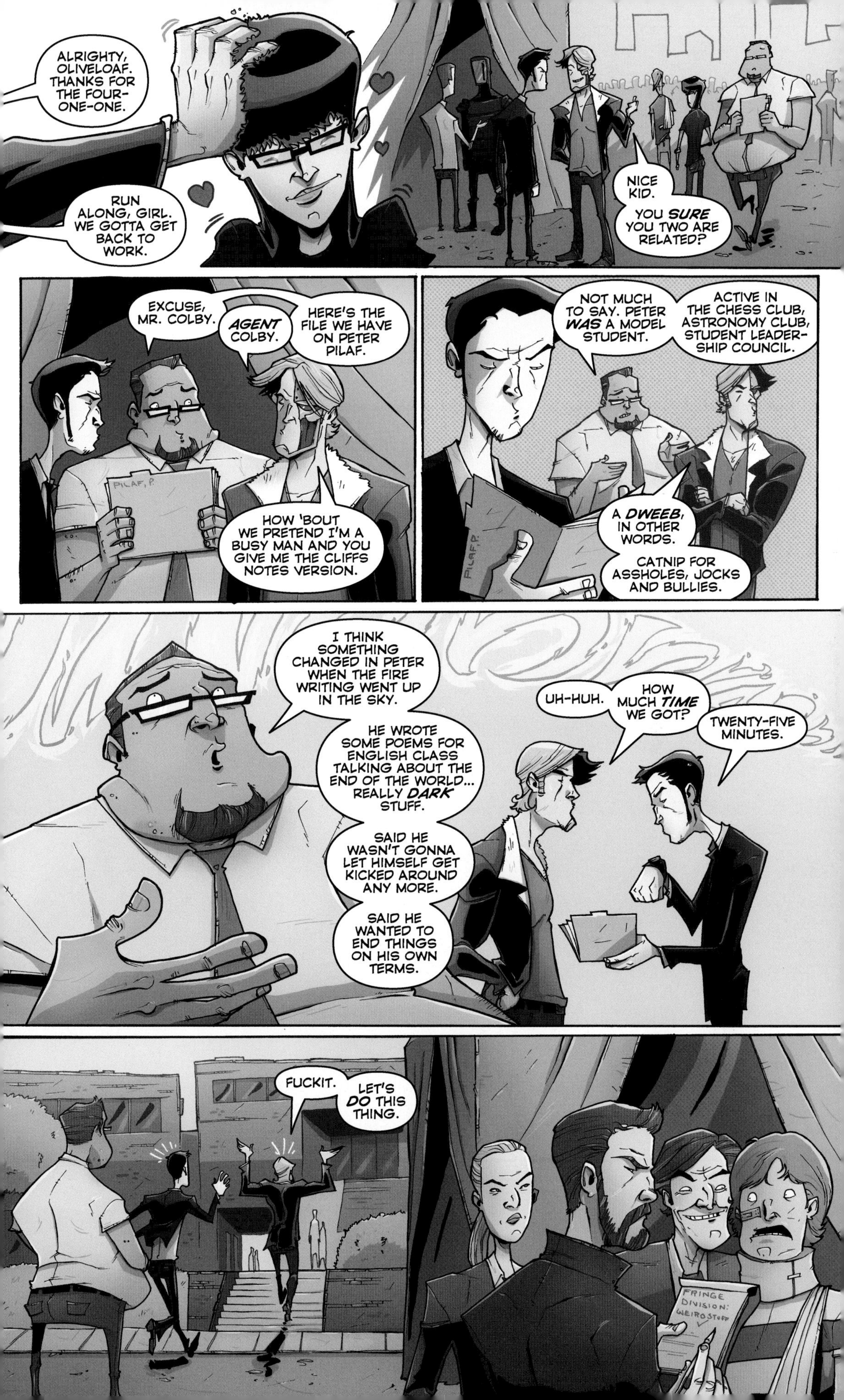
ALRIGHTY, OLIVELOAF. THANKS FOR THE FOUR-ONE-ONE.
RUN ALONG, GIRL. WE GOTTA GET BACK TO WORK.
NICE KID.
YOU SURE YOU TWO ARE RELATED?
EXCUSE, MR. COLBY.
AGENT COLBY.
HERE'S THE FILE WE HAVE ON PETER PILAF.
PILAF, P.
HOW 'BOUT WE PRETEND I'M A BUSY MAN AND YOU GIVE ME THE CLIFFS NOTES VERSION.
NOT MUCH TO SAY. PETER WAS A MODEL STUDENT.
ACTIVE IN THE CHESS CLUB, ASTRONOMY CLUB, STUDENT LEADERSHIP COUNCIL.
PILAF, P.
A DWEEB, IN OTHER WORDS.
CATNIP FOR ASSHOLES, JOCKS AND BULLIES.
I THINK SOMETHING CHANGED IN PETER WHEN THE FIRE WRITING WENT UP IN THE SKY.
HE WROTE SOME POEMS FOR ENGLISH CLASS TALKING ABOUT THE END OF THE WORLD... REALLY DARK STUFF.
SAID HE WASN'T GONNA LET HIMSELF GET KICKED AROUND ANY MORE.
SAID HE WANTED TO END THINGS ON HIS OWN TERMS.
UH-HUH.
HOW MUCH TIME WE GOT?
TWENTY-FIVE MINUTES.
FUCKIT.
LET'S DO THIS THING.
FRINGE DIVISION: WEIRD STUFF

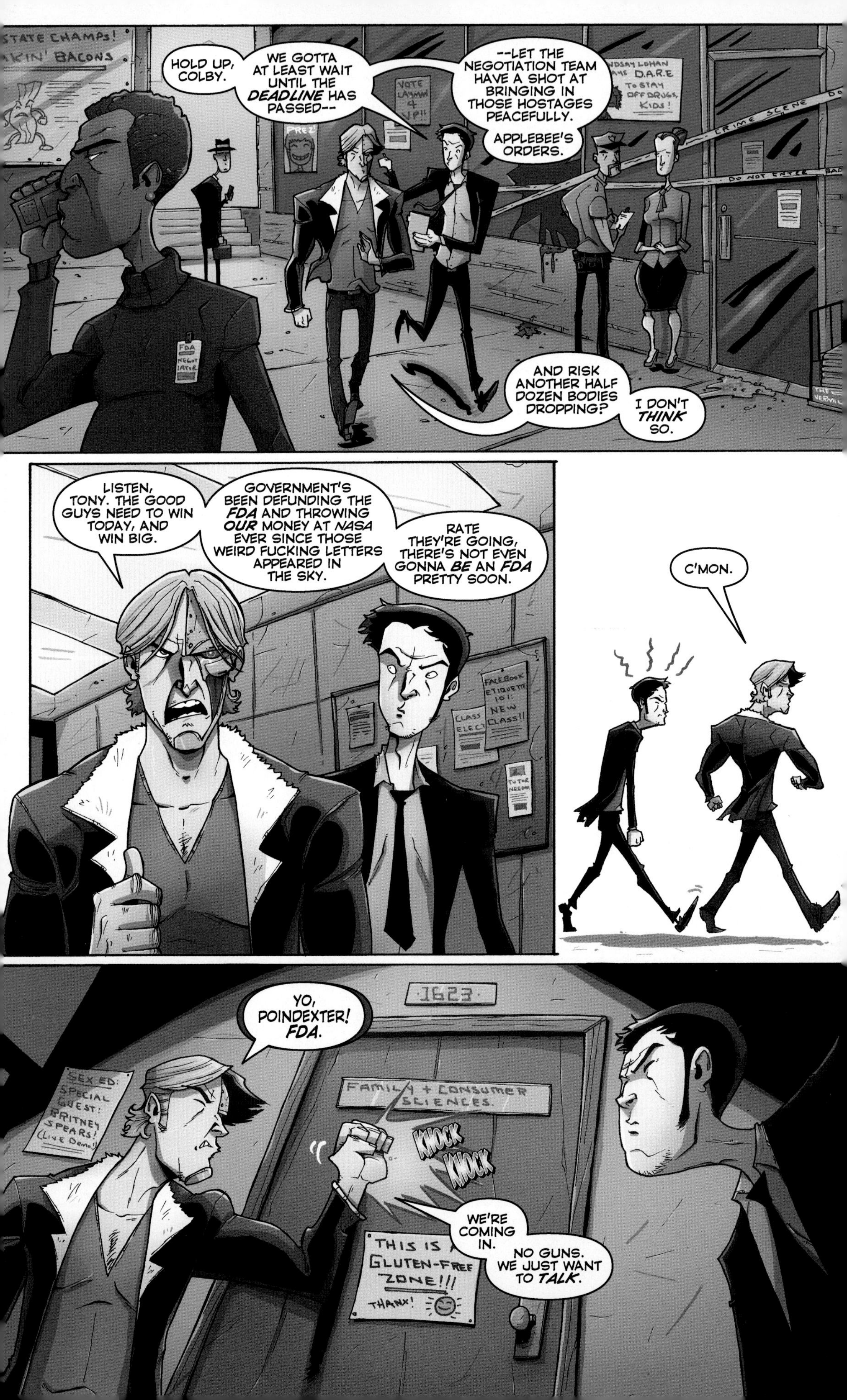

STATE CHAMPS!
HOLD UP, COLBY.
WE GOTTA AT LEAST WAIT UNTIL THE DEADLINE HAS PASSED--
--LET THE NEGOTIATION TEAM HAVE A SHOT AT BRINGING IN THOSE HOSTAGES PEACEFULLY.
APPLEBEE'S ORDERS.
FDA NEGOTIATOR
AND RISK ANOTHER HALF DOZEN BODIES DROPPING?
I DON'T THINK SO.
LISTEN, TONY. THE GOOD GUYS NEED TO WIN TODAY, AND WIN BIG.
GOVERNMENT'S BEEN DEFUNDING THE FDA AND THROWING OUR MONEY AT NASA EVER SINCE THOSE WEIRD FUCKING LETTERS APPEARED IN THE SKY.
RATE THEY'RE GOING, THERE'S NOT EVEN GONNA BE AN FDA PRETTY SOON.
FACEBOOK ETIQUETTE 101: NEW CLASS!!
C'MON.
·1623·
YO, POINDEXTER! FDA.
SEX ED: SPECIAL GUEST: BRITNEY SPEARS! (LIVE DEMO!)
FAMILY + CONSUMER SCIENCES.
KNOCK KNOCK
WE'RE COMING IN.
NO GUNS. WE JUST WANT TO TALK.
GLUTEN-FREE ZONE!!!
THANX!

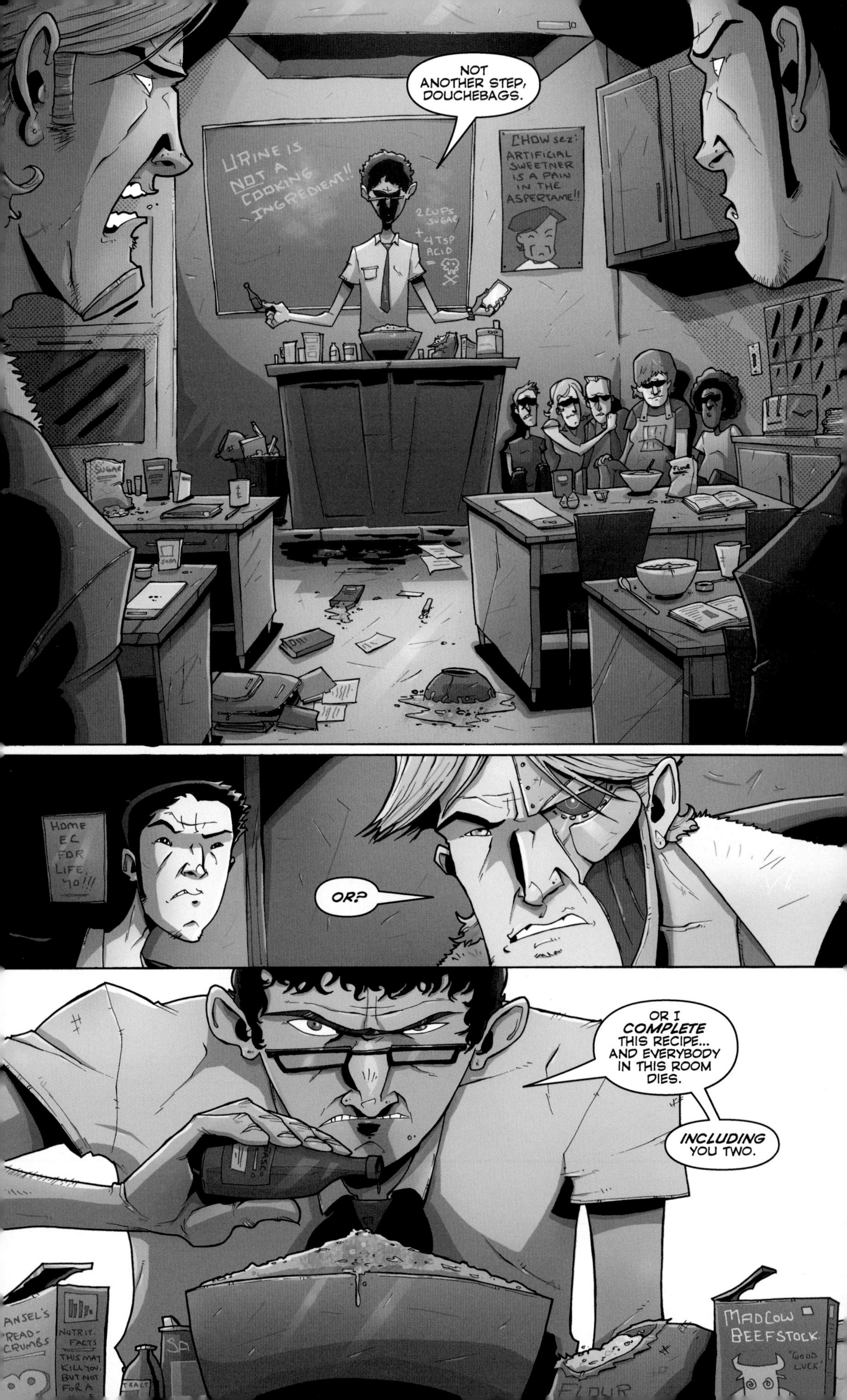

NOT ANOTHER STEP, DOUCHEBAGS.
URINE IS NOT A COOKING INGREDIENT!!
2 CUPS SUGAR + 4 TSP ACID =
CHOW sez: ARTIFICIAL SWEETNER IS A PAIN IN THE ASPERTAME!!
SUGAR
FLOUR
HOME EC FOR LIFE, YO!!!
OR?
OR I COMPLETE THIS RECIPE... AND EVERYBODY IN THIS ROOM DIES.
INCLUDING YOU TWO.
NUTRIT. FACTS THIS MAY KILL YOU. BUT NOT FOR A
MADCOW BEEFSTOCK
"GOOD LUCK"

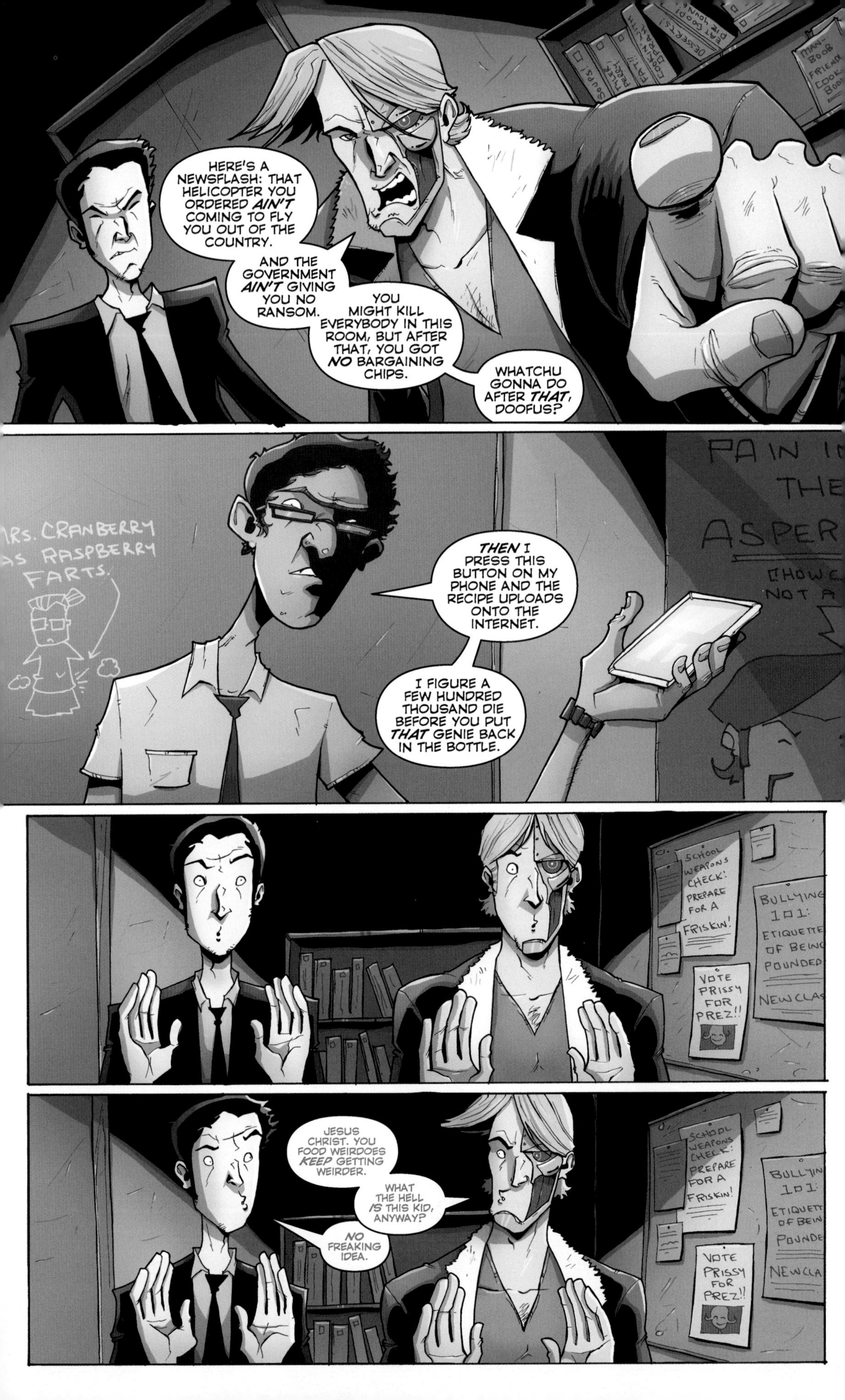
HERE'S A NEWSFLASH: THAT HELICOPTER YOU ORDERED AIN'T COMING TO FLY YOU OUT OF THE COUNTRY.
AND THE GOVERNMENT AIN'T GIVING YOU NO RANSOM.
YOU MIGHT KILL EVERYBODY IN THIS ROOM, BUT AFTER THAT, YOU GOT NO BARGAINING CHIPS.
WHATCHU GONNA DO AFTER THAT, DOOFUS?
THEN I PRESS THIS BUTTON ON MY PHONE AND THE RECIPE UPLOADS ONTO THE INTERNET.
I FIGURE A FEW HUNDRED THOUSAND DIE BEFORE YOU PUT THAT GENIE BACK IN THE BOTTLE.
SCHOOL WEAPONS CHECK: PREPARE FOR A FRISKIN!
VOTE PRISSY FOR PREZ!!
JESUS CHRIST. YOU FOOD WEIRDOES KEEP GETTING WEIRDER.
WHAT THE HELL IS THIS KID, ANYWAY?
NO FREAKING IDEA.

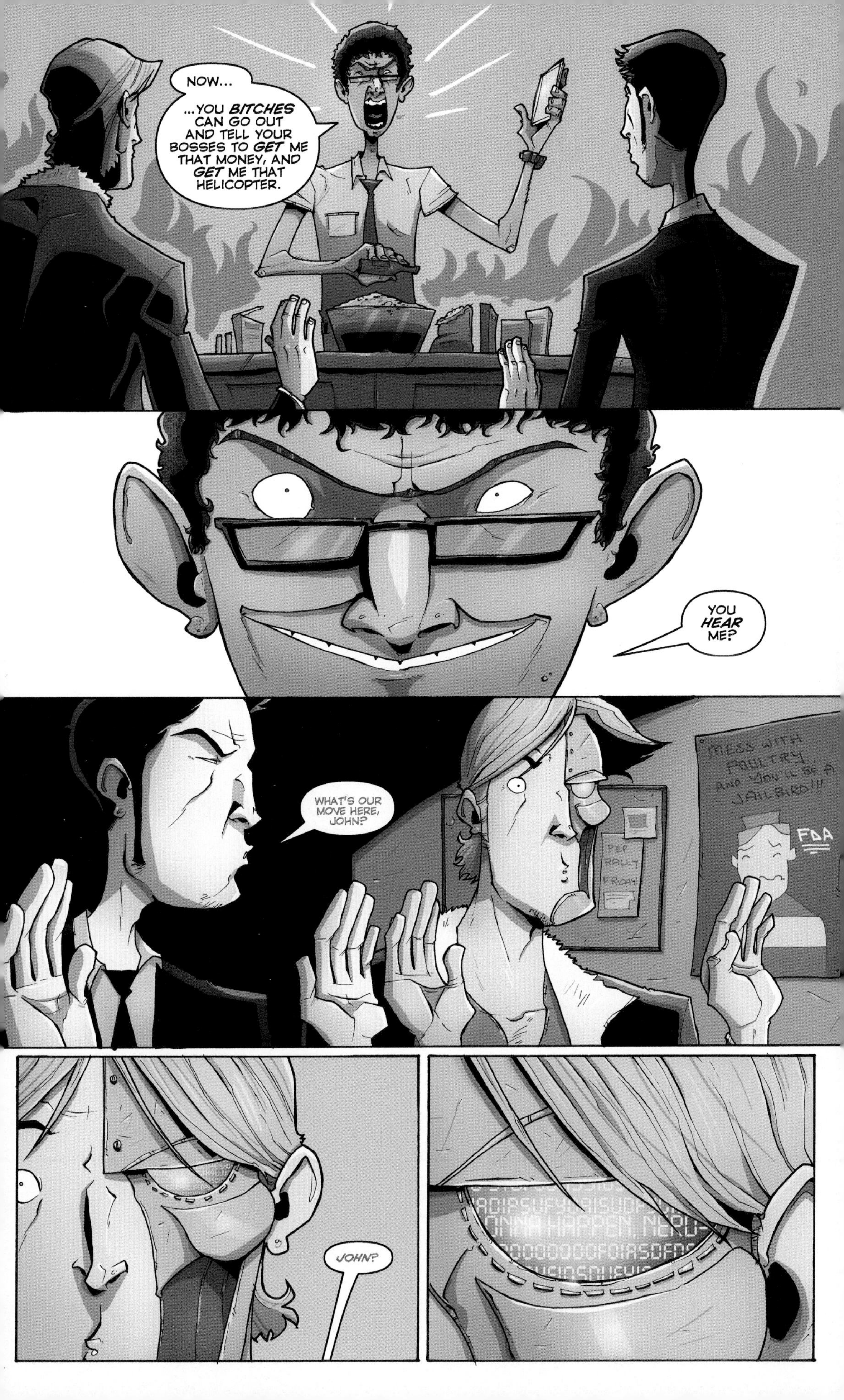

NOW...
...YOU BITCHES CAN GO OUT AND TELL YOUR BOSSES TO GET ME THAT MONEY, AND GET ME THAT HELICOPTER.
YOU HEAR ME?
WHAT'S OUR MOVE HERE, JOHN?
MESS WITH POULTRY... AND YOU'LL BE A JAILBIRD!!!
FDA
PEP RALLY FRIDAY!
JOHN?

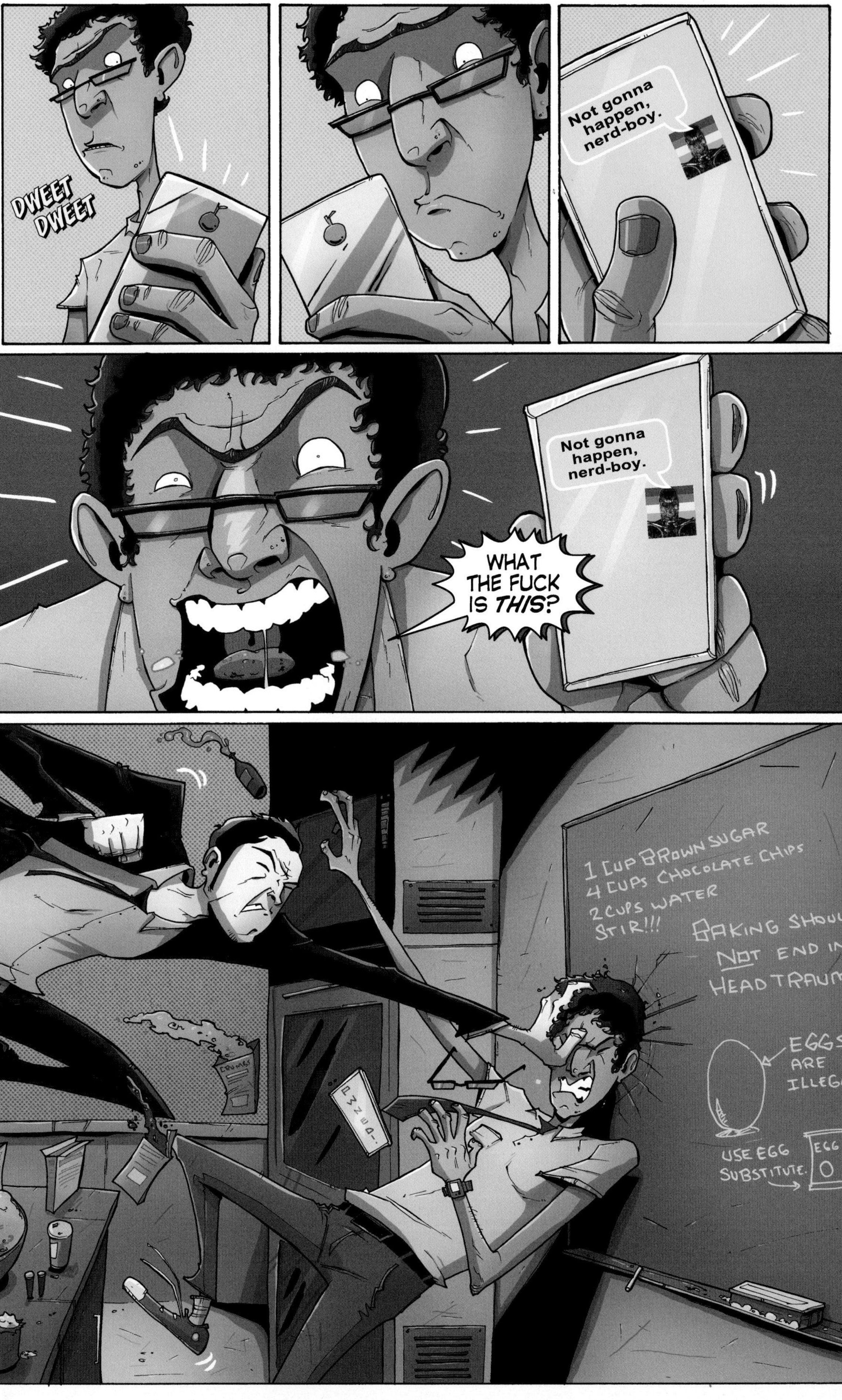
DWEET DWEET
Not gonna happen, nerd-boy.
Not gonna happen, nerd-boy.
WHAT THE FUCK IS *THIS*?
1 CUP BROWN SUGAR
4 CUPS CHOCOLATE CHIPS
2 CUPS WATER
STIR!!!
BAKING SHOUL
NOT END IN
HEAD TRAUM
EGGS ARE ILLEGA
USE EGG SUBSTITUTE.
EGG
CRUMBS
PWNED.

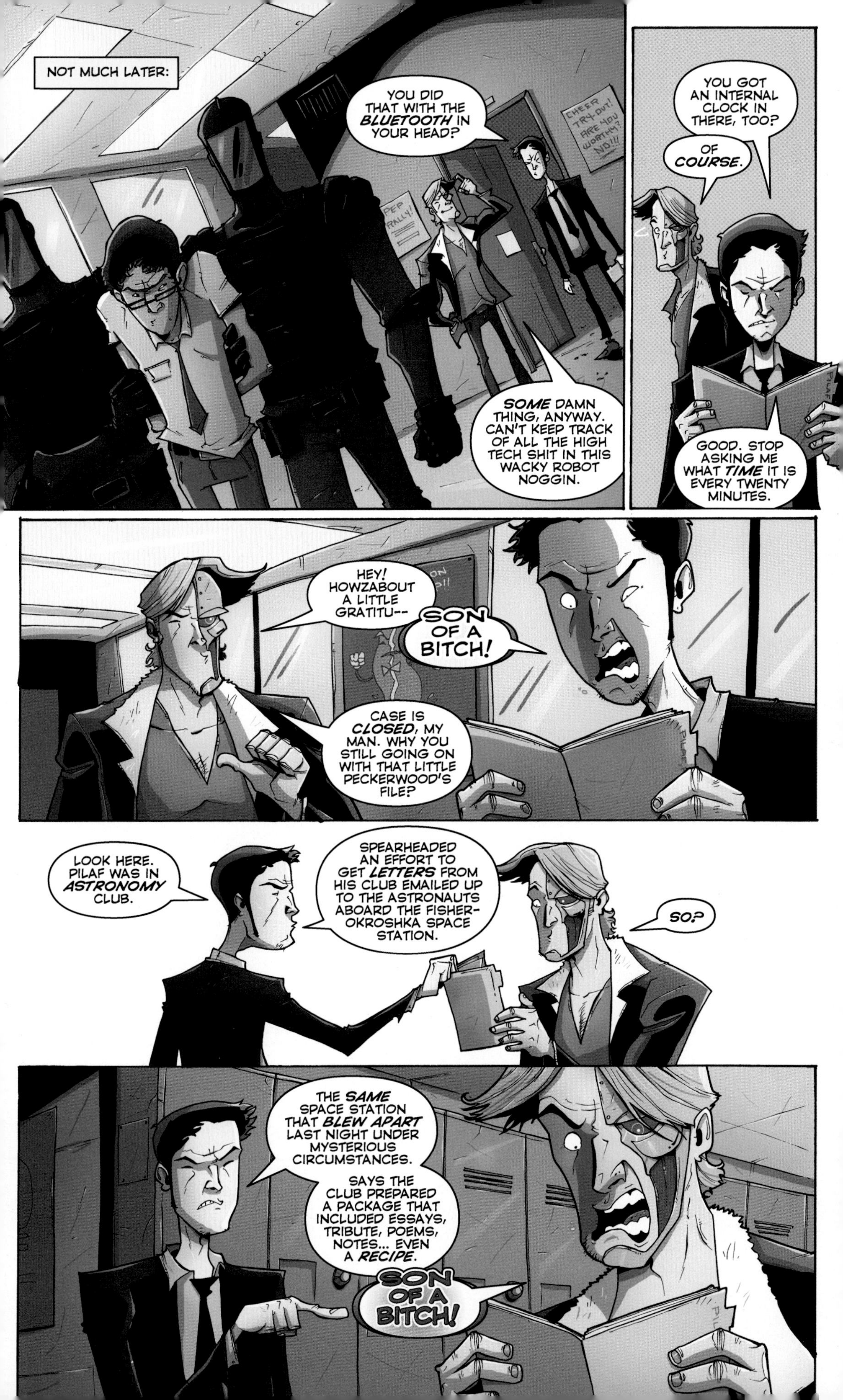
NOT MUCH LATER:
YOU DID THAT WITH THE BLUETOOTH IN YOUR HEAD?
CHEER TRY-OUT! ARE YOU WORTHY? NO!!!
PEP RALLY!
SOME DAMN THING, ANYWAY. CAN'T KEEP TRACK OF ALL THE HIGH TECH SHIT IN THIS WACKY ROBOT NOGGIN.
YOU GOT AN INTERNAL CLOCK IN THERE, TOO?
OF COURSE.
GOOD. STOP ASKING ME WHAT TIME IT IS EVERY TWENTY MINUTES.
HEY! HOWZABOUT A LITTLE GRATITU--
SON OF A BITCH!
CASE IS CLOSED, MY MAN. WHY YOU STILL GOING ON WITH THAT LITTLE PECKERWOOD'S FILE?
LOOK HERE. PILAF WAS IN ASTRONOMY CLUB.
SPEARHEADED AN EFFORT TO GET LETTERS FROM HIS CLUB EMAILED UP TO THE ASTRONAUTS ABOARD THE FISHER-OKROSHKA SPACE STATION.
SO?
THE SAME SPACE STATION THAT BLEW APART LAST NIGHT UNDER MYSTERIOUS CIRCUMSTANCES.
SAYS THE CLUB PREPARED A PACKAGE THAT INCLUDED ESSAYS, TRIBUTE, POEMS, NOTES... EVEN A RECIPE.
SON OF A BITCH!

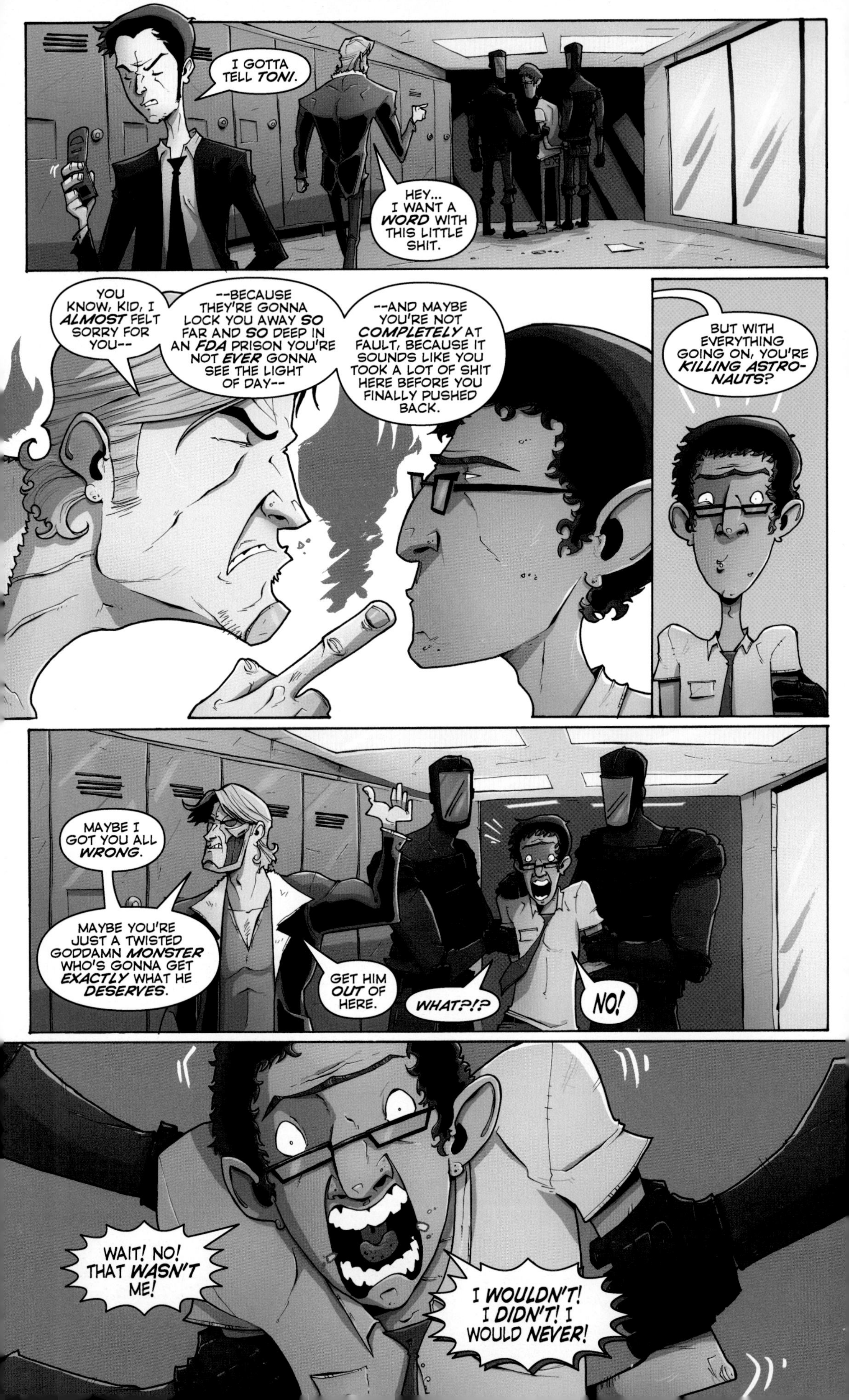
I GOTTA TELL TONI.
HEY... I WANT A WORD WITH THIS LITTLE SHIT.
YOU KNOW, KID, I ALMOST FELT SORRY FOR YOU--
--BECAUSE THEY'RE GONNA LOCK YOU AWAY SO FAR AND SO DEEP IN AN FDA PRISON YOU'RE NOT EVER GONNA SEE THE LIGHT OF DAY--
--AND MAYBE YOU'RE NOT COMPLETELY AT FAULT, BECAUSE IT SOUNDS LIKE YOU TOOK A LOT OF SHIT HERE BEFORE YOU FINALLY PUSHED BACK.
BUT WITH EVERYTHING GOING ON, YOU'RE KILLING ASTRO-NAUTS?
MAYBE I GOT YOU ALL WRONG.
MAYBE YOU'RE JUST A TWISTED GODDAMN MONSTER WHO'S GONNA GET EXACTLY WHAT HE DESERVES.
GET HIM OUT OF HERE.
WHAT?!?
NO!
WAIT! NO! THAT WASN'T ME!
I WOULDN'T! I DIDN'T! I WOULD NEVER!

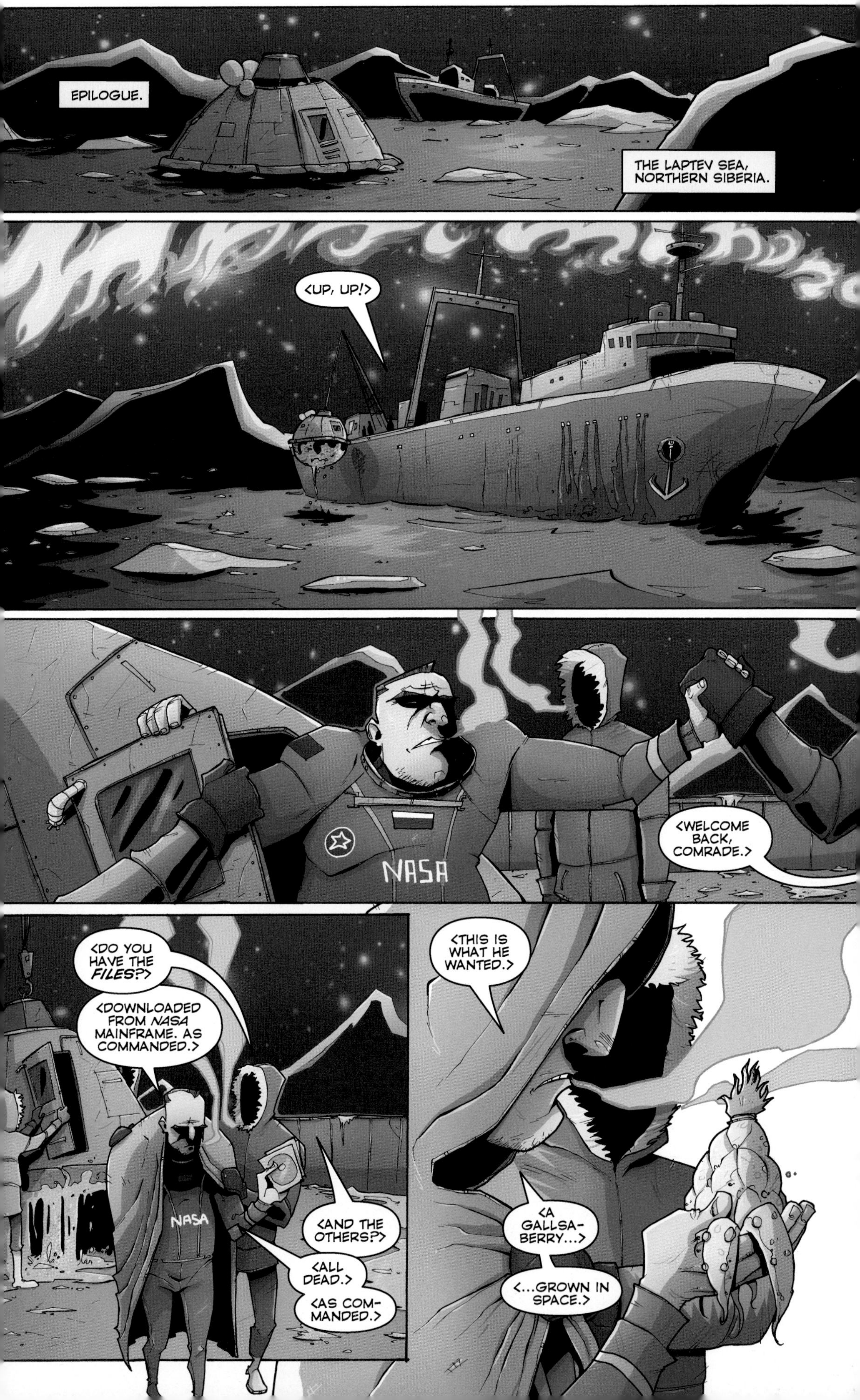
EPILOGUE.
THE LAPTEV SEA, NORTHERN SIBERIA.
<UP, UP!>
NASA
<WELCOME BACK, COMRADE.>
<DO YOU HAVE THE *FILES*?>
<DOWNLOADED FROM *NASA* MAINFRAME. AS COMMANDED.>
NASA
<AND THE OTHERS?>
<ALL DEAD.>
<AS COMMANDED.>
<THIS IS WHAT HE WANTED.>
<A GALLSABERRY...>
<...GROWN IN SPACE.>

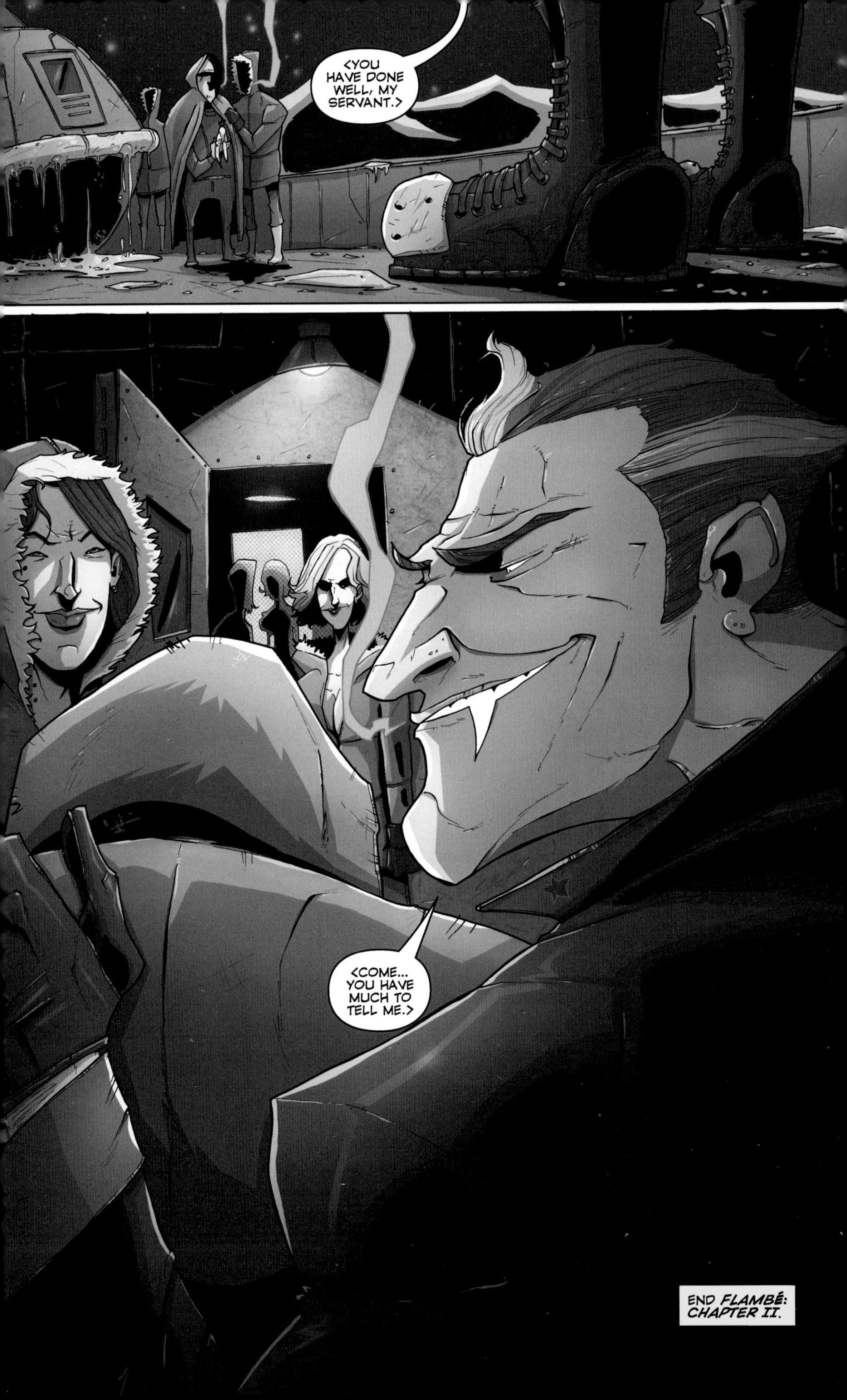
<YOU HAVE DONE WELL, MY SERVANT.>
<COME... YOU HAVE MUCH TO TELL ME.>
END FLAMBÉ: CHAPTER II.

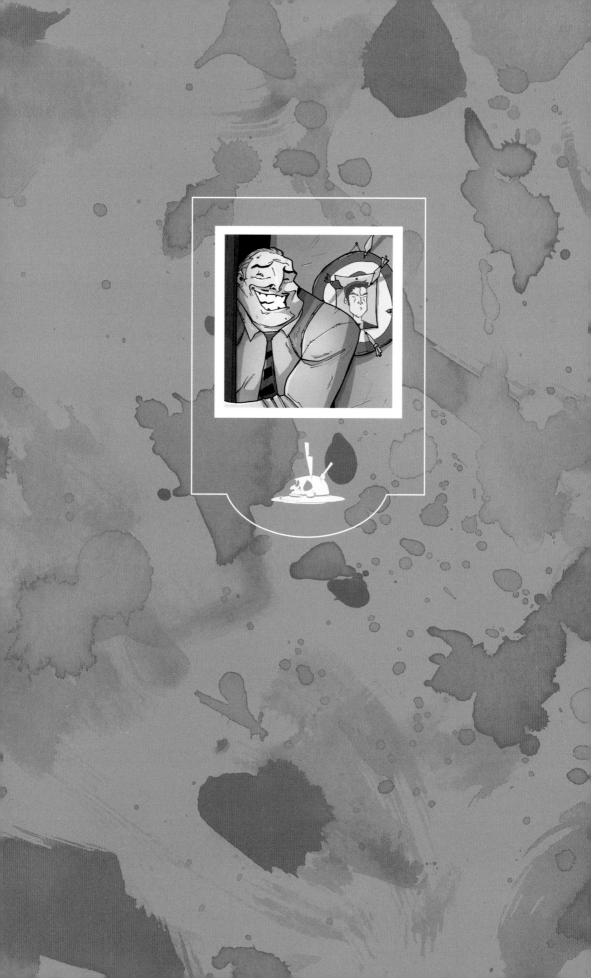

Chapter 3

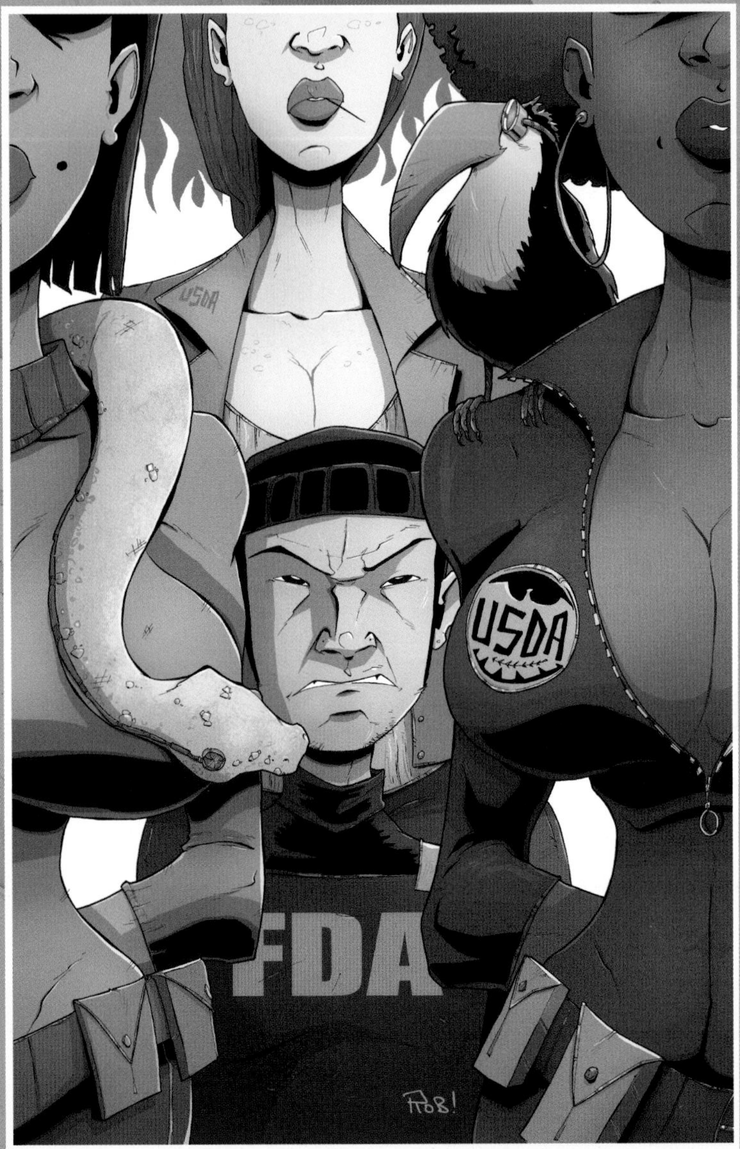
USDA
USDA
FDA
ROB!

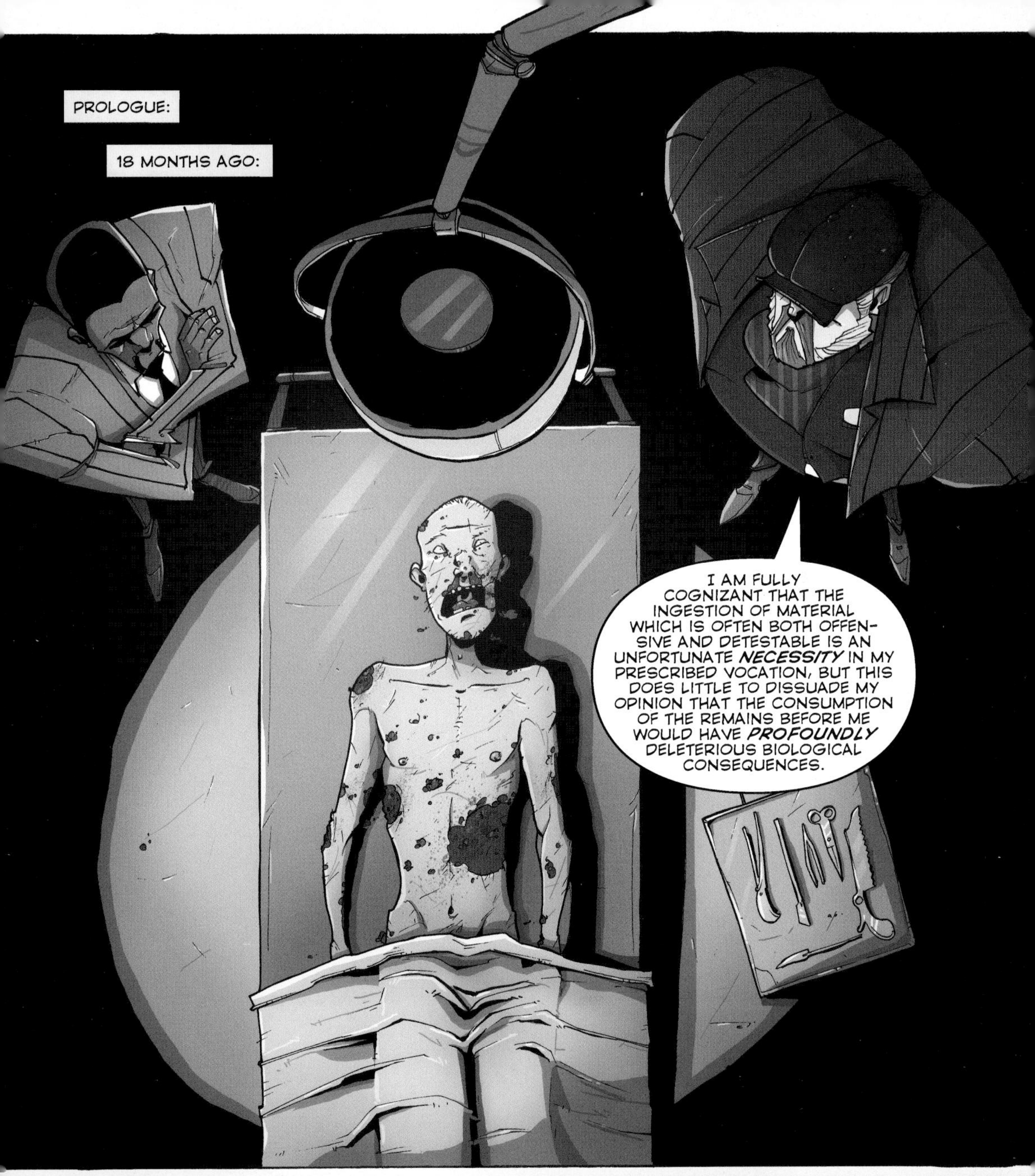
PROLOGUE:
18 MONTHS AGO:
I AM FULLY COGNIZANT THAT THE INGESTION OF MATERIAL WHICH IS OFTEN BOTH OFFENSIVE AND DETESTABLE IS AN UNFORTUNATE *NECESSITY* IN MY PRESCRIBED VOCATION, BUT THIS DOES LITTLE TO DISSUADE MY OPINION THAT THE CONSUMPTION OF THE REMAINS BEFORE ME WOULD HAVE *PROFOUNDLY* DELETERIOUS BIOLOGICAL CONSEQUENCES.

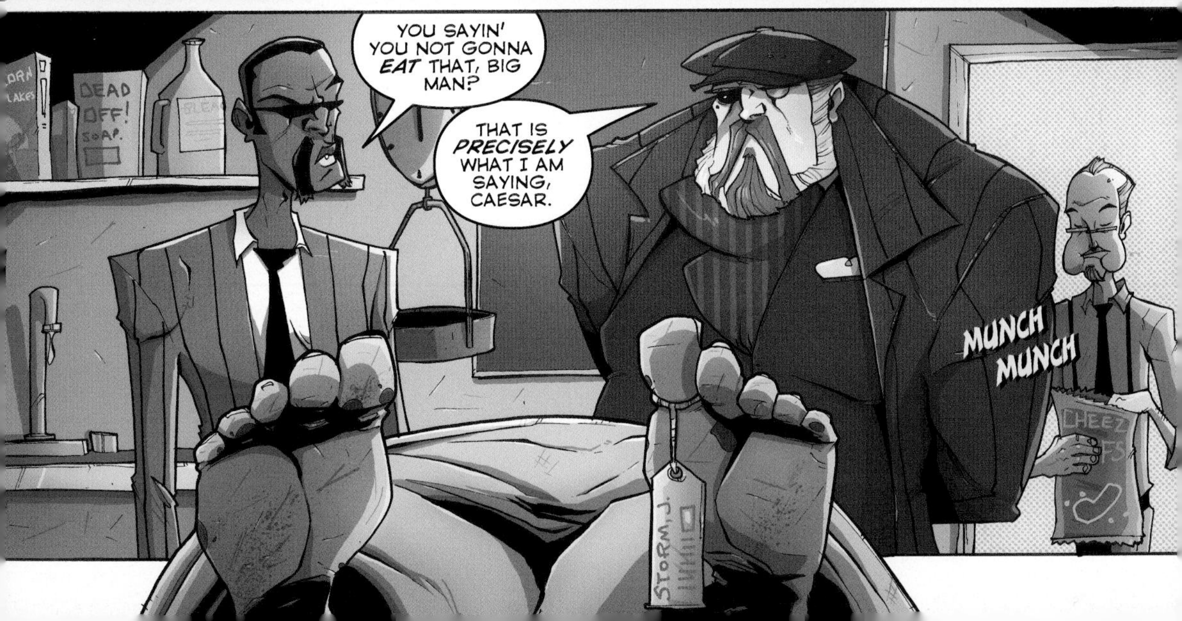
YOU SAYIN' YOU NOT GONNA *EAT* THAT, BIG MAN?
THAT IS *PRECISELY* WHAT I AM SAYING, CAESAR.
DEAD OFF! SOAP
MUNCH MUNCH
STORM, J.

MUNCH MUNCH

MUNCH MUNCH MUNCH

CHEEZ PUFFS

TAP TAP

DON'T THINK YOU HAVE TO WORRY ABOUT EATING HIM.

I GOT IT *ALL* FIGURED OUT.

DANIEL *MIGDALO.*

THE *VORESOPH?*

MASON *SAVOY.*

THE *CIBOPATH?*

PLEASURE TO MEET YOU.

CHEEZ PUFFS

ANYWAY, I THINK WE GOT ALL THE INFO WE NEED ON *THIS* GUY.

HE'S ONE OF *US,* RIGHT? *FDA?*

SPOOK'S DIVISION?

DOIN' SOME CLOAK AND DAGGER ASSIGNMENT IN NORTH KOREA?

CHEEZ PUFFS

SHAKE SHAKE

PIZZA!!!

PIZZA
PIZZA
PIZZA
PIZZA

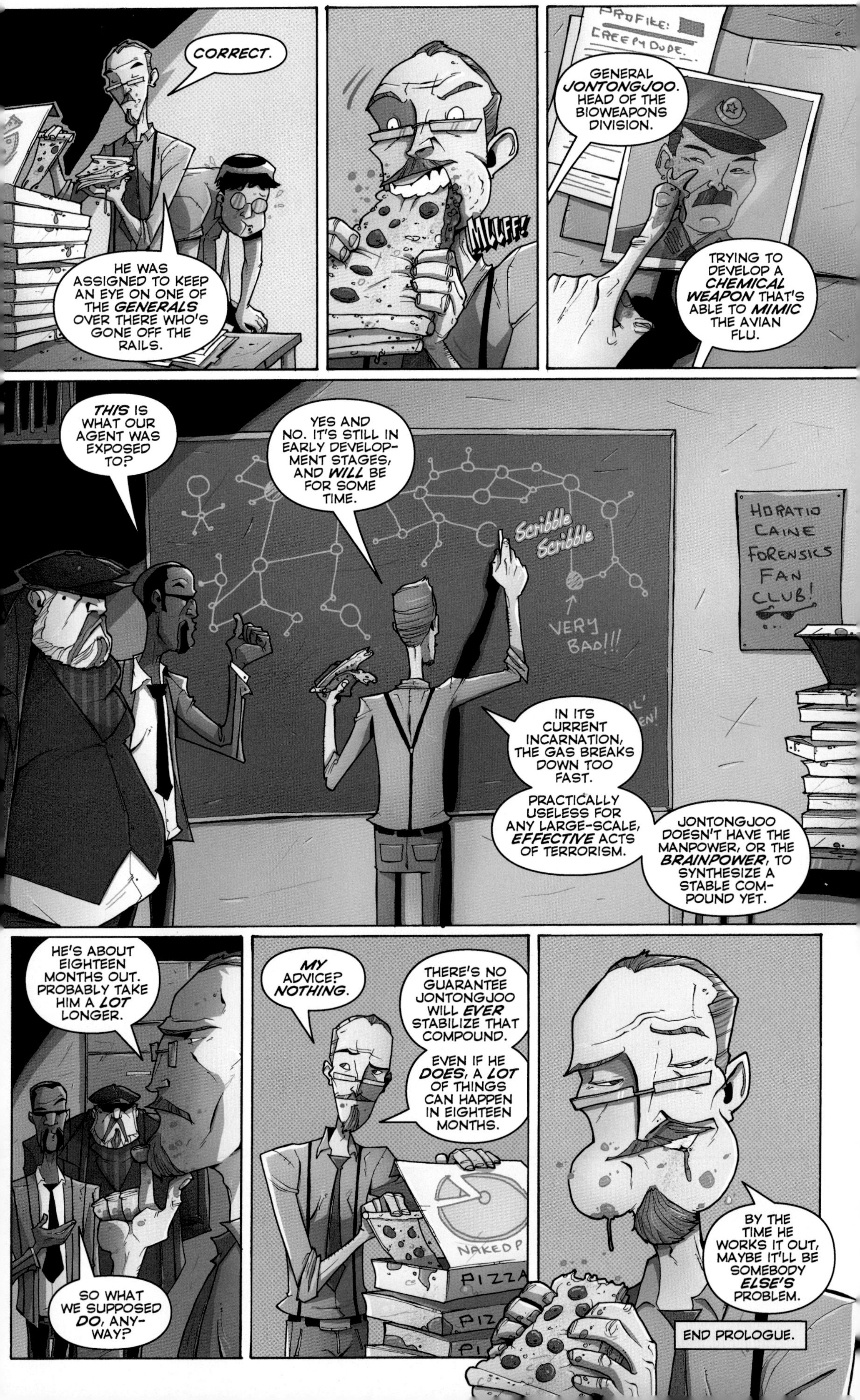
CORRECT.
HE WAS ASSIGNED TO KEEP AN EYE ON ONE OF THE GENERALS OVER THERE WHO'S GONE OFF THE RAILS.
MLLLFF!
PROFILE:
CREEPY DUDE.
GENERAL JONTONGJOO. HEAD OF THE BIOWEAPONS DIVISION.
TRYING TO DEVELOP A CHEMICAL WEAPON THAT'S ABLE TO MIMIC THE AVIAN FLU.
THIS IS WHAT OUR AGENT WAS EXPOSED TO?
YES AND NO. IT'S STILL IN EARLY DEVELOPMENT STAGES, AND WILL BE FOR SOME TIME.
Scribble Scribble
VERY BAD!!!
HORATIO CAINE FORENSICS FAN CLUB!
IN ITS CURRENT INCARNATION, THE GAS BREAKS DOWN TOO FAST.
PRACTICALLY USELESS FOR ANY LARGE-SCALE, EFFECTIVE ACTS OF TERRORISM.
JONTONGJOO DOESN'T HAVE THE MANPOWER, OR THE BRAINPOWER, TO SYNTHESIZE A STABLE COMPOUND YET.
HE'S ABOUT EIGHTEEN MONTHS OUT. PROBABLY TAKE HIM A LOT LONGER.
SO WHAT WE SUPPOSED DO, ANYWAY?
MY ADVICE? NOTHING.
THERE'S NO GUARANTEE JONTONGJOO WILL EVER STABILIZE THAT COMPOUND.
EVEN IF HE DOES, A LOT OF THINGS CAN HAPPEN IN EIGHTEEN MONTHS.
NAKED P
PIZZA
PIZ
BY THE TIME HE WORKS IT OUT, MAYBE IT'LL BE SOMEBODY ELSE'S PROBLEM.
END PROLOGUE.

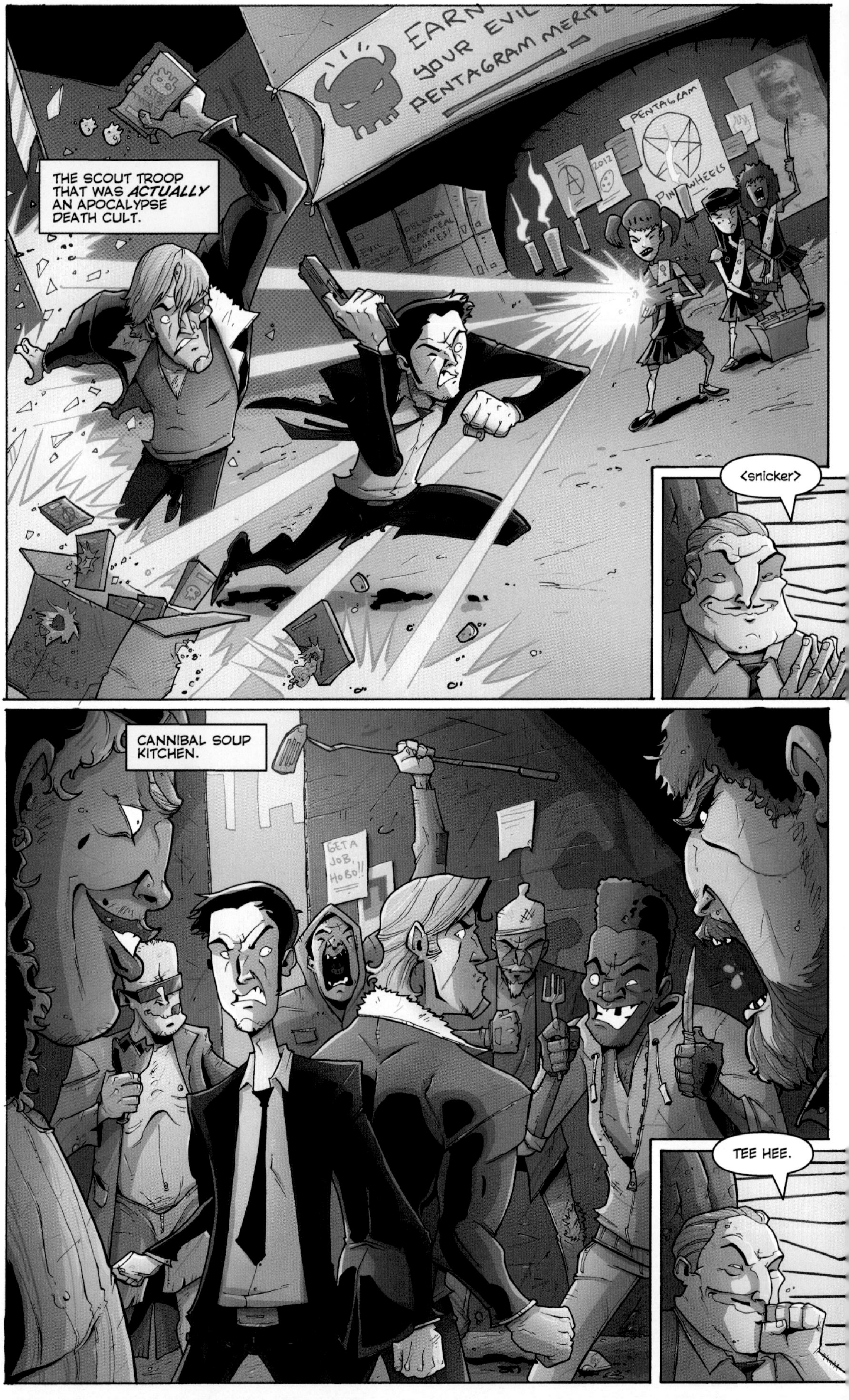
THE SCOUT TROOP THAT WAS *ACTUALLY* AN APOCALYPSE DEATH CULT.
EARN YOUR EVIL PENTAGRAM MERIT
PENTAGRAM PINWHEELS
OBLIVION OATMEAL COOKIES!
EVIL COOKIES
<snicker>
CANNIBAL SOUP KITCHEN.
GET A JOB, HOBO!!
TEE HEE.

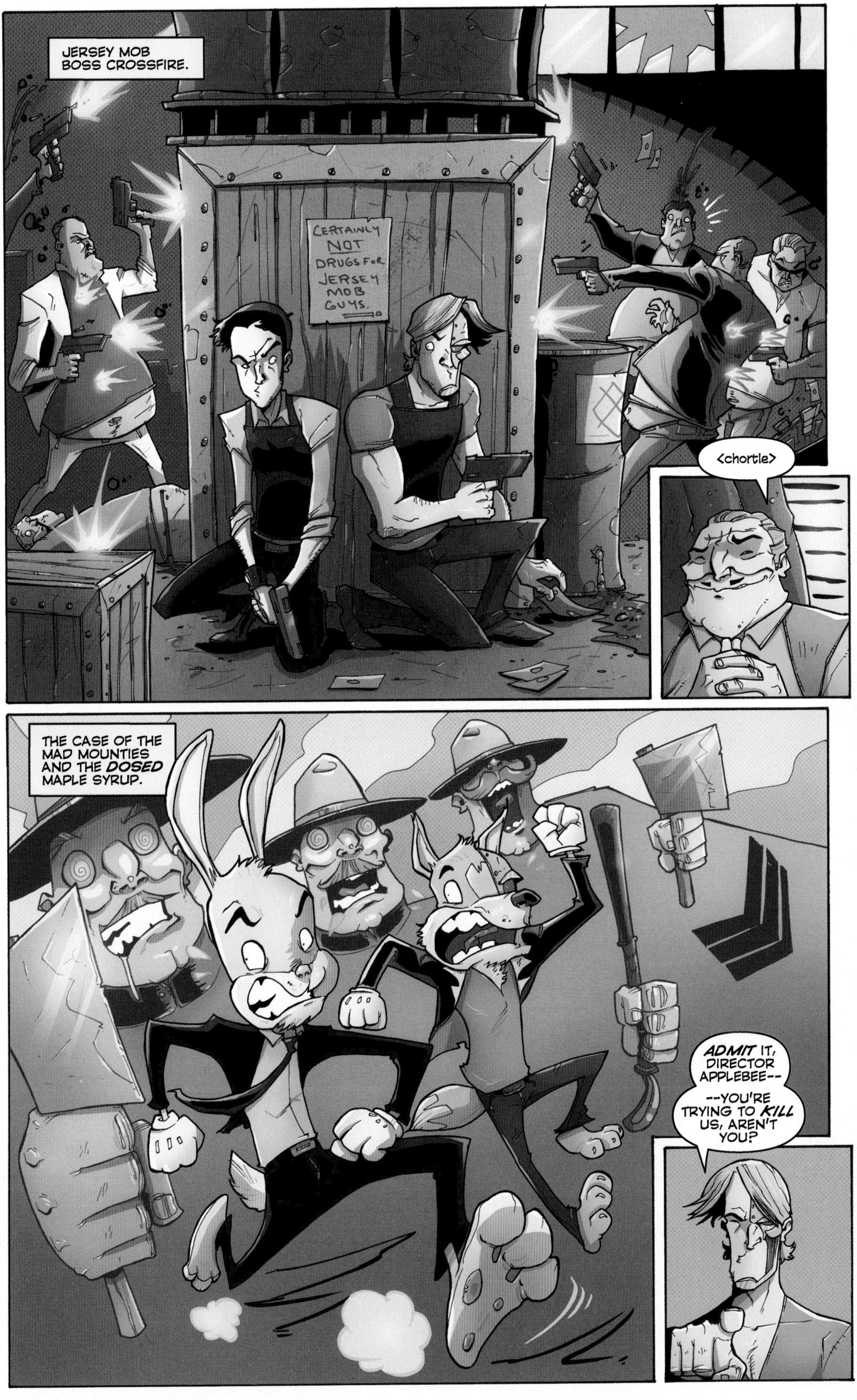

JERSEY MOB BOSS CROSSFIRE.
CERTAINLY NOT DRUGS FOR JERSEY MOB GUYS.
<chortle>
THE CASE OF THE MAD MOUNTIES AND THE *DOSED* MAPLE SYRUP.
ADMIT IT, DIRECTOR APPLEBEE--
--YOU'RE TRYING TO *KILL* US, AREN'T YOU?

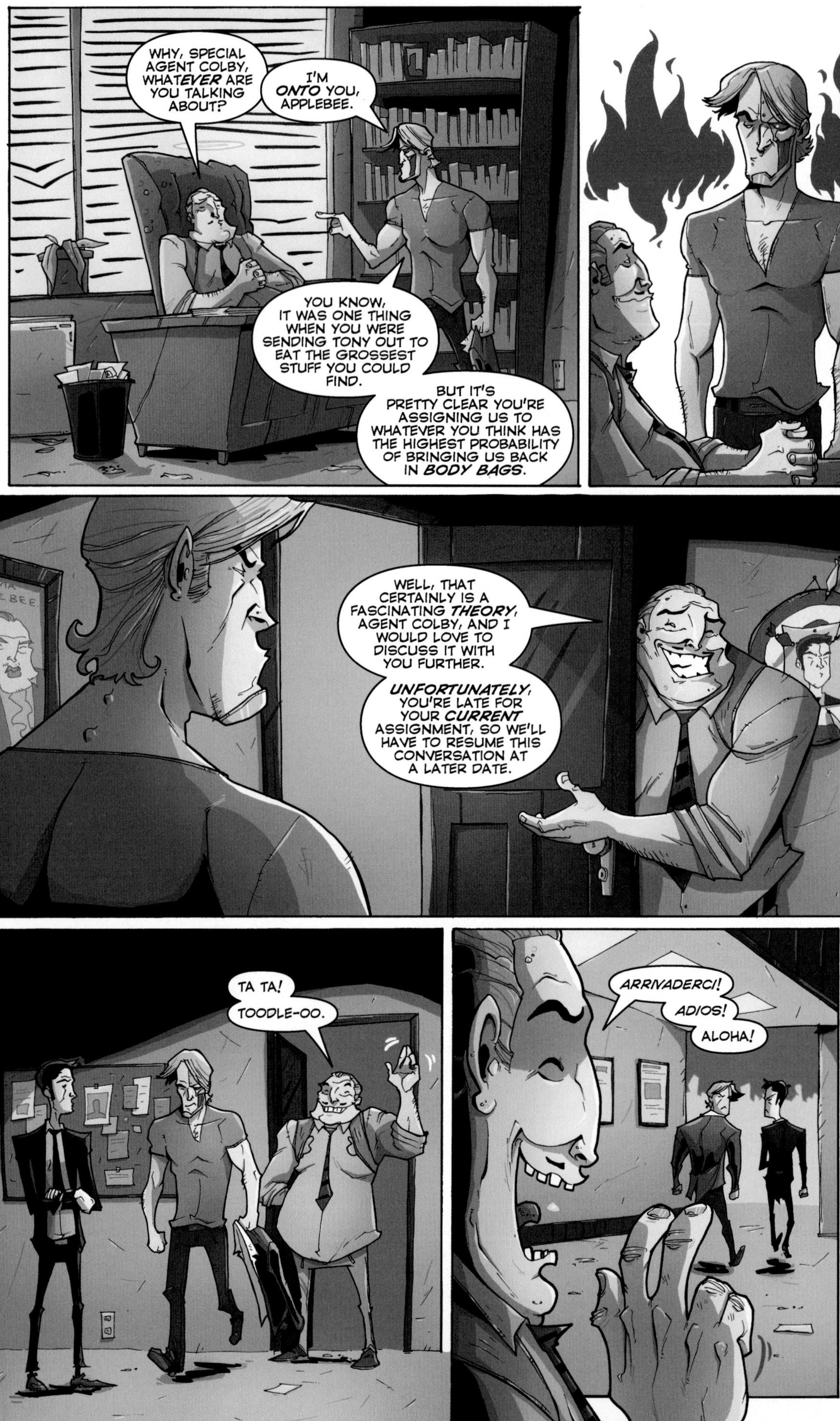
WHY, SPECIAL AGENT COLBY, WHATEVER ARE YOU TALKING ABOUT?
I'M ONTO YOU, APPLEBEE.
YOU KNOW, IT WAS ONE THING WHEN YOU WERE SENDING TONY OUT TO EAT THE GROSSEST STUFF YOU COULD FIND.
BUT IT'S PRETTY CLEAR YOU'RE ASSIGNING US TO WHATEVER YOU THINK HAS THE HIGHEST PROBABILITY OF BRINGING US BACK IN BODY BAGS.
WELL, THAT CERTAINLY IS A FASCINATING THEORY, AGENT COLBY, AND I WOULD LOVE TO DISCUSS IT WITH YOU FURTHER.
UNFORTUNATELY, YOU'RE LATE FOR YOUR CURRENT ASSIGNMENT, SO WE'LL HAVE TO RESUME THIS CONVERSATION AT A LATER DATE.
TA TA!
TOODLE-OO.
ARRIVADERCI!
ADIOS!
ALOHA!

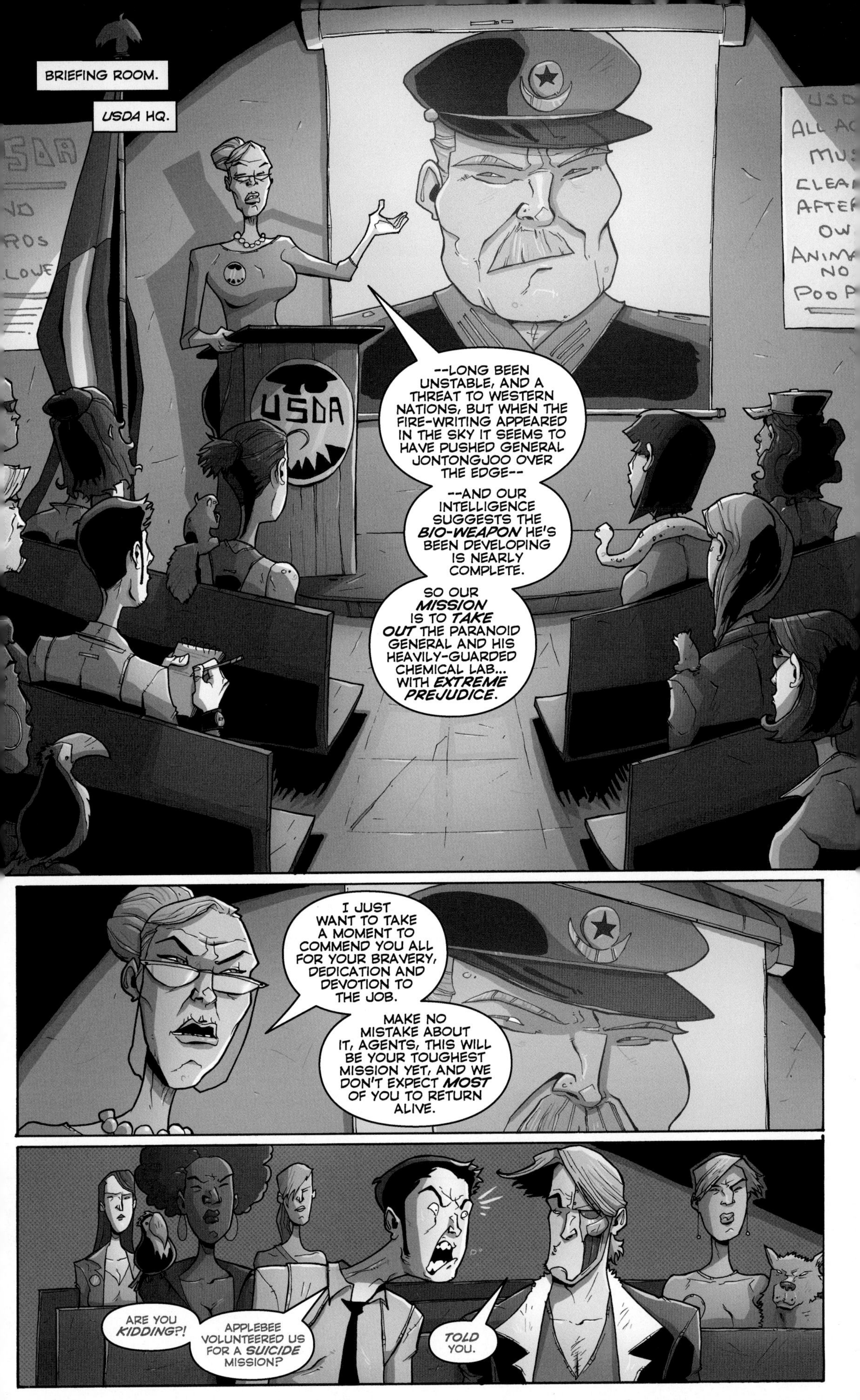
BRIEFING ROOM.
USDA HQ.
USDA
--LONG BEEN UNSTABLE, AND A THREAT TO WESTERN NATIONS, BUT WHEN THE FIRE-WRITING APPEARED IN THE SKY IT SEEMS TO HAVE PUSHED GENERAL JONTONGJOO OVER THE EDGE--
--AND OUR INTELLIGENCE SUGGESTS THE *BIO-WEAPON* HE'S BEEN DEVELOPING IS NEARLY COMPLETE.
SO OUR ***MISSION*** IS TO ***TAKE OUT*** THE PARANOID GENERAL AND HIS HEAVILY-GUARDED CHEMICAL LAB... WITH ***EXTREME PREJUDICE***.
I JUST WANT TO TAKE A MOMENT TO COMMEND YOU ALL FOR YOUR BRAVERY, DEDICATION AND DEVOTION TO THE JOB.
MAKE NO MISTAKE ABOUT IT, AGENTS, THIS WILL BE YOUR TOUGHEST MISSION YET, AND WE DON'T EXPECT ***MOST*** OF YOU TO RETURN ALIVE.
ARE YOU ***KIDDING***?!
APPLEBEE VOLUNTEERED US FOR A ***SUICIDE*** MISSION?
TOLD YOU.

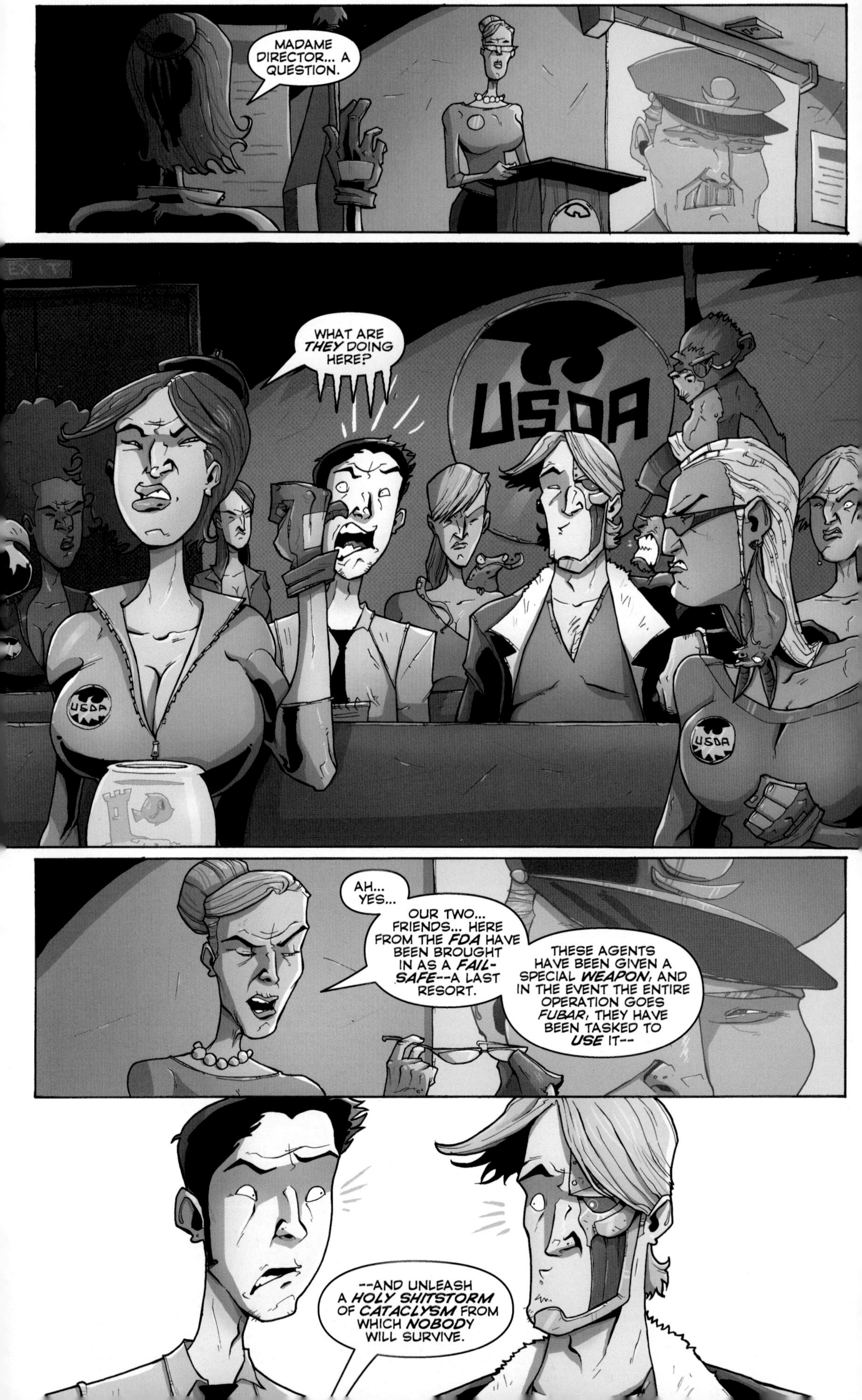
MADAME DIRECTOR... A QUESTION.
WHAT ARE *THEY* DOING HERE?
USDA
AH... YES...
OUR TWO... FRIENDS... HERE FROM THE *FDA* HAVE BEEN BROUGHT IN AS A *FAIL-SAFE*--A LAST RESORT.
THESE AGENTS HAVE BEEN GIVEN A SPECIAL *WEAPON*, AND IN THE EVENT THE ENTIRE OPERATION GOES *FUBAR*, THEY HAVE BEEN TASKED TO *USE* IT--
--AND UNLEASH A *HOLY SHITSTORM* OF *CATACLYSM* FROM WHICH *NOBODY* WILL SURVIVE.

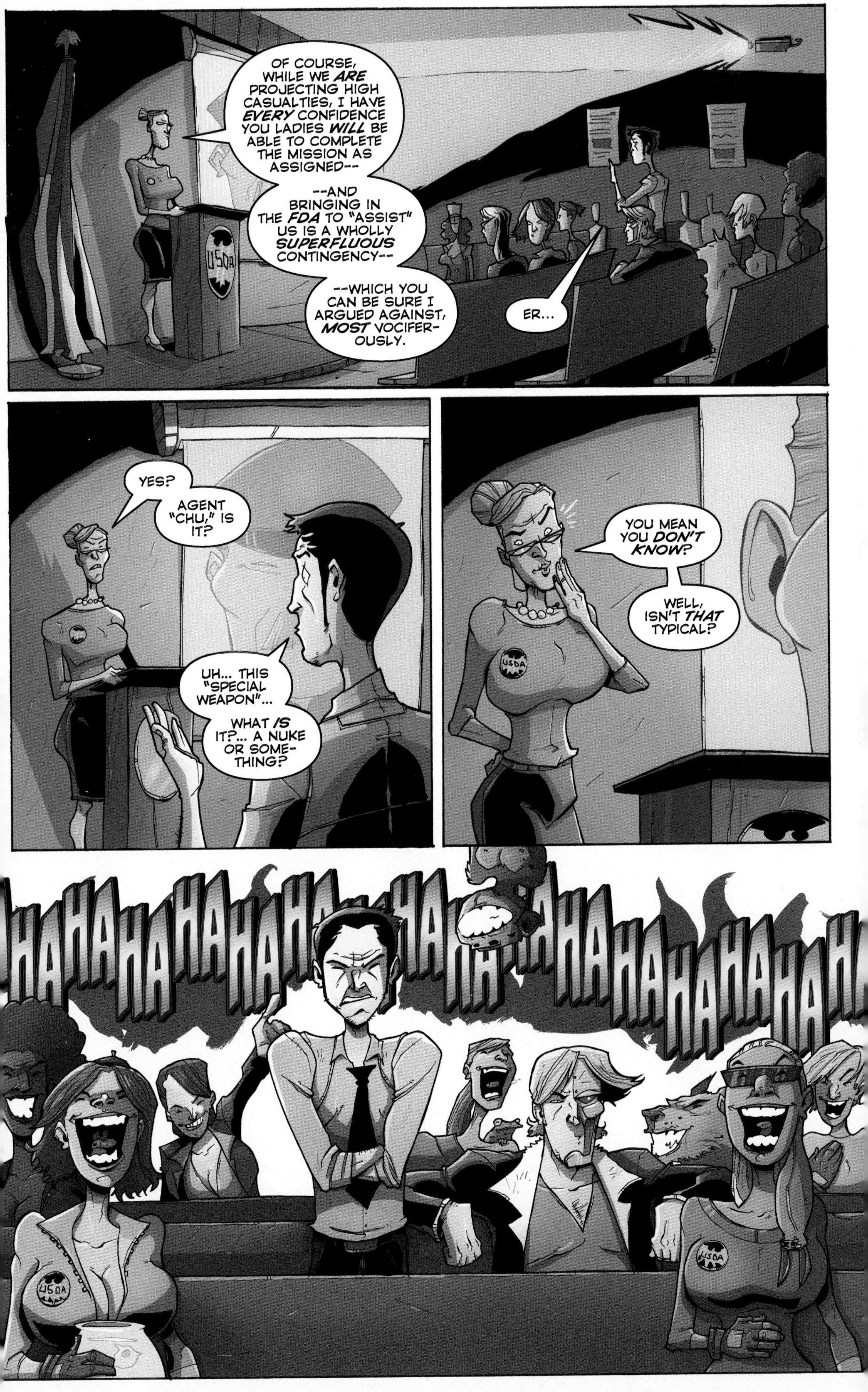
OF COURSE, WHILE WE ARE PROJECTING HIGH CASUALTIES, I HAVE EVERY CONFIDENCE YOU LADIES WILL BE ABLE TO COMPLETE THE MISSION AS ASSIGNED--
--AND BRINGING IN THE FDA TO "ASSIST" US IS A WHOLLY SUPERFLUOUS CONTINGENCY--
--WHICH YOU CAN BE SURE I ARGUED AGAINST, MOST VOCIFEROUSLY.
ER...
YES?
AGENT "CHU," IS IT?
UH... THIS "SPECIAL WEAPON"...
WHAT IS IT?... A NUKE OR SOMETHING?
YOU MEAN YOU DON'T KNOW?
WELL, ISN'T THAT TYPICAL?
HAHAHAHAHAHAHAHAHAHAHAHAHAHAHAHAH

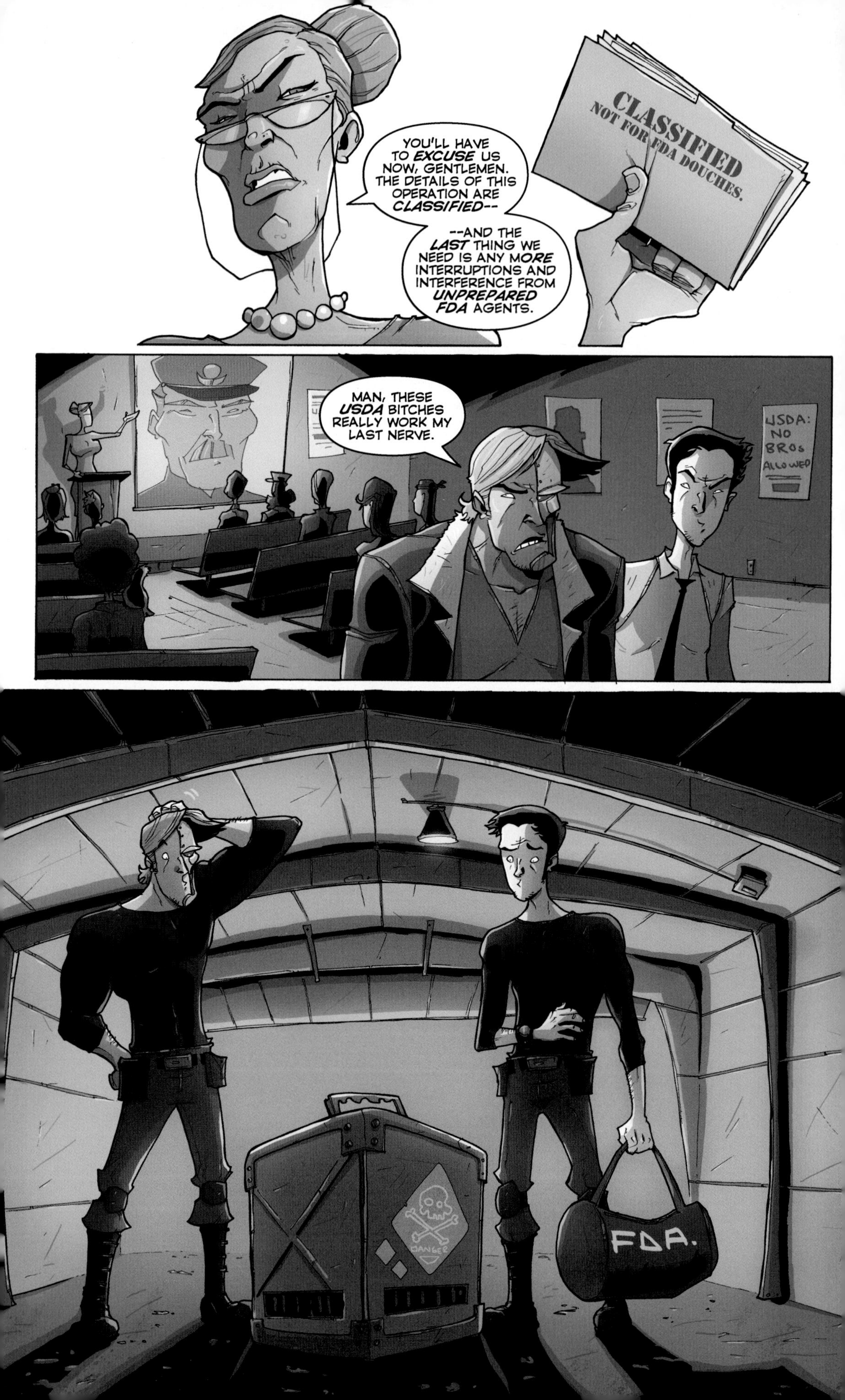

YOU'LL HAVE TO *EXCUSE* US NOW, GENTLEMEN. THE DETAILS OF THIS OPERATION ARE *CLASSIFIED*--
CLASSIFIED
NOT FOR FDA DOUCHES.
--AND THE *LAST* THING WE NEED IS ANY *MORE* INTERRUPTIONS AND INTERFERENCE FROM *UNPREPARED FDA* AGENTS.
MAN, THESE *USDA* BITCHES REALLY WORK MY LAST NERVE.
USDA: NO BROS ALLOWED
DANGER
FDA.

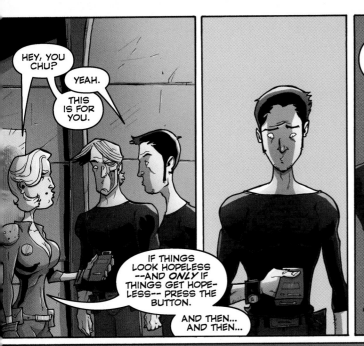

HEY, YOU CHU?

YEAH.

THIS IS FOR YOU.

IF THINGS LOOK HOPELESS --AND *ONLY* IF THINGS GET HOPE-LESS-- PRESS THE BUTTON.

AND THEN... AND THEN...

AND THEN WHATEVER'S IN OUR LITTLE *MYSTERY* BOX--

LET'S JUST HOPE TO HELL IT DOESN'T COME TO THAT, OKAY?

ALRIGHTY, LADIES... *MOVE OUT!*

THANKS FOR FLYING CLASSIFIED AIRLINES!!! (TELL ANYONE AND WE SHALL KILL YOU.)

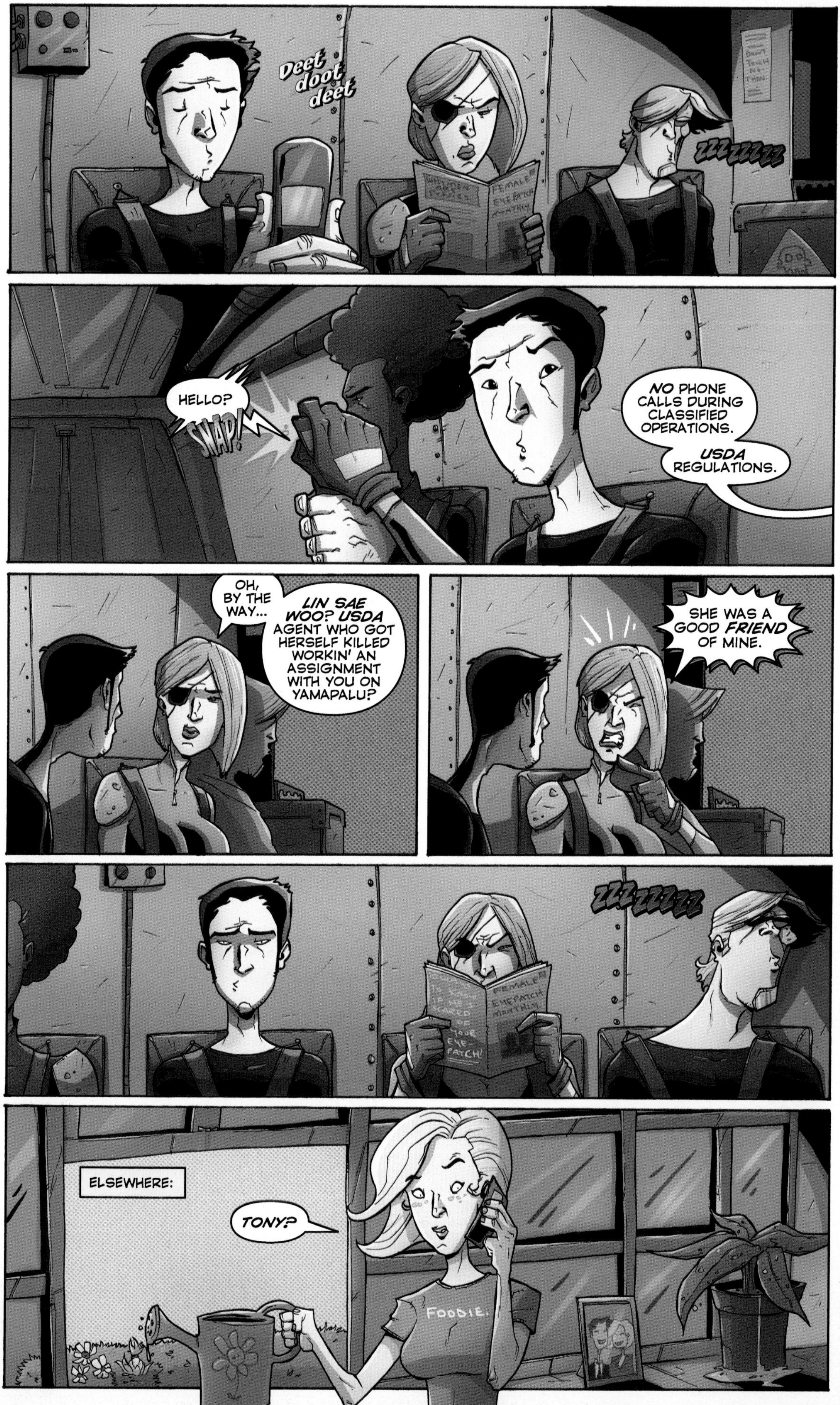

Deet doot deet
WHITE MEN ARE PUZZLES
FEMALE EYEPATCH MONTHLY
ZZZZZZZZ
HELLO?
SNAP!
NO PHONE CALLS DURING CLASSIFIED OPERATIONS.
USDA REGULATIONS.
OH, BY THE WAY...
LIN SAE WOO? USDA AGENT WHO GOT HERSELF KILLED WORKIN' AN ASSIGNMENT WITH YOU ON YAMAPALU?
SHE WAS A GOOD FRIEND OF MINE.
ZZZZZZZZ
10 WAYS TO KNOW IF HE'S SCARED OF YOUR EYE-PATCH!
FEMALE EYEPATCH MONTHLY
ELSEWHERE:
TONY?
FOODIE.

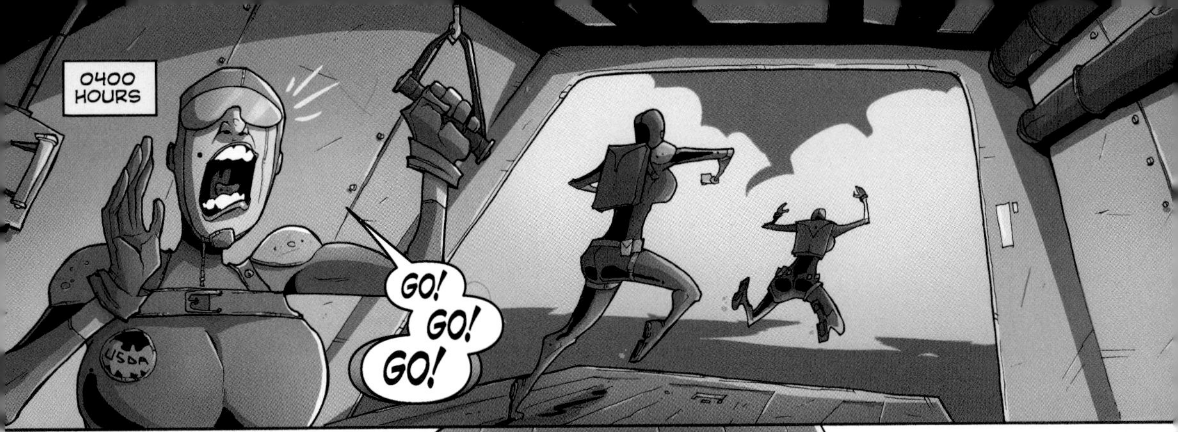
0400 HOURS
GO! GO! GO!

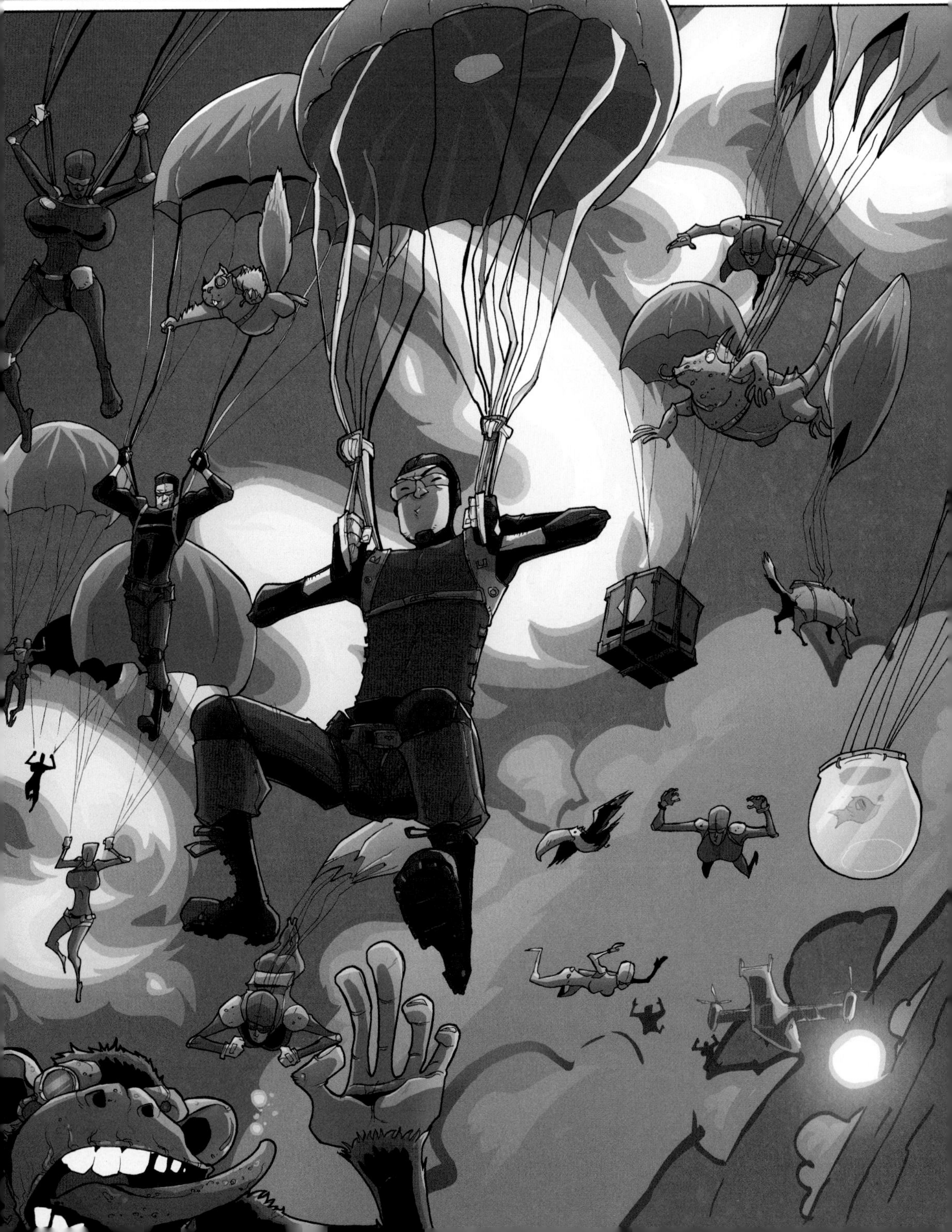

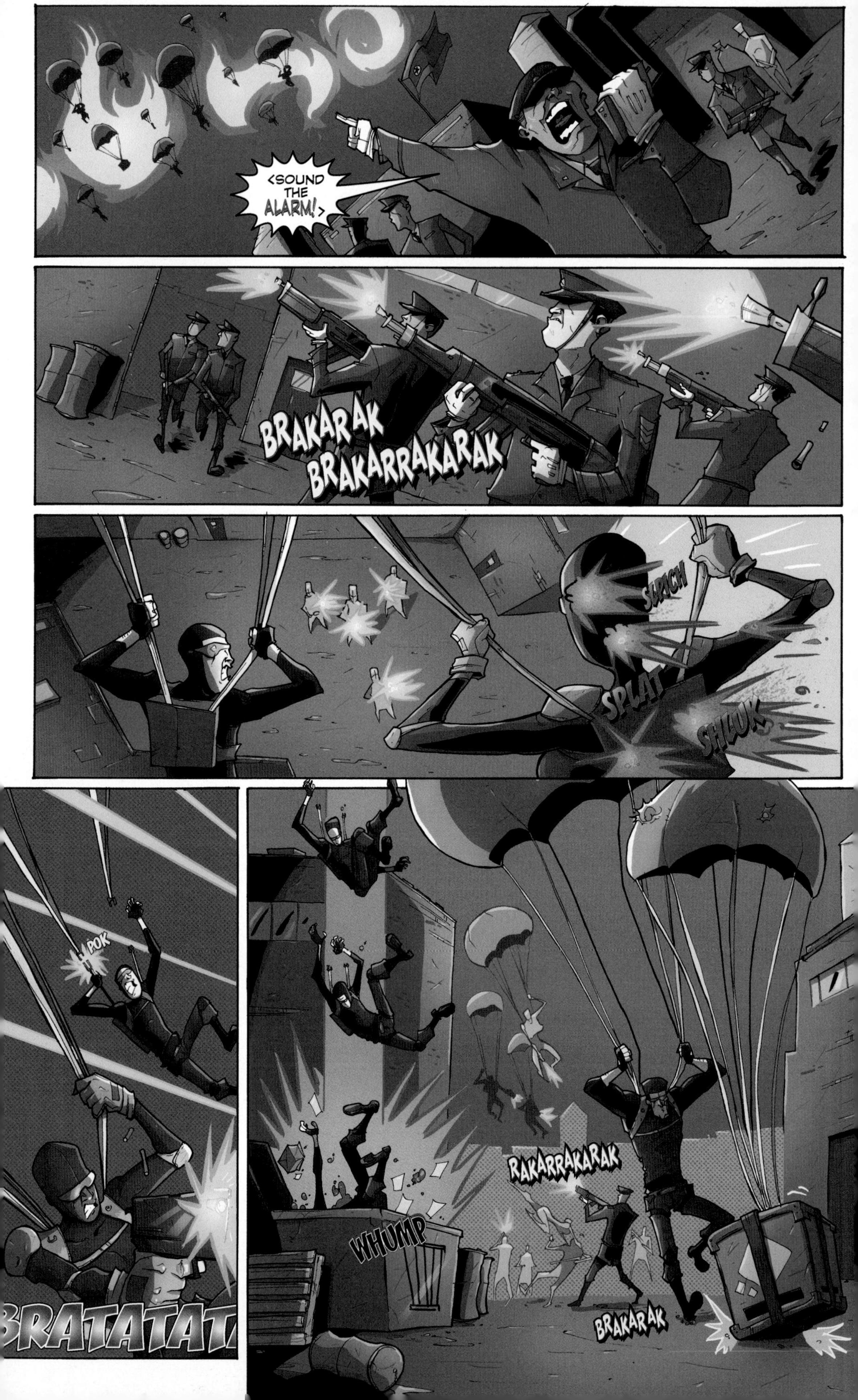
<SOUND THE ALARM!>
BRAKARAK
BRAKARRAKARAK
SPLICH
SPLAT
SHLUK
POK
BRATATAT
WHUMP
RAKARRAKARAK
BRAKARAK

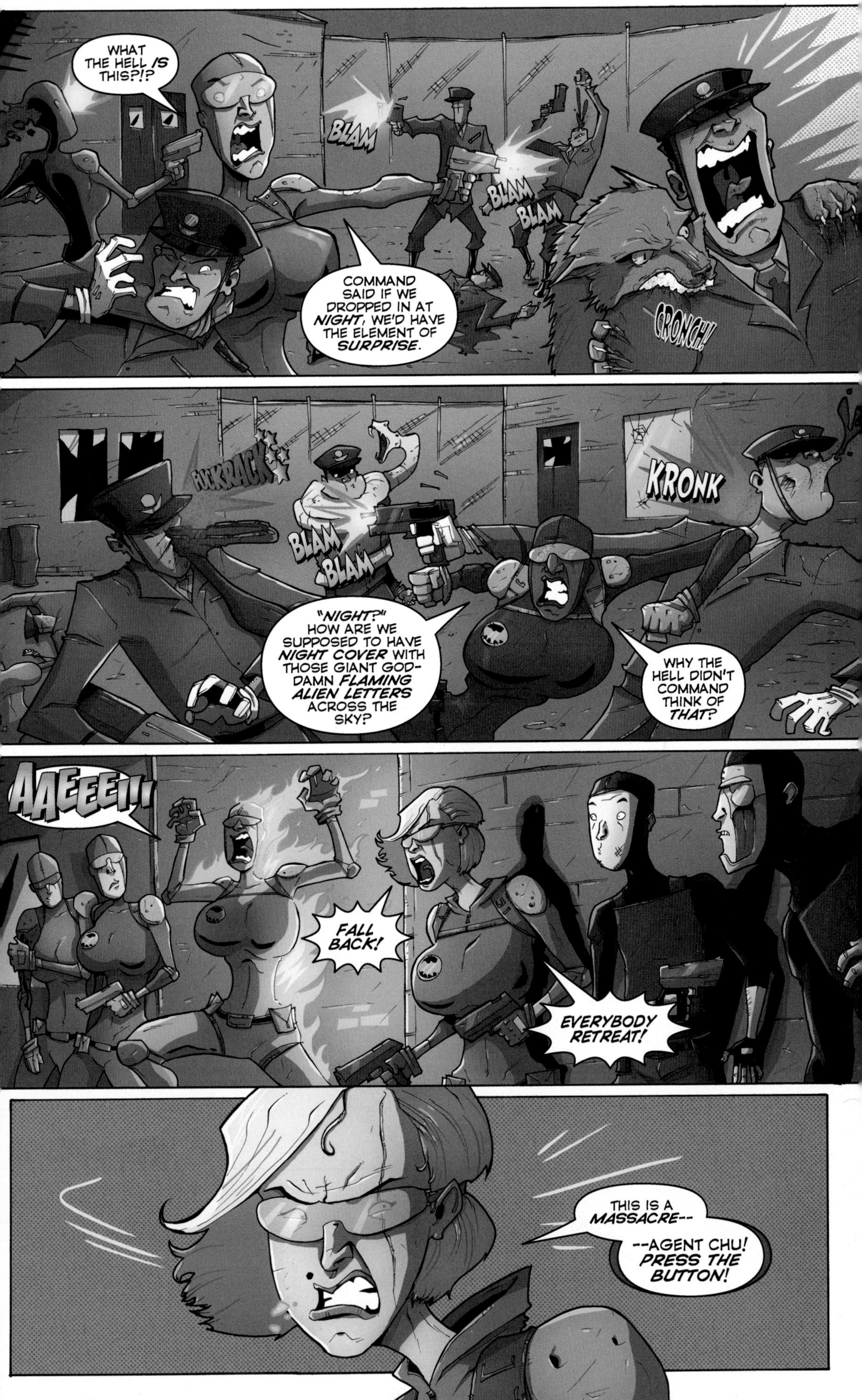
WHAT THE HELL IS THIS?!?
BLAM
BLAM
BLAM
COMMAND SAID IF WE DROPPED IN AT NIGHT, WE'D HAVE THE ELEMENT OF SURPRISE.
CRONCH!
FUCKRACK
BLAM
BLAM
KRONK
"NIGHT?" HOW ARE WE SUPPOSED TO HAVE NIGHT COVER WITH THOSE GIANT GOD-DAMN FLAMING ALIEN LETTERS ACROSS THE SKY?
WHY THE HELL DIDN'T COMMAND THINK OF THAT?
AAEEE!!!
FALL BACK!
EVERYBODY RETREAT!
THIS IS A MASSACRE--
--AGENT CHU! PRESS THE BUTTON!

YOU *HEAR* ME? PRESS THE GODDA--

SPLUT

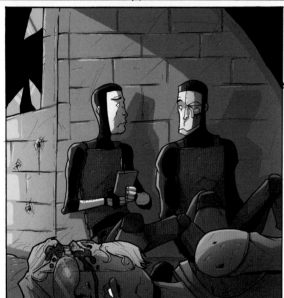

I GUESS THIS IS *IT,* PARTNER--

NO TIME TO GET SAPPY ON ME, PRINCESS.

PRESS THE FREAKIN--

CLIK

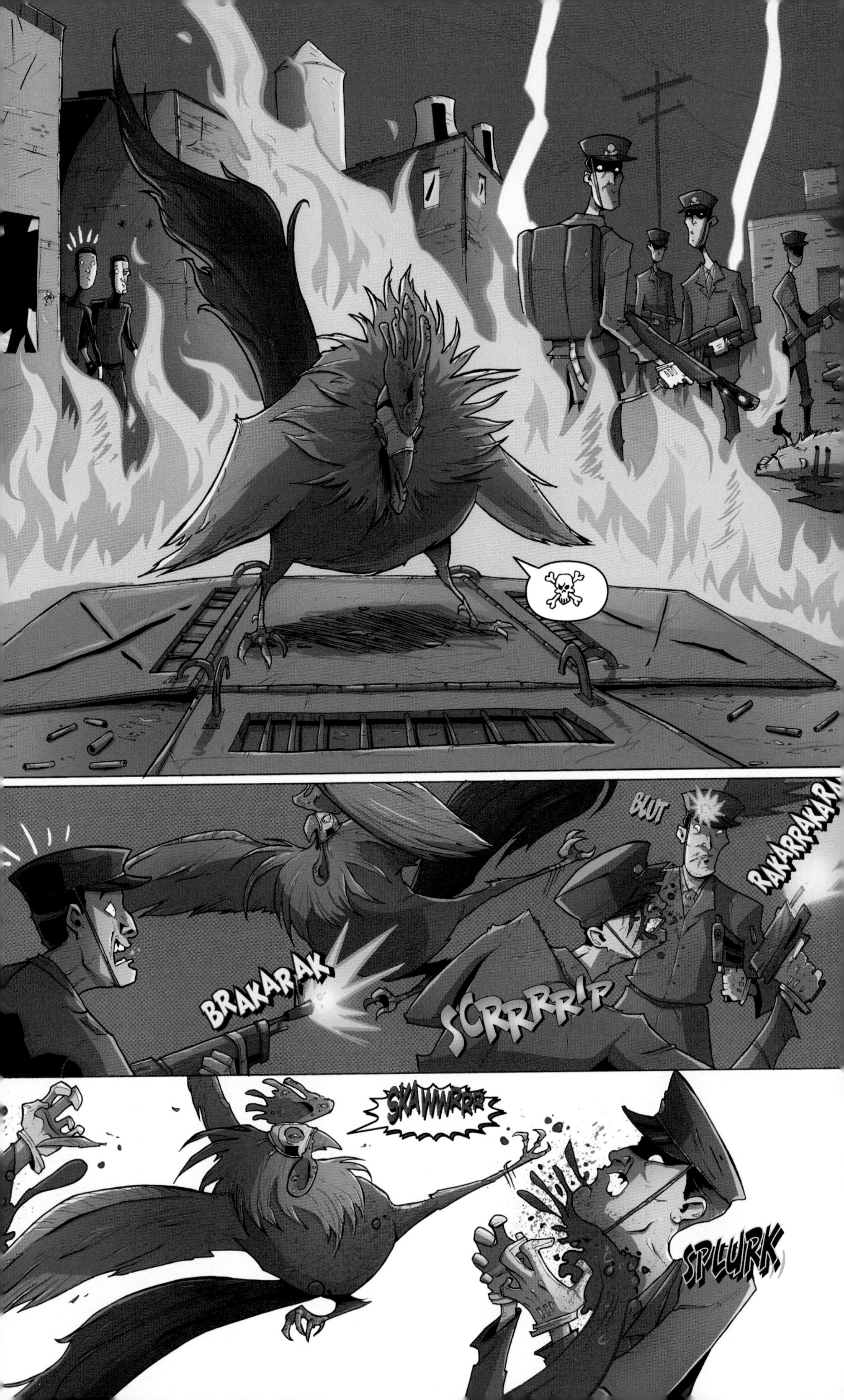
BLUT
RAKARRAKARA
BRAKARAK
SCRRRRIP
SKAWWRRR
SPLURK

THIS IS
POYO.

POYO WAS EXPOSED TO A NEAR-LETHAL AMOUNT OF RADIATION AS AN EGG, DURING THE FIRST STAGES OF A GOVERNMENT EXPERIMENT TO CREATE MUTANT SUPER SOLDIERS--

HI-YA!

HI-YA!

BA-KAW!

--TRAINED IN EXOTIC MARTIAL ARTS TECHNIQUE BY TIBETAN KUNG FU FIGHTIN' MONKS--

--AND GIVEN STRANGE BIO-ENHANCEMENTS DURING A RASH OF FARM ANIMAL ABDUCTIONS BY EXTRA-TERRESTRIALS.

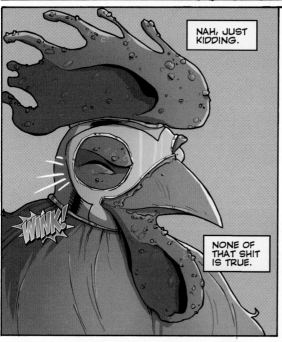

NAH, JUST KIDDING.

WINK!

NONE OF THAT SHIT IS TRUE.

POYO IS JUST REALLY, *REALLY* BAD ASS.

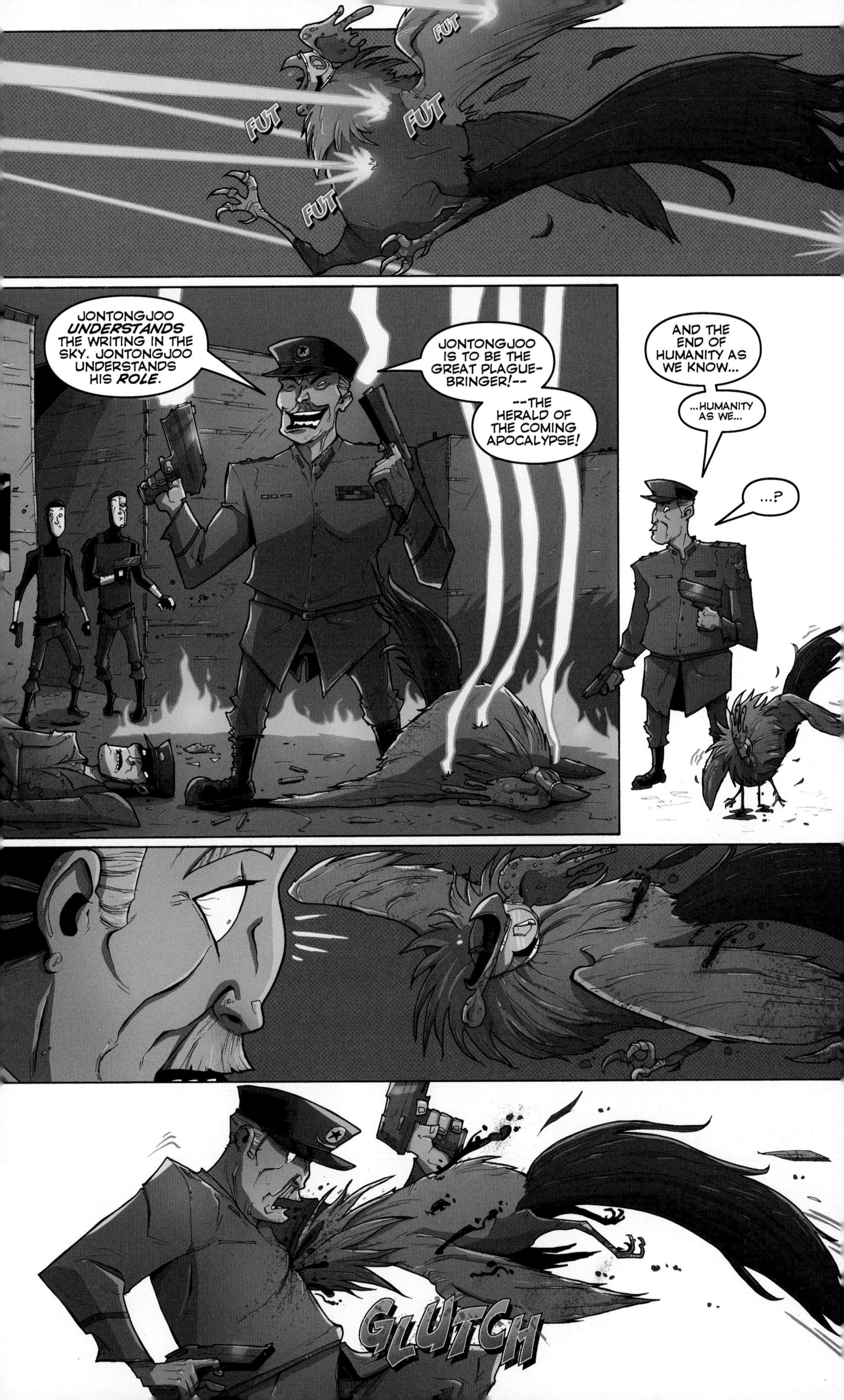
FUT
FUT
FUT
FUT
JONTONGJOO UNDERSTANDS THE WRITING IN THE SKY. JONTONGJOO UNDERSTANDS HIS ROLE.
JONTONGJOO IS TO BE THE GREAT PLAGUE-BRINGER!--
--THE HERALD OF THE COMING APOCALYPSE!
AND THE END OF HUMANITY AS WE KNOW...
...HUMANITY AS WE...
...?
GLUTCH

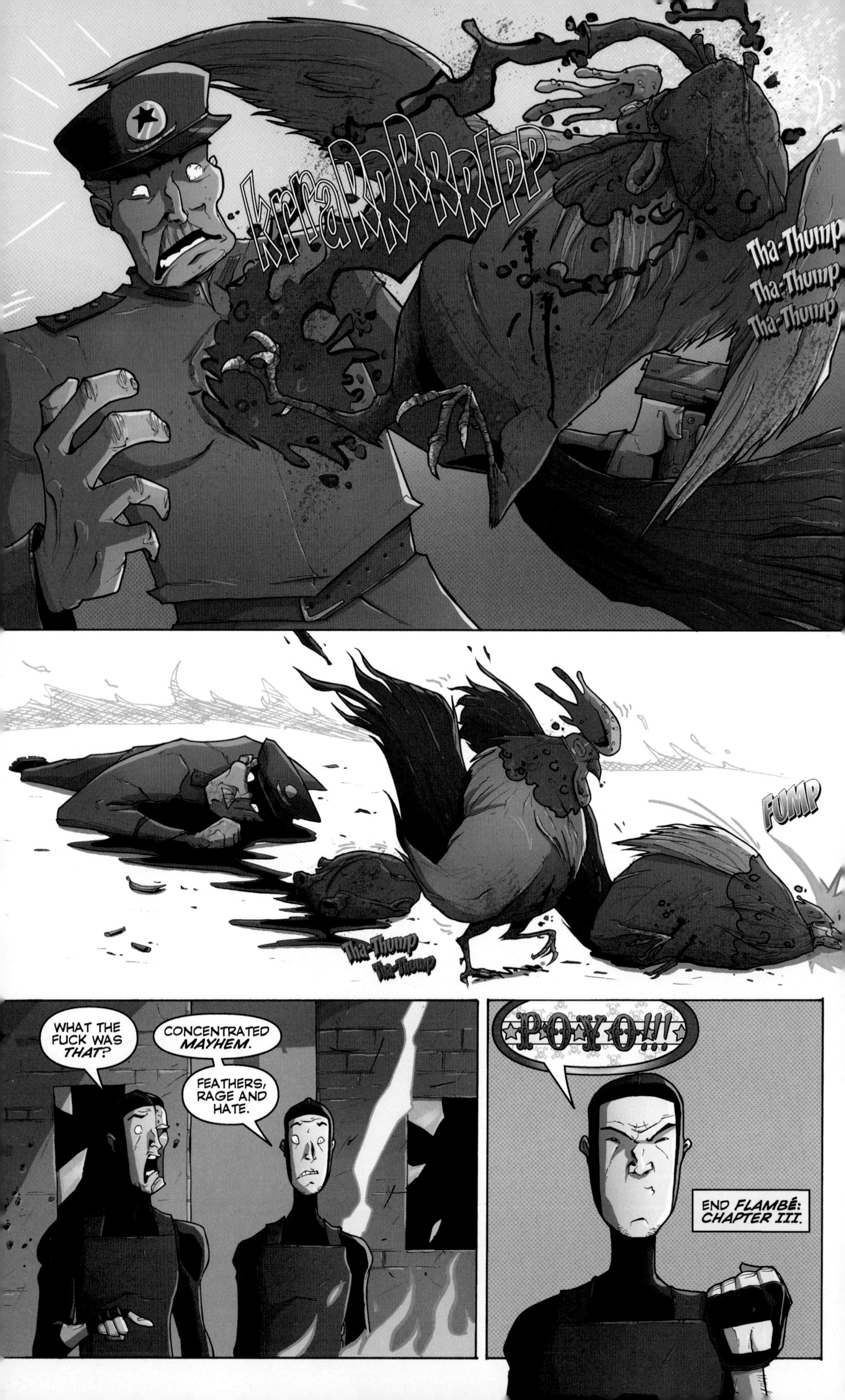
krraRRRRRIPP
Tha-Thump
Tha-Thump
Tha-Thump
FUMP
Tha-Thump
Tha-Thump
WHAT THE FUCK WAS THAT?
CONCENTRATED MAYHEM.
FEATHERS, RAGE AND HATE.
POYO!!!
END FLAMBÉ: CHAPTER III.

Chapter 4

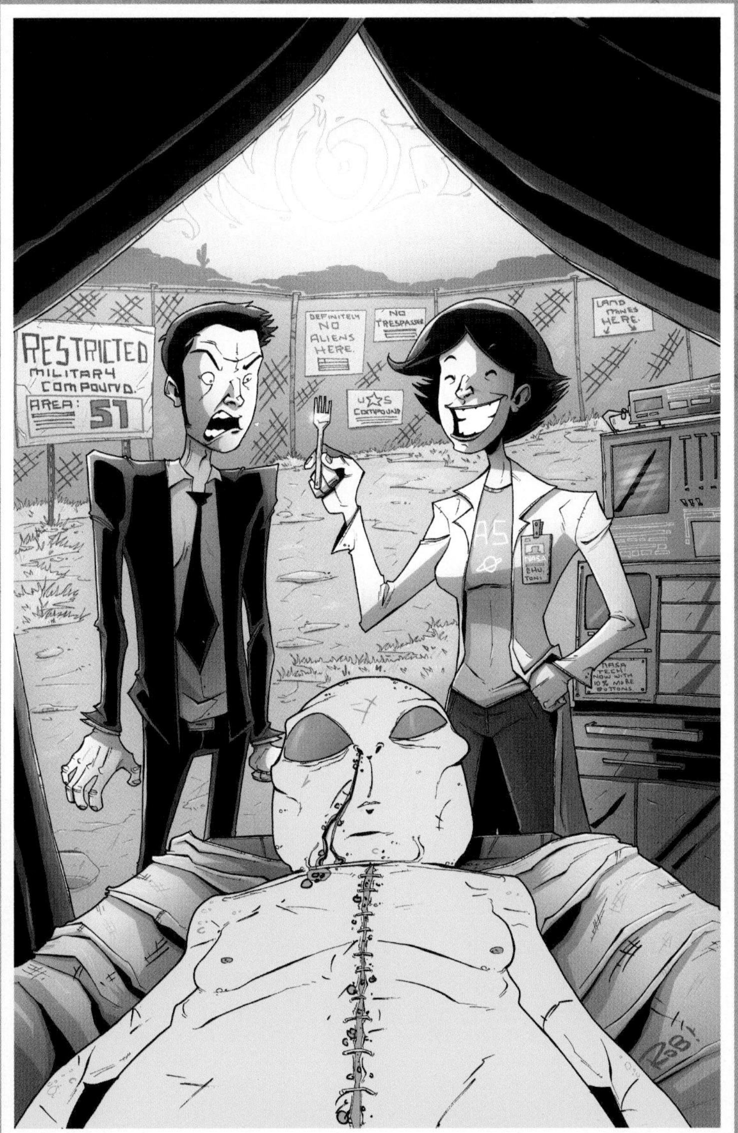

RESTRICTED
MILITARY
COMPOUND.
AREA: 51
DEFINITELY NO ALIENS HERE.
NO TRESPASSING
LAND MINES HERE.
U.S COMPOUND

NASA

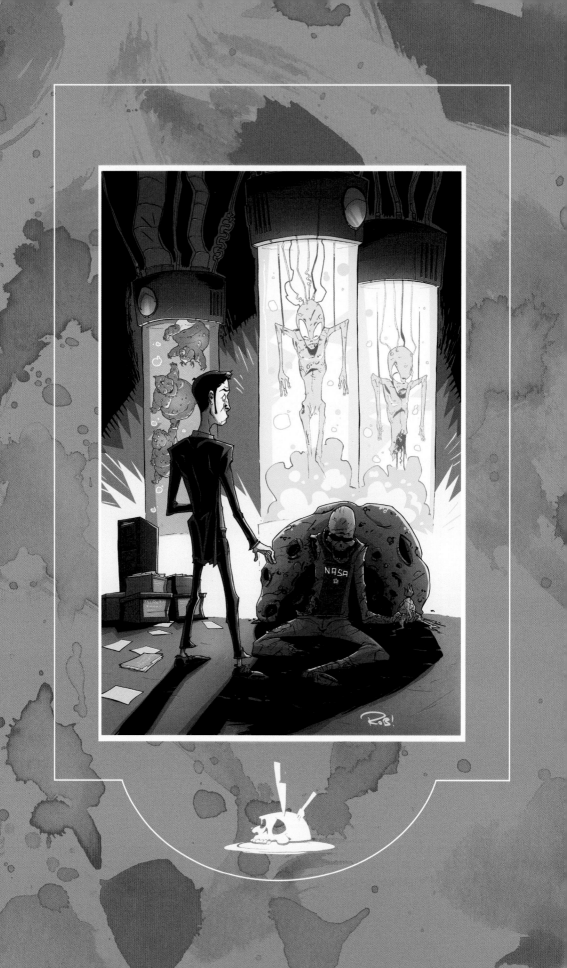

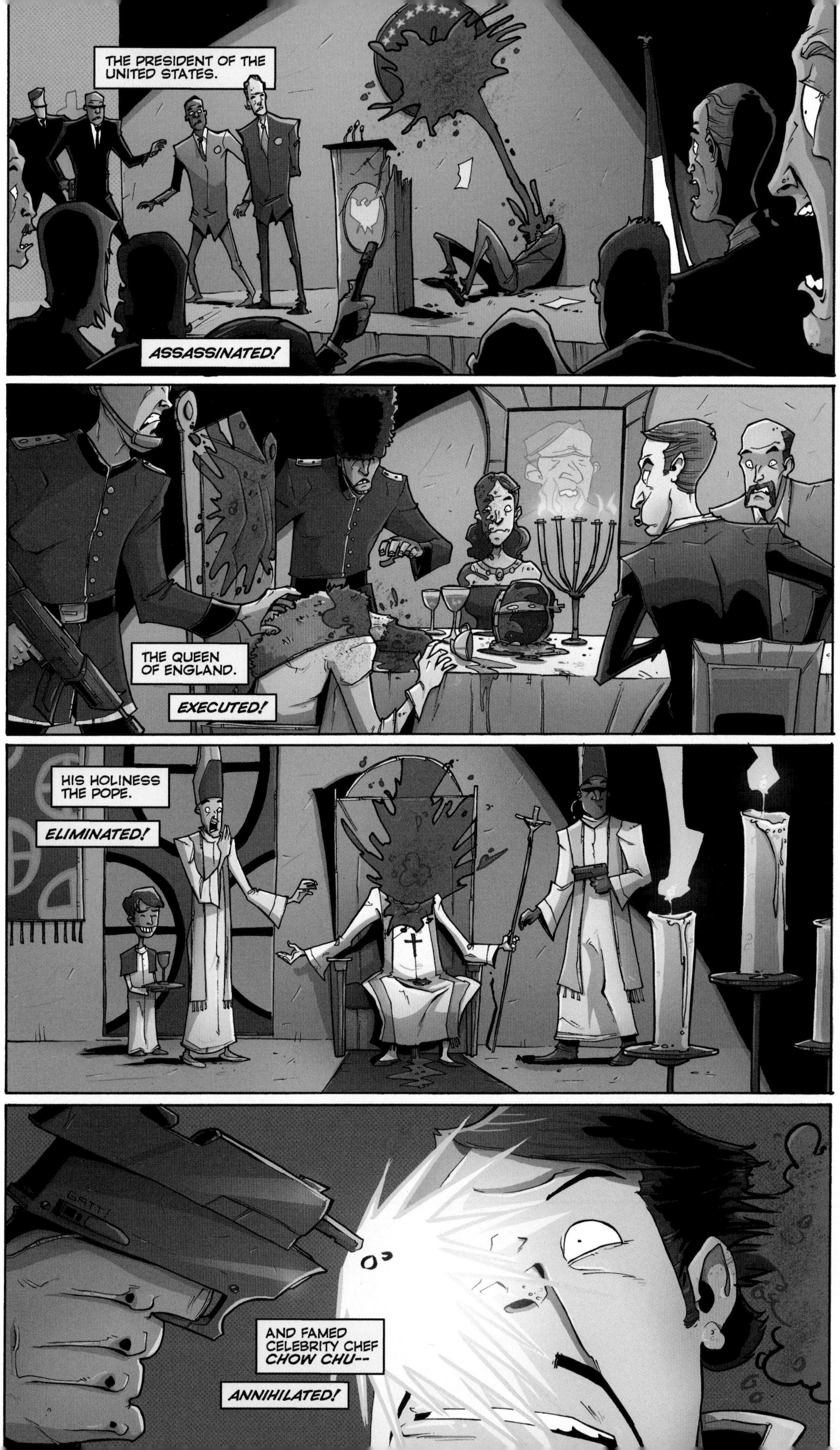
THE PRESIDENT OF THE UNITED STATES.
ASSASSINATED!
THE QUEEN OF ENGLAND.
EXECUTED!
HIS HOLINESS THE POPE.
ELIMINATED!
AND FAMED CELEBRITY CHEF CHOW CHU--
ANNIHILATED!

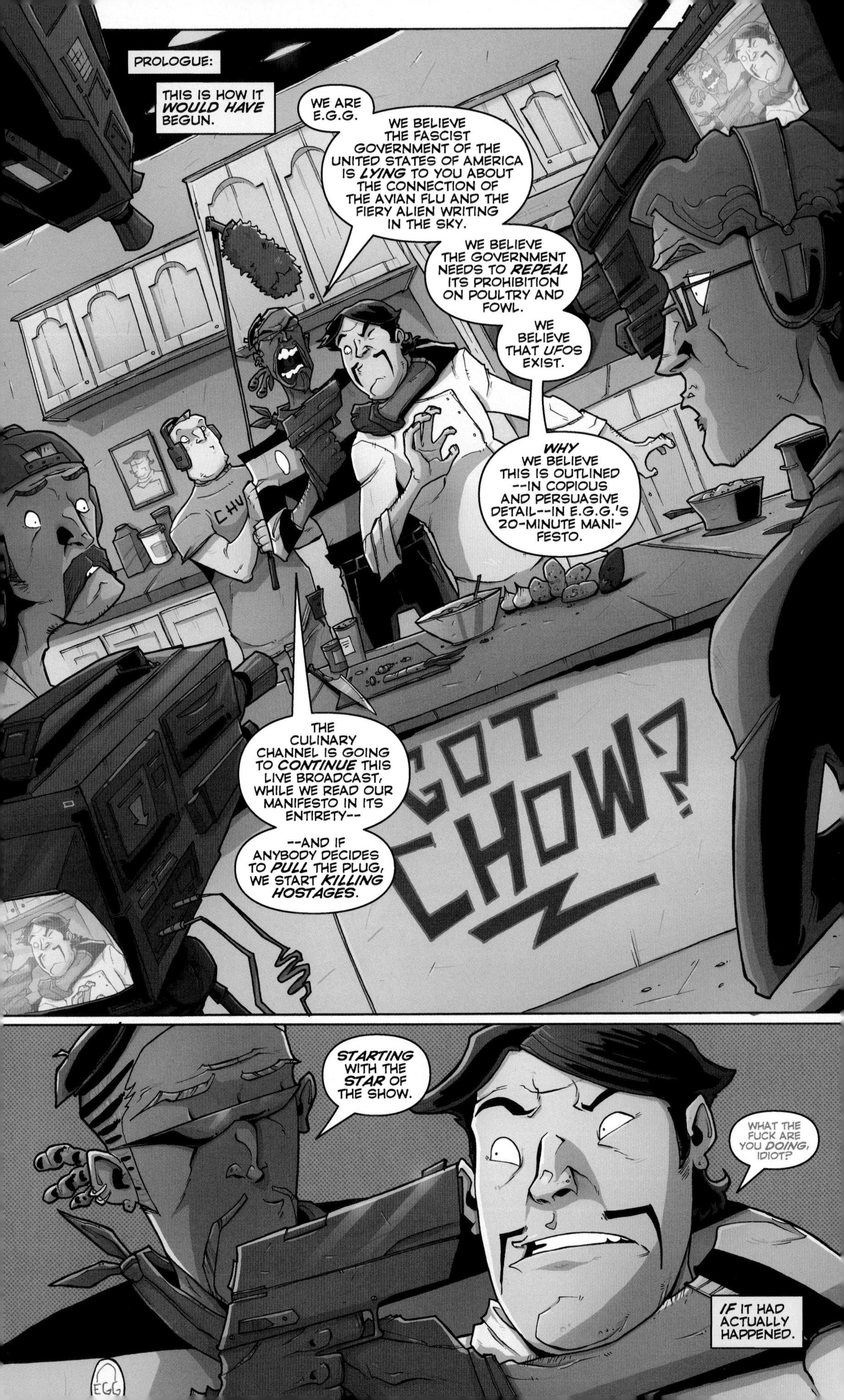
PROLOGUE:
THIS IS HOW IT WOULD HAVE BEGUN.
WE ARE E.G.G.
WE BELIEVE THE FASCIST GOVERNMENT OF THE UNITED STATES OF AMERICA IS LYING TO YOU ABOUT THE CONNECTION OF THE AVIAN FLU AND THE FIERY ALIEN WRITING IN THE SKY.
WE BELIEVE THE GOVERNMENT NEEDS TO REPEAL ITS PROHIBITION ON POULTRY AND FOWL.
WE BELIEVE THAT UFOS EXIST.
WHY WE BELIEVE THIS IS OUTLINED --IN COPIOUS AND PERSUASIVE DETAIL--IN E.G.G.'S 20-MINUTE MANI-FESTO.
CHU
THE CULINARY CHANNEL IS GOING TO CONTINUE THIS LIVE BROADCAST, WHILE WE READ OUR MANIFESTO IN ITS ENTIRETY--
--AND IF ANYBODY DECIDES TO PULL THE PLUG, WE START KILLING HOSTAGES.
GOT CHOW?
STARTING WITH THE STAR OF THE SHOW.
WHAT THE FUCK ARE YOU DOING, IDIOT?
IF IT HAD ACTUALLY HAPPENED.
EGG

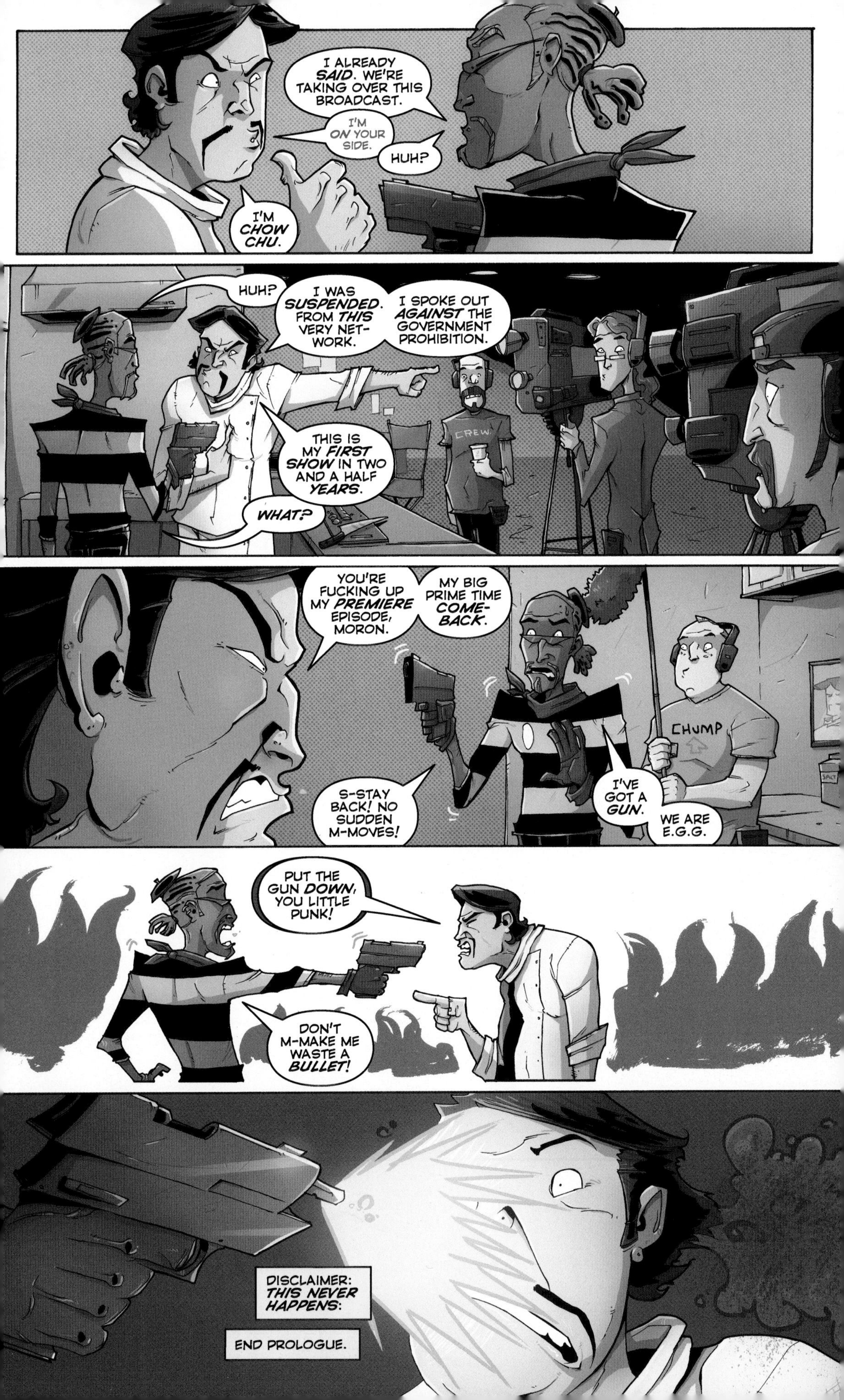
I ALREADY SAID. WE'RE TAKING OVER THIS BROADCAST.
I'M ON YOUR SIDE.
HUH?
I'M CHOW CHU.
HUH?
I WAS SUSPENDED. FROM THIS VERY NET-WORK.
I SPOKE OUT AGAINST THE GOVERNMENT PROHIBITION.
CREW
THIS IS MY FIRST SHOW IN TWO AND A HALF YEARS.
WHAT?
YOU'RE FUCKING UP MY PREMIERE EPISODE, MORON.
MY BIG PRIME TIME COME-BACK.
CHUMP
S-STAY BACK! NO SUDDEN M-MOVES!
I'VE GOT A GUN.
WE ARE E.G.G.
PUT THE GUN DOWN, YOU LITTLE PUNK!
DON'T M-MAKE ME WASTE A BULLET!
DISCLAIMER: THIS NEVER HAPPENS:
END PROLOGUE.

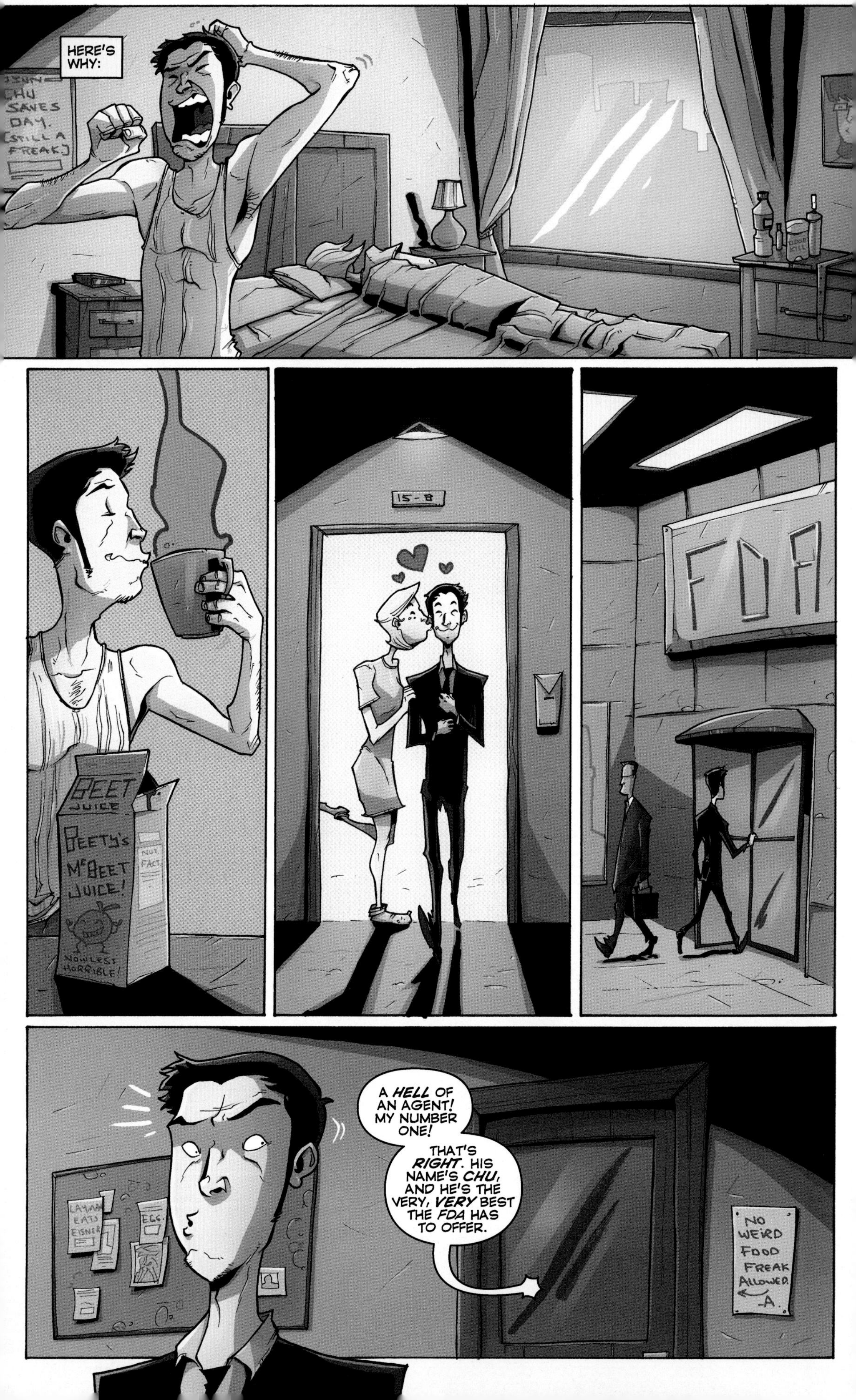
HERE'S WHY:
CHU SAVES DAY. [STILL A FREAK]
BEET JUICE
BEETY'S McBEET JUICE!
NUT. FACT.
NOW LESS HORRIBLE!
15-B
FDA
A HELL OF AN AGENT! MY NUMBER ONE!
THAT'S RIGHT. HIS NAME'S CHU, AND HE'S THE VERY, VERY BEST THE FDA HAS TO OFFER.
LAYMAN EATS EISNER
EGG.
NO WEIRD FOOD FREAK ALLOWED -A.

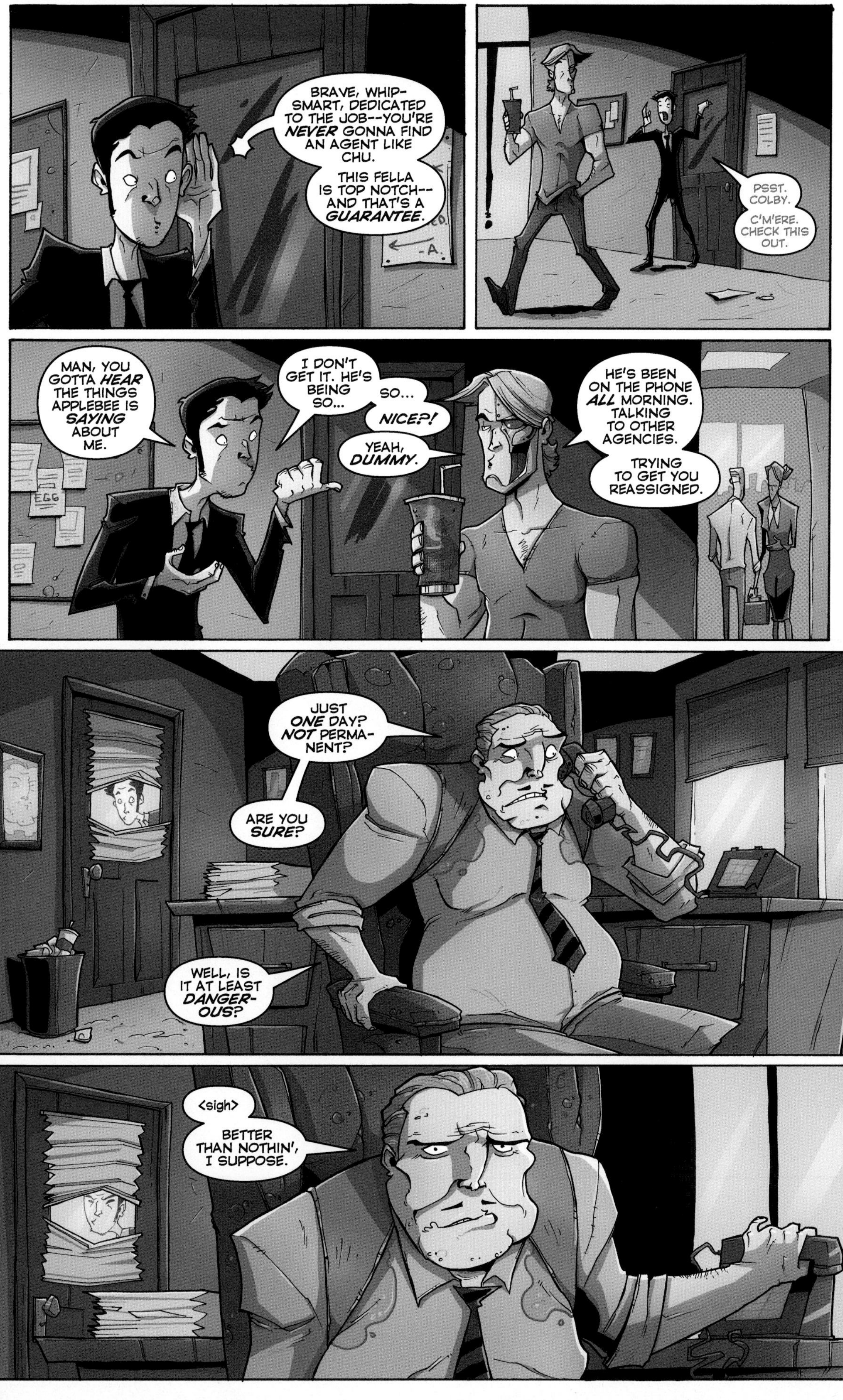

BRAVE, WHIP-SMART, DEDICATED TO THE JOB--YOU'RE NEVER GONNA FIND AN AGENT LIKE CHU.
THIS FELLA IS TOP NOTCH--AND THAT'S A GUARANTEE.
PSST. COLBY.
C'M'ERE. CHECK THIS OUT.
MAN, YOU GOTTA HEAR THE THINGS APPLEBEE IS SAYING ABOUT ME.
I DON'T GET IT. HE'S BEING SO...
SO... NICE?!
YEAH, DUMMY.
HE'S BEEN ON THE PHONE ALL MORNING. TALKING TO OTHER AGENCIES.
TRYING TO GET YOU REASSIGNED.
JUST ONE DAY? NOT PERMA-NENT?
ARE YOU SURE?
WELL, IS IT AT LEAST DANGER-OUS?
<sigh>
BETTER THAN NOTHIN', I SUPPOSE.

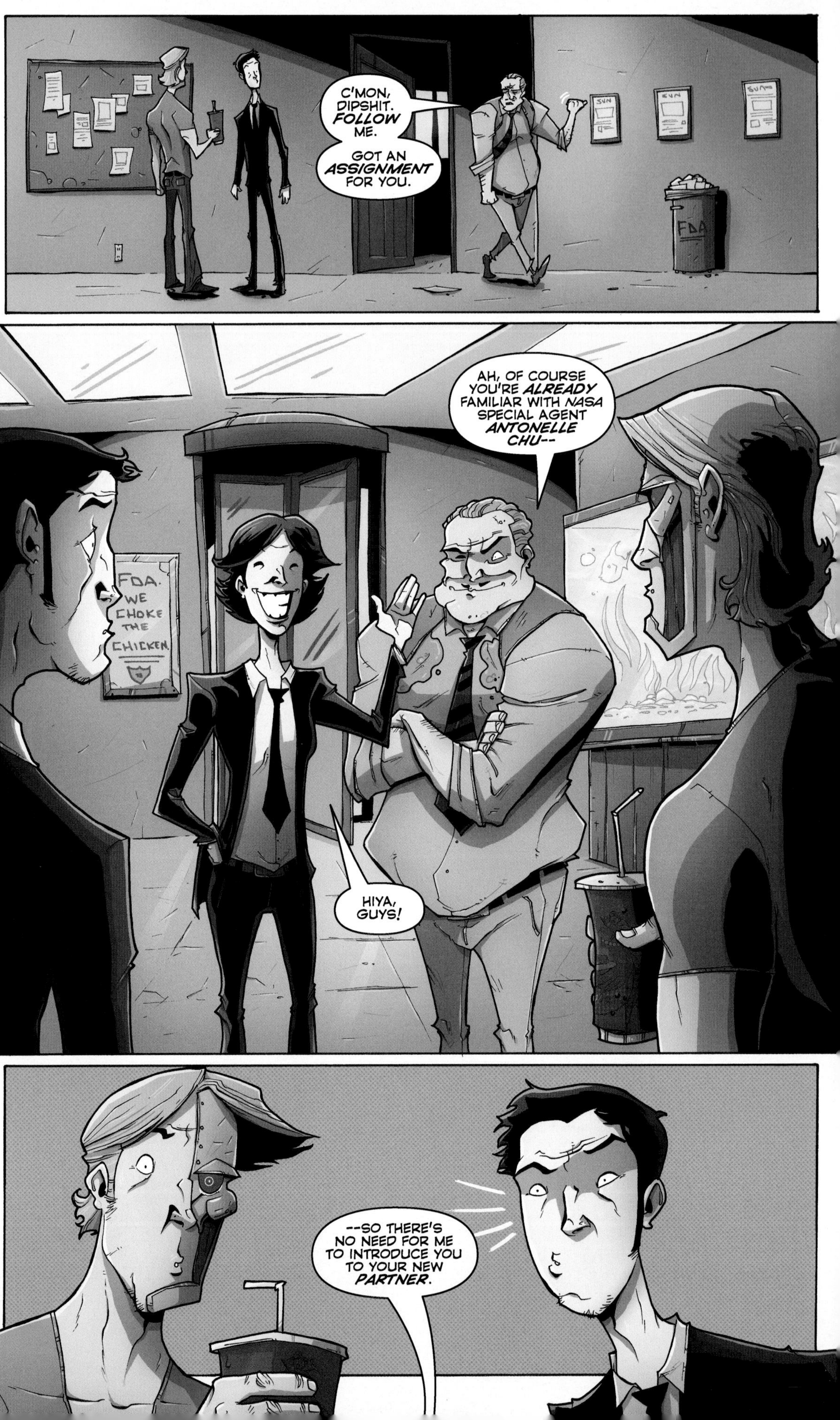
C'MON, DIPSHIT. *FOLLOW* ME.
GOT AN *ASSIGNMENT* FOR YOU.
SUN
SUN
SUN
FDA
AH, OF COURSE YOU'RE *ALREADY* FAMILIAR WITH *NASA* SPECIAL AGENT *ANTONELLE CHU*--
FDA. WE CHOKE THE CHICKEN.
HIYA, GUYS!
--SO THERE'S NO NEED FOR ME TO INTRODUCE YOU TO YOUR NEW *PARTNER*.

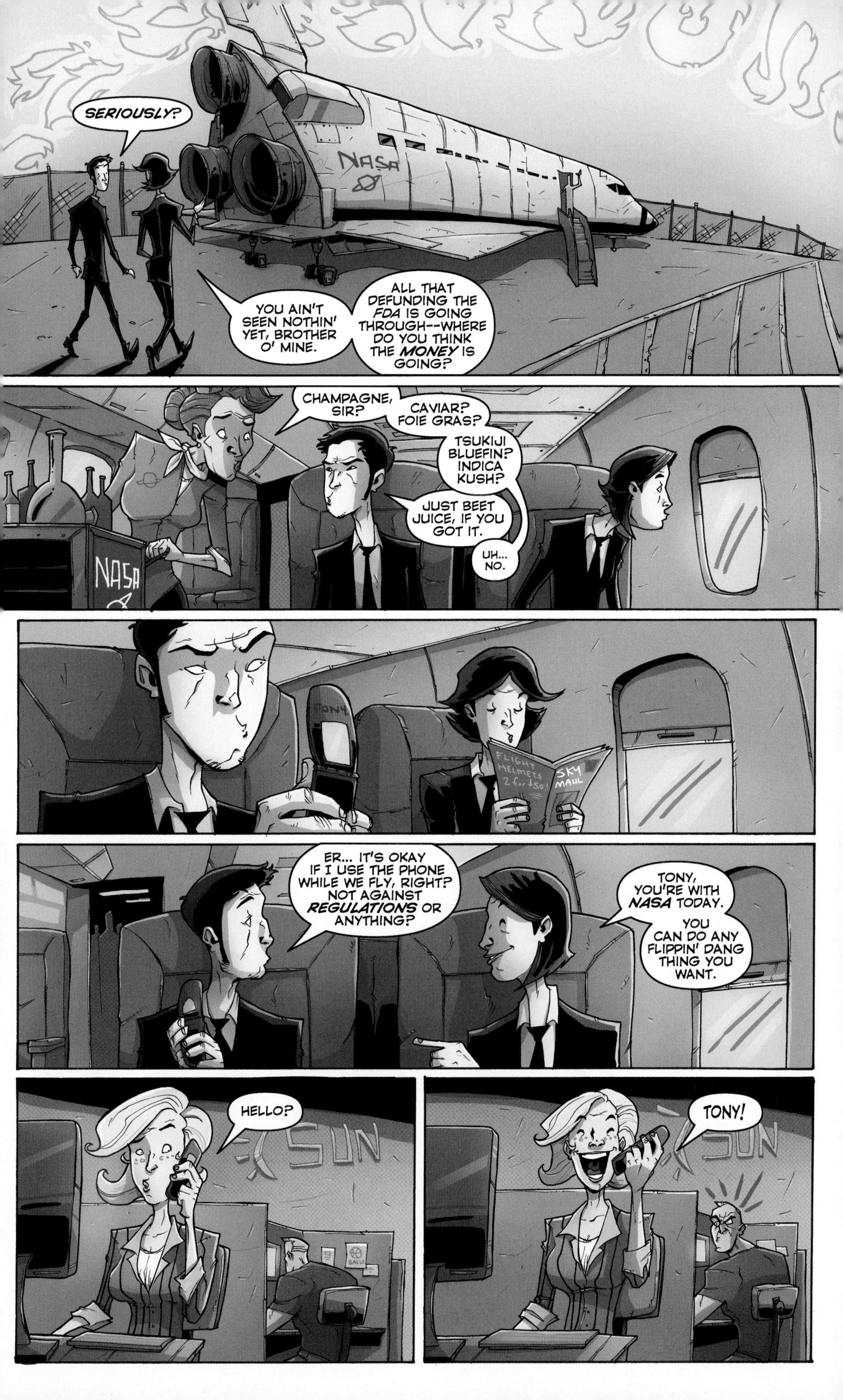
SERIOUSLY?
YOU AIN'T SEEN NOTHIN' YET, BROTHER O' MINE.
ALL THAT DEFUNDING THE FDA IS GOING THROUGH--WHERE DO YOU THINK THE MONEY IS GOING?
NASA
CHAMPAGNE, SIR?
CAVIAR? FOIE GRAS?
TSUKIJI BLUEFIN? INDICA KUSH?
JUST BEET JUICE, IF YOU GOT IT.
UH... NO.
NASA
TONY
FLIGHT HELMETS 2 for $50!
SKY MAUL
ER... IT'S OKAY IF I USE THE PHONE WHILE WE FLY, RIGHT? NOT AGAINST REGULATIONS OR ANYTHING?
TONY, YOU'RE WITH NASA TODAY.
YOU CAN DO ANY FLIPPIN' DANG THING YOU WANT.
HELLO?
SUN
TONY!
SUN

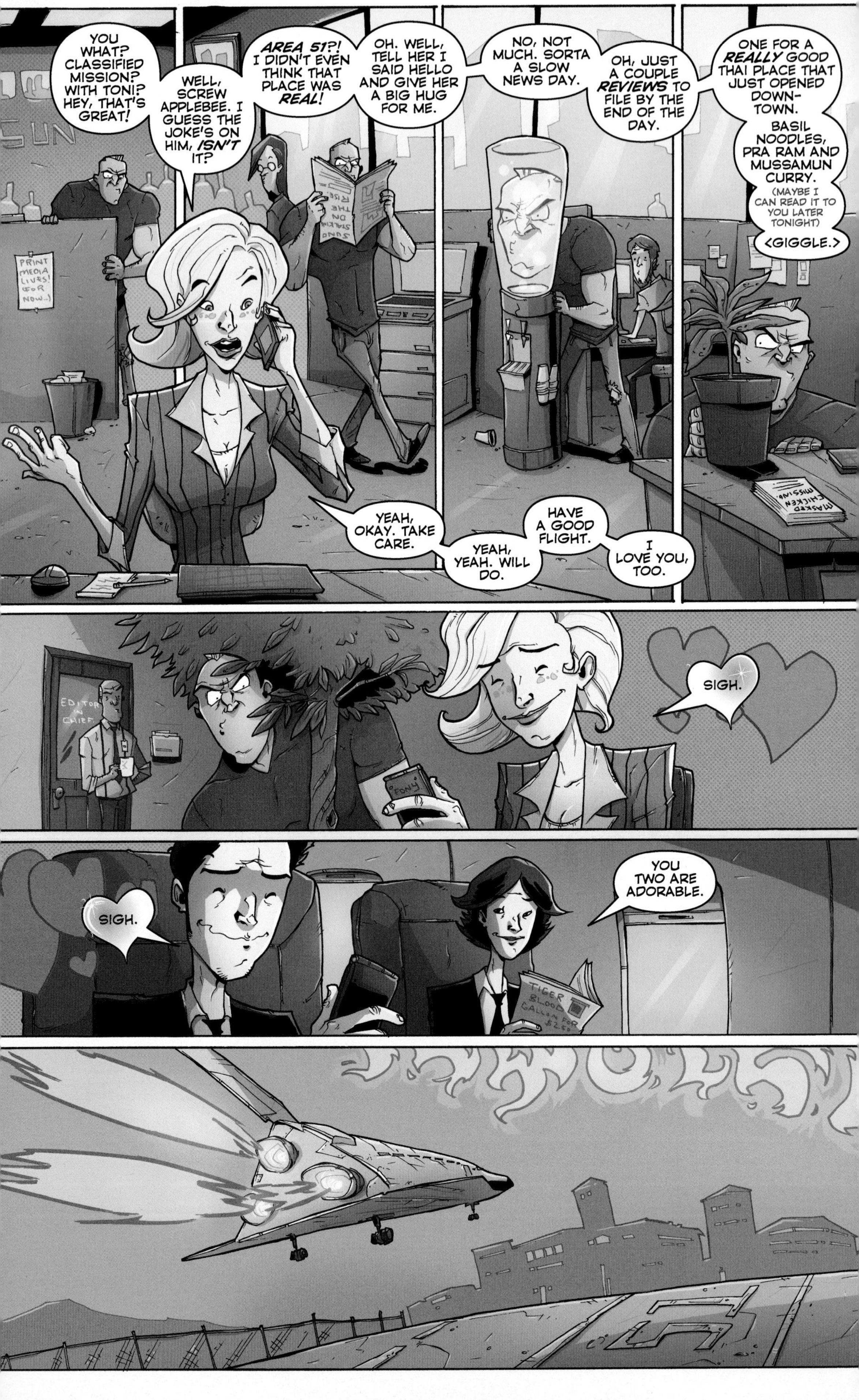
YOU WHAT? CLASSIFIED MISSION? WITH TONI? HEY, THAT'S GREAT!
WELL, SCREW APPLEBEE. I GUESS THE JOKE'S ON HIM, *ISN'T* IT?
AREA 51?! I DIDN'T EVEN THINK THAT PLACE WAS *REAL!*
OH. WELL, TELL HER I SAID HELLO AND GIVE HER A BIG HUG FOR ME.
NO, NOT MUCH. SORTA A SLOW NEWS DAY.
OH, JUST A COUPLE *REVIEWS* TO FILE BY THE END OF THE DAY.
ONE FOR A *REALLY* GOOD THAI PLACE THAT JUST OPENED DOWN-TOWN.
BASIL NOODLES, PRA RAM AND MUSSAMUN CURRY.
(MAYBE I CAN READ IT TO YOU LATER TONIGHT)
<GIGGLE.>
PRINT MEDIA LIVES! (FOR NOW...)
YEAH, OKAY. TAKE CARE.
YEAH, YEAH. WILL DO.
HAVE A GOOD FLIGHT.
I LOVE YOU, TOO.
EDITOR IN CHIEF
SIGH.
SIGH.
YOU TWO ARE ADORABLE.

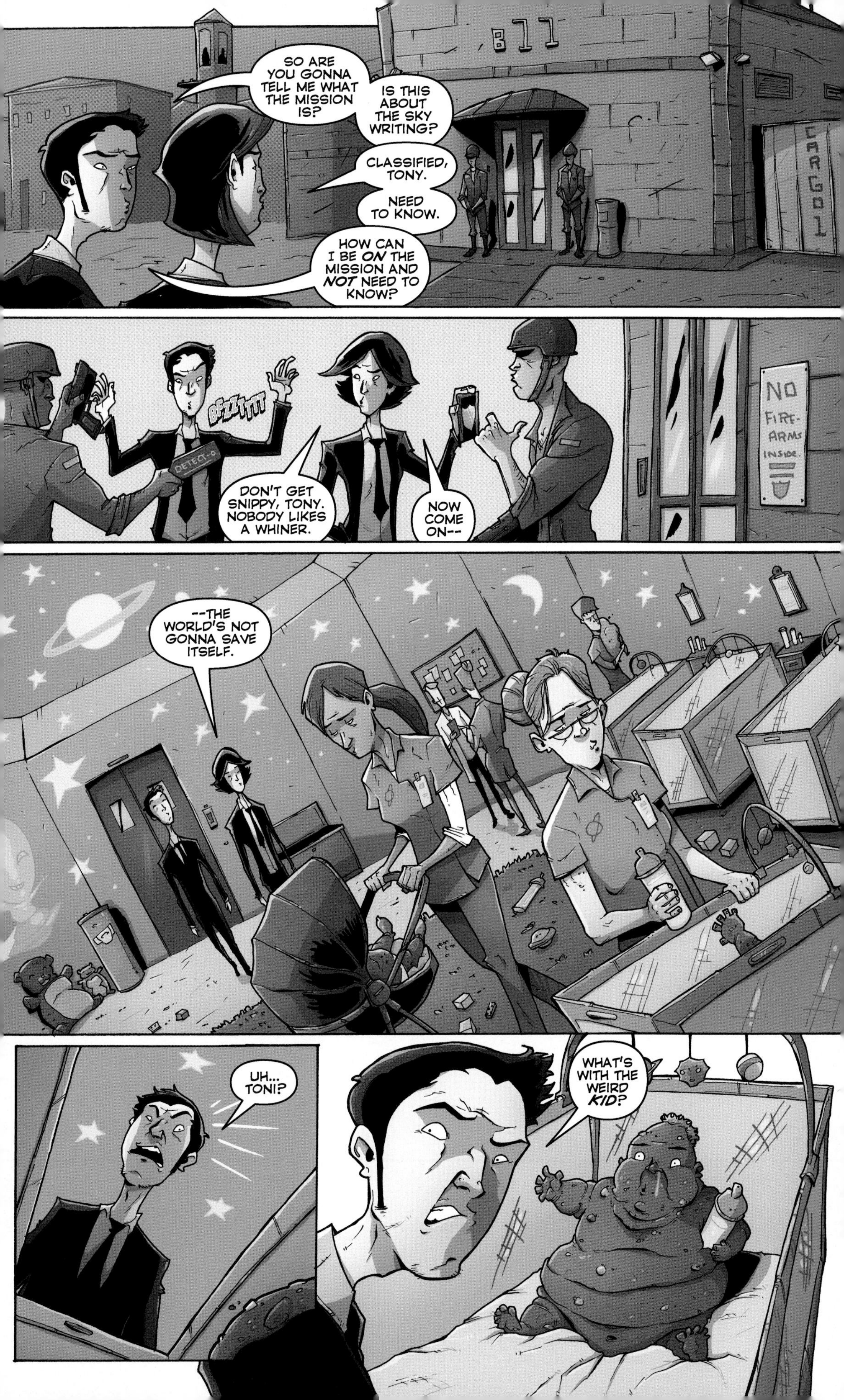
B11
SO ARE YOU GONNA TELL ME WHAT THE MISSION IS?
IS THIS ABOUT THE SKY WRITING?
CLASSIFIED, TONY.
NEED TO KNOW.
HOW CAN I BE ON THE MISSION AND NOT NEED TO KNOW?
CARGO 1
BZZZTTTT
DETECT-O
DON'T GET SNIPPY, TONY. NOBODY LIKES A WHINER.
NOW COME ON--
NO FIRE-ARMS INSIDE.
--THE WORLD'S NOT GONNA SAVE ITSELF.
UH... TONI?
WHAT'S WITH THE WEIRD KID?

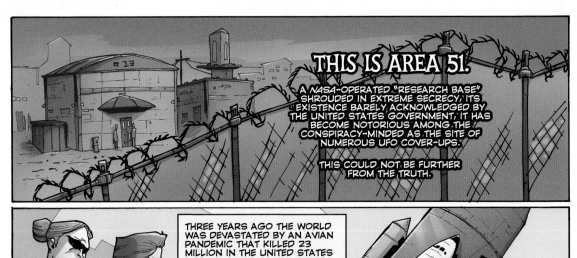

THIS IS AREA 51.

A *NASA*-OPERATED "RESEARCH BASE" SHROUDED IN EXTREME SECRECY, ITS EXISTENCE BARELY ACKNOWLEDGED BY THE UNITED STATES GOVERNMENT, IT HAS BECOME NOTORIOUS AMONG THE CONSPIRACY-MINDED AS THE SITE OF NUMEROUS UFO COVER-UPS.

THIS COULD NOT BE FURTHER FROM THE TRUTH.

THREE YEARS AGO THE WORLD WAS DEVASTATED BY AN AVIAN PANDEMIC THAT KILLED 23 MILLION IN THE UNITED STATES AND 116 MILLION WORLDWIDE.

A FAILSAFE FOR CATASTRO-PHIC EXTINCTION EVENTS WAS ENACTED, WHERE IN A DESPERATE ATTEMPT TO PROTECT HUMANITY--

--EVERY AVAILABLE ASTRONAUT WAS SENT INTO SPACE WITH PAYLOADS OF WHITE WINE, VIAGRA AND MP3S OF SMOOTH JAZZ--

--AND GIVEN ONLY A SINGLE DIRECTIVE:

SMOOTH JAMS INITIATED.

"START FUCKIN'!"

NINE MONTHS LATER, THE PANDEMIC HAD PASSED, AND *NASA* HAD A *NEW* PROBLEM TO CONTEND WITH.

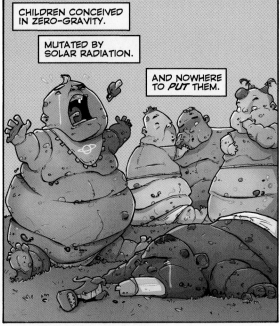

CHILDREN CONCEIVED IN ZERO-GRAVITY.

MUTATED BY SOLAR RADIATION.

AND NOWHERE TO *PUT* THEM.

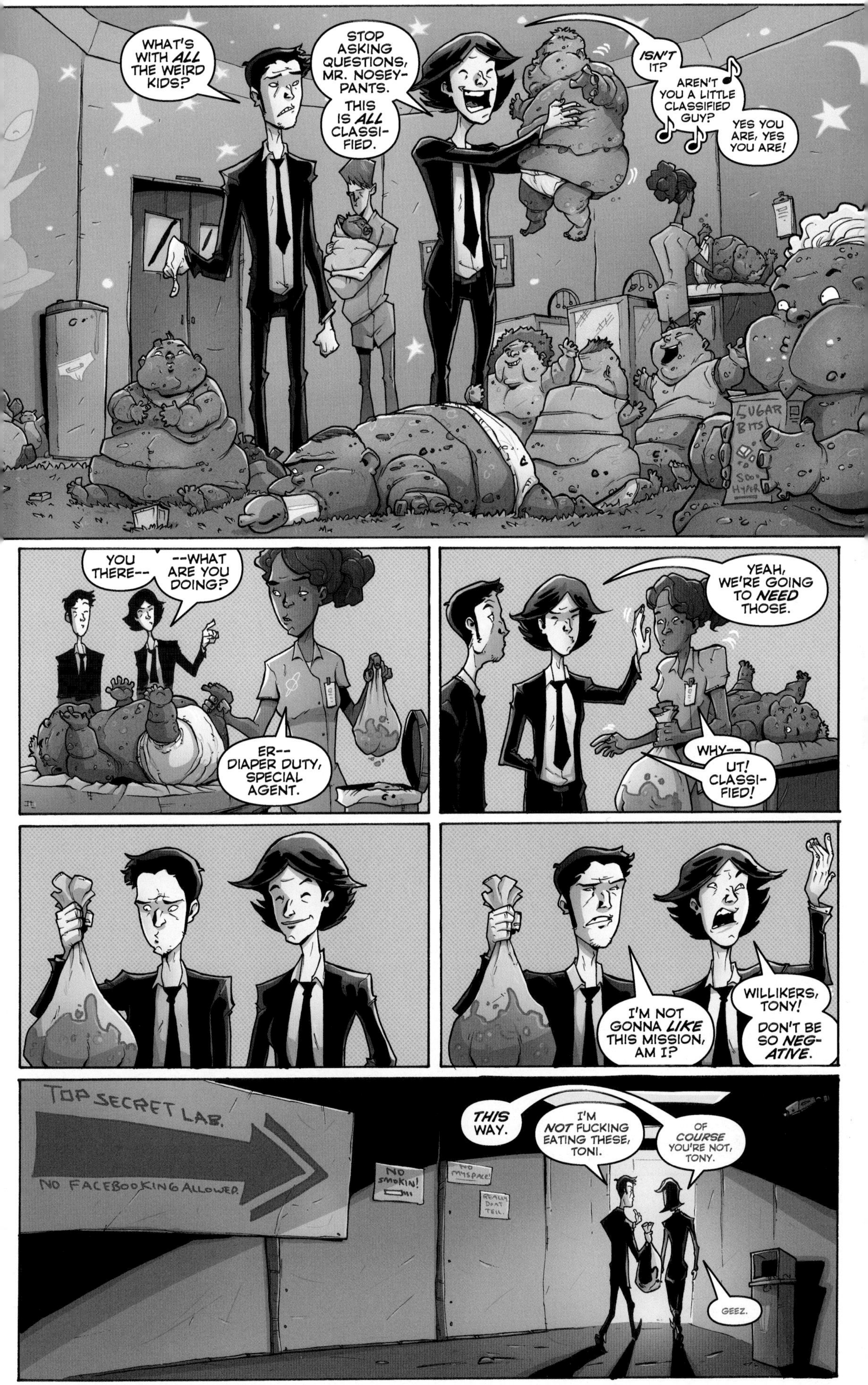

WHAT'S WITH ALL THE WEIRD KIDS?
STOP ASKING QUESTIONS, MR. NOSEY-PANTS.
THIS IS ALL CLASSI-FIED.
ISN'T IT?
AREN'T YOU A LITTLE CLASSIFIED GUY?
YES YOU ARE, YES YOU ARE!
SUGAR BITS
SOO HYPER
YOU THERE--
--WHAT ARE YOU DOING?
ER-- DIAPER DUTY, SPECIAL AGENT.
YEAH, WE'RE GOING TO NEED THOSE.
WHY--
UT! CLASSI-FIED!
I'M NOT GONNA LIKE THIS MISSION, AM I?
WILLIKERS, TONY!
DON'T BE SO NEG-ATIVE.
TOP SECRET LAB.
NO FACEBOOKING ALLOWED.
NO SMOKIN!
NO MYSPACE!
REALLY DON'T TELL.
THIS WAY.
I'M NOT FUCKING EATING THESE, TONI.
OF COURSE YOU'RE NOT, TONY.
GEEZ.

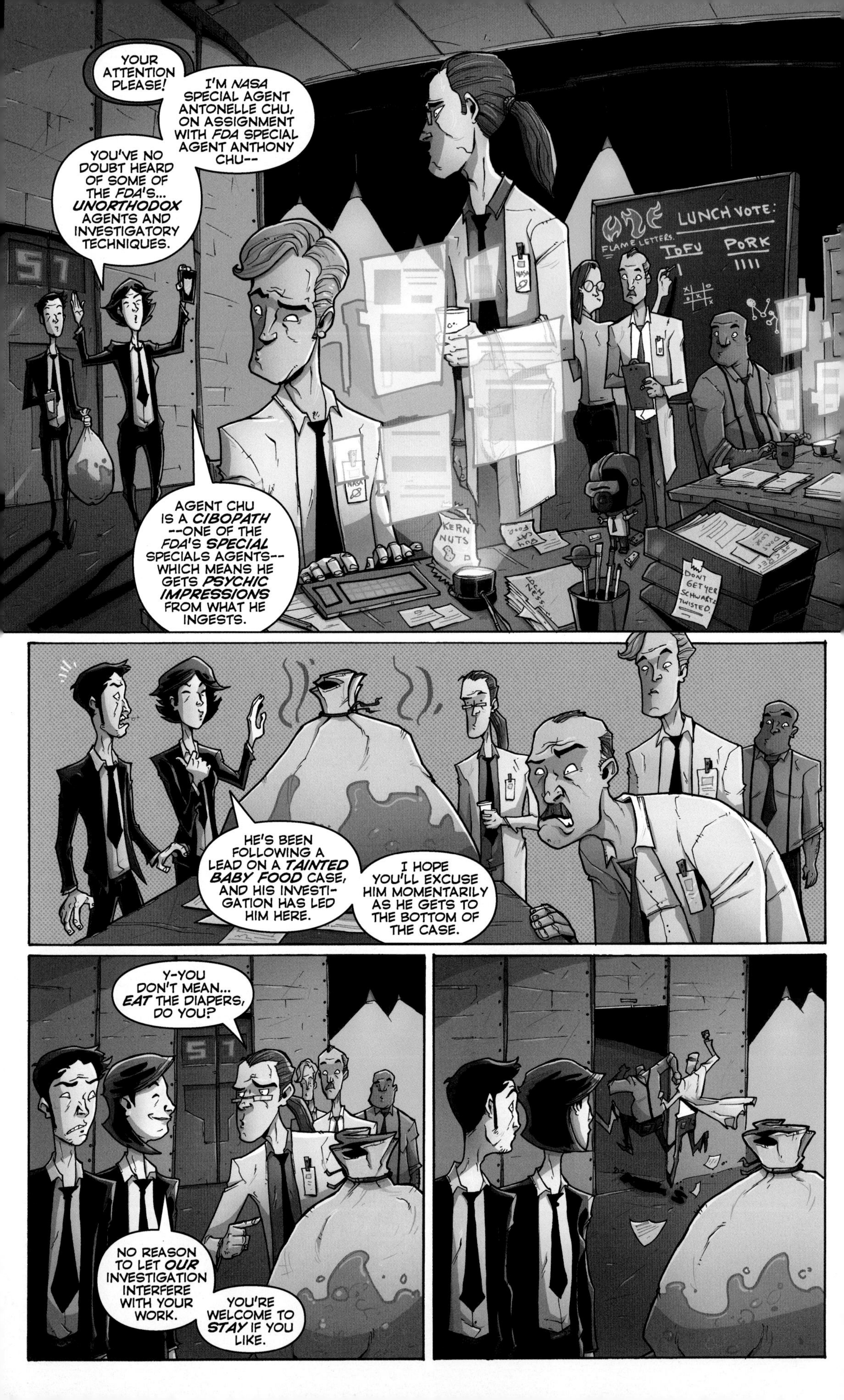
YOUR ATTENTION PLEASE!
I'M NASA SPECIAL AGENT ANTONELLE CHU, ON ASSIGNMENT WITH FDA SPECIAL AGENT ANTHONY CHU--
YOU'VE NO DOUBT HEARD OF SOME OF THE FDA'S... UNORTHODOX AGENTS AND INVESTIGATORY TECHNIQUES.
57
LUNCH VOTE:
FLAME LETTERS.
TOFU
PORK
KERN NUTS
DON'T GET YER SCHWARTZ TWISTED.
AGENT CHU IS A CIBOPATH --ONE OF THE FDA'S SPECIAL SPECIALS AGENTS-- WHICH MEANS HE GETS PSYCHIC IMPRESSIONS FROM WHAT HE INGESTS.
HE'S BEEN FOLLOWING A LEAD ON A TAINTED BABY FOOD CASE, AND HIS INVESTIGATION HAS LED HIM HERE.
I HOPE YOU'LL EXCUSE HIM MOMENTARILY AS HE GETS TO THE BOTTOM OF THE CASE.
Y-YOU DON'T MEAN... EAT THE DIAPERS, DO YOU?
57
NO REASON TO LET OUR INVESTIGATION INTERFERE WITH YOUR WORK.
YOU'RE WELCOME TO STAY IF YOU LIKE.

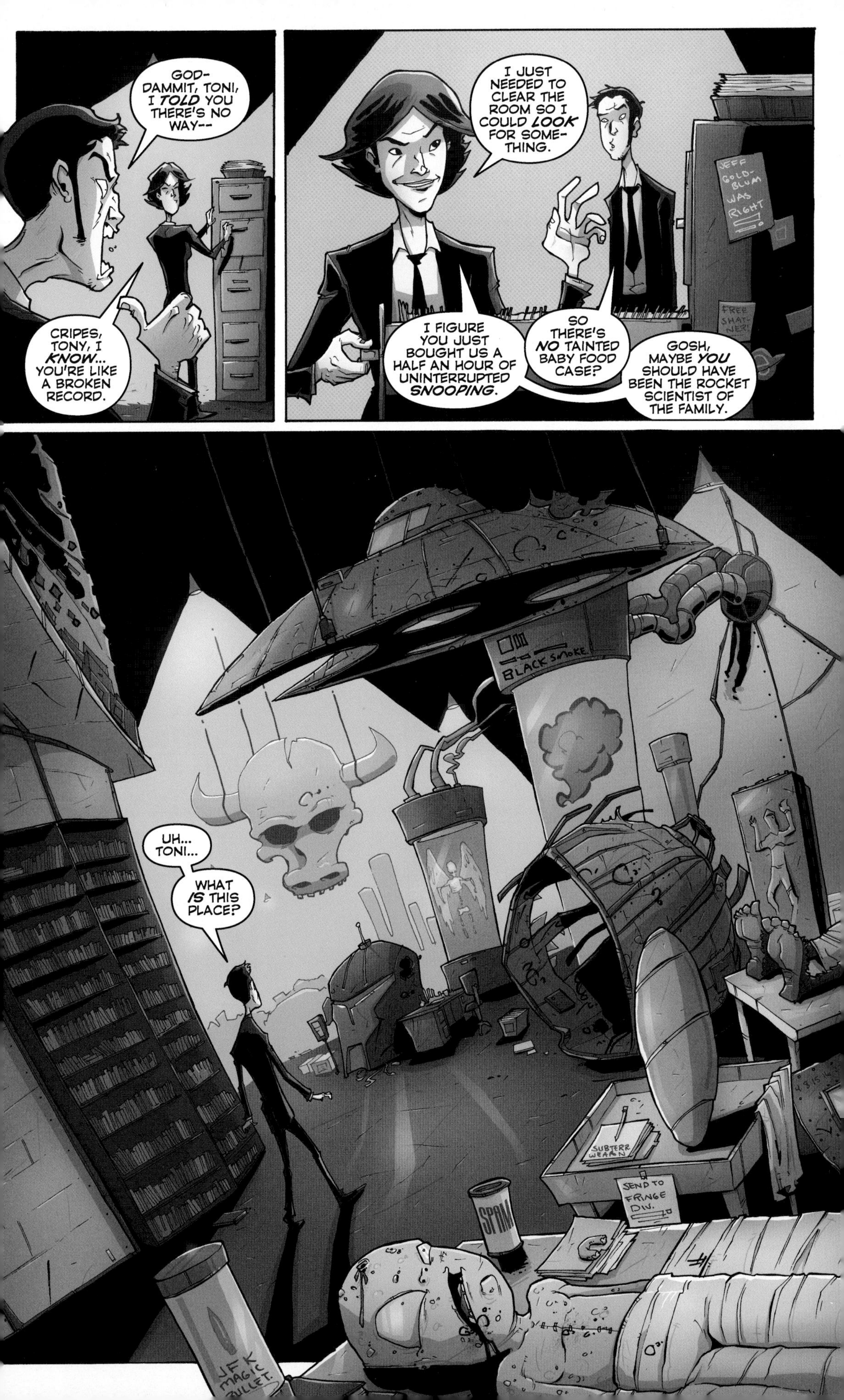
GOD-DAMMIT, TONI, I *TOLD* YOU THERE'S NO WAY--
CRIPES, TONY, I *KNOW*... YOU'RE LIKE A BROKEN RECORD.
I JUST NEEDED TO CLEAR THE ROOM SO I COULD *LOOK* FOR SOME-THING.
JEFF GOLDBLUM WAS RIGHT
FREE SHATNER!
I FIGURE YOU JUST BOUGHT US A HALF AN HOUR OF UNINTERRUPTED *SNOOPING*.
SO THERE'S *NO* TAINTED BABY FOOD CASE?
GOSH, MAYBE *YOU* SHOULD HAVE BEEN THE ROCKET SCIENTIST OF THE FAMILY.
BLACK SMOKE
UH... TONI...
WHAT *IS* THIS PLACE?
SEND TO FRINGE DIV.
SPAM
JFK MAGIC BULLET

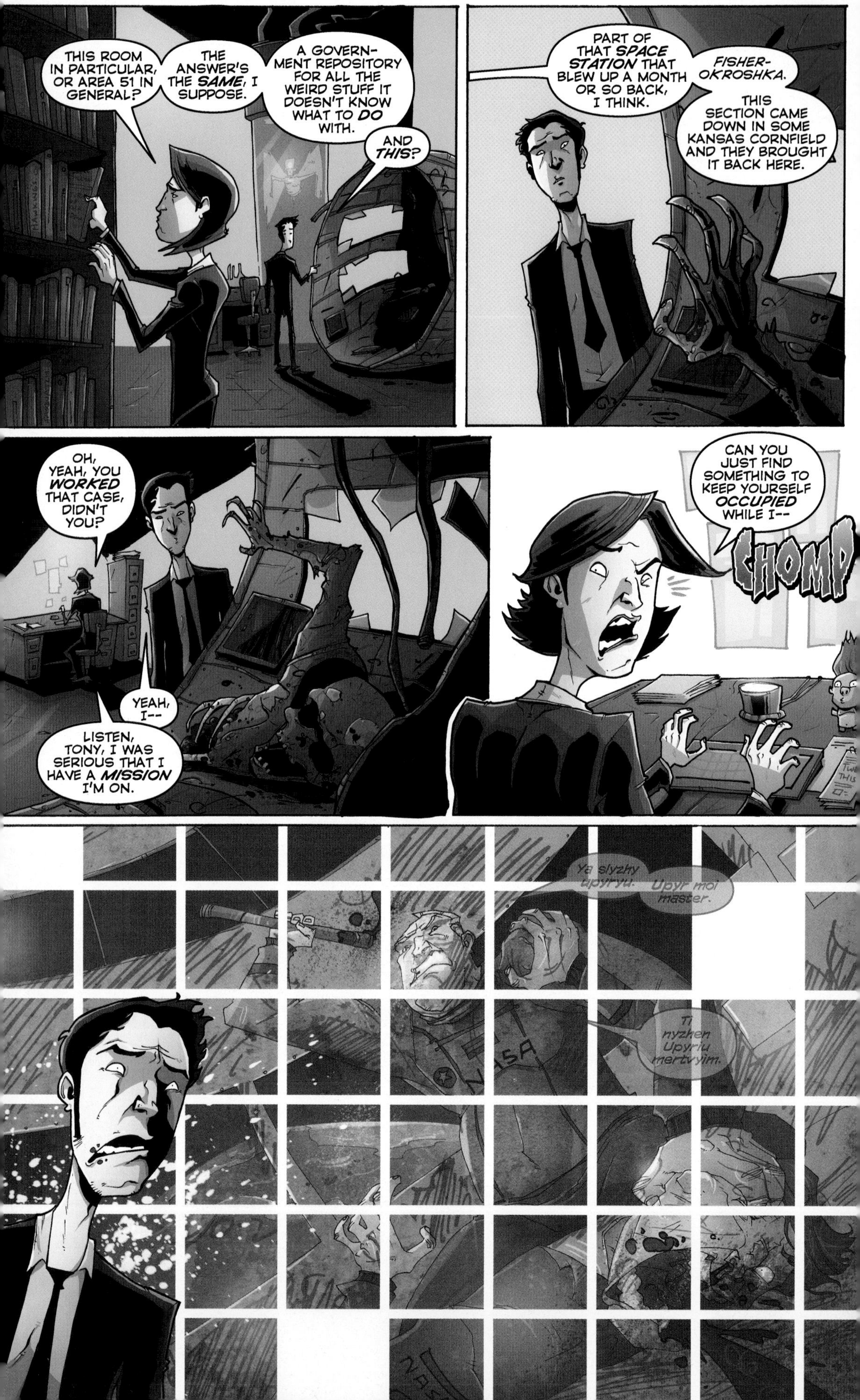
THIS ROOM IN PARTICULAR, OR AREA 51 IN GENERAL?
THE ANSWER'S THE SAME, I SUPPOSE.
A GOVERNMENT REPOSITORY FOR ALL THE WEIRD STUFF IT DOESN'T KNOW WHAT TO DO WITH.
AND THIS?
PART OF THAT SPACE STATION THAT BLEW UP A MONTH OR SO BACK, I THINK.
FISHER-OKROSHKA.
THIS SECTION CAME DOWN IN SOME KANSAS CORNFIELD AND THEY BROUGHT IT BACK HERE.
OH, YEAH, YOU WORKED THAT CASE, DIDN'T YOU?
YEAH, I--
LISTEN, TONY, I WAS SERIOUS THAT I HAVE A MISSION I'M ON.
CAN YOU JUST FIND SOMETHING TO KEEP YOURSELF OCCUPIED WHILE I--
CHOMP
Ya slyzhy upyryu.
Upyr moi master.
Ti nyzhen Upyriu mertvyim.

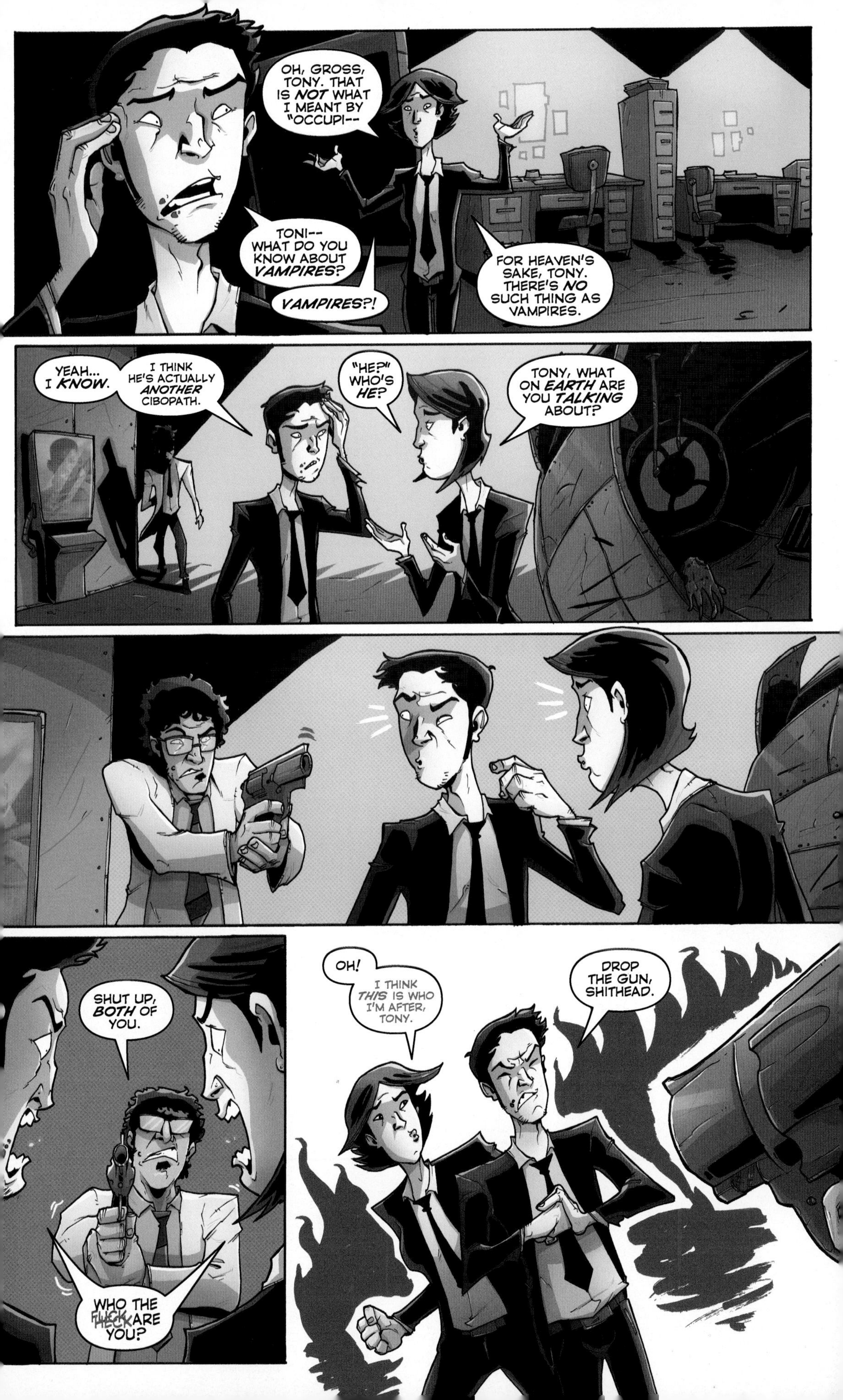
OH, GROSS, TONY. THAT IS *NOT* WHAT I MEANT BY "OCCUPI--
TONI-- WHAT DO YOU KNOW ABOUT *VAMPIRES*?
VAMPIRES?!
FOR HEAVEN'S SAKE, TONY. THERE'S *NO* SUCH THING AS VAMPIRES.
YEAH... I *KNOW*.
I THINK HE'S ACTUALLY *ANOTHER* CIBOPATH.
"HE?" WHO'S *HE*?
TONY, WHAT ON *EARTH* ARE YOU *TALKING* ABOUT?
SHUT UP, *BOTH* OF YOU.
WHO THE FUCK HECK ARE YOU?
OH!
I THINK *THIS* IS WHO I'M AFTER, TONY.
DROP THE GUN, SHITHEAD.

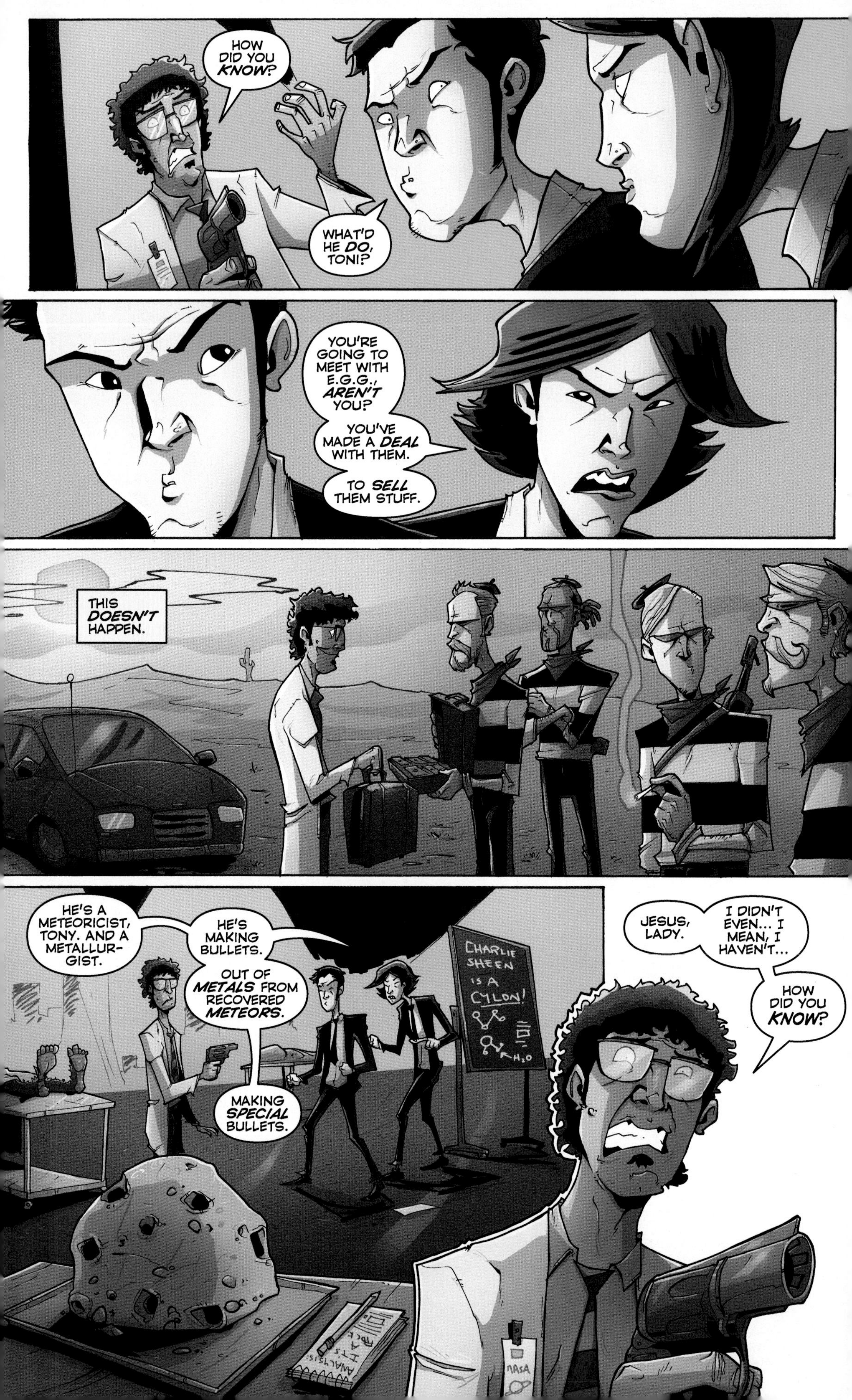
HOW DID YOU KNOW?
WHAT'D HE DO, TONI?
YOU'RE GOING TO MEET WITH E.G.G., AREN'T YOU?
YOU'VE MADE A DEAL WITH THEM.
TO SELL THEM STUFF.
THIS DOESN'T HAPPEN.
HE'S A METEORICIST, TONY. AND A METALLURGIST.
HE'S MAKING BULLETS.
OUT OF METALS FROM RECOVERED METEORS.
MAKING SPECIAL BULLETS.
CHARLIE SHEEN IS A CYLON!
JESUS, LADY.
I DIDN'T EVEN... I MEAN, I HAVEN'T...
HOW DID YOU KNOW?
NASA

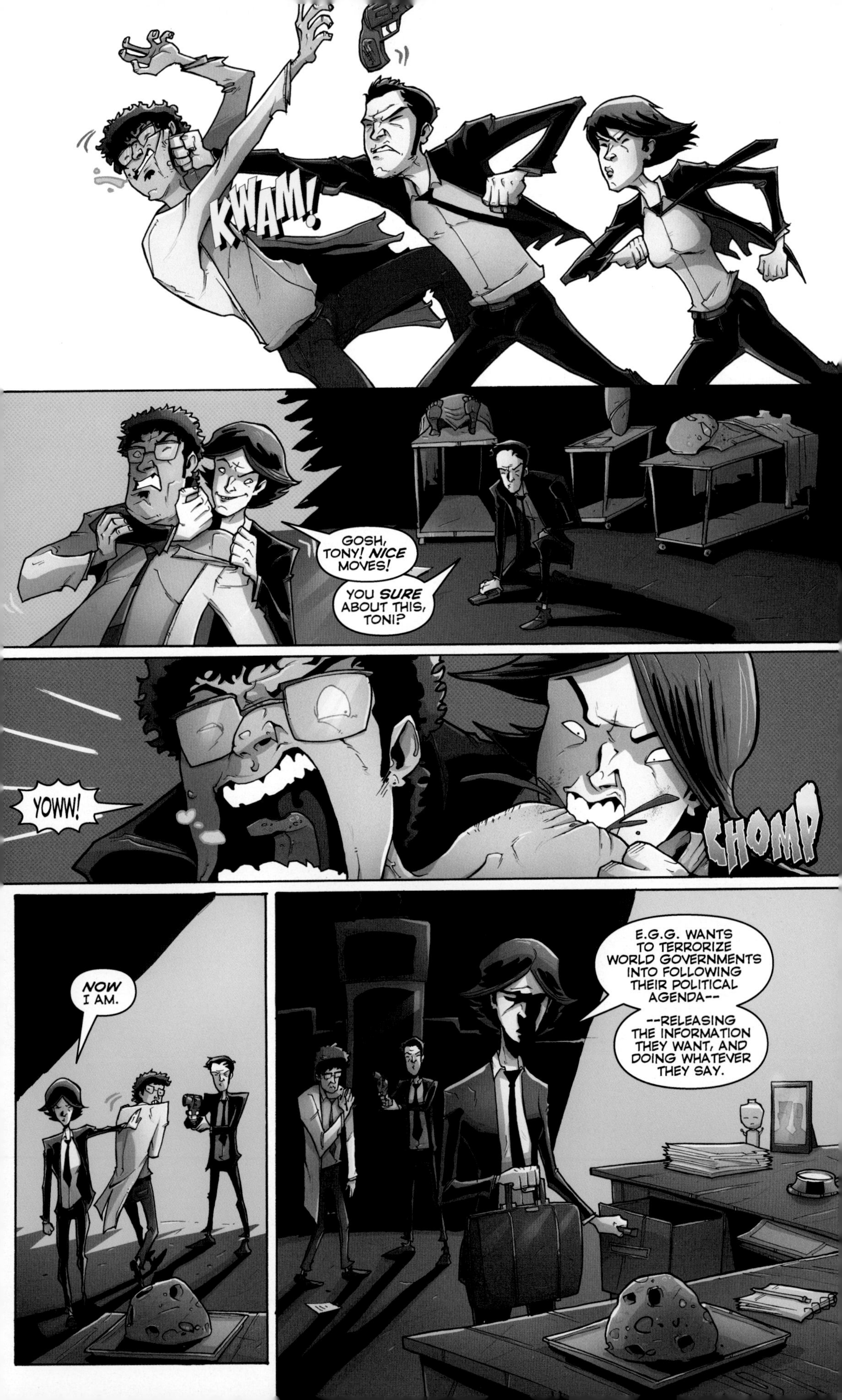
KWAM!
GOSH, TONY! NICE MOVES!
YOU SURE ABOUT THIS, TONI?
YOWW!
CHOMP
NOW I AM.
E.G.G. WANTS TO TERRORIZE WORLD GOVERNMENTS INTO FOLLOWING THEIR POLITICAL AGENDA--
--RELEASING THE INFORMATION THEY WANT, AND DOING WHATEVER THEY SAY.

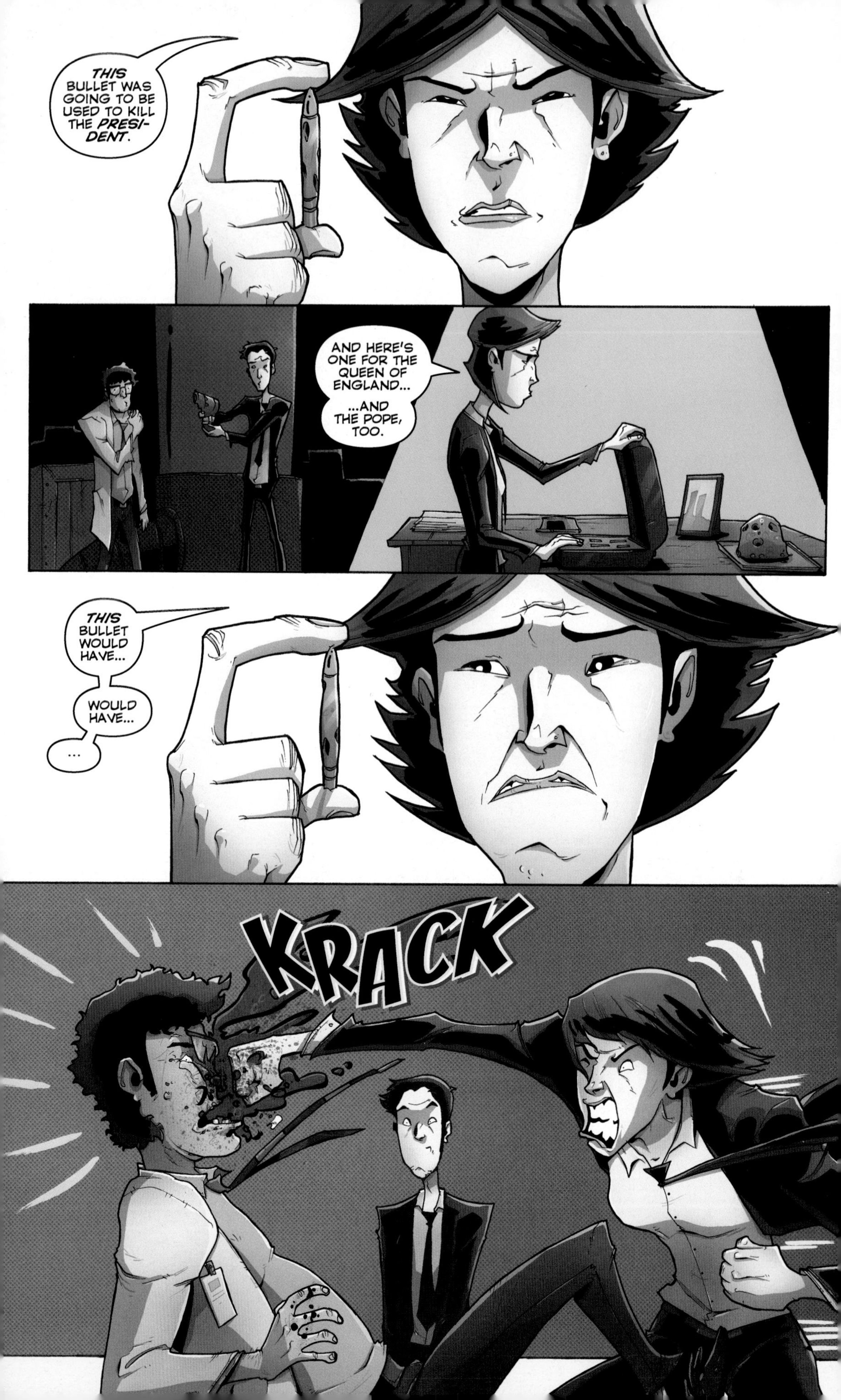
THIS BULLET WAS GOING TO BE USED TO KILL THE PRESIDENT.
AND HERE'S ONE FOR THE QUEEN OF ENGLAND...
...AND THE POPE, TOO.
THIS BULLET WOULD HAVE...
WOULD HAVE...
...
KRACK

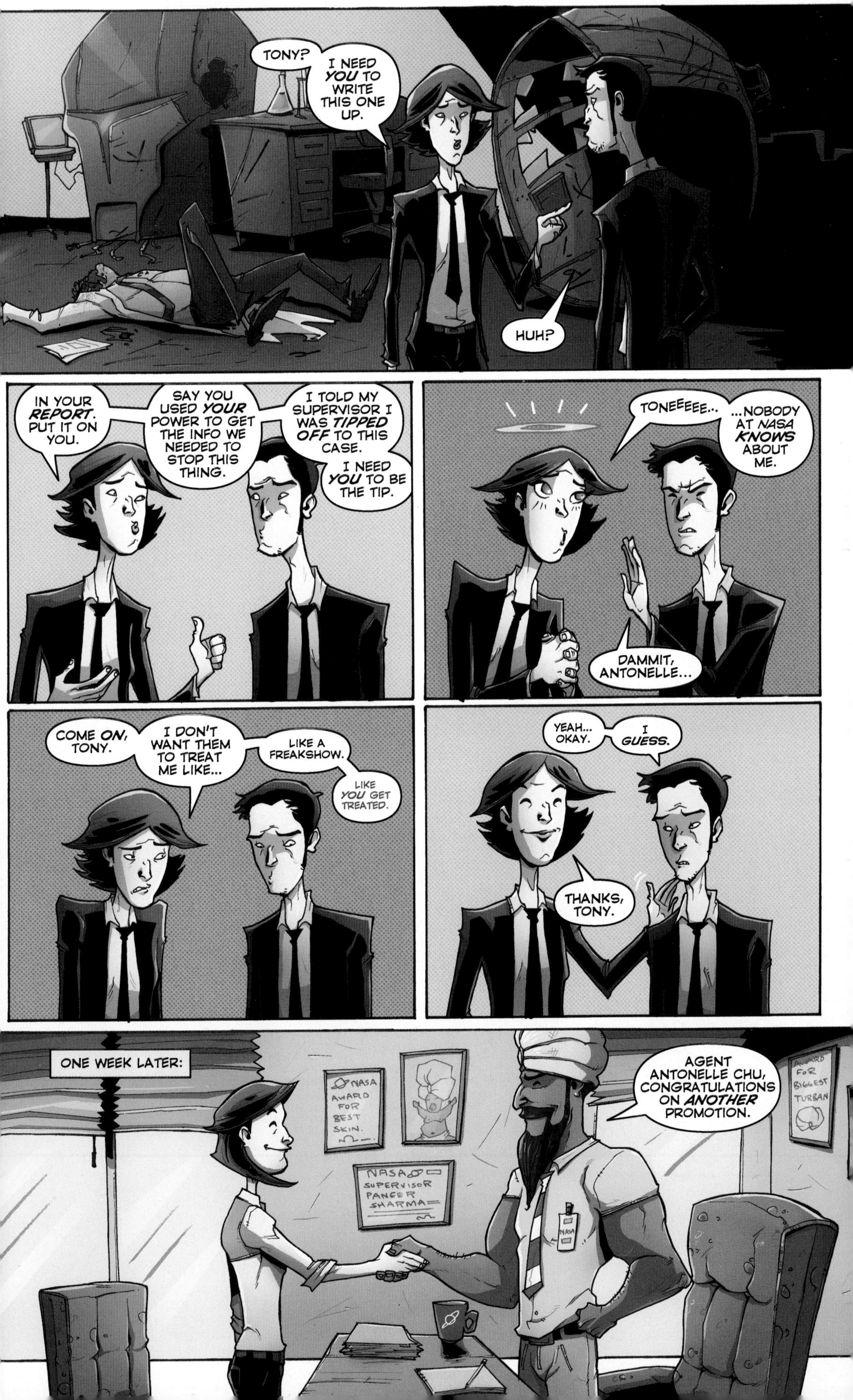
TONY?
I NEED *YOU* TO WRITE THIS ONE UP.
HUH?
IN YOUR *REPORT*. PUT IT ON YOU.
SAY YOU USED *YOUR* POWER TO GET THE INFO WE NEEDED TO STOP THIS THING.
I TOLD MY SUPERVISOR I WAS *TIPPED OFF* TO THIS CASE.
I NEED *YOU* TO BE THE TIP.
TONEEEEEE...
...NOBODY AT *NASA* *KNOWS* ABOUT ME.
DAMMIT, ANTONELLE...
COME *ON*, TONY.
I DON'T WANT THEM TO TREAT ME LIKE...
LIKE A FREAKSHOW.
LIKE *YOU* GET TREATED.
YEAH... OKAY.
I *GUESS*.
THANKS, TONY.
ONE WEEK LATER:
NASA AWARD FOR BEST SKIN
NASA SUPERVISOR PANEER SHARMA
AWARD FOR BIGGEST TURBAN
AGENT ANTONELLE CHU, CONGRATULATIONS ON *ANOTHER* PROMOTION.
NASA

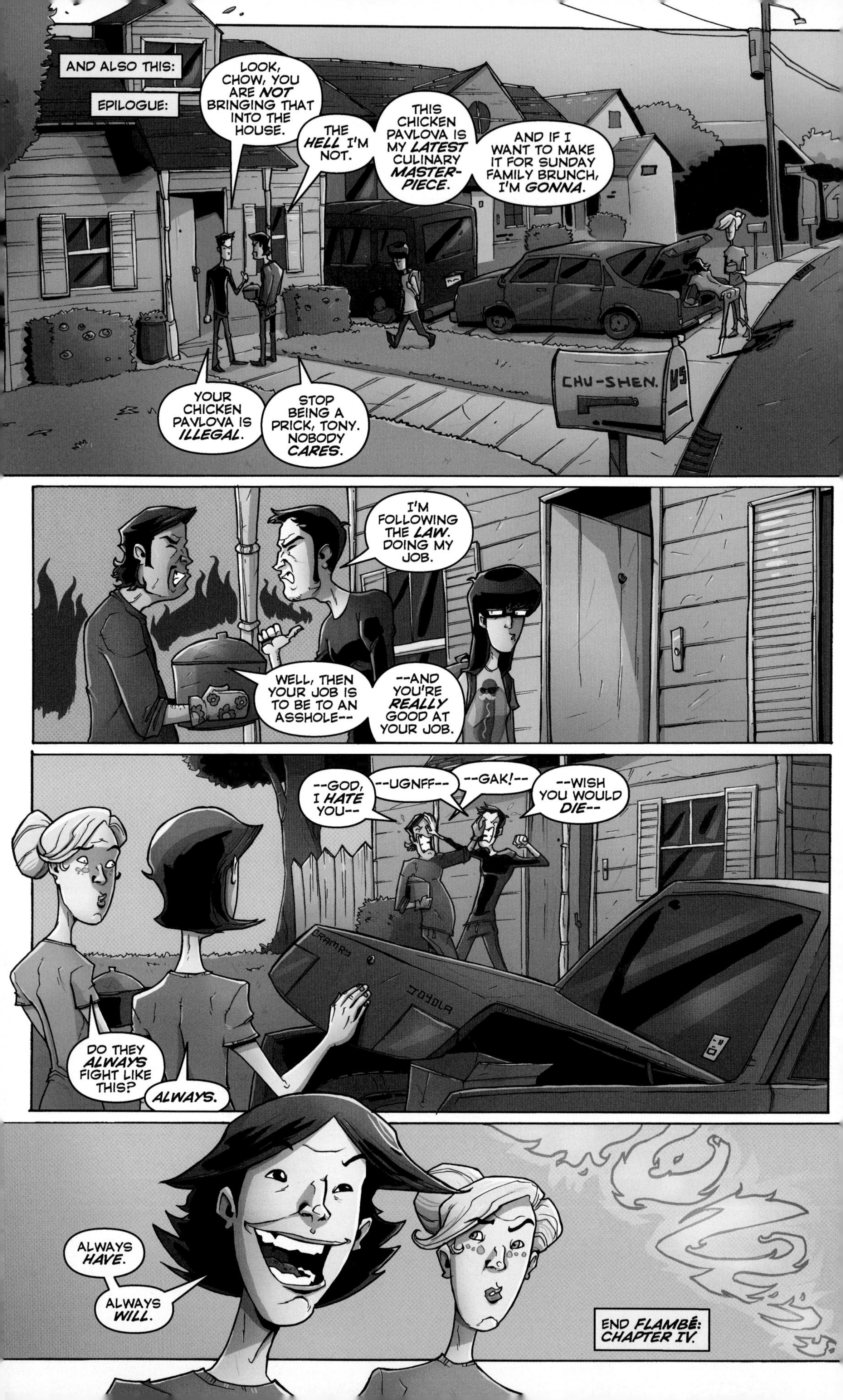
AND ALSO THIS:
EPILOGUE:
LOOK, CHOW, YOU ARE NOT BRINGING THAT INTO THE HOUSE.
THE HELL I'M NOT.
THIS CHICKEN PAVLOVA IS MY LATEST CULINARY MASTERPIECE.
AND IF I WANT TO MAKE IT FOR SUNDAY FAMILY BRUNCH, I'M GONNA.
YOUR CHICKEN PAVLOVA IS ILLEGAL.
STOP BEING A PRICK, TONY. NOBODY CARES.
CHU-SHEN.
I'M FOLLOWING THE LAW. DOING MY JOB.
WELL, THEN YOUR JOB IS TO BE TO AN ASSHOLE--
--AND YOU'RE REALLY GOOD AT YOUR JOB.
--GOD, I HATE YOU--
--UGNFF--
--GAK!--
--WISH YOU WOULD DIE--
DO THEY ALWAYS FIGHT LIKE THIS?
ALWAYS.
ALWAYS HAVE.
ALWAYS WILL.
END FLAMBÉ: CHAPTER IV.

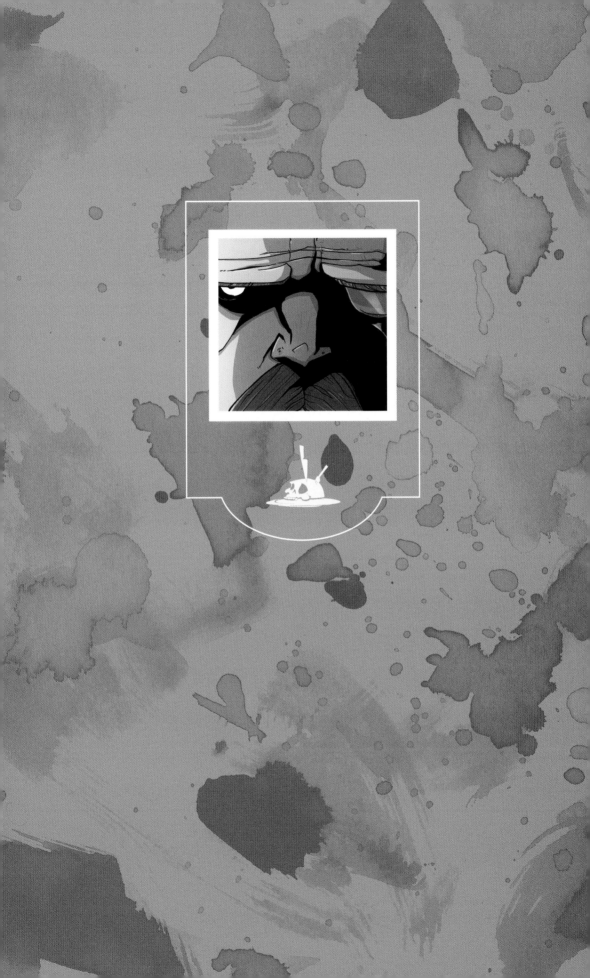

Chapter 5

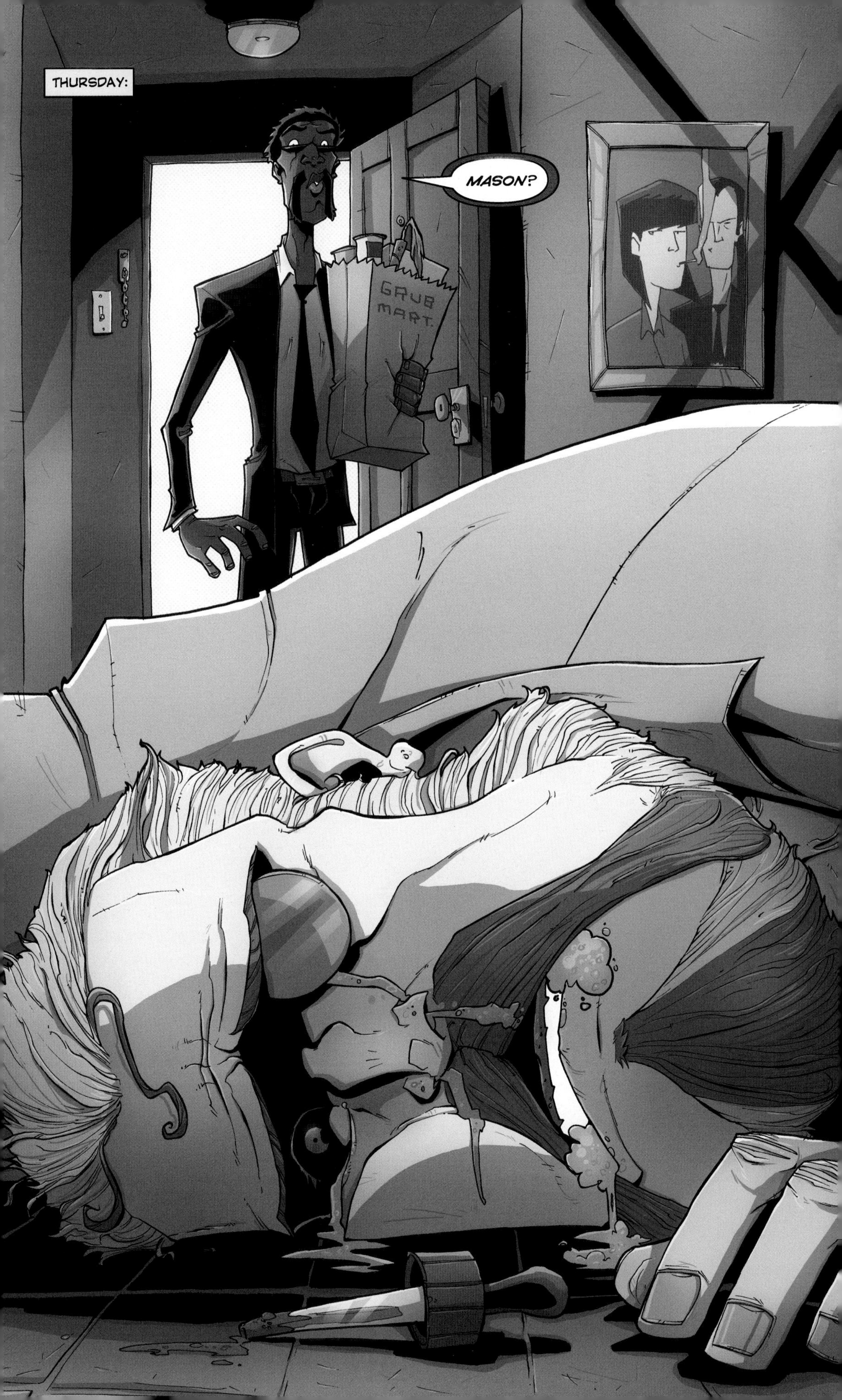
THURSDAY:
MASON?
GRUB MART.

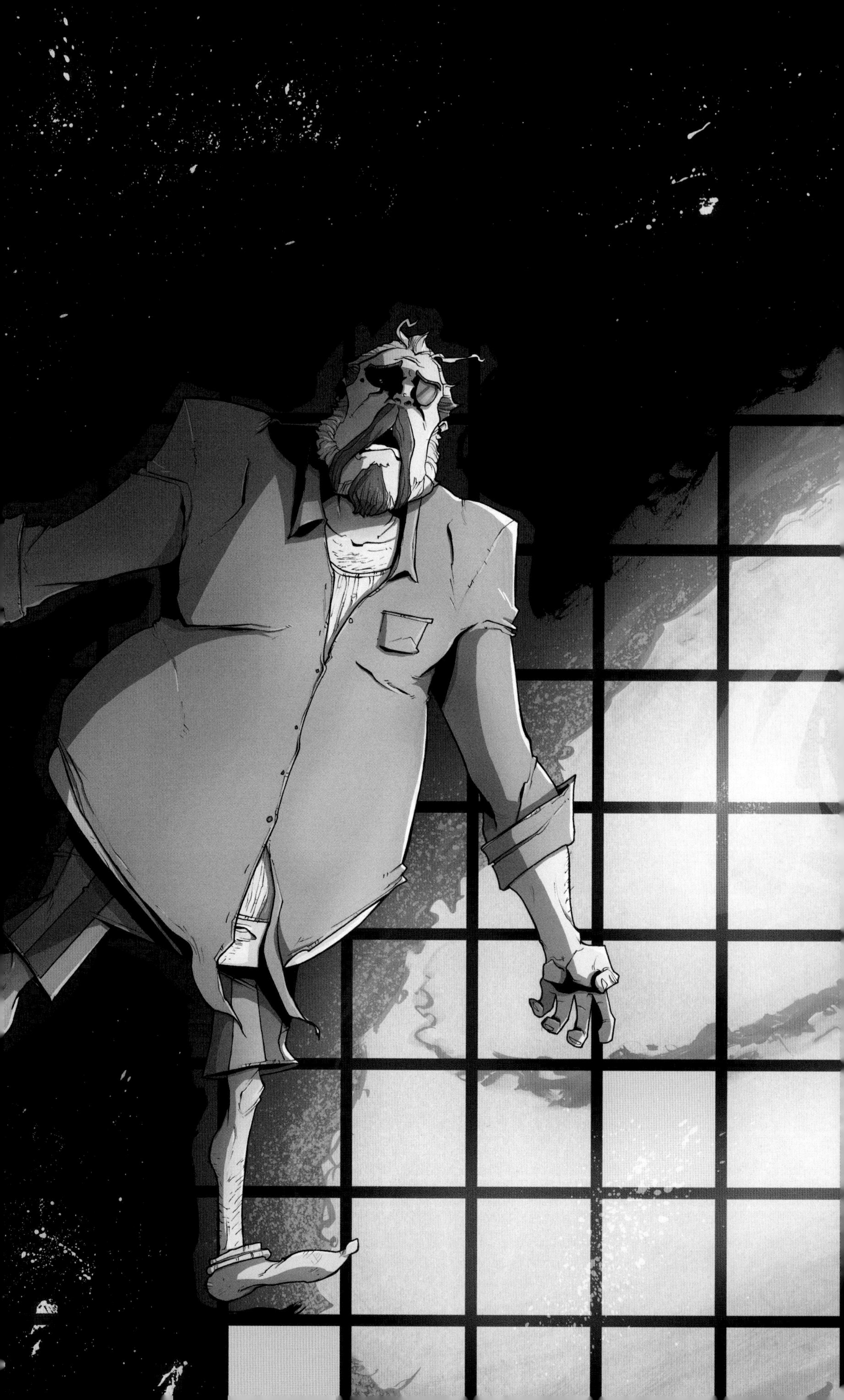

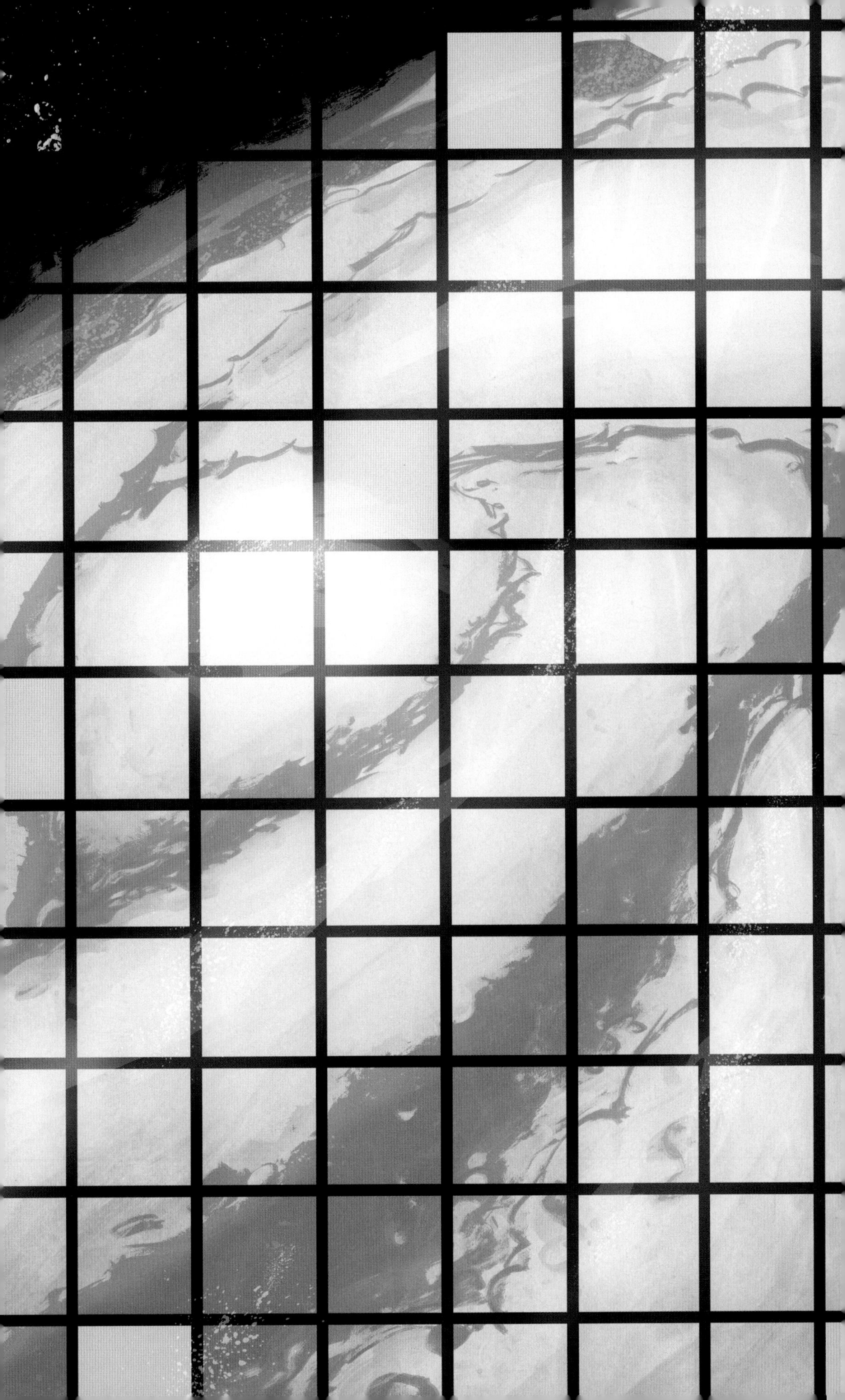

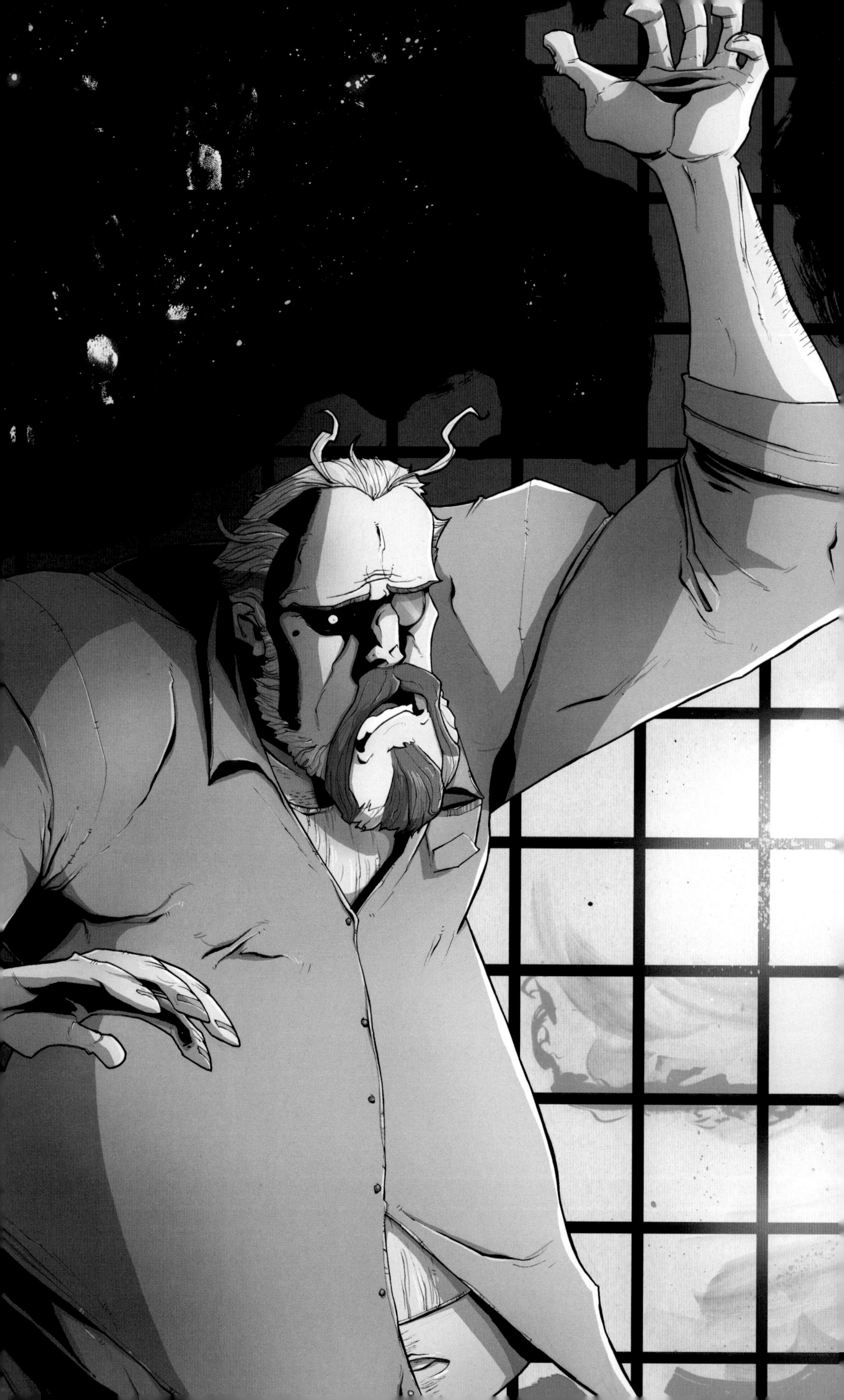

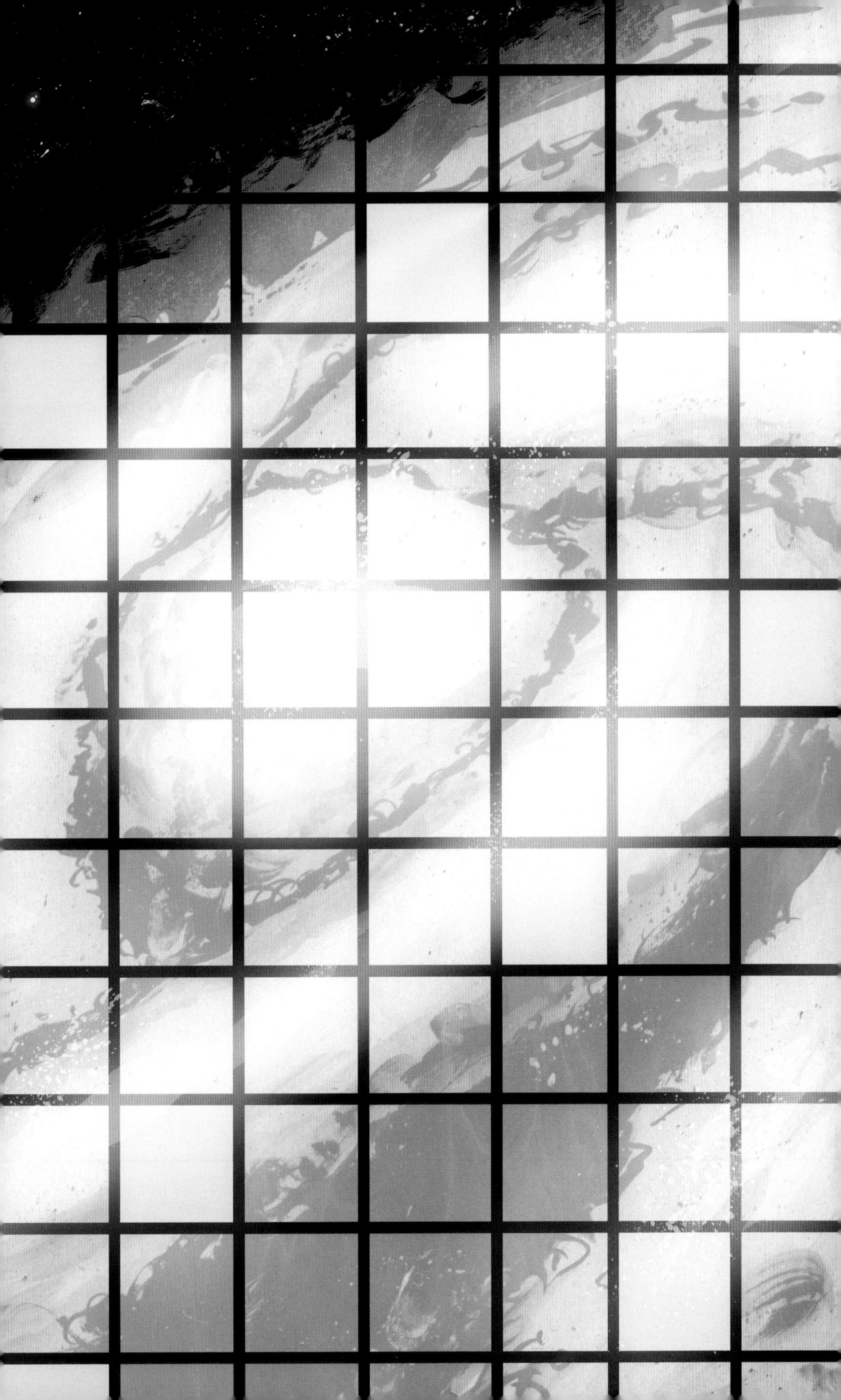

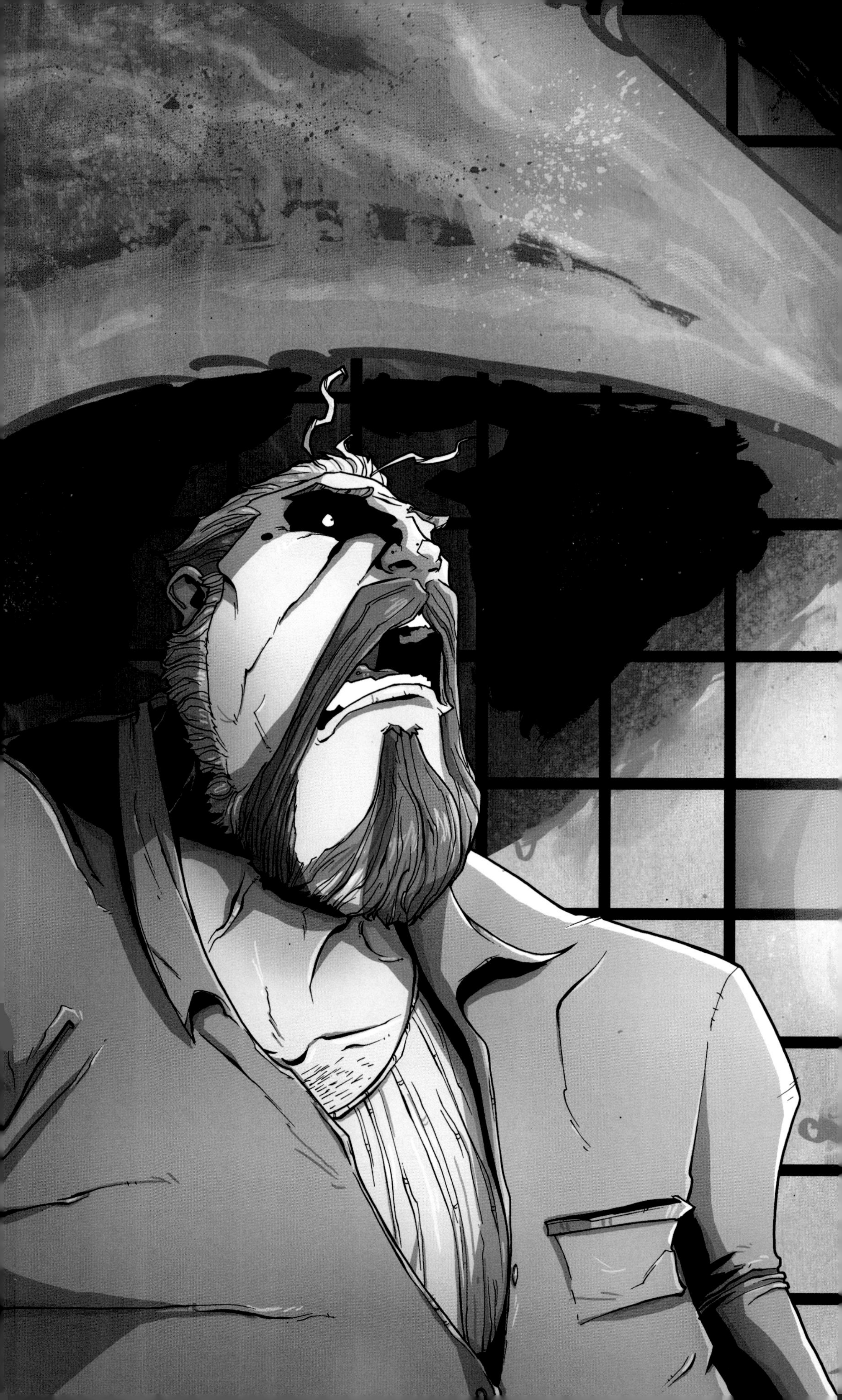

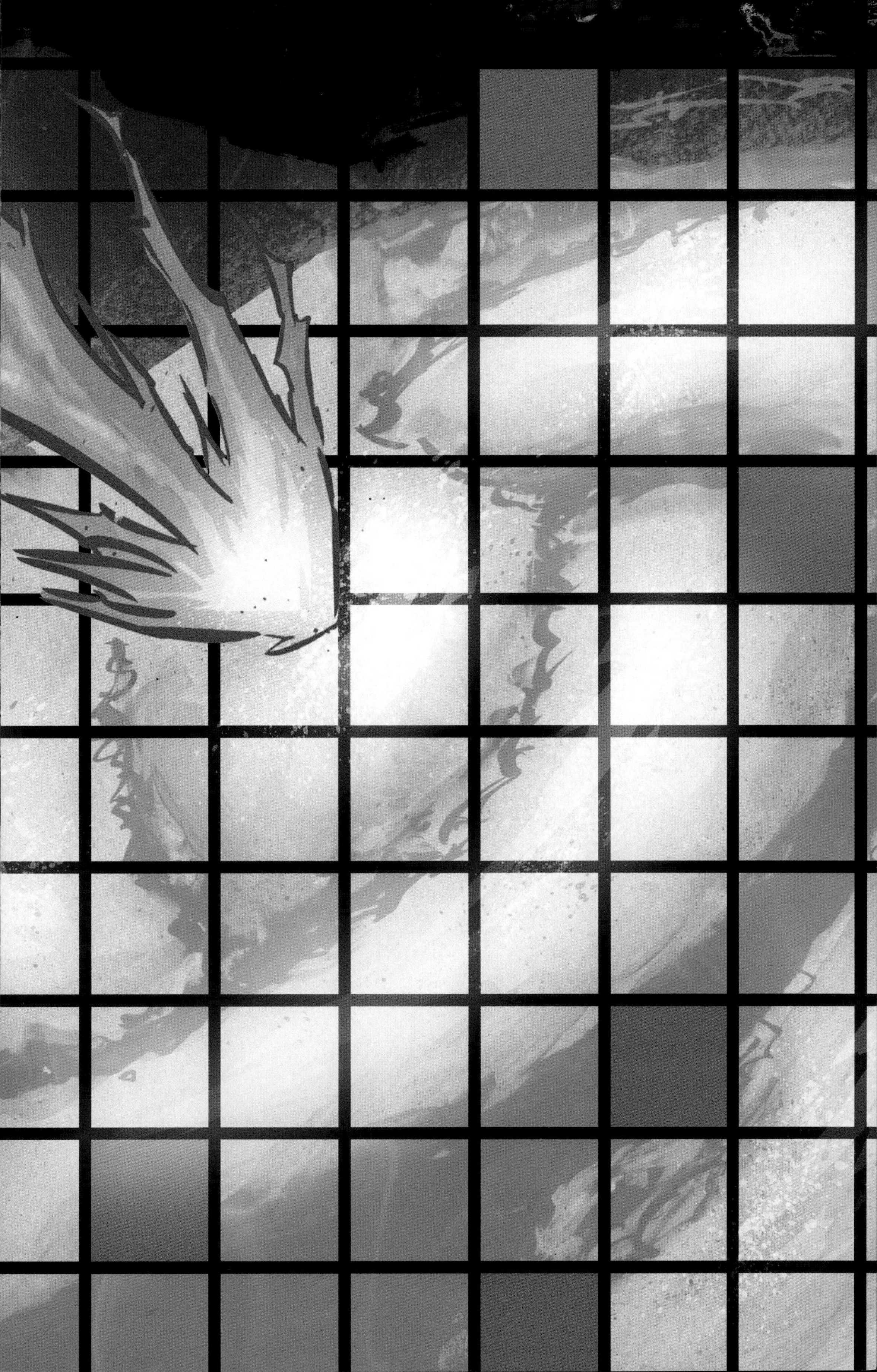

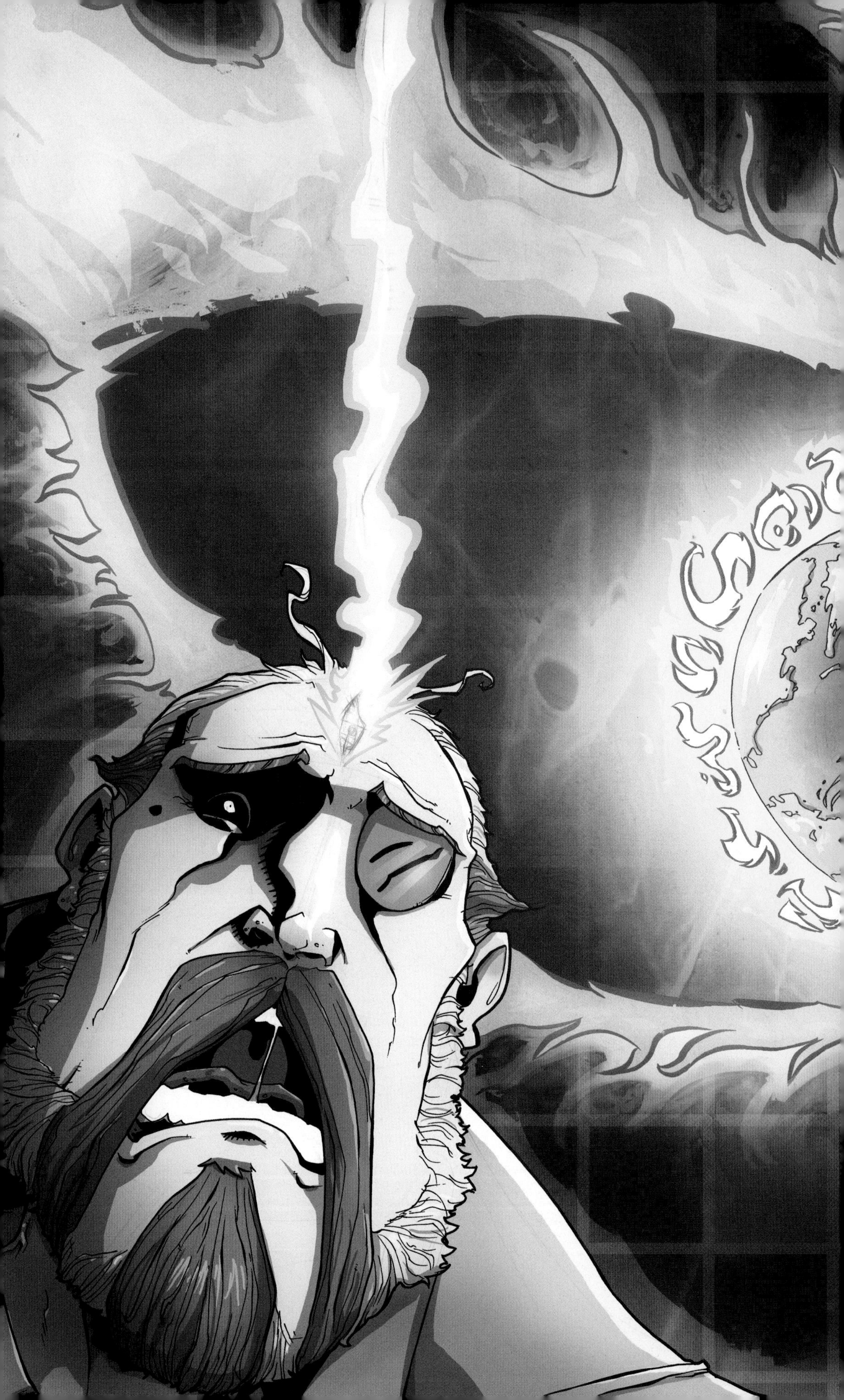

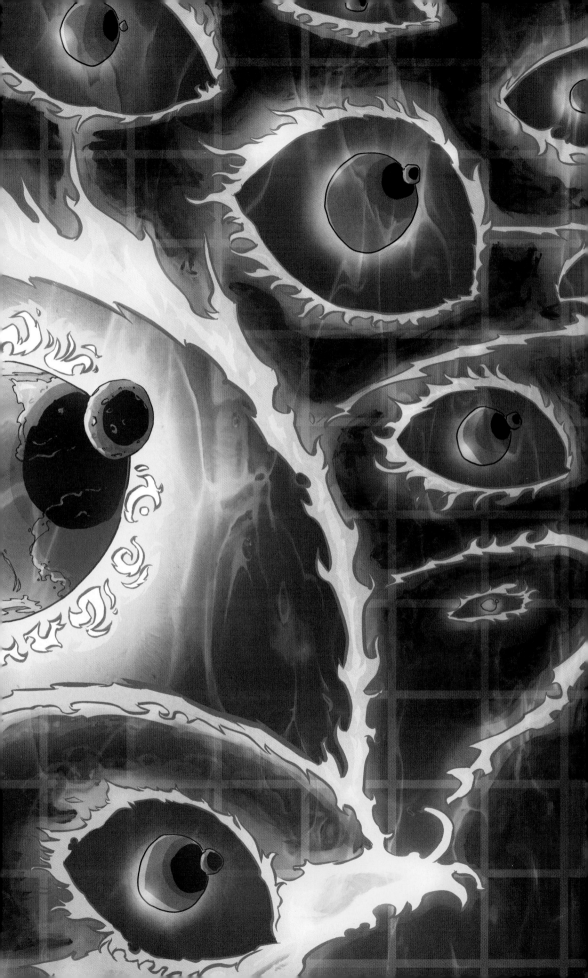

SNAP *OUT* OF IT, BIG MAN.

UHHHHH...

WHAT THE *HELL*, MASON?

THE *BLOOD*. FROM MIGDALO.

YOU *DRANK* IT?

A *DROP*, CAESAR.

I INGESTED BUT A *SINGLE* DROP.

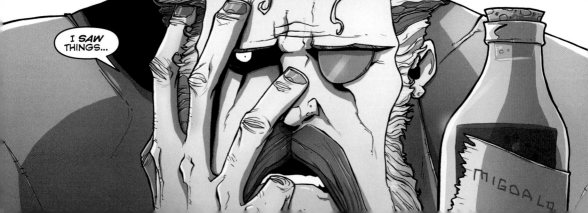

I *SAW* THINGS...

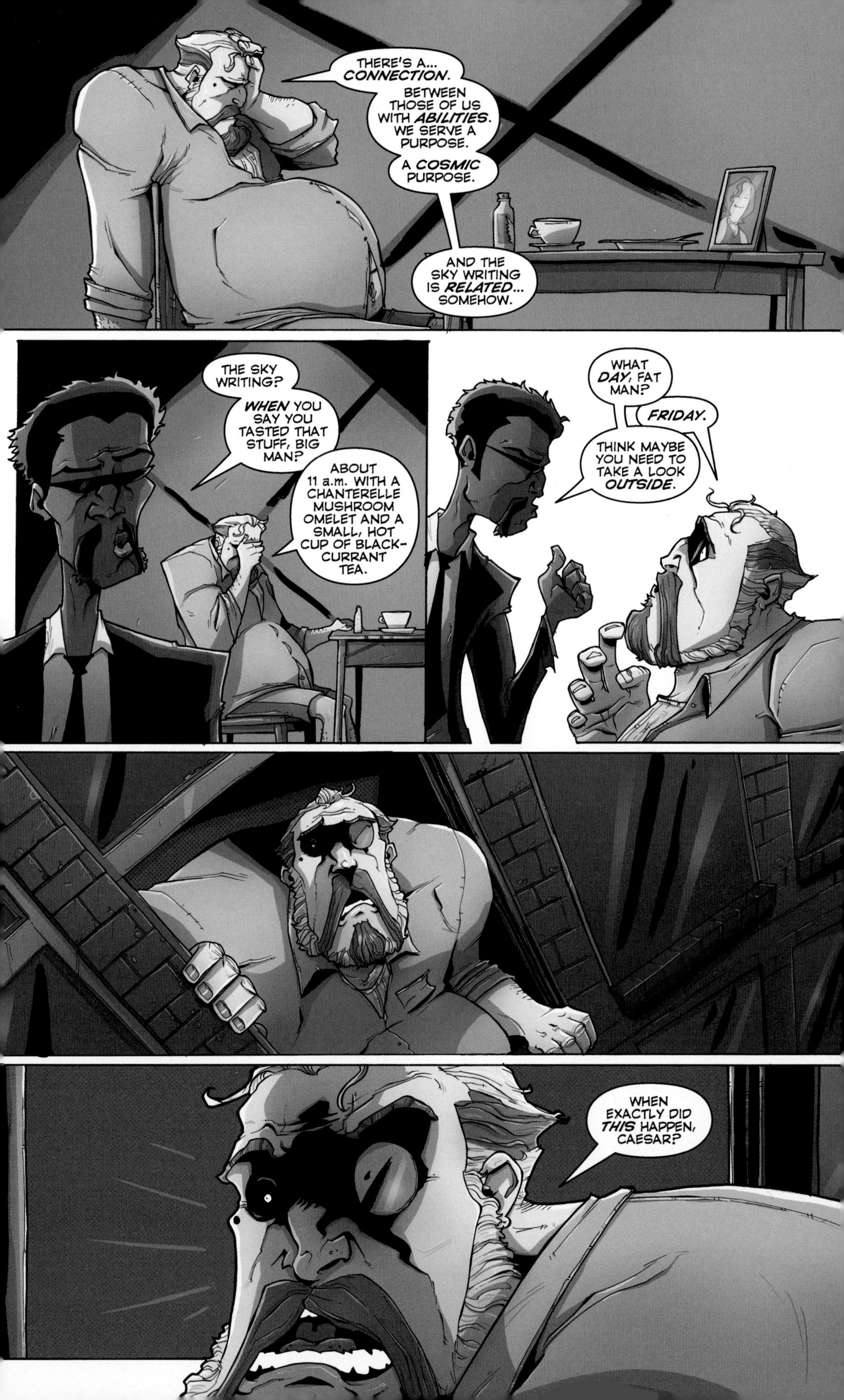
THERE'S A... CONNECTION.
BETWEEN THOSE OF US WITH ABILITIES. WE SERVE A PURPOSE.
A COSMIC PURPOSE.
AND THE SKY WRITING IS RELATED... SOMEHOW.
THE SKY WRITING?
WHEN YOU SAY YOU TASTED THAT STUFF, BIG MAN?
ABOUT 11 a.m. WITH A CHANTERELLE MUSHROOM OMELET AND A SMALL, HOT CUP OF BLACK-CURRANT TEA.
WHAT DAY, FAT MAN?
FRIDAY.
THINK MAYBE YOU NEED TO TAKE A LOOK OUTSIDE.
WHEN EXACTLY DID THIS HAPPEN, CAESAR?

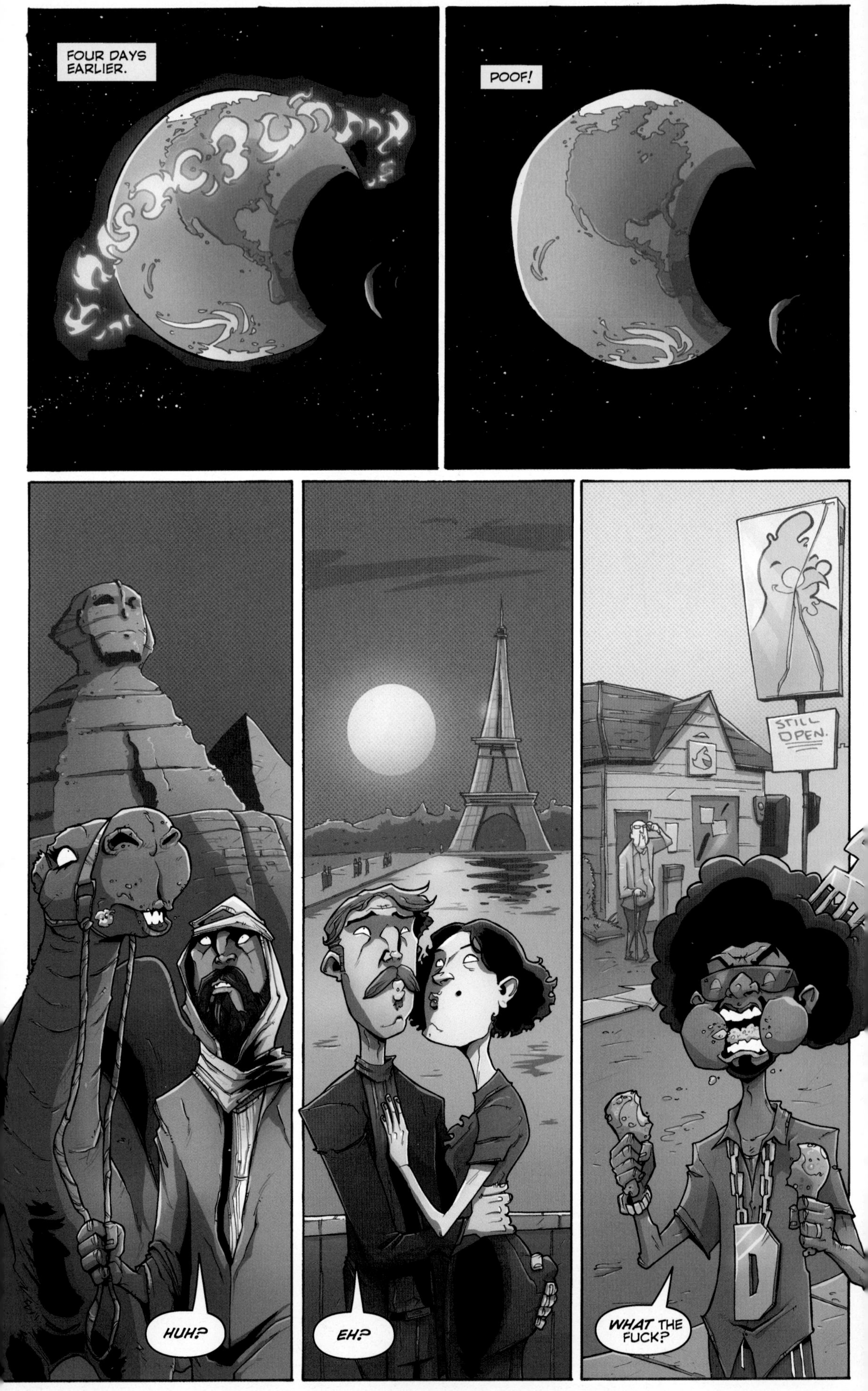
FOUR DAYS EARLIER.
POOF!
STILL OPEN.
HUH?
EH?
WHAT THE FUCK?

SIMPLY *DISAPPEARED*, LEAVING *NO* TRACE IN THE UPPER ATMOSPHERE THAT IT WAS EVER THERE--

--AND NOBODY HAS ANY IDEA HOW... OR WHY.

FDA Headquarters

In Memory of the 23 million Americans that lost their lives in the pandemic.

DOESN'T MATTER. THAT'S *NASA'S* JURIS-DICTION.

FDA

FDA: WE PUNCH FACES.

FDA: WE KICK THROATS.

THIS IS OURS:

"THE CHURCH OF THE DIVINITY OF THE IMMACULATE OVA."

EGG WORSHIPPERS?

WHAT KIND OF CRACKPOT SHIT IS *THAT*?

FDA

THE KIND THAT *PREDICTED* THE SKY WRITING WOULD COME DOWN, AGENT COLBY.

TO THE DAY. EVEN TO THE MINUTE.

AT LEAST, SISTER *ALANI ADOBO* DID.

THE CULT'S SELF-PROCLAIMED *PROPHET* AND *LEADER*.

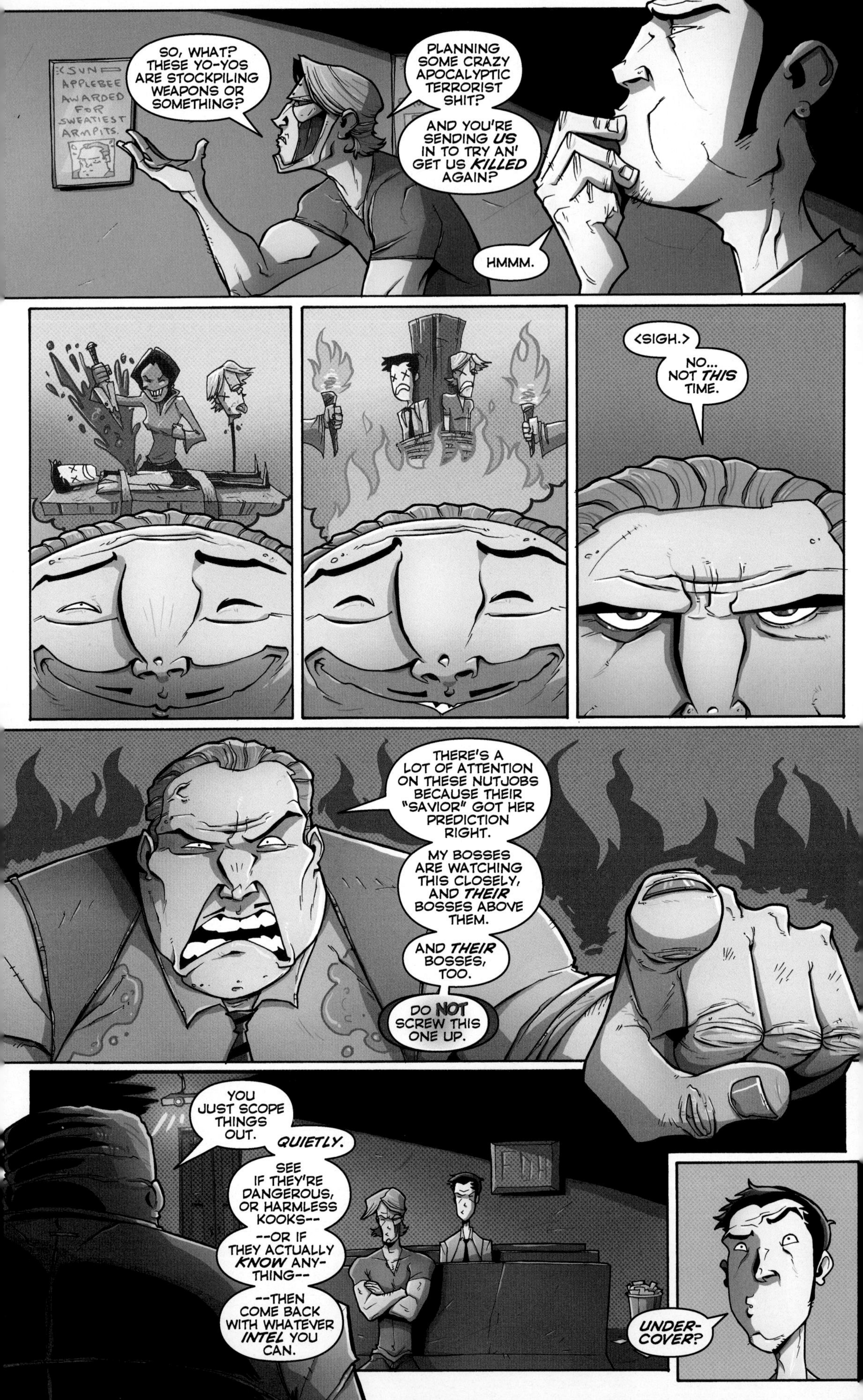

<SUN
APPLEBEE AWARDED FOR SWEATIEST ARMPITS.
SO, WHAT? THESE YO-YOS ARE STOCKPILING WEAPONS OR SOMETHING?
PLANNING SOME CRAZY APOCALYPTIC TERRORIST SHIT?
AND YOU'RE SENDING *US* IN TO TRY AN' GET US *KILLED* AGAIN?
HMMM.
<SIGH.>
NO... NOT *THIS* TIME.
THERE'S A LOT OF ATTENTION ON THESE NUTJOBS BECAUSE THEIR "SAVIOR" GOT HER PREDICTION RIGHT.
MY BOSSES ARE WATCHING THIS CLOSELY, AND *THEIR* BOSSES ABOVE THEM.
AND *THEIR* BOSSES, TOO.
DO **NOT** SCREW THIS ONE UP.
YOU JUST SCOPE THINGS OUT. *QUIETLY.*
SEE IF THEY'RE DANGEROUS, OR HARMLESS KOOKS--
--OR IF THEY ACTUALLY *KNOW* ANY-THING--
--THEN COME BACK WITH WHATEVER *INTEL* YOU CAN.
UNDER-COVER?

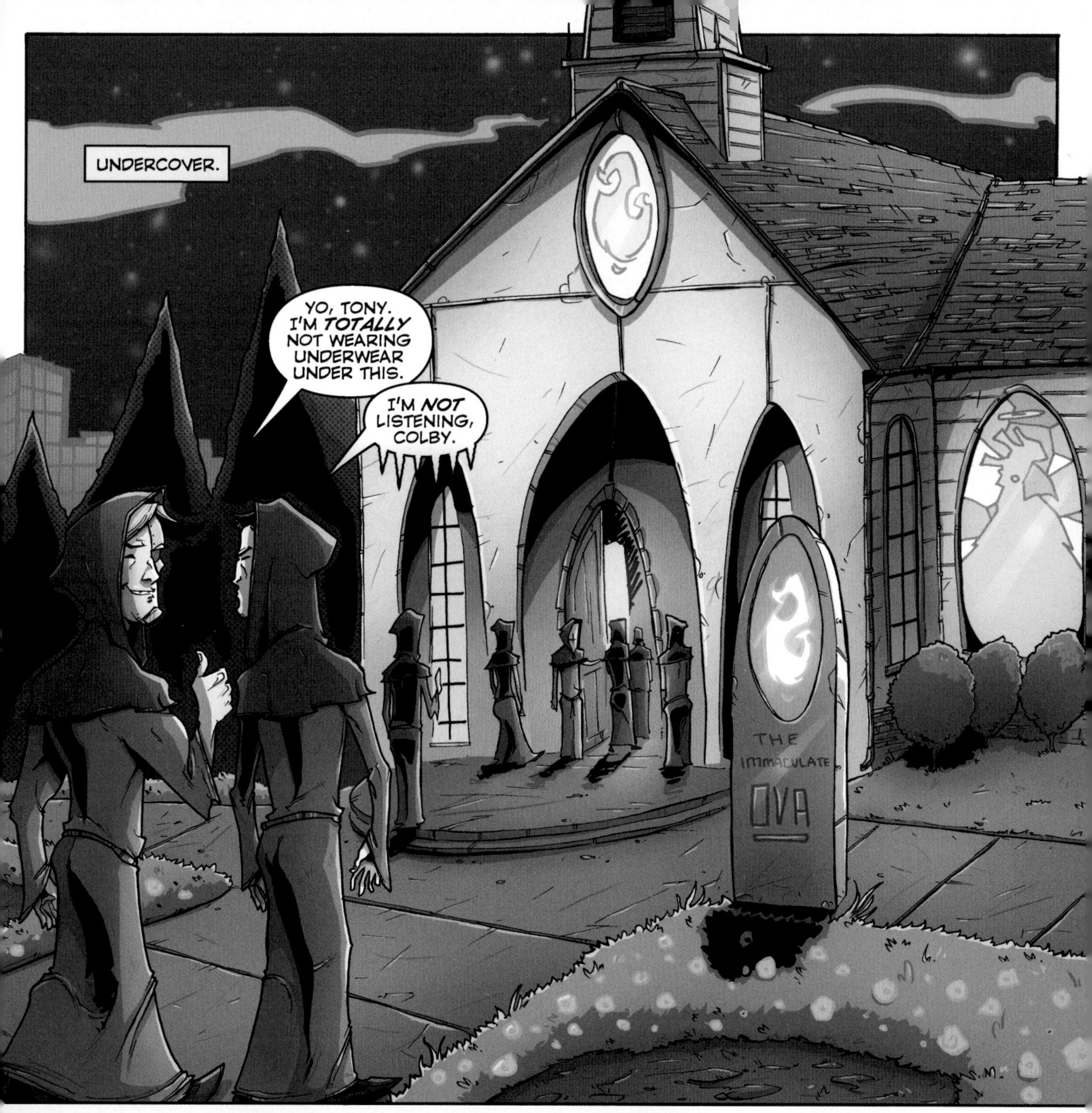
UNDERCOVER.
YO, TONY. I'M TOTALLY NOT WEARING UNDERWEAR UNDER THIS.
I'M NOT LISTENING, COLBY.
THE IMMACULATE OVA

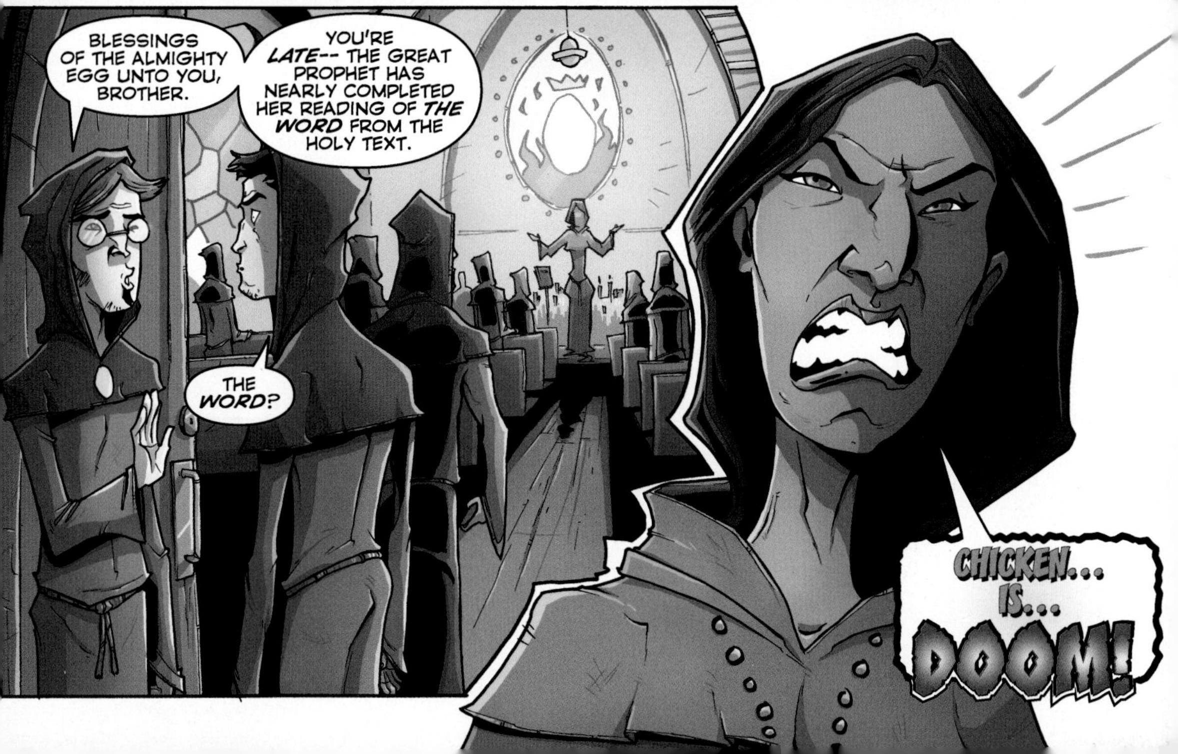
BLESSINGS OF THE ALMIGHTY EGG UNTO YOU, BROTHER.
YOU'RE LATE-- THE GREAT PROPHET HAS NEARLY COMPLETED HER READING OF THE WORD FROM THE HOLY TEXT.
THE WORD?
CHICKEN... IS... DOOM!

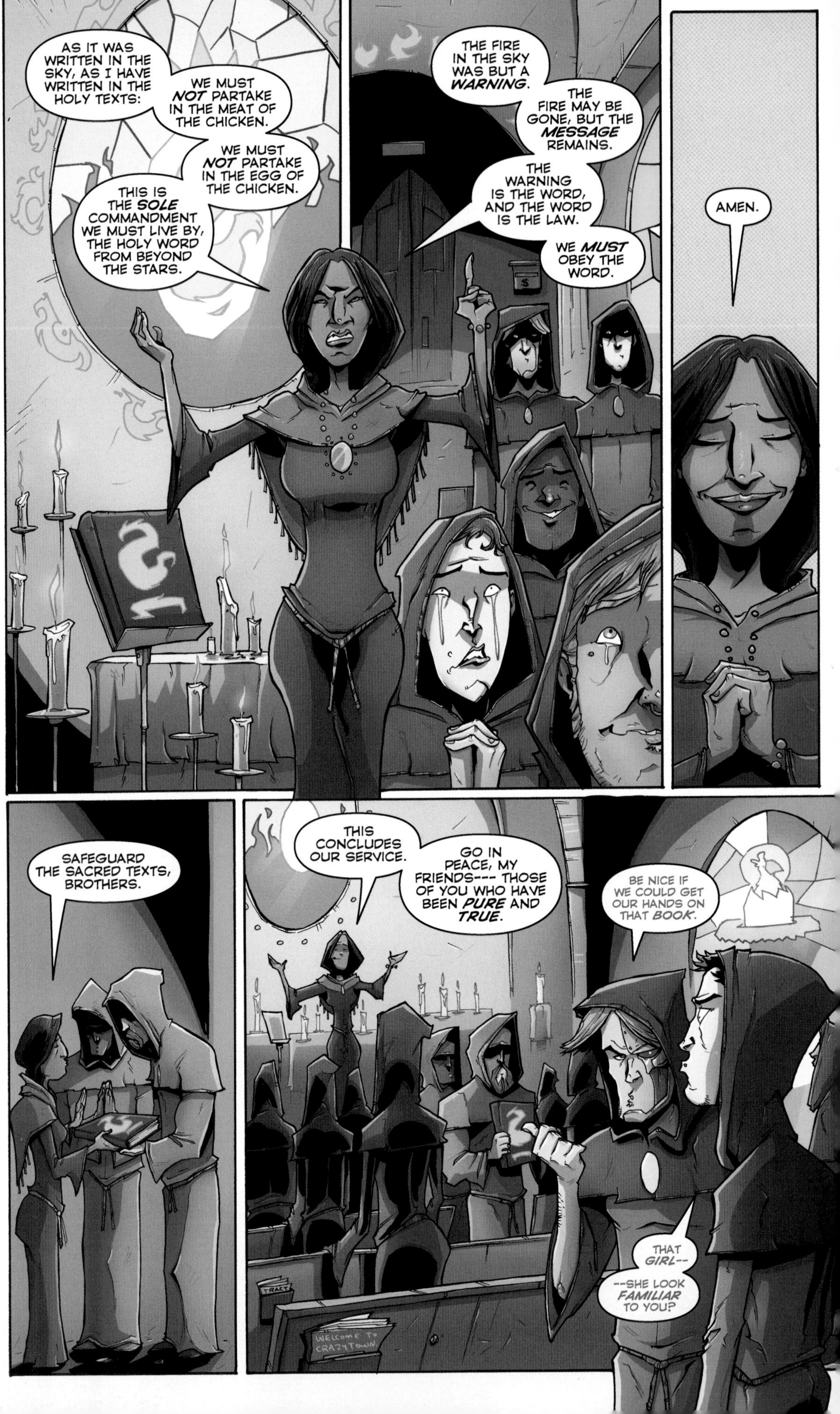
AS IT WAS WRITTEN IN THE SKY, AS I HAVE WRITTEN IN THE HOLY TEXTS:
WE MUST *NOT* PARTAKE IN THE MEAT OF THE CHICKEN.
WE MUST *NOT* PARTAKE IN THE EGG OF THE CHICKEN.
THIS IS THE *SOLE* COMMANDMENT WE MUST LIVE BY, THE HOLY WORD FROM BEYOND THE STARS.
THE FIRE IN THE SKY WAS BUT A *WARNING*.
THE FIRE MAY BE GONE, BUT THE *MESSAGE* REMAINS.
THE WARNING IS THE WORD, AND THE WORD IS THE LAW.
WE *MUST* OBEY THE WORD.
AMEN.
SAFEGUARD THE SACRED TEXTS, BROTHERS.
THIS CONCLUDES OUR SERVICE.
GO IN PEACE, MY FRIENDS--- THOSE OF YOU WHO HAVE BEEN *PURE* AND *TRUE*.
TRACT
WELCOME TO CRAZYTOWN
BE NICE IF WE COULD GET OUR HANDS ON THAT *BOOK*.
THAT *GIRL*--
--SHE LOOK *FAMILIAR* TO YOU?

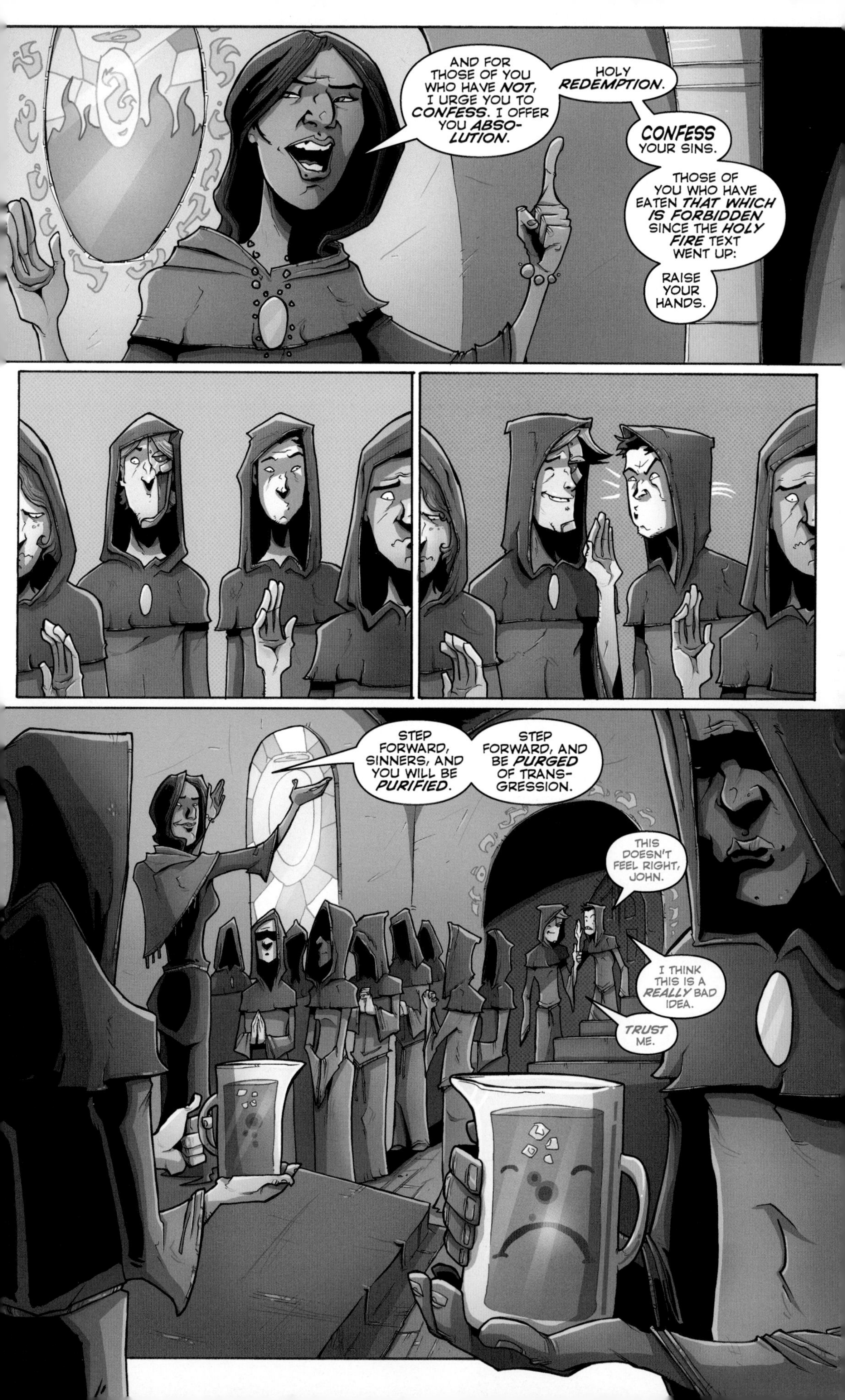
AND FOR THOSE OF YOU WHO HAVE NOT, I URGE YOU TO CONFESS. I OFFER YOU ABSO-LUTION.
HOLY REDEMPTION.
CONFESS YOUR SINS.
THOSE OF YOU WHO HAVE EATEN THAT WHICH IS FORBIDDEN SINCE THE HOLY FIRE TEXT WENT UP:
RAISE YOUR HANDS.
STEP FORWARD, SINNERS, AND YOU WILL BE PURIFIED.
STEP FORWARD, AND BE PURGED OF TRANS-GRESSION.
THIS DOESN'T FEEL RIGHT, JOHN.
I THINK THIS IS A REALLY BAD IDEA.
TRUST ME.

DRINK, MY FRIENDS, AND SIN SHALL *WASH* AWAY. ALL WILL BE FOR-GIVEN.

BUT FIRST... CLOSE YOUR EYES--

--AND LET US PRAY.

SNIFF

OH GREAT AND POWERFUL EGG-- *YOINK*

C'MON!

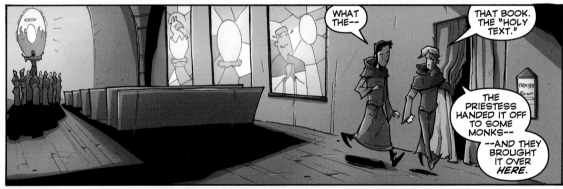

WHAT THE--

THAT BOOK. THE "HOLY TEXT."

THE PRIESTESS HANDED IT OFF TO SOME MONKS--

--AND THEY BROUGHT IT OVER *HERE.*

PRAYER ROOM

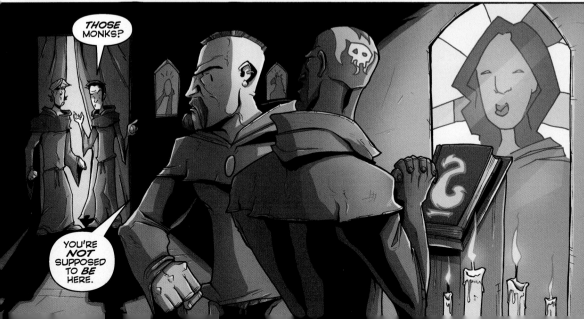

THOSE MONKS?

YOU'RE *NOT* SUPPOSED TO *BE* HERE.

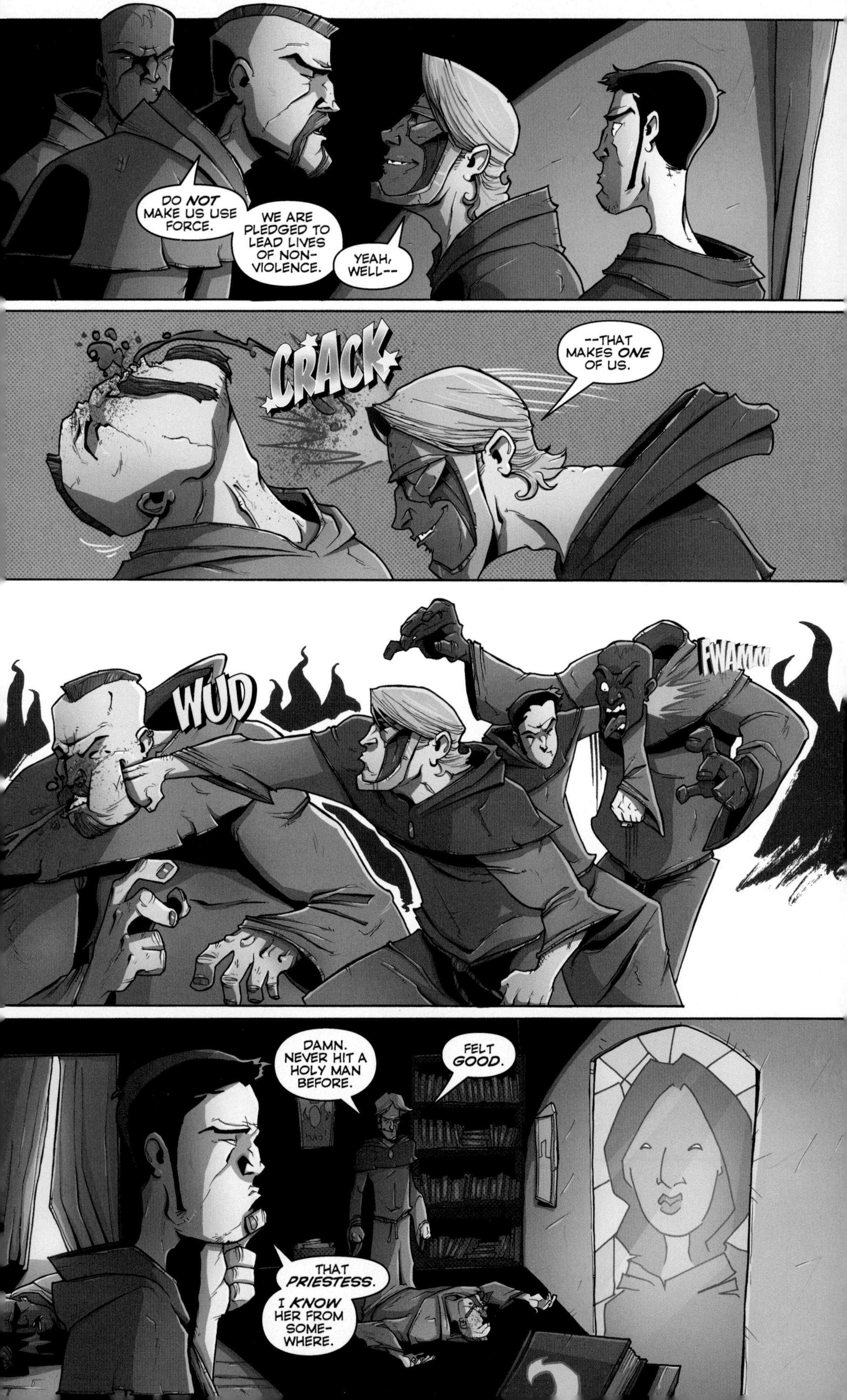
DO NOT MAKE US USE FORCE.
WE ARE PLEDGED TO LEAD LIVES OF NON-VIOLENCE.
YEAH, WELL--
CRACK
--THAT MAKES ONE OF US.
WUD
FWAMM
DAMN. NEVER HIT A HOLY MAN BEFORE.
FELT GOOD.
THAT PRIESTESS. I KNOW HER FROM SOME-WHERE.

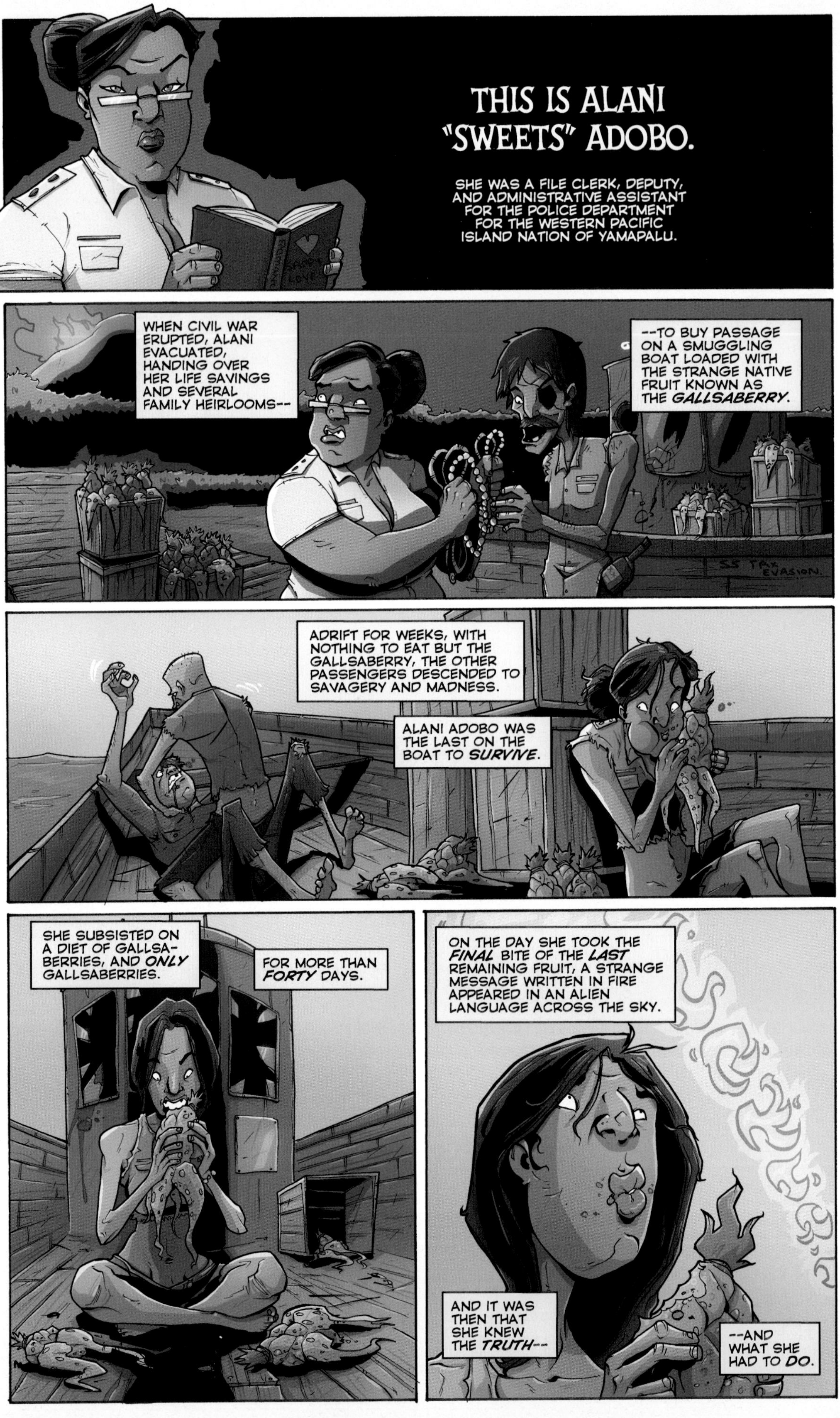
THIS IS ALANI "SWEETS" ADOBO.
SHE WAS A FILE CLERK, DEPUTY, AND ADMINISTRATIVE ASSISTANT FOR THE POLICE DEPARTMENT FOR THE WESTERN PACIFIC ISLAND NATION OF YAMAPALU.
WHEN CIVIL WAR ERUPTED, ALANI EVACUATED, HANDING OVER HER LIFE SAVINGS AND SEVERAL FAMILY HEIRLOOMS--
--TO BUY PASSAGE ON A SMUGGLING BOAT LOADED WITH THE STRANGE NATIVE FRUIT KNOWN AS THE GALLSABERRY.
SS TAX EVASION
ADRIFT FOR WEEKS, WITH NOTHING TO EAT BUT THE GALLSABERRY, THE OTHER PASSENGERS DESCENDED TO SAVAGERY AND MADNESS.
ALANI ADOBO WAS THE LAST ON THE BOAT TO SURVIVE.
SHE SUBSISTED ON A DIET OF GALLSA-BERRIES, AND ONLY GALLSABERRIES.
FOR MORE THAN FORTY DAYS.
ON THE DAY SHE TOOK THE FINAL BITE OF THE LAST REMAINING FRUIT, A STRANGE MESSAGE WRITTEN IN FIRE APPEARED IN AN ALIEN LANGUAGE ACROSS THE SKY.
AND IT WAS THEN THAT SHE KNEW THE TRUTH--
--AND WHAT SHE HAD TO DO.

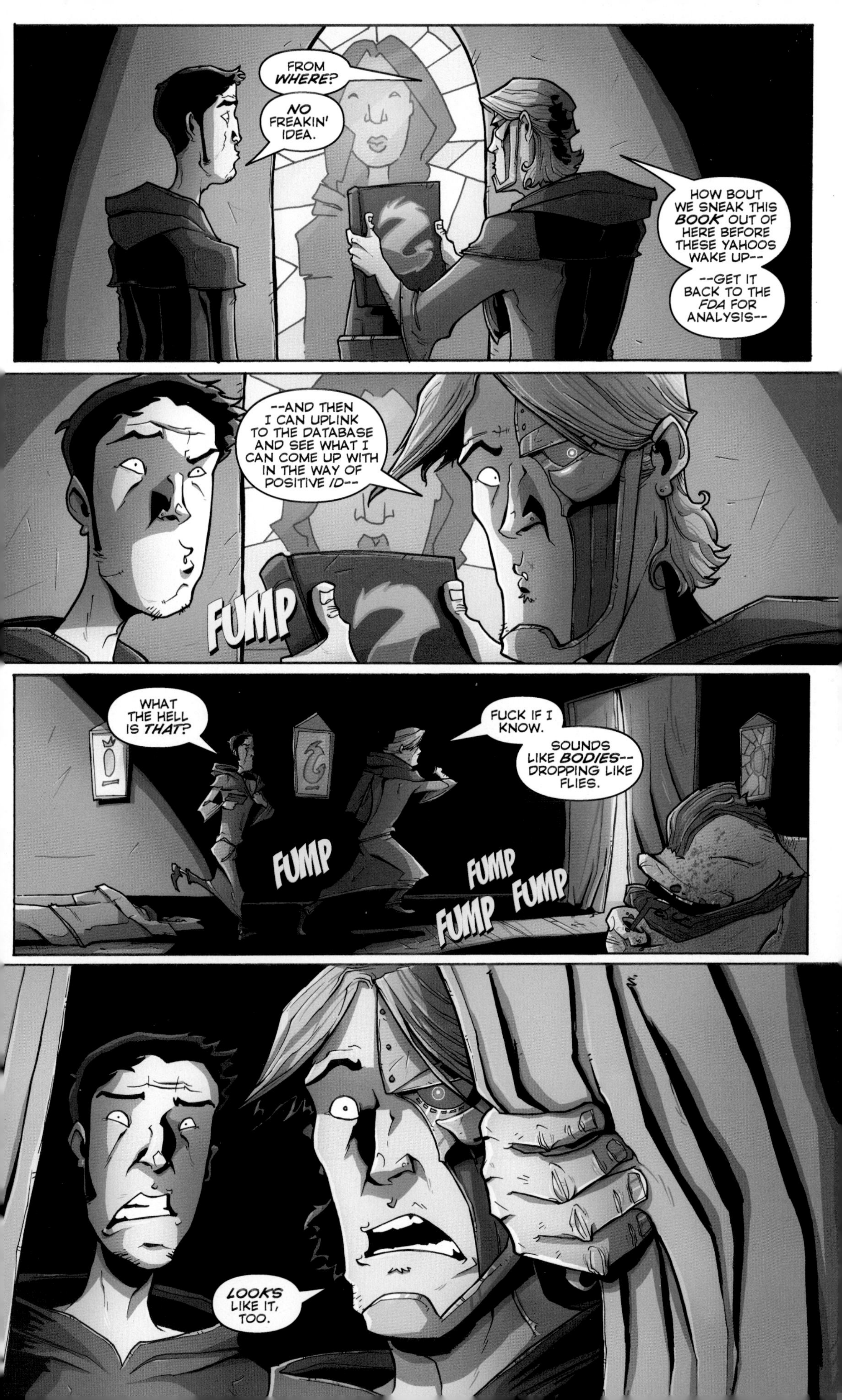
FROM *WHERE?*
NO FREAKIN' IDEA.
HOW BOUT WE SNEAK THIS *BOOK* OUT OF HERE BEFORE THESE YAHOOS WAKE UP--
--GET IT BACK TO THE *FDA* FOR ANALYSIS--
--AND THEN I CAN UPLINK TO THE DATABASE AND SEE WHAT I CAN COME UP WITH IN THE WAY OF POSITIVE *ID*--
FUMP
WHAT THE HELL IS *THAT?*
FUCK IF I KNOW.
SOUNDS LIKE *BODIES*-- DROPPING LIKE FLIES.
FUMP
FUMP
FUMP
FUMP
LOOKS LIKE IT, TOO.

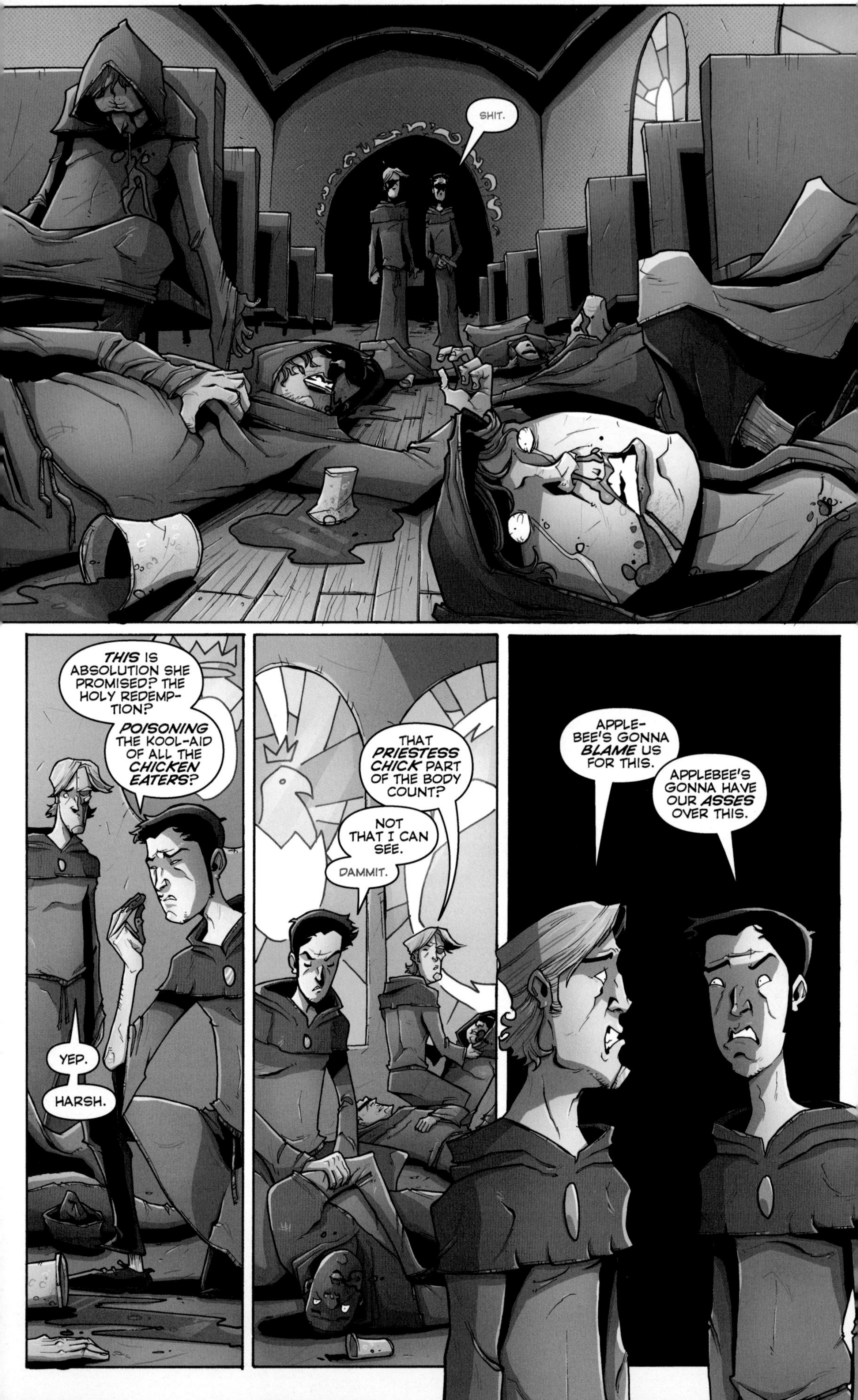
SHIT.
THIS IS ABSOLUTION SHE PROMISED? THE HOLY REDEMPTION?
POISONING THE KOOL-AID OF ALL THE CHICKEN EATERS?
YEP.
HARSH.
THAT PRIESTESS CHICK PART OF THE BODY COUNT?
NOT THAT I CAN SEE.
DAMMIT.
APPLEBEE'S GONNA BLAME US FOR THIS.
APPLEBEE'S GONNA HAVE OUR ASSES OVER THIS.

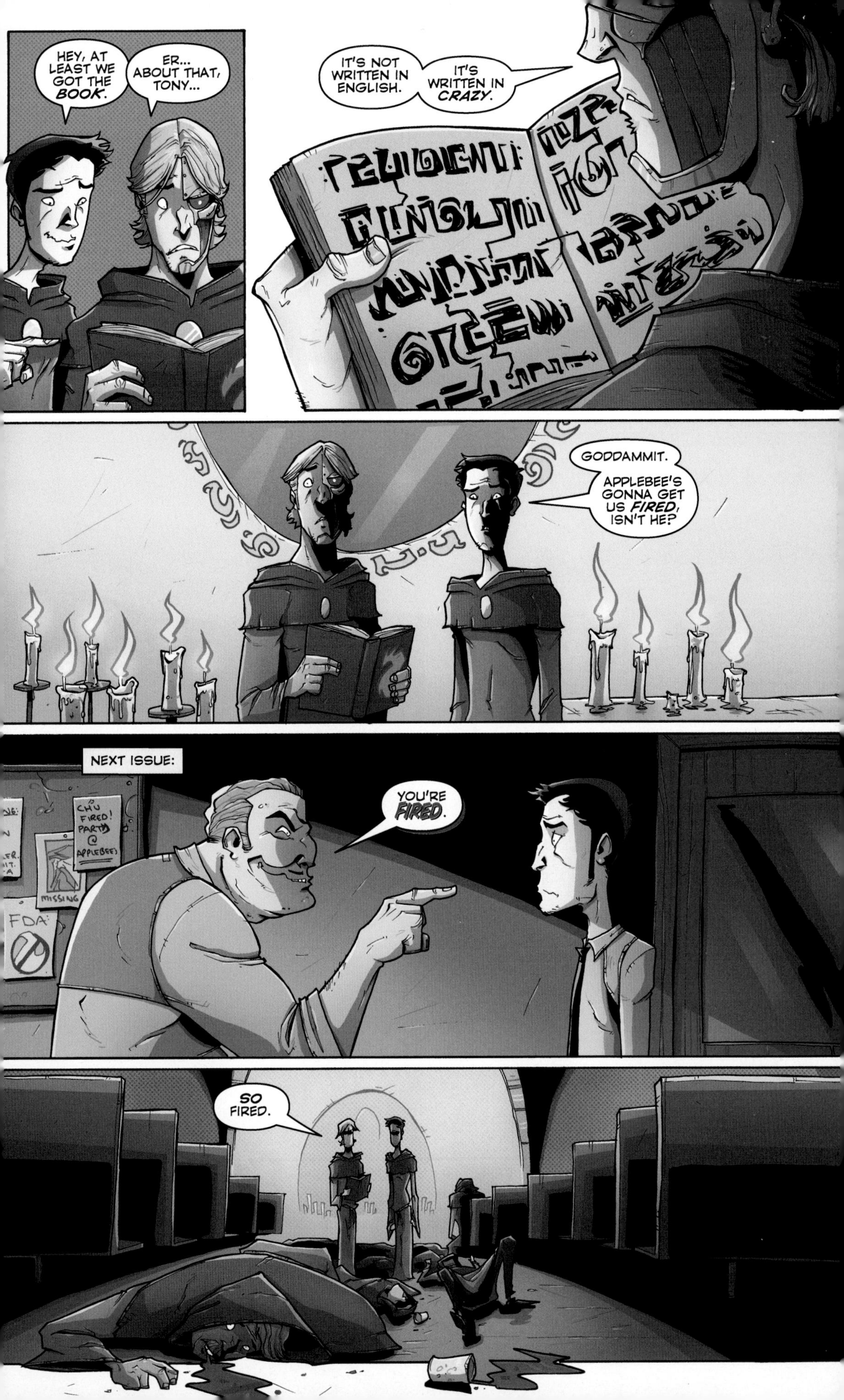
HEY, AT LEAST WE GOT THE BOOK.
ER... ABOUT THAT, TONY...
IT'S NOT WRITTEN IN ENGLISH.
IT'S WRITTEN IN CRAZY.
GODDAMMIT.
APPLEBEE'S GONNA GET US FIRED, ISN'T HE?
NEXT ISSUE:
CHU FIRED! PARTY @ APPLEBEES
MISSING
FDA
YOU'RE FIRED.
SO FIRED.

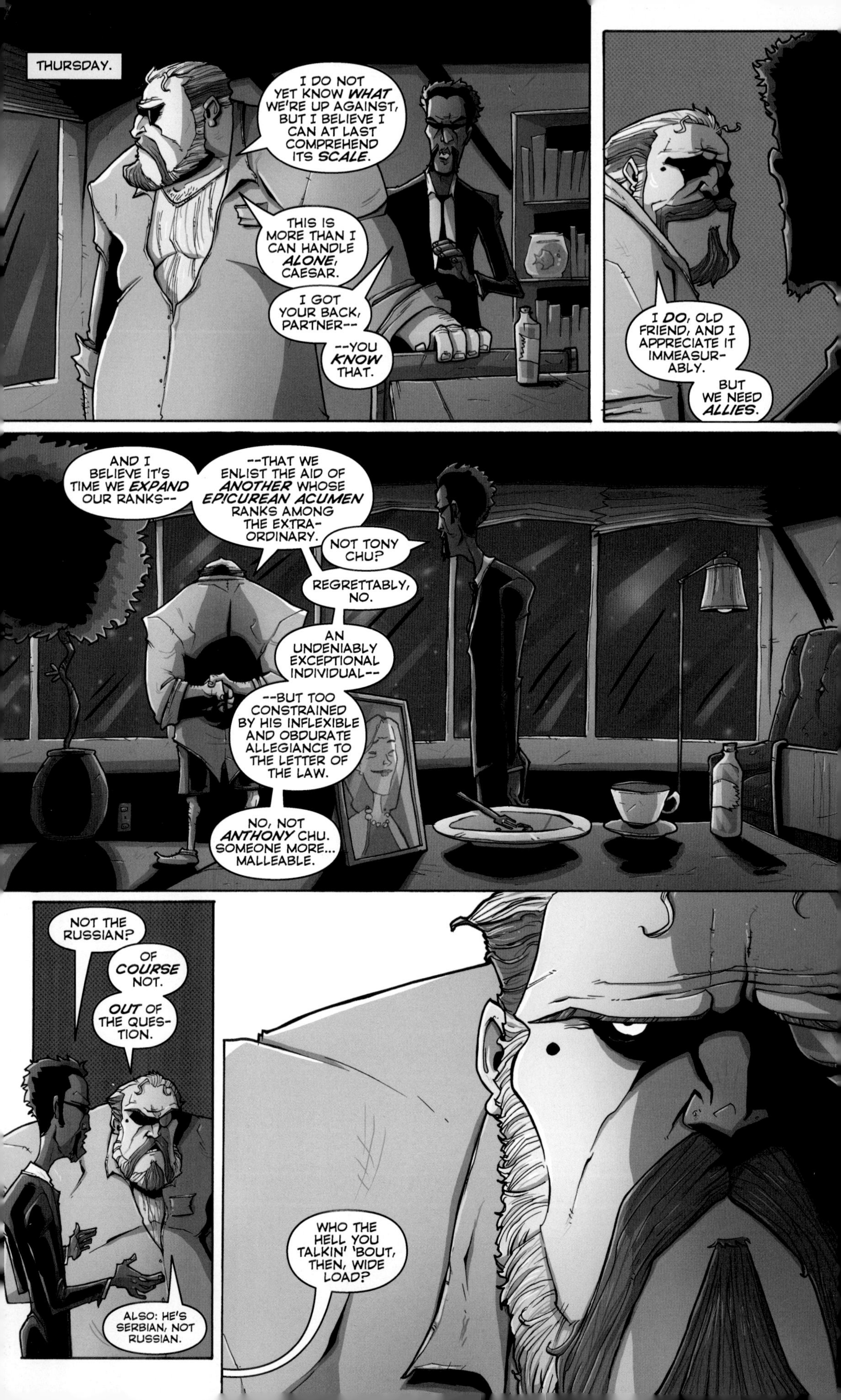
THURSDAY.
I DO NOT YET KNOW WHAT WE'RE UP AGAINST, BUT I BELIEVE I CAN AT LAST COMPREHEND ITS SCALE.
THIS IS MORE THAN I CAN HANDLE ALONE, CAESAR.
I GOT YOUR BACK, PARTNER--
--YOU KNOW THAT.
I DO, OLD FRIEND, AND I APPRECIATE IT IMMEASUR-ABLY.
BUT WE NEED ALLIES.
AND I BELIEVE IT'S TIME WE EXPAND OUR RANKS--
--THAT WE ENLIST THE AID OF ANOTHER WHOSE EPICUREAN ACUMEN RANKS AMONG THE EXTRA-ORDINARY.
NOT TONY CHU?
REGRETTABLY, NO.
AN UNDENIABLY EXCEPTIONAL INDIVIDUAL--
--BUT TOO CONSTRAINED BY HIS INFLEXIBLE AND OBDURATE ALLEGIANCE TO THE LETTER OF THE LAW.
NO, NOT ANTHONY CHU. SOMEONE MORE... MALLEABLE.
NOT THE RUSSIAN?
OF COURSE NOT.
OUT OF THE QUES-TION.
ALSO: HE'S SERBIAN, NOT RUSSIAN.
WHO THE HELL YOU TALKIN' 'BOUT, THEN, WIDE LOAD?

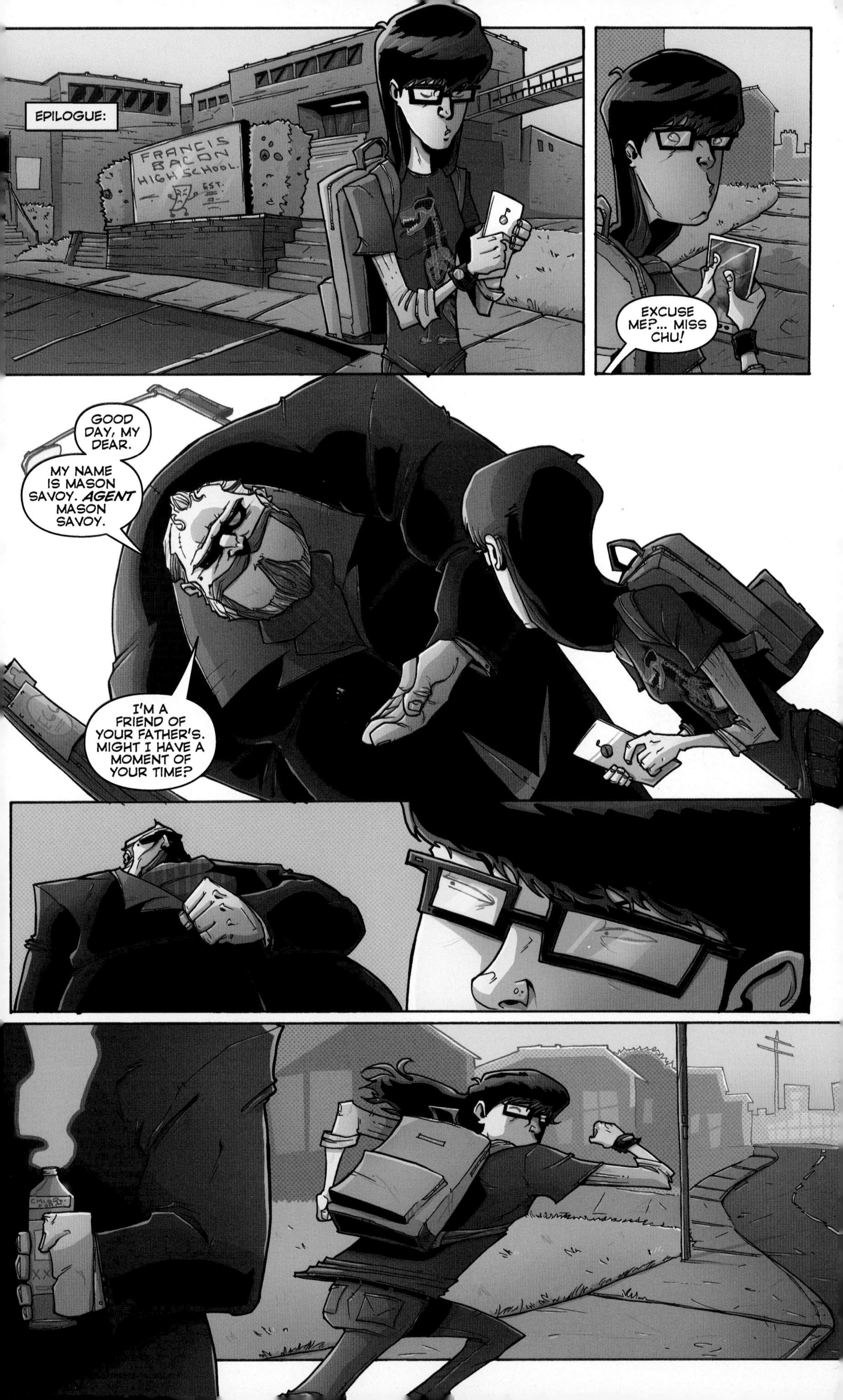
EPILOGUE:
FRANCIS BACON HIGH SCHOOL. EST.
EXCUSE ME?... MISS CHU!
GOOD DAY, MY DEAR.
MY NAME IS MASON SAVOY. *AGENT* MASON SAVOY.
I'M A FRIEND OF YOUR FATHER'S. MIGHT I HAVE A MOMENT OF YOUR TIME?

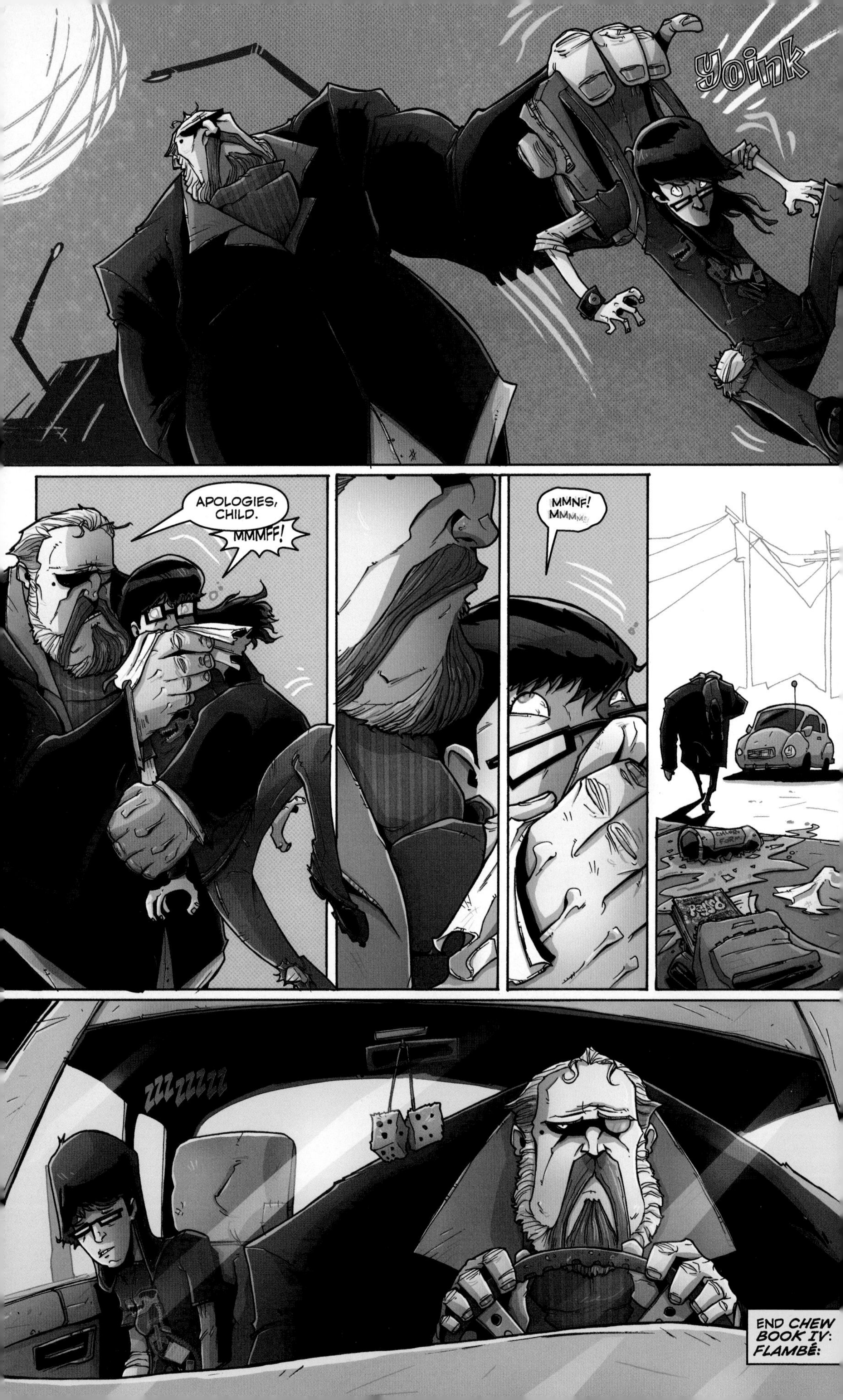
yoink
APOLOGIES, CHILD.
MMMFF!
MMNF! MMMM!!
ZZZZZZZ
END CHEW BOOK IV: FLAMBÉ:

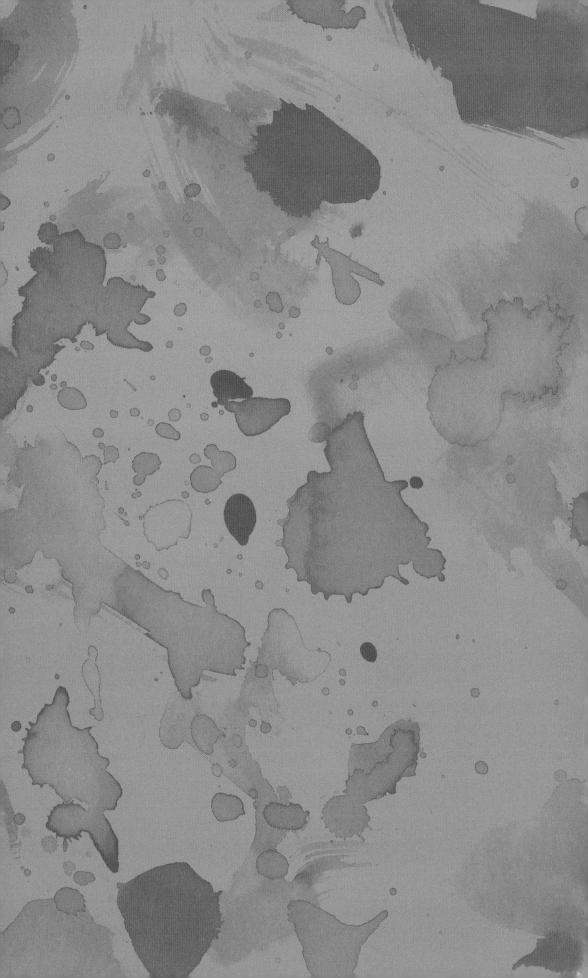

JOHN LAYMAN

If a unicorn and a rainbow could mate on a bed of hearts and smiles, the name of their firstborn would be **"Layman."**

Layman has three cats: Rufus, Ash and Ruby.

ROB GUILLORY

In addition to working on CHEW, Rob is in the process of breeding his Eisners with his Harveys. It's not going well...

Rob's son Aiden was born during the making of this book, right between pages 8 & 9 of Chapter 2. He's pretty spectacular.
Visit **RobGuillory.com** *for all your sporadic blogging needs.*

ChewComic.com

For Original Art Sales, please email
ChewComicSales@gmail.com.